Also available in
Random House Large Print

BLACK NOTICE

THE
LAST
PRECINCT

PATRICIA CORNWELL

THE
LAST
PRECINCT

RANDOM HOUSE
LARGE PRINT

A Division of Random House, Inc.
Published in association with G.P. Putnam's Sons,
a member of Penguin Putnam, Inc.
New York 2000

Published in the United States of America by Random House Large Print in association with G.P. Putnam's Sons, a member of Penguin Putnam, Inc. New York, and simultaneously in Canada by Random House of Canada Limited, Toronto.
Distributed by Random House, Inc., New York.

Library of Congress Cataloging-in-Publication Data

Cornwell, Patricia Daniels.
The last precinct / by Patricia Cornwell—1st large print ed.
p.   cm.
ISBN 0-375-43068-7
1. Scarpetta, Kay (Fictitious character)—Fiction.
2. Medical examiners (Law)—Virginia—Richmond—Fiction.   3. Women detectives—Virginia—Richmond—Fiction.   4. Jamestown (Va.)—Fiction.   5. Richmond (Va.)—Fiction.   6. Large type books.   I. Title.

PS3553.O692 L37 2000
813'.54—dc21
00-021645

Random House Web Address: www.randomlargeprint.com

FIRST LARGE PRINT EDITION

10 9 8 7 6 5 4 3 2 1

This Large Print edition published in accord with the standards of the N.A.V.H.

To Linda Fairstein—

Prosecutor. Novelist. Mentor.
Best Friend.
(This one's for you)

THE
LAST
PRECINCT

PROLOGUE:
AFTER THE FACT

THE COLD DUSK GIVES UP ITS bruised color to complete darkness, and I am grateful that the draperies in my bedroom are heavy enough to absorb even the faintest hint of my silhouette as I move about packing my bags. Life could not be more abnormal than it is right now.

"I want a drink," I announce as I open a dresser drawer. "I want to build a fire and have a drink and make pasta. Yellow and green broad noodles, sweet peppers, sausage. *Le papparedelle del cantunzein.* I've always wanted to take a sabbatical, go to Italy, learn Italian, really learn it. Speak it. Not just know the names of food. Or maybe France. I will go to France. Maybe I'll go there right this minute," I add with a double edge of helplessness and rage. "I could live in Paris. Easily." It is my way of rejecting Virginia and everybody in it.

Richmond Police Captain Pete Marino dominates my bedroom like a thick lighthouse, his giant hands shoved into the pockets of his jeans. He doesn't offer to help me pack the suit bag and tote bags laid open on the bed, knowing me well enough to not even think about it. Marino may look like a redneck, talk like a redneck, act like a redneck, but he is as smart as hell, sensitive and very perceptive. This very moment, for example, he realizes a simple fact: Not even twenty-four hours ago, a man named Jean-Baptiste Chandonne tracked through snow beneath a full moon and tricked his way into my house. I was already intimately familiar with Chandonne's modus operandi, so I can safely project what he would have done to me given the chance. But I haven't quite been able to subject myself to anatomically correct images of my own mauled dead body, and nobody could more accurately describe such a thing than I. I am a forensic pathologist with a law degree, the chief medical examiner of Virginia. I autopsied the two women Chandonne recently killed here in Richmond and reviewed the cases of seven others he murdered in Paris.

Safer for me to say what he did to those victims, which was to savagely beat them, to bite their breasts, hands and feet, and to play with their blood. He doesn't always use the same weapon. Last night, he was armed with a chipping hammer, a peculiar tool used in masonry. It looks very much like a pickaxe. I know for a fact what a chipping hammer can do to a human body because Chandonne used a chipping hammer—the same one, I presume—on Diane Bray, his second Richmond victim, the policewoman he murdered two days ago, on Thursday.

"What day is it?" I ask Captain Marino. "Saturday, isn't it?"

"Yeah. Saturday."

"December eighteenth. One week before Christmas. Happy holidays." I unzip a side pocket of the suit bag.

"Yeah, December eighteenth."

He watches me as if I am someone who might spring into irrationality any second, his bloodshot eyes reflecting a wariness that pervades my house. Distrust is palpable in the air. I taste it like dust. I smell it like ozone. I feel it like dampness. The wet swishing of tires on the street, the discord of feet, of voices and radio chatter are a disharmony from hell as law enforcement continues its occupation of my property. I am violated. Every inch of my home is exposed, every facet of my life is laid bare. I may as well be a naked body on one of my own steel tables in the morgue. So Marino knows not to ask if he can help me pack. Oh yes, he sure as hell knows he better dare not even think about touching a damn thing, not a shoe, not a sock, not a hairbrush, not a bottle of shampoo, not the smallest item. Police have asked me to leave the sturdy stone house of dreams I built in my quiet, gated West End neighborhood. Imagine that. I am quite certain Jean-Baptiste Chandonne—*Le Loup-Garou* or *The Werewolf,* as he calls himself—is getting better treatment than I am. The law provides people like him with every human right conceivable: comfort, confidentiality, free room, free food and drink, and free medical care in the forensic ward of the Medical College of Virginia, where I am a member of the faculty.

Marino hasn't bathed or been to bed in at least twenty-four hours. When I move past him, I smell Chandonne's hideous body odor and am stabbed by nausea, a burning wrenching of my stomach that locks my brain and causes me to break out in a cold sweat. I straighten up and take a deep breath to dispel the olfactory hallucination as my attention is drawn beyond the windows to the slowing of a car. I have come to recognize the subtlest pause in traffic and know when it will become someone parking out front. It is a rhythm I have listened to for hours. People gawk. Neighbors rubberneck and stop in the middle of the road. I reel in an uncanny intoxication of emotions, one minute bewildered and then frightened the next. I swing from exhaustion to mania, from depression to tranquility, and beneath it all, excitement fizzes as if my blood is filled with gas.

A car door shuts out front. "Now what?" I complain. "Who this time? The FBI?" I open another drawer. "Marino, that's it." I gesture with a fuck-you wave of my hands. "Get them out of my house, all of them. Now." Fury shimmers like mirages on hot blacktop. "So I can finish packing and get the hell out of here. Can't they just leave long enough for me to get out?" My hands shake as I pick through socks. "It's bad enough they're in my yard." I toss a pair of socks in the tote bag. "It's bad enough they're here at all." Another pair. "They can come back when I leave." And I throw another pair and miss, and stoop over to pick it up. "They can at least let me walk through my own house." Another pair. "And let me get out in peace and privacy." I put a pair back in the drawer. "Why the hell are they in my kitchen?" I change my mind and get out the socks I just put back. "Why are they in my study? I told them he didn't go in there."

"We gotta look around, Doc," is what Marino has to say about it.

He sits down on the foot of my bed, and that is wrong, too. I want to tell him to get off my bed and out of my room. It is all I can do not to order him out of my house and possibly out of my life. It doesn't matter how long I have known him or how much we have been through together.

"How's the elbow, Doc?" He indicates the cast that immobilizes my left arm like a stovepipe.

"It's fractured. It hurts like hell." I shut the drawer too hard.

"Taking your medicine?"

"I'll survive."

He watches my every move. "You need to be taking that stuff they gave you."

We have suddenly reversed roles. I act like the rude cop while he is logical and calm like the lawyer-physician I am supposed to be. I walk back into the cedar-lined closet and begin gathering blouses and laying them in the suit bag, making sure top buttons are buttoned, smoothing silk and polished cotton with my right hand. My left elbow throbs like a toothache, my flesh sweating and itching inside plaster. I spent most of the day in the hospital—not that getting a cast put on a fractured limb is a lengthy procedure, but doctors insisted on checking me very carefully to make sure I didn't have other injuries. I repeatedly explained that when I fled from my house, I fell down my front steps and fractured my elbow, nothing more. Jean-Baptiste Chandonne never had a chance to touch me. I got away and am okay, I kept saying during X ray after X ray. Hospital staff held me for observation until late afternoon and detectives were in and out of the examination room. They took my clothes. My niece, Lucy, had to bring me something to wear. I have had no sleep.

The telephone pierces the air like a foil. I pick

up the extension by the bed. "Dr. Scarpetta," I announce into the handset, and my own voice saying my name reminds me of calls in the middle of the night when I answer my phone and some detective gives me very bad news about a death scene somewhere. Hearing my usual businesslike self-announcement triggers the image I have so far evaded: my savaged body on my bed, blood spattered all over the room, this room, and my assistant chief medical examiner getting the call and the look on his face as police—probably Marino—tell him I have been murdered and someone, God knows who, needs to respond to the scene. It occurs to me that no one from my office could possibly respond. I have helped Virginia design the best disaster plan of any state in the country. We can handle a major airline crash or a bombing in the coliseum or a flood, but what would we do if something happened to me? Bring in a forensic pathologist from a nearby jurisdiction, maybe Washington, I suppose. Problem is, I know almost every forensic pathologist on the East Coast and would feel terribly sorry for whoever had to deal with my dead body. It is very difficult working a case when you are acquainted with the victim. These thoughts fly through my mind like startled birds as Lucy asks me over the phone if I need anything, and I assure her I am fine, which is perfectly ridiculous.

"Well, you can't be fine," she replies.

"Packing," I tell her what I am doing. "Marino's with me and I'm packing," I repeat myself as my eyes fix on Marino in a frozen way. His attention wanders around and it seeps into my awareness that he has never been inside my bedroom. I don't want to imagine his fantasies. I have known him for many years and have always been aware that his respect for me is potently laced with insecurity and sexual attraction. He is a hulk of a man with a swollen beer belly, and a big disgruntled face, and his hair is colorless and has unattractively migrated from his head to other parts of his body. I listen to my niece on the phone as Marino's eyes feel their way around my private spaces: my dressers, my closet, the open drawers, what I am packing and my breasts. When Lucy brought tennis shoes, socks and a warm-up suit to the hospital, she didn't think to include a bra, and the best I could do when I got here was to cover up with an old, voluminous lab coat that I wear like a smock when I do odd jobs around the house.

"I guess they don't want you in there, either," Lucy's voice sounds over the line.

It is a long story, but my niece is an agent with the Bureau of Alcohol, Tobacco and Firearms, and when the police responded, they couldn't exile her from my property fast enough. Maybe a little knowledge is a dangerous thing and they feared a big-shot federal agent would insert herself into the investigation. I don't know, but she is feeling guilty because she wasn't here for me last night and I almost got murdered, and now she isn't here for me again. I make it clear I don't blame her in the least. I also can't stop wondering how different my life would be had she been home with me when Chandonne showed up— instead of out taking care of a girlfriend. Maybe Chandonne would have known I wasn't alone and would have stayed away, or he would have been surprised by another person in the house and would have fled, or he would have put off murdering me until tomorrow or the next night or Christmas or the new millennium.

I pace as I listen to Lucy's breathless explanations and comments over the cordless phone and catch my reflection as I go past the full-length mirror. My short blond hair is wild, my blue eyes glassy and puckered with exhaustion and stress, my brow gathered in what is a mixture of a frown and near-tears. The lab coat is dingy and stained and not the least bit chiefly. I am very pale. The craving for a drink and a cigarette are atypically strong, almost unbearable, as if almost being murdered has turned me into an instant junkie. I imagine being alone in my own home. Nothing has happened. I am enjoying a fire, a cigarette, a glass of French wine, maybe a Bordeaux because Bordeaux is less complicated than Burgundy. Bordeaux is like a fine old friend you don't have to figure out. I dispel the fantasy with fact: It doesn't matter what Lucy did or didn't do. Chandonne would have come to murder me eventually, and I feel as if a terrible judgment has been waiting for me all of my life, marking my door like the Angel of Death. Bizarrely, I am still here.

CHAPTER 1

I KNOW FROM LUCY'S VOICE that she is scared. Rarely is my brilliant, forceful, helicopter-piloting, fitness-obsessed, federal-law-enforcement-agent niece scared.

"I feel really bad," she continues to repeat herself over the phone as Marino maintains his position on my bed and I pace.

"You shouldn't," I tell her. "The police don't want anybody here, and believe me, you don't want to be here. I guess you're staying with Jo and that's good." I say this to her as if it makes no difference to me, as if it doesn't bother me that she is not here and I haven't seen her all day. It does make a difference. It does bother me. But it is my old habit to give people an out. I don't like to be rejected, especially by Lucy Farinelli, whom I have raised like a daughter.

She hesitates before answering. "Actually, I'm downtown at the Jefferson."

I try to make sense of this. The Jefferson is the grandest hotel in the city, and I don't know why she would go to a hotel at all, much less an elegant, expensive one. Tears sting my eyes and I force them back, clearing my throat, shoving down hurt. "Oh," is all I say. "Well, that's good. I guess Jo's with you at the hotel, then."

"No, with her family. Look, I just checked in. I've got a room for you. Why don't I come get you?"

"A hotel's probably not a good idea right now." She thought of me and wants me with her. I feel a little better. "Anna's asked me to stay with her. In light of everything, I think it's best for me to go on to her house. She's invited you, too. But I guess you're settled."

"How did Anna know?" Lucy inquires. "She hear about it on the news?"

Since the attempt on my life happened at a very late hour, it won't be in the newspapers until tomorrow morning. But I expect there has been a storm of news breaks over the radio and on television. I don't know how Anna knew, now that I think about it. Lucy says she needs to stay put but will try to drop by later tonight. We hang up.

"The media finds out you're in a hotel, that's all you need. They'll be behind every bush," Marino says with a hard frown, looking like hell. "Where's Lucy staying?"

I repeat what she told me and almost wish I hadn't talked to her. All it did was make me feel worse. Trapped, I feel trapped, as if I am inside a diving bell a thousand feet under the sea, detached, light-headed, the world beyond me suddenly unrecognizable and surreal. I am numb yet every nerve is on fire.

"The Jefferson?" Marino is saying. "You gotta be kidding! She win the lottery or something? She not worried about the media finding her, too? What the shit's gotten into her?"

I resume packing. I can't answer his questions. I am so tired of questions.

"And she ain't at Jo's house. Huh," he goes on, "that's interesting. Huh. Never thought that would last." He yawns loudly and rubs his thick-featured, stubbly face as he watches me drape suits over a chair, continuing to pick out clothes for the office. To give Marino credit, he has tried to be even-tempered, even considerate, since I got home from the hospital. Decent behavior is difficult for him given the best of circumstances, which certainly are not the ones he finds himself in at present. He is strung out, sleep-deprived and fueled by caffeine and junk food, and I won't allow him to smoke inside my house. It was simply a matter of time before his self-control began to erode and he stepped back into his rude, big-mouthed character. I witness the metamorphosis and am strangely relieved by it. I am desperate for things familiar, no matter how unpleasant. Marino starts talking about what Lucy did last night when she pulled up in front of the house and discovered Jean-Baptiste Chandonne and me in my snowy front yard.

"Hey, it's not that I blame her for wanting to blow the squirrel's brains out," Marino gives me his commentary. "But that's where your training's got to come in. Don't matter if it's your aunt or your kid involved, you got to do what you're trained to do, and she didn't. She sure as hell didn't. What she did was go ape-shit."

"I've seen you go ape-shit a few times in your life," I remind him.

"Well, it's my personal opinion they never should have thrown her into that undercover work down there in Miami." Lucy is assigned to the Miami field office and is here for the holidays, among other reasons. "Sometimes people get too close to the bad guys and start identifying with them. Lucy's in a kill mode. She's gotten trigger-happy, Doc."

"That's not fair." I realize I have packed too many pairs of shoes. "Tell me what you would have done if you'd gotten to my house first instead of her." I stop what I am doing and look at him.

"At least take a nanosecond to assess the situation before I went in there and put a gun to the asshole's head. Shit. The guy was so fucked up he couldn't even see what he was doing. He's screaming bloody murder because he's got this chemical shit you threw in his eyes. He wasn't armed by this point. He wasn't going to be hurting nobody. That was obvious right away. And it was obvious you was hurt, too. So if it had been me, I'd called for an ambulance, and Lucy didn't think to even do that. She's a wild card, Doc. And no, I didn't want her in the house with all this going on. That's why we interviewed her down at the station, got her statements in a neutral place to get her calmed down."

"I don't consider an interrogation room a neutral place," I reply.

"Well, being inside the house where your Aunt Kay almost got whacked ain't exactly neutral, either."

I don't disagree with him, but sarcasm is poisoning his tone. I begin to resent it.

"All the same, I got to tell you I've got a really bad feeling about her being alone in a hotel right now," he adds, rubbing his face again, and no matter what he says to the contrary, he thinks the world of my niece and would do anything for her. He has known her since she was ten, and he introduced her to trucks and big engines and guns and all sorts of so-called manly interests that he now criticizes her for having in her life. "I might

just check on the little shit after I drop you off at
Anna's. Not that anybody seems to care about my
bad feelings," he jumps back several thoughts.
"Like Jay Talley. Of course, it ain't my business.
The self-centered bastard."

"He waited with me the entire time at the hospital," I defend Jay yet one more time, deflecting
Marino's naked jealousy. Jay is ATF's Interpol liaison. I don't know him very well but slept with
him in Paris four days ago. "And I was there
thirteen or fourteen hours," I go on as Marino
practically rolls his eyes. "I don't call that self-
centered."

"Jesus!" Marino exclaims. "Where'd you hear
that fairy tale?" His eyes burn with resentment.
He despises Jay and did the first time he ever laid
eyes on him in France. "I can't believe it. He lets
you think he was at the hospital all that time? He
didn't wait for you! That's total bullshit. He took
you there on his fucking white horse and came
right back here. Then he called to see when you
was going to be ready to check out and slithered
back to the hospital and picked you up."

"Which makes good sense." I don't show my
dismay. "No point in sitting and doing nothing.
And he never said he was there the entire time. I
just assumed it."

"Yeah, why? Because he let you assume it. He
lets you think something that isn't true, and you

ain't bothered by that? In my book, that's known as a character flaw. It's called lying. . . . What?" He abruptly changes his tone. Someone is in my doorway.

A uniformed officer whose nameplate reads M. I. Calloway steps inside my bedroom. "I'm sorry," she addresses Marino right off. "Captain, I didn't know you were back here."

"Well, now you know." He gives her a black look.

"Dr. Scarpetta?" Her wide eyes are like Ping-Pong balls, bouncing back and forth between Marino and me. "I need to ask you about the jar. Where the jar of the chemical, the formulin . . ."

"Formalin," I quietly correct her.

"Right," she says. "Exactly, I mean, where exactly was the jar when you picked it up?"

Marino remains on the bed, as if he makes himself at home on the foot of my bed every day of his life. He starts feeling for his cigarettes.

"The coffee table in the great room," I answer Calloway. "I've already told everybody that."

"Yes, ma'am, but where on the coffee table? It's a pretty big coffee table. I'm really sorry to bother you with all this. It's just we're trying to reconstruct how it all happened, because later it's only going to get harder to remember."

Marino slowly shakes a Lucky Strike loose from the pack. "Calloway?" He doesn't even look at

her. "Since when are you a detective? Don't seem
I remember you being in A Squad." He is the head
of the Richmond Police Department's violent
crime unit known as A Squad.

"We just aren't sure where the jar was, Captain." Her cheeks burn.

The cops probably assumed a woman coming
back here to question me would be less intrusive
than a male. Perhaps her comrades sent her back
here for that reason, or maybe it was simply that
she got the assignment because no one else wanted
to tangle with me.

"When you walk into the great room and face
the coffee table, it's the right corner of the table
closest to you," I say to her. I have been through
this many times. Nothing is clear. What happened
is a blur, an unreal torquing of reality.

"And that's approximately where you were
standing when you threw the chemical on him?"
Calloway asks me.

"No. I was on the other side of the couch. Near
the sliding glass door. He was chasing me and
that's where I ended up," I explain.

"And after that you ran directly out of the
house . . . ?" Calloway scratches through something she is writing on her small memo pad.

"Through the dining room," I interrupt her.
"Where my gun was, where I happened to have
set it on the dining room table earlier in the

evening. Not a good place to leave it, I admit." My mind meanders. I feel as if I have severe jet lag. "I hit the panic alarm and went out the front door. With the gun, the Glock. But I slipped on ice and fractured my elbow. I couldn't pull the slide back, not with just one hand."

She writes this down, too. My story is tired and the same. If I have to tell it one more time, I might become irrational, and no cop on this planet has ever seen me irrational.

"You never fired it?" She glances up at me and wets her lips.

"I couldn't cock it."

"You never tried to fire it?"

"I don't know what you mean by *try*. I couldn't cock it."

"But you tried to?"

"You need a translator or something?" Marino erupts. The ominous way he stares at M. I. Calloway reminds me of the red dot a laser sight marks on a person before a bullet follows. "The gun wasn't cocked and she didn't fire it, you got that?" he repeats slowly and rudely. "How many cartridges you have in the magazine?" He directs this to me. "Eighteen? It's a Glock Seventeen, takes eighteen in the mag, one in the chamber, right?"

"I don't know," I tell him. "Probably not eighteen, definitely not. It's hard to get that many rounds in it because the spring's stiff, the spring in the magazine."

"Right, right. You remember the last time you shot that gun?" he then asks me.

"Whenever I was at the range last. Months at least."

"You always clean your guns after you go to the range, don't you, Doc." This is a statement, not an inquiry. Marino knows my habits and routines.

"Yes." I am standing in the middle of my bedroom, blinking. I have a headache and the lights hurt my eyes.

"You looked at the gun, Calloway? I mean, you've examined it, right?" He fixes her in his laser sight again. "So what's the deal?" He flaps a hand at her as if she is a stupid nuisance. "Tell me what you found."

She hesitates. I sense she doesn't want to give out information in front of me. Marino's question hangs heavy like moisture about to precipitate. I decide on two skirts, one navy blue, one gray, and drape them over the chair.

"There are fourteen rounds in the magazine," Calloway tells him in a robotic military tone. "There wasn't one in the chamber. It wasn't cocked. And it looks clean."

"Well, well. Then it wasn't cocked and she didn't shoot it. *And it was a dark and stormy night and three Indians sat around a campfire.* We want to go round and round, or can we fucking move along?" He is sweating and his body odor rises with his heat.

"Look, there's nothing new to add," I say, suddenly on the verge of tears, cold and trembling and smelling Chandonne's awful stench again.

"And why was it you had the jar in your home? And what exactly was in it? That stuff you use in the morgue, right?" Calloway positions herself to take Marino out of her sight line.

"Formalin. A ten percent dilution of formaldehyde known as formalin," I say. "It's used in the morgue to fix tissue, yes. Sections of organs. Skin, in this case."

I dashed a caustic chemical into the eyes of another human being. I maimed him. Maybe I permanently blinded him. I imagine him strapped to a bed on the ninth-floor prison ward of the Medical College of Virginia. I saved my own life and feel no satisfaction in that fact. All I feel is ruined.

"So you had human tissue in your house. The skin. A tattoo. From that unidentified body at the port? The one in the cargo container?" The sound of Calloway's voice, of her pen, of pages flipping, reminds me of reporters. "I don't mean to be dense, but why would you have something like that at your house?"

I go on to explain that we have had a very difficult time identifying the body from the port. We had nothing beyond a tattoo, really, and last week I drove to Petersburg and had an experienced tattoo artist look at the tattoo from my case. I came directly home afterward, which is why the tattoo in its jar of formalin happened to be in my house last night. "Ordinarily, I wouldn't have something like that in my house," I add.

"You kept it at your house for a week?" she asks with a dubious expression.

"A lot was happening. Kim Luong was murdered. My niece was almost killed in a shoot-out in Miami. I was called out of the country, to Lyon, France. Interpol wanted to see me, wanted to talk about seven women he"—I mean Chandonne—"probably murdered in Paris and the suspicion that the dead man in the cargo container might be Thomas Chandonne, the brother, the killer's brother, both of them sons of this Chandonne criminal cartel that half of law enforcement in the universe has been trying to bring down forever. Then Deputy Police Chief Diane Bray was murdered. Should I have returned the tattoo to the morgue?" My head pounds. "Yes, I certainly should have. But I was distracted. I just forgot." I almost snap at her.

"You just forgot," Officer Calloway repeats

while Marino listens with gathering fury, trying to let her do her job and despising her at the same time. "Dr. Scarpetta, do you have other body parts in your house?" Calloway then asks.

A stabbing pain penetrates my right eye. I am getting a migraine.

"What kind of fucking question is that?" Marino raises his voice another decibel.

"I just didn't want us walking in on anything else like body fluids or other chemicals or . . ."

"No, no." I shake my head and turn my attention to a stack of neatly folded slacks and polo shirts. "Just slides."

"Slides?"

"For histology," I vaguely explain.

"For what?"

"Calloway, you're done." Marino's words crack like a gavel as he rises from the bed.

"I just want to make sure we don't need to worry about any other hazards," she says to him, and her hot cheeks and the flash in her eyes belie her subordination. She hates Marino. A lot of people do.

"The only hazard you gotta worry about is the one you're looking at," Marino snaps at her. "How 'bout giving the Doc a little privacy, a little reprieve from dumb-ass questions?"

Calloway is an unattractive chinless woman

with thick hips and narrow shoulders, her body tense with anger and embarrassment. She spins around and walks out of my bedroom, her footsteps absorbed by the Persian runner in the hallway.

"What's she think? You collect trophies or something?" Marino says to me. "You bring home souvenirs like fucking Jeffrey Dahmer? Jesus Christ."

"I can't take any more of this." I tuck perfectly folded polo shirts into the tote bag.

"You're gonna have to take it, Doc. But you don't have to take any more of it today." He wearily sits back down on the foot of my bed.

"Keep your detectives off me," I warn him. "I don't want to see another cop in my face. I'm not the one who did something wrong."

"If they got anything else, they'll run it through me. This is my investigation, even if people like Calloway ain't figured that out yet. But I also ain't the one you got to worry about. It's like *take a number* in the deli line, there's so many people who insist they got to talk to you."

I stack slacks on top of the polo shirts, and then reverse the order, placing the shirts on top so they don't wrinkle.

"Course, nowhere near as many people as the ones who want to talk to him." He means Chandonne. "All these profilers and forensic psychia-

trists and the media and shit," Marino goes
through the Who's Who list.

I stop packing. I have no intention of picking
through lingerie while Marino watches. I refuse
to sort through toiletries with him witness to it
all. "I need a few minutes alone," I tell him.

He stares at me, his eyes red, his face flushed the
deep color of wine. Even his balding head is red,
and he is disheveled in his jeans and a sweatshirt,
his belly nine months pregnant, his Red Wing
boots huge and dirty. I can see his mind working.
He doesn't want to leave me alone and seems to
be weighing concerns that he will not share with
me. A paranoid thought rises like dark smoke in
my mind. He doesn't trust me. Maybe he thinks
I am suicidal.

"Marino, please. Can you just stand outside and
keep people away while I finish up in here? Go
to my car and get my crime scene case out of the
trunk. If I get called out on something . . . well,
I need to have it. The key's in the kitchen desk
drawer, the top right—where I keep all my keys.
Please. And I need my car, by the way. I guess I'll
just take my car and you can leave the scene case
in it." Confusion eddies.

He hesitates. "You can't take your car."

"Damn it!" I blurt out. "Don't tell me they've
got to go through my car, too. This is insane."

"Look. The first time your alarm went off last

night, it was because someone tried to break into your garage."

"What do you mean, *someone*?" I retort as migraine pain sears my temples and blurs my vision. "We know exactly who. He forced my garage door open because he *wanted* the alarm to go off. He *wanted* the police to show up. So it wouldn't seem odd if the police came back a little later because a neighbor reported a prowler on my property, supposedly."

It was Jean-Baptiste Chandonne who came back. He impersonated the police. I still can't believe I fell for it.

"We ain't got all the answers yet," Marino replies.

"Why is it I keep getting this feeling you don't believe me?"

"You need to get to Anna's and sleep."

"He didn't touch my car," I assert. "He never got inside my garage. I don't want anyone touching my car. I want to take it tonight. Just leave the scene case inside the trunk."

"Not tonight."

Marino walks out and shuts the door behind him. I am desperate for a drink to override the electrical spikes in my central nervous system, but what do I do? Walk out to the bar and tell the cops to get the hell out of my way while I find the Scotch? Knowing that liquor probably won't help my headache doesn't have an impact. I am so miserable in my own skin, I don't care what is good or not good for me right now. In the bathroom I dig through more drawers and spill several lipsticks on the floor. They roll between the toilet and the tub. I am unsteady as I bend over to retrieve them, groping awkwardly with my right arm, all of this made more difficult because I am left-handed. I stop to ponder the perfumes neatly arranged on the vanity and gently pick up the small gold metal bottle of Hermès 24 Faubourg. It is cool in my hand. I lift the spray nozzle to my nose and the spicy, erotic scent that Benton Wesley loved fills my eyes with tears and my heart feels as if it will fatally fly out of rhythm. I have not used the perfume in more than a year, not once since Benton was murdered. Now I have been murdered, I tell him in my throbbing mind. And I am still here, Benton, I am still here. You were a psychological profiler for the FBI, an expert in dissecting the psyches of monsters and interpreting and predicting their behavior. You would have seen this coming, wouldn't you? You would have predicted it, prevented it. Why weren't you here, Benton? I would be all right if you had been here.

I realize someone is knocking on my bedroom

door. "Just a minute," I call out, clearing my throat and wiping my eyes. I splash cold water on my face and tuck the Hermès perfume into the tote bag. I go to the door, expecting Marino. Instead, Jay Talley walks in wearing ATF battle dress and a day's growth of beard that turns his dark beauty sinister. He is one of the handsomest men I have ever known, his body exquisitely sculpted, sensuality exuding from his pores like musk.

"Just checking on you before you head out." His eyes burn into mine. They seem to feel and explore me the way his hands and mouth did four days ago in France.

"What can I tell you?" I let him into my bedroom and am suddenly self-conscious about the way I look. I don't want him to see me like this. "I have to leave my own house. It's almost Christmas. My arm hurts. My head hurts. Other than that, I'm fine."

"I'll drive you to Dr. Zenner's. I would like to, Kay."

It vaguely penetrates that he knows where I am staying tonight. Marino promised my whereabouts would be secret. Jay shuts the door and takes my hand, and all I can think about is that he didn't wait at the hospital for me and now he wants to drive me someplace else.

"Let me help you through this. I care about you," he says to me.

"No one seemed to care very much last night," I reply as I recall that when he drove me home from the hospital and I thanked him for waiting, for being there for me, he never once even intimated that he hadn't been there. "You and all your IRTs out there and the bastard just walks right up to my front door," I go on. "You fly all the way here from Paris to lead a goddamn International Response Team in your big-game hunt for this guy, and what a joke. What a bad movie—all these big cops with all their gear and assault rifles and the monster just strolls right up to my house."

Jay's eyes have begun wandering over areas of my anatomy as if they are rest stops he is entitled to revisit. It shocks and repulses me that he can think about my body at a time like this. In Paris I thought I was falling in love with him. As I stand here with him in my bedroom and he is openly interested in what is under my old lab coat, I realize I don't love him in the least.

"You're just upset. God, why wouldn't you be? I'm concerned about you. I'm here for you." He tries to touch me and I move away.

"We had an afternoon." I have told him this before, but now I mean it. "A few hours. An encounter, Jay."

"A mistake?" Hurt sharpens his voice. Dark anger flashes in his eyes.

"Don't try to turn an afternoon into a life, into something of permanent meaning. It isn't there. I'm sorry. For God's sake." My indignation rises. "Don't want anything from me right now." I walk away from him, gesturing with my one good arm. "What are you doing? What the hell are you doing?"

He raises a hand and hangs his head, warding off my blows, acknowledging his mistake. I am not sure if he is sincere. "I don't know what I'm doing. Being stupid, that's what," he says. "I don't mean to want anything. Stupid, I'm stupid because of how I feel about you. Don't hold it against me. Please." He casts me an intense look and opens the door. "I'm here for you, Kay. *Je t'aime.*" I realize Jay has a way of saying good-bye that makes me feel I might never see him again. An atavistic panic thrills my deepest psyche and I resist the temptation to call after him, to apologize, to promise we will have dinner or drinks soon. I shut my eyes and rub my temples, briefly leaning against the bedpost. I tell myself I don't know what I am doing right now and should not do anything.

Marino is in the hallway, an unlit cigarette clamped in the corner of his mouth, and I can feel him trying to read me and what might have just happened while Jay was inside my bedroom with the door shut. My gaze lingers on the empty hallway, halfway hoping Jay will reappear and dreading it at the same time. Marino grabs my bags and cops fall silent as I approach. They avoid looking in my direction as they move about my great room, duty belts creaking, equipment they manipulate clicking and clacking. An investigator takes photographs of the coffee table, the flash gun popping bright white. Someone else is videotaping while a crime scene technician sets up an alternative light source called a Luma-Lite that can detect fingerprints, drugs and body fluids not visible to the unaided eye. My downtown office has a Luma-Lite I routinely use on bodies at scenes and in the morgue. To see a Luma-Lite inside my house gives me a feeling that is indescribable.

Dark dusting powder smudges furniture and walls, and the colorful Persian rug is pulled back, exposing antique French oak underneath. An endtable lamp is unplugged and on the floor. The sectional sofa has craters where cushions used to be, the air oily and acrid with the residual odor of formalin. Off the great room and near the front door is the dining room and through the open doorway I am greeted with the sight of a brown paper bag sealed with yellow evidence tape, dated, initialed and labeled *clothing Scarpetta.* Inside it are the slacks, sweater, socks, shoes, bra and panties I was wearing last night, clothes taken from me in the hospital. That bag and other evidence and flashlights and equipment are on top of my favorite red Jarrah Wood dining room table, as if it is a workbench. Cops have draped coats over chairs, and wet, dirty footprints are everywhere. My mouth is dry, my joints weak with shame and rage.

"Yo Marino!" a cop barks. "Righter's looking for you."

Buford Righter is the city commonwealth's attorney. I look around for Jay. He is nowhere to be seen.

"Tell him to take a number and wait in line." Marino sticks to his deli-line allusion.

He lights the cigarette as I open the front door, and cold air bites my face and makes my eyes water. "Did you get my crime scene case?" I ask him.

"It's in the truck." He says this like a condescending husband who has been asked to fetch his wife's pocketbook.

"Why's Righter calling?" I want to know.

"Bunch of fucking voyeurs," he mutters.

Marino's truck is on the street out front and two massive tires have chewed tracks into my snowy churned-up lawn. Buford Righter and I have worked many cases together over the years and it stings that he did not ask me directly if he could come to my house. He has not, for that matter, contacted me to see how I am and let me know he is glad I am alive.

"You ask me, people just want to see your joint," Marino says. "So they give these excuses about needing to check this and that."

Slush seeps into my shoes as I carefully make my way along the driveway.

"You got no idea how many people ask me what your house is like. You'd think you was Lady Di or something. Plus, Righter's got his nose in everything, can't stand to be left out of the loop. Biggest fucking case since Jack the Ripper. Righter's bugging the hell out of us."

Flash guns suddenly explode in bright white stutters and I almost slip. I swear out loud. Photographers have gotten past the neighborhood guard gate. Three of them hurry toward me in a blaze of flashes as I struggle with one arm to climb into the truck's high front seat.

"Hey!" Marino yells at the nearest offender, a woman. "Goddamn bitch!" He lunges, trying to block her camera, and her feet go out from under her. She sits down hard on the slick street, camera equipment thudding and scattering.

"Fuckhead!" she screams at him. "Fuckhead!"

"Get in the truck! Get in the truck!" Marino yells at me.

"Motherfucker!"

My heart drills my ribs.

"I'm going to sue you, motherfucker!"

More flashes and I shut my coat in the door and

have to open it again and shut it again while Marino shoves my bags in back and jumps into the driver's seat, the engine turning over and rumbling like a yacht. The photographer is trying to get up, and it occurs to me I ought to make sure she isn't injured. "We should see if she's hurt," I say, staring out the side window.

"Hell no. Fuck no." The truck lurches onto the street, fishtails and accelerates.

"Who are they?" Adrenaline pumps. Blue dots float before my eyes.

"Assholes. That's who." He snatches up the hand mike. "Unit nine," he announces over the air.

"Unit nine," the dispatcher comes back.

"I don't need pictures of me, my house . . ." I raise my voice. Every cell in my body lights up to protest the unfairness of it all.

"Ten-five unit three-twenty, ask him to call me on my portable." Marino holds the mike against his mouth. Unit three-twenty gets back to him right away, the portable phone vibrating like a huge insect. Marino flips it open and talks. "Somehow the media's gotten in the neighborhood. Photographers. I'm thinking they parked somewhere in Windsor Farms, came in on foot over the fence, through that open grassy area behind the guard booth. Send units to look for any cars parked where they shouldn't be and tow 'em. They step foot on the Doc's property, arrest 'em." He ends the call, flipping the phone shut as if he is Captain Kirk and has just ordered the *Enterprise* to attack.

We slow down at the guard booth and Joe steps out. He is an old man who has always been proud to wear his brown Pinkerton's uniform, and he is very nice, polite and protective, but I would not want to depend on him or his colleagues for more than nuisance control. It shouldn't surprise me a bit that Chandonne got inside my neighborhood or that now the media has. Joe's slack, wrinkled face turns uneasy when he notices me sitting inside the truck.

"Hey, man," Marino gruffly says through the open window, "how'd the photographers get in here?"

"What?" Joe instantly goes into protect mode, eyes narrowing as he stares down the slick, empty street, sodium vapor lights casting yellow auras high up on poles.

"In front of the Doc's house. At least three of 'em."

"They didn't come through here," Joe declares. He ducks back inside the booth and grabs the phone.

We drive off. "We can do but so much, Doc,"

Marino says to me. "You may as well duck your head in the sand because there's gonna be pictures and shit all over the place."

I stare out the window at lovely Georgian homes glowing with holiday festivity.

"Bad news is, your security risk just went up another mile." He is preaching to me, telling me what I already know and have no interest in dwelling on right now. "Because now half the world's gonna see your big fancy house and know exactly where you live. Problem is, and what worries the hell out of me, is stuff like this brings out other squirrels. Gives 'em ideas. They start imagining you as a victim and get off on it, like those assholes who go to the courthouse, cruising for rape cases to sit in on."

He eases to a stop at the intersection of Canterbury Road and West Cary Street, and headlights sweep over us as a compact dark-colored sedan turns in and slows. I recognize the narrow, insipid face of Buford Righter looking over at Marino's truck. Righter and Marino roll down their windows.

"You leaving . . . ?" Righter starts to say when his eyes shoot past Marino and land on me in surprise. I have the unnerving sense that I am the last person he wants to see. "Sorry for your trouble," Righter weirdly says to me, as if what is happening in my life is nothing more than trouble, an inconvenience, an unpleasantness.

"Yeah, heading out." Marino sucks on the cigarette, not the least bit helpful. He has already expressed his opinion about Righter's showing up at my house. It is unnecessary, and even if he truly thinks it is so important to eyeball the crime scene himself, why didn't he do it earlier when I was at the hospital?

Righter pulls his overcoat more tightly around his neck, light from street lamps glinting off his glasses. He nods and says to me, "Take care. Glad you're okay," deciding to acknowledge my so-called trouble. "This is real hard on all of us." A thought catches before it is out in words. Whatever he was going to say next is gone, retracted, struck from the record. "I'll be talking to you," he promises Marino.

Windows go up. We drive off.

"Give me a cigarette," I tell Marino. "I'm assuming he didn't come to my house earlier today," I then say.

"Yeah, actually he did. About ten o'clock this morning." He offers me the pack of unfiltered Lucky Strikes and flame spits out of a lighter he holds my way.

Anger coils through my entrails, and the back of my neck is hot, the pressure in my head almost unbearable. Fear stirs inside me like a waking beast. I turn mean, punching in the lighter on the dash, ungraciously leaving Marino's arm extended with the Bic lighter flaming. "Thanks for telling me," I sharply reply. "You mind my asking who the hell else has been in my house? And how many times? And how long they stayed and what they touched?"

"Hey, don't take it out on me," he warns.

I know the tone. He is about to lose his patience with me and my mess. We are like weather systems about to collide, and I don't want that. The last thing I need right now is a war with Marino. I touch the tip of the cigarette to bright orange coils and inhale deeply, the punch of pure tobacco spinning me. We drive several minutes in flinty silence, and when I finally speak, I sound numb, my feverish brain glazing over like the streets, depression a heavy pain spreading along my ribs. "I know you're just doing what has to be done. I appreciate it," I force the words. "Even if I'm not showing it."

"You don't got to explain nothing." He sucks on the cigarette, both of us shooting streams of smoke toward our partially open windows. "I know exactly what you feel," he adds.

"You couldn't possibly." Resentment seeps up my throat like bile. "I don't even know."

"I understand a lot more than you give me

credit for," he says. "Someday you'll see that, Doc. No way you can see shit right now, and I'm telling you it ain't gonna get no better in days and weeks to come. That's the way it works. The real damage hasn't even hit. I can't tell you how many times I've seen it, seen what happens to people when they're victimized."

I absolutely do not want to hear a single word of this.

"Damn good thing you're going where you are," he says. "Exactly what the doctor ordered, in more ways than one."

"I'm not staying with Anna because it's what the doctor ordered," I reply testily. "I'm staying with her because she's my friend."

"Look, you're a victim and you got to deal with it, and you need help dealing with it. Don't matter you're a doctor–lawyer–Indian chief." Marino will not shut up, in part because he is looking for a fight. He wants a focus for his anger. I can see what is coming, and anger crawls up my neck and heats up the roots of my hair. "Being a victim's the great equalizer," Marino, the world's authority, goes on.

I draw out the words slowly. "I am not a victim." My voice wavers around its edges like fire. "There's a difference between being victimized and *being a victim.* I'm not a sideshow for character disorders." My tone sears. "I haven't become what he wanted to turn me into"—of course, I mean Chandonne—"even if he'd had his way, I wouldn't be what he tried to project onto me. I would just be dead. Not changed. Not something less than I am. Just dead."

I feel Marino recoil in his dark, loud space on the other side of his huge, manly truck. He doesn't understand what I mean or feel and probably never will. He reacts as if I slapped him across the face or kneed him in the groin.

"I'm talking reality." He strikes back. "One of us has to."

"Reality is, I'm alive."

"Yeah. A fuckin' goddamn miracle."

"I should have known you would do this." I get quiet and cold. "So predictable. People blame the prey not the predator, criticize the injured not the asshole who did it." I tremble in the dark. "Goddamn you. Goddamn you, Marino."

"I still can't believe you opened your door!" he shouts. What happened to me makes him feel powerless.

"And where were you guys?" I again remind him of an unpleasant fact. "It might have been nice if at least one or two of you could have kept an eye on my property. Since you were so concerned that he might come after me."

"I talked to you on the phone, remember?" He attacks from another angle. "You said you was fine. I told you to sit tight, that we'd found where the son of a bitch was hiding, that we knew he was out somewhere, probably looking for another woman to beat and bite the shit out of. And what do you do, Doctor Law Enforcement? You open your fucking door when someone knocks! At *fucking midnight!*"

I thought the person was the police. He said he was the police.

"Why?" Marino is yelling now, pounding the steering wheel like an out-of-control child. "Huh? Why? Goddamn it, tell me!"

We knew for days who the killer is, that he is the spiritual and physical freak Chandonne. We knew he is French and where his organized crime family lives in Paris. The person outside my door did not have even a hint of a French accent.

Police.

I didn't call the police, I said through the shut door.

Ma'am, we've gotten a call about a suspicious person on your property. Are you all right?

He had no accent. I never expected him to speak without an accent. It never occurred to me, not once. Were I to relive last night, it still would not occur to me. The police had just been at my house when the alarm went off. It didn't seem the least bit suspicious that they would be back. I incorrectly assumed they were keeping a close eye on my property. It was so quick. I opened the door and the porch light was off and I smelled that dirty, wet animal smell in the deep, frigid night.

"Yo! Anybody home?" Marino yells, poking my shoulder hard.

"Don't touch me!" I come to with a start, and gasp and jerk away from him and the truck swerves. The ensuing silence turns the air heavy like water a hundred feet deep, and awful images swim back into my blackest thoughts. A forgotten ash is so long I can't steer it to the ashtray in time. I brush off my lap. "You can turn at Stonypoint Shopping Center, if you want," I say to Marino. "It's quicker."

CHAPTER 2

DR. ANNA ZENNER'S IMPOS-
ing Greek Revival house soars up—lit
into the night on the southern bank of the
James River. Her mansion, as the neighbors call
it, has large Corinthian columns and is a local example of Thomas Jefferson and George Washington's belief that the new nation's architecture
should express the grandeur and dignity of the ancient world. Anna is from the ancient world, a
German of the first order. I believe she is from
Germany. Now that I think about it, I do not recall her ever telling me where she was born.

White holiday lights wink from trees, and candles in Anna's many windows glow warmly, reminding me of Christmases in Miami during the
late fifties, when I was a child. On the rare occasion when my father's leukemia was in remission,
he loved to drive us through Coral Gables to
gawk at houses he called villas, as if somehow his

ability to show us such places made him part of
that world. I remember fantasizing about the privileged people who lived inside those homes with
their graceful walls and Bentleys and their feasts
of steak or shrimp seven days a week. No one
who lived like that could possibly be poor or sick
or regarded as trash by people who did not like
Italians or Catholics or immigrants called Scarpetta.

It is an unusual name of a lineage I really don't
know much about. The Scarpettas have lived in
this country for two generations, or so my mother
claims, but I don't know who these other Scarpettas are. I have never met them. I have been told
we are traced back to Verona, that my ancestors
were farmers and railway workers. I do know for
a fact that I have only one sibling, a younger sister named Dorothy. She was briefly married to a
Brazilian twice her age who supposedly fathered
Lucy. I say *supposedly,* because when it comes to
Dorothy, only DNA would convince me of who
she happened to be in bed with on the occasion
my niece was conceived. My sister's fourth marriage was to a Farinelli, and after that Lucy stopped
changing her name. Except for my mother, I am
the only Scarpetta left, as far as I know.

Marino brakes at formidable black iron gates
and his big arm stretches out to stab an intercom
button. An electronic buzz and a loud click, and

the gates slowly open like a raven's wings. I don't know why Anna left her homeland for Virginia and never married. I have never asked her why she set up a psychiatric practice in this modest southern city when she could have gone anywhere. I don't know why I am suddenly wondering about her life. Thoughts are odd misfires. I carefully get out of Marino's truck and step down on granite pavers. It is as if I am having software problems. All sorts of files are being opened and closed unprovoked, and system messages are flashing. I am not sure of Anna's exact age, only that she is in her mid-seventies. As far as I know, she has never told me where she went to college or medical school. We have shared opinions and information for years, but rarely our vulnerabilities and intimate facts.

It suddenly bothers me considerably that I know so little about Anna, and I feel ashamed as I make my way up her neatly swept front steps, one at a time, sliding my good hand along the frigid iron railing. She opens the front door and her keen face softens. She looks at my thick, crooked cast and blue sling, and meets my eyes. "Kay, I am so glad to see you," she says, greeting me the same way she always does.

"How'ya doin', Dr. Zenner!" Marino announces. His enthusiasm is overblown as he goes out of his way to show how popular and charming he is and how little I matter to him. "Something sure smells mmm-mmm-good. You cooking for me again?"

"Not tonight, Captain." Anna has no interest in him or his bluster. She kisses both of my cheeks, careful of my injury and not hugging me hard, but I feel her heart in the light touch of her fingers. Marino sets my bags inside the foyer on a splendid silk rug beneath a crystal chandelier that sparkles like ice forming in space.

"You can take some soup with you," she tells Marino. "There is plenty. Very healthy. No fat."

"If it don't got fat, it's against my religion. I'm gonna head out." He avoids looking at me.

"Where is Lucy?" Anna helps me off with my coat, and I struggle to pull the sleeve over the cast, and then am dismayed to realize I still have my old lab coat on. "You have no autographs on it," she says to me, because no one has signed my plaster and no one ever will. Anna has an arid, elitist sense of humor. She can be very funny without so much as a hint of a smile, and if one is not attentive and quick-witted, he will completely miss the joke.

"Your joint ain't nice enough so she's at the Jefferson," Marino ironically comments.

Anna goes inside the hall closet to hang up my coat. My nervous energy is dissipating fast. Depression tightens its grip on my chest and increases pressure around my heart. Marino continues to pretend I don't exist.

"Of course, she can stay here. She is always welcome and I would very much like to see her," Anna says to me. Her German accent has not softened over the decades. She still talks in square meals, going to awkward angles to get a thought from her brain to her tongue and rarely using contractions. I have always believed she prefers German and speaks English because she has no choice.

Through the open doorway I watch Marino leave. "Why did you move here, Anna?" Now I am talking in non sequiturs.

"Here? You mean this house?" She studies me.

"Richmond. Why Richmond?"

"That is easy. Love." She says this flatly with no trace of feeling one way or another about it.

The temperature has dropped as the night deepens, and Marino's big, booted feet crunch through crusty snow.

"What love?" I ask her.

"A person who proved to be a waste of time."

Marino kicks the running board to knock snow loose before climbing inside his throbbing truck, engine rumbling like the bowels of a great ship, exhaust rushing out. He senses I am looking and puts on a bigger act of pretending he is unaware or doesn't care as he pulls his door shut and shoves his behemoth into gear. Snow spits out from huge tires as he drives off. Anna shuts the front door while I stand before it, lost in a vortex of spiraling thoughts and feelings.

"We must get you settled," she says to me, touching my arm and motioning for me to follow her.

I come to. "He's angry with me."

"If he were not angry about something—or rude—I would think he is ill."

"He's angry at me because I almost got murdered." I sound very tired. "Everybody's angry with me."

"You are exhausted." She pauses in the entrance hallway to hear what I have to say.

"I'm supposed to apologize because someone tried to kill me?" The protests tumble out. "I asked for it? I did something wrong? So I opened my door. I wasn't perfect, but I'm here, aren't I? I'm alive, aren't I? We're all alive and well, aren't we? Why is everybody angry with me?"

"Everybody isn't," Anna replies.

"Why is it my fault?"

"Do you think it is your fault?" She studies me with an expression that can only be described as radiological. Anna sees right through to my bones.

"Of course not," I reply. "I know it's not my fault."

She deadbolts the door, then sets the alarm and

takes me into the kitchen. I try to remember the last time I ate or what day of the week it is. Then it glimmers. Saturday. I have already asked that several times now. Twenty hours have passed since I almost died. The table is set for two, and a large pot of soup simmers on the stove. I smell baking bread and am suddenly nauseous and starved at the same time, and despite all this, a detail registers. If Anna was expecting Lucy, why isn't the table set for three?

"When will Lucy go back to Miami?" Anna seems to read my thoughts as she lifts the lid off the pot and stirs with a long wooden spoon. "What would you like? Scotch?"

"A strong one."

She pulls the cork out of a bottle of Glenmorangie Sherry Wood Finish single malt whisky and pours its precious rosy essence over ice in cut crystal tumblers.

"I don't know when Lucy will go back. Have no idea, really." I begin to fill in the blanks for her. "ATF was involved in a takedown in Miami that turned bad, very bad. There was a shooting. Lucy . . ."

"Yes, yes, Kay, I know that part." Anna hands me my drink. She can sound impatient even when she is very calm. "It was all over the news. And I called you. Remember? We talked about Lucy."

"Oh, that's right," I mutter.

Anna takes the chair across from me, elbows on the table, leaning into our conversation. She is an amazingly intense, fit woman, tall and firm, a Leni Riefenstahl enlightened beyond her time and undaunted by the years. Her blue warm-up suit turns her eyes the same startling shade of cornflowers, and her silver hair is pulled back in a neat ponytail held by a black velvet band. I don't know for a fact that she had a face-lift or any other cosmetic work, but I suspect modern medicine has something to do with the way she looks. Anna could easily pass for a woman in her fifties.

"I assume Lucy came to stay with you while the incident is investigated," she comments. "I can only imagine the red tape."

The takedown had gone about as badly as one could. Lucy killed two members of an international gun smuggling cartel that we now believe is connected to Chandonne's crime family. She inadvertently wounded Jo, a DEA agent who at the time was her lover. Red tape is not the word for it.

"But I'm not sure you know the part about Jo," I tell Anna. "Her HIDTA partner."

"I do not know what HIDTA is."

"High Intensity Drug Trafficking Area. A squad made up of different law enforcement agencies working violent crimes. ATF, DEA, FBI, Miami-Dade," I tell her. "When the takedown went to hell two weeks ago, Jo got shot in the leg. It turned out the bullet was fired from Lucy's own gun."

Anna listens, sipping Scotch.

"So Lucy accidentally shot Jo, and then, of course, what comes out next is their personal relationship," I continue. "Which has been very strained. I don't know what's going on with them now, to tell you the truth. But Lucy is here. I guess she'll stay through the holidays, and then who knows?"

"I did not know she and Janet had broken up," Anna observes.

"Quite a while ago."

"I am very sorry." She is sincerely bothered by the news. "I liked Janet very much."

I look down at my soup. It has been a long time since Janet was a topic of conversation. Lucy never says a word about her. I realize I miss Janet very much and still think she was a very stabilizing, mature influence on my niece. If I am honest, I really don't like Jo. I am not sure why. Maybe, I consider as I reach for my drink, it is simply because she isn't Janet.

"And Jo's in Richmond?" Anna digs for more of the story.

"Ironically, she's from here, even though that's not how she and Lucy ended up together. They met in Miami through work. Jo will be recovering for a while, staying in Richmond with her parents, I guess. Don't ask me how that's going to work. They're fundamentalist Christians and not exactly supportive of their daughter's lifestyle."

"Lucy never picks anything easy," Anna says, and she is right. "Shootings and more shootings. What is it with her and shooting people? Thank goodness she did not kill again."

The weight in my chest presses down harder. My blood seems to have turned into a heavy metal.

"What is it with her and killing?" Anna pushes. "What happened this time worries me. If what I've heard on TV is to be believed."

"I haven't turned on TV. I don't know what they're saying." I sip my drink and think about cigarettes again. I have quit so many times in my life.

"She almost killed him, that Frenchman, Jean-Baptiste Chandonne. She had the gun pointed at him but you stopped her." Anna's eyes bore through my skull, probing for secrets. "You tell me."

I describe to her what happened. Lucy had gone to the Medical College of Virginia to bring Jo home from the hospital, and when they pulled up to my house after midnight, Chandonne and I were in the front yard. The Lucy I conjure up in my memory seems a stranger, a violent person I don't know, her face unrecognizably twisted by rage as she pointed the pistol at him, finger on the trigger, and I pleaded with her not to shoot. She was screaming at him, cursing him as I called out to her, no, no, Lucy, no! Chandonne was in unspeakable pain, blind and thrashing, rubbing snow into his chemically burned eyes, howling and begging for someone to help him. At this point, Anna interrupts my story.

"Was he speaking French?" she asks.

The question catches me off guard. I try to remember. "I think so."

"Then you understand French."

I pause again. "Well, I took it in high school. I just know it seemed at the time he was screaming for me to help him. I seemed to understand what he was saying."

"Did you try to help him?"

"I was trying to save his life, trying to stop Lucy from killing him."

"But that was for Lucy, not for him. You weren't really trying to save his life. You were trying to stop Lucy from ruining her own."

Thoughts collide, canceling each other out. I don't reply.

"She wanted to kill him," Anna goes on. "This was clearly her intention."

I nod, staring off, reliving it. *Lucy, Lucy.* I repeatedly called out her name, trying to shatter the
homicidal spell she was under. *Lucy.* I crawled
closer to her in the snowy front yard. *Put the gun
down. Lucy, you don't want to do this. Please. Put the
gun down.* Chandonne rolled and writhed, making the horrible sounds of a wounded animal,
and Lucy was on her knees, in combat position,
gun shaking in both hands as she pointed it at his
head. Then feet and legs were all around us. ATF
agents and police in dark battle dress clutching rifles and pistols had swarmed into my yard. Not
one of them knew what to do as I begged my
niece not to kill Chandonne in cold blood. *There's
been enough killing*, I pled with Lucy as I pulled
myself within inches of her, my left arm fractured
and useless. *Don't do this. Don't do this, please. We
love you.*

"You are quite certain it was Lucy's intention
to kill him, even though it wasn't self-defense?"
Anna asks again.

"Yes," I reply. "I'm certain."

"Then should we reconsider that perhaps it was
not necessary for her to kill those men down in
Miami?"

"That was totally different, Anna," I reply. "And
I can't blame Lucy for the way she reacted when
she saw him in front of my house—saw him and
me on the ground in the snow, not even ten feet

from each other. She knew about the other cases here, the murders of Kim Luong and Diane Bray. She knew damn well why he had come to my house, what he planned for me. How would you feel if you had been Lucy?"

"I cannot imagine."

"That's right," I reply. "I don't think anyone can imagine something like that until it happens. I know if I were the one driving up and it was Lucy in the yard, and he had tried to murder her, then . . ." I pause, analyzing, not really able to complete the thought.

"You would have killed him," Anna finishes what she must suspect I was going to say.

"Well, I might have."

"Even though he was no threat? He was in terrible pain, blind and helpless?"

"It's hard to know the other person is helpless, Anna. What did I know outside in the snow, in the dark, with a broken arm, terrorized?"

"Ah. But you knew enough to talk Lucy out of killing him." She gets up and I watch as she unhooks a ladle from the iron rack of pots and pans suspended overhead and fills big earthenware bowls, steam rising in aromatic clouds. She sets the soup on the table, giving me time to think about what she just said. "Have you ever considered that your life reads like one of your more complicated death certificates." Anna then says. "*Due to, due to, due to, due to."* She motions with her hands, conducting her own orchestra of emphasis. "Where you find yourself now *is due to* this and that and *due to* on and on, and it all goes back to the original injury. Your father's death."

I search to remember what I have told her about my past.

"You are who you are in life because you became a student of death at a very young age," she continues. "Most of your childhood you lived with your father's dying."

The soup is chicken vegetable and I detect bay leaves and sherry. I am not sure I can eat. Anna slips mitts over her hands and slides sourdough rolls out of the oven. She serves hot bread on small plates with butter and honey. "It seems to be your karma to return to the scene, so to speak, over and over," she analyzes. "The scene of your father's death, of that original loss. As if somehow you will undo it. But all you do is repeat it. The oldest pattern in human nature. I see it daily."

"This isn't about my father." I pick up my spoon. "This isn't about my childhood, and to tell you the truth, the last thing I care about right now is my childhood."

"It is about *not feeling.*" She pulls out her chair and sits back down. "About learning not to feel because it was too painful to feel." The soup is too hot to eat and she idly stirs it with a heavy, engraved silver spoon. "When you were a child, you could not live with the impending doom in your house, the fear, the grief, the anger. You shut down."

"Sometimes you have to do that."

"It is never good to do that." She shakes her head.

"Sometimes it's survival to do that," I disagree.

"Shutting down is denial. When you deny the past, you will repeat it. You are living proof. Your life has been one loss after another ever since that original loss. Ironically, you have turned loss into a profession, the doctor who hears the dead, the doctor who sits at the bedside of the dead. Your divorce from Tony. Mark's death. Then last year, Benton's murder. Then Lucy in a shoot-out and you almost lose her. And now, finally, you. This terrible man comes to your house and you almost lost you. Losses and more losses."

The pain from Benton's murder is frighteningly fresh. I fear it will always be fresh, that I will never escape the hollowness, the echo of empty rooms in my soul and the anguish in my heart. I am outraged all over again as I think of the police in my house unwittingly touching items that belonged to Benton, brushing past his paintings, tracking mud over the fine rug in the dining room he gave me for Christmas one year. No one knowing. No one caring.

"A pattern like this," Anna comments, "if it isn't arrested, takes on an unstoppable energy and sucks everything into its black hole."

I tell her my life is not in a black hole. I don't deny there is a pattern. I would have to be as dense as dirt not to see it. But on one point I am in adamant disagreement. "It bothers me considerably to hear you imply I brought him to my door," I tell her, referring again to Chandonne, whom I can scarcely bear to call by name. "That somehow I set everything into motion to bring a killer to my house. If that's what I hear you saying. If that *is* what you're saying."

"It is what I am asking." She butters a roll. "It is what I am asking you, Kay," she somberly repeats.

"Anna, how in God's name can you think I would somehow bring about my own murder?"

"Because you would not be the first or last person to do something like that. It is not conscious."

"Not me. Not subconsciously or unconsciously," I claim.

"There is much self-fulfilled prophecy here. You. Then Lucy. She almost became what she fights. Be careful who you choose for an enemy because that is who you become most like," Anna tosses Nietzsche's quote up into the air. She serves up words she has heard me say in the past.

"I didn't will him to come to my house," I repeat slowly and flatly. I continue to avoid saying Chandonne's name because I don't want to give him the power of being a real person to me.

"How did he know where you live?" Anna continues her questioning.

"It's been in the news numerous times over the years, unfortunately," I conjecture. "I don't know how he knew."

"What? He went to the library and looked up your address on microfilm? This creature so hideously deformed who rarely went out in the light of day? This dog-faced congenital anomaly, almost every inch of his face, his body covered with long lanugo hair, pale baby-fine hair? He went to the public library?" She lets the absurdity of this hover over us.

"I don't know how he knew," I repeat. "Where he was hiding isn't far from my house." I am getting upset. "Don't blame me. No one has a right to blame me for what he did. Why are you blaming me?"

"We create our own worlds. We destroy our own worlds. It is that simple, Kay," she answers me.

"I can't believe you think for a minute I wanted

him coming after me. I, of all people." An image of Kim Luong flashes. I remember fractured facial bones crunching beneath my latex-gloved fingers. I remember the pungent sweet odor of coagulating blood in the airless, hot storeroom where Chandonne dragged her dying body so he could release his frenzied lust, beating and biting and smearing her blood. "Those women didn't bring this upon themselves, either," I say with emotion.

"I did not know those women," Anna says. "I cannot speak to what they did or did not do."

An image of Diane Bray flashes, her arrogant beauty savaged, destroyed and crudely displayed on the bare mattress inside her bedroom. She was completely unrecognizable by the time he finished with her, seeming to hate her more completely than he did Kim Luong—more completely than the women we believe he murdered in Paris before he came to Richmond. I wonder out loud to Anna if Chandonne recognized himself in Bray and it excited his self-hate to its highest level. Diane Bray was cunning and cold. She was cruel and abused power as readily as she breathed air.

"You had every good reason to hate her," is Anna's reply.

This stops me in my mental tracks. I don't respond right away. I try to remember if I have ever said I hate someone, or worse, if I have actually been guilty of it. To hate another person is wrong. It is never right. Hate is a crime of the spirit that leads to crimes of the flesh. Hate is what brings so many of my patients to my door. I tell Anna that I didn't hate Diane Bray, even though she made it her mission to overpower me and almost succeeded in getting me fired. Bray was pathologically jealous and ambitious. But no, I tell Anna, I didn't hate Diane Bray. She was evil, I conclude. But she didn't deserve what he did to her. Certainly, she didn't invite it.

"You don't think so?" Anna questions all of it. "You do not think he did to her, symbolically, what she was doing to you? Obsession. Forcing her way into your life when you were vulnerable. Attacking, degrading, destroying—an overpowering that aroused her, perhaps even sexually. What is it you have told me so many times? People die the way they lived."

"Many of them do."

"Did she?"

"Symbolically, as you put it?" I reply. "Maybe."

"And you, Kay? Did you almost die the way you lived?"

"I didn't die, Anna."

"But you almost did," she says again. "And before he came to your door, you had almost given up. You almost stopped living when Benton did."

Tears touch my eyes.

"What do you think might have happened to you had Diane Bray not died?" Anna then asks.

Bray ran the Richmond police department and fooled people who mattered. In a very short time, she made a name for herself throughout Virginia, and ironically, her narcissism, her lust for power and recognition, it appears, may be what lured Chandonne to her. I wonder if he stalked her first. I wonder if he stalked me, and suppose the answer to both questions is that he must have.

"Do you think you'd still be the chief medical examiner if Diane Bray were alive?" Anna's stare is unwavering.

"I wouldn't have let her win." I taste my soup and my stomach flops. "I don't care how diabolical she was, I wouldn't have allowed it. My life is up to me. It was never up to her. My life is mine to make or ruin."

"Perhaps you are glad she is dead," Anna says.

"The world's better off without her." I push the place mat and everything on it well away from me. "That's the truth. The world is better off without people like her. The world would be better off without him."

"Better off without Chandonne?"

I nod.

"Then perhaps you wish Lucy had killed him after all?" she quietly suggests, and Anna has a way of demanding truth without being aggressive or judging. "Maybe you would pull the switch, as they say?"

"No." I shake my head. "No, I would not pull the switch on anyone. I can't eat. I'm sorry you went to so much trouble. I hope I'm not coming down with something."

"We have talked enough for now." Anna is suddenly the parent deciding it is time for bed. "Tomorrow is Sunday, a good day to stay in and be quiet and rest. I am clearing my calendar, canceling all my appointments for Monday. And then I'll cancel Tuesday and Wednesday and the rest of the week, if need be."

I try to object but she won't hear it.

"The good thing about being my age is I can do whatever the hell I want," she adds. "I am on call for emergencies. But that is all. And right now, you are my biggest emergency, Kay."

"I'm not an emergency." I get up from the table.

Anna helps me with my luggage and takes me down a long hallway that leads to the west wing of her majestic home. The guest room where I am to stay for an undetermined period of time is dominated by a large yew wood bed that, like much of the furniture in her house, is pale gold Biedermeier. Her decor is restrained, with straight and simple lines, but cumulus down-filled duvets and pillows and heavy draperies that flow in champagne silk waterfalls to the hardwood floor hint at her true nature. Anna's motivation in life is the comfort of others, to heal and to banish pain and celebrate pure beauty.

"What else do you need?" She hangs up my clothes.

I help put away other items in dresser drawers and realize I am trembling again.

"Do you need something to sleep?" She lines up my shoes on the closet floor.

Taking an Ativan or some other sedative is a tempting proposition that I resist. "I've always been afraid to make it a habit," I vaguely respond. "You can see how I am with cigarettes. I can't be trusted."

Anna looks at me. "It is very important you get sleep, Kay. No better friend to depression."

I am not sure what she is saying, but I know what she means. I *am* depressed. I am probably going to be depressed, and sleep deprivation makes everything so much worse. Throughout my life, insomnia has flared up like arthritis, and when I became a physician I had to resist the easy habit of indulging in one's own candy store. Prescription drugs have always been there. I have always stayed away from them.

Anna leaves me and I sit up in bed with the lights off, staring into the dark, halfway believing that when morning comes, I will find what has happened is just another one of my bad dreams, another horror that crept out from my deeper layers when I was not quite conscious. My rational voice probes my interior like a flashlight but dispels nothing. I can't illuminate any meaning to my almost being mutilated and killed and how that fact will affect the rest of my life. I can't feel it. I can't make sense of it. God, help me. I turn over on my side and shut my eyes. Now I lay me down to sleep, my mother used to pray with me, but I always thought the words were really more for my father in his sickbed down the hall. Sometimes when my mother would leave my room I would insert masculine pronouns into the verses. If he should die before he wakes, I pray the Lord his soul to take, and I would cry myself to sleep.

CHAPTER 3

I WAKE UP THE FOLLOWING morning to voices in the house and have the unsettling sensation that the telephone rang all night. I am not sure if I dreamed it. For an awful moment I have no idea where I am, then it comes to me in a sick, fearful wave. I work my way up against pillows and am still for a moment. I can tell through drawn curtains that the sun is aloof again, offering nothing but gray.

I help myself to a thick terry-cloth robe hanging on the back of the bathroom door and put on a pair of socks before venturing out to see who else is in the house. I hope the visitor is Lucy, and it is. She and Anna are in the kitchen. Small snowflakes sprinkle down past expansive windows overlooking the backyard and the flat pewter river. Bare trees etched darkly against the day move slightly in the wind, and wood smoke rises from the house of the nearest neighbor. Lucy has on a faded warm-up suit left over from when she took computer and robotics courses at MIT. It appears she has styled her short auburn hair with her fingers, and she seems unusually grim and has a glassy-eyed, bloodshot look that I associate with too much booze the night before.

"Did you just get here?" I hug her good morning.

"Actually, last night," she replies, squeezing me tight. "I couldn't resist. Thought I'd drop by and we'd have a slumber party. But you were down for the count. It's my fault for getting here so late."

"Oh no." I go hollow inside. "You should have gotten me up. Why didn't you?"

"No way. How's the arm?"

"It doesn't hurt as much." This is not at all true. "You checked out of the Jefferson?"

"Nope, still there." Lucy's expression is unreadable. She drops to the floor and pulls off her warm-up pants, revealing bright spandex running tights underneath.

"I am afraid your niece was a bad influence," Anna says. "She brought over a very nice bottle of Veuve Cliquot and we stayed up much too late. I would not let her drive back downtown."

I feel a twinge of hurt, or maybe it is jealousy. "Champagne? Are we celebrating something?" I inquire.

Anna replies with a slight shrug. She is preoccupied. I sense she carries very heavy thoughts that she does not want to set down before me, and I wonder if the phone really did ring last night. Lucy unzips her jacket, revealing more bright blue and black nylon that fits her strong, athletic body like paint.

"Yeah. Celebrating," Lucy says, bitterness lacing her voice. "ATF's put me on admin leave."

I can't believe I heard her right. Administrative leave is the same thing as being suspended. It is the first step in being fired. I glance at Anna for any sign that she already knows about this, but she seems just as surprised as I am.

"They've put me on the beach." ATF slang for suspension. "I'll get a letter in the next week or so that will cite all my transgressions." Lucy acts blasé but I know her too well to be fooled. Anger is about all I have seen boiling out of her over recent months and years, and it is there now, molten beneath her many complex layers. "They'll give me all the reasons I should be terminated and I get to appeal. Unless I decide to just fuck it and quit. Which I might. I don't need them."

"Why? What on earth happened? Not because of him." I mean Chandonne.

With rare exception, when an agent has been in a shooting or some other critical incident, the routine is to immediately involve him in peer support and reassign him to a less stressful job, such as arson investigation instead of the dangerous undercover work Lucy was doing in Miami. If the individual is emotionally unable to cope, he might even be granted traumatic leave time. But administrative leave is another matter. It is punishment, plain and simple.

Lucy looks up at me from her seat on the floor, legs straight out, hands planted behind her back. "It's the old damned if you do, damned if you don't," she retorts. "If I'd shot him, I'd have hell to pay. I didn't shoot him and I have hell to pay."

"You were in a shoot-out in Miami, then very soon after you come to Richmond and almost shot someone else." Anna states the truth. It doesn't matter if the *someone else* is a serial killer who broke into my house. Lucy has a history of resorting to force that predates even the incident in Miami. Her troubled past presses down heavily in Anna's kitchen like a low-pressure front.

"I'm the first to admit it," Lucy replies. "All of us wanted to blow him away. You don't think Marino did?" She meets my eyes. "You don't think every cop, every agent who showed up at your house didn't want to pull the trigger? They think I'm some kind of soldier of fortune, some psycho who gets off on killing people. At least, that's what they're hinting at."

"You do need time off," Anna says bluntly. "Maybe it is about that and nothing more."

"That's not what this is about. Come on, if one of the guys had done what I did in Miami, he'd be a hero. If one of the guys almost killed Chandonne, the suits in D.C. would be applauding his restraint, not nailing him for *almost* doing something. How can you punish someone for *almost* doing something? In fact, how can you even prove someone *almost* did something?"

"Well, they'll have to prove it," the lawyer, the investigator in me tells her. At the same time I am reminded that Chandonne almost did something to me. He didn't actually do it, no matter his intention, and his eventual legal defense will make a big issue of this fact.

"They can do whatever they want," Lucy replies, as hurt and outrage swell. "They can fire me. Or bring me back in and park my butt at a desk in some little windowless room somewhere in South Dakota or Alaska. Or bury me in some chicken-shit department like audio-visual."

"Kay, you haven't had coffee yet." Anna attempts to dispel the mounting tension.

"So maybe that's my problem. Maybe that's why nothing's making any sense this morning." I head to the drip machine near the sink. "Anybody else?"

There are no other takers. I pour a cup as Lucy

leans into deep stretches, and it is always amazing to watch her move, liquid and supple, her muscles calling attention to themselves without deliberation or fanfare. Having started life pudgy and slow, she has spent years engineering herself into a machine that will respond the way she demands, very much like the helicopters she flies. Maybe it is her Brazilian blood that adds the dark fire to her beauty, but Lucy is electrifying. People fix their eyes on her wherever she goes, and her reaction is a shrug, at most.

"I don't know how you can go out and run in weather like this," Anna says to her.

"I like pain." Lucy snaps on her butt pack, a pistol inside it.

"We need to talk more about this, figure out what you're going to do." Caffeine defibrillates my slow heart and jolts me back into a clear head.

"After I run, I'm going to work out in the gym," Lucy tells us. "I'll be gone for a while."

"Pain and more pain," Anna muses.

All I can think of when I look at my niece is how extraordinary she is and how much unfairness life has dealt her. She never knew her biological father, and then Benton came along and was the father she never had, and she lost him, too. Her mother is a self-centered woman who is too competitive with Lucy to love her, if my sister, Dorothy, is capable of loving anyone, and I really

don't believe she is. Lucy is possibly the most intelligent, intricate person I know. It has not earned
her many fans. She has always been irrepressible
and as I watch her spring out of the kitchen like
an Olympic runner, armed and dangerous, I am
reminded of when she began the first grade at age
four and a half and flunked conduct.

"How do you flunk conduct?" I asked Dorothy
when she called me in a rage to complain about
the horrible hardship of being Lucy's mother.

"She talks all the time and interrupts the other
students and is always raising her hand to answer
questions!" Dorothy blurted over the phone. "Do
you know what her teacher wrote on her report
card? Here! Let me read it to you! *Lucy does not
work and play well with others. She is a show-off and
a know-it-all and is constantly taking things apart, such
as the pencil sharpener and doorknobs.*"

Lucy is gay. That is probably most unfair of all
because she can't outgrow it or get over it. Homosexuality is unfair because it creates unfairness.
For that reason, it broke my heart when I found
out this part of my niece's life. I desperately don't
want her to suffer. I also force myself to admit that
I have managed to ignore the obvious up until
now. ATF isn't going to be generous or forgiv-
ing, and Lucy has probably known this for a while.
Administration in D.C. won't look at all she has

accomplished, but will focus on her through the distorting lens of prejudice and jealousy.

"It'll be a witch hunt," I say after Lucy has left the house.

Anna cracks eggs into a bowl.

"They want her gone, Anna."

She drops shells into the sink and opens the refrigerator, pulling out a carton of milk, glancing at the expiration date. "There are those who think she is a hero," she says.

"Law enforcement tolerates women. It doesn't celebrate them and punishes those who become heroes. That's the dirty little secret no one wants to talk about," I say.

Anna vigorously whips eggs with a fork.

"It's our same story," I continue. "We went to medical school in a day when we had to apologize for taking men's slots. In some cases, we were shunned, sabotaged. I had three other women in my first-year medical school class. How many did you have?"

"It was different in Vienna."

"Vienna?" My thoughts evaporate.

"Where I was trained," she informs me.

"Oh." I experience guilt again as I learn another detail I don't know about my good friend.

"When I came here, everything you are saying about how it is for women was exactly like that."

Anna's mouth is set in a hard line as she pours egg batter into a cast-iron skillet. "I remember what it was like when I moved to Virginia. How I was treated."

"Believe me, I know all about it."

"I was thirty years ahead of you, Kay. You really don't know all about it."

Eggs steam and bubble. I lean against the counter, drinking black coffee, wishing I had been awake when Lucy came in last night, aching because I didn't talk to her. I had to find out her news like this, almost as a *by the way.* "Did she talk to you?" I ask Anna. "About what she just told us?"

She folds the eggs over and over. "Looking back on it, I think she showed up with champagne because she wanted to tell you. Rather an inappropriate effect, considering her news." She pops multi-grain English muffins out of the toaster. "It is easy to assume that psychiatrists have such deep conversations with everyone, when in truth, people rarely tell me their true feelings, even when they pay me by the hour." She carries our plates to the table. "Mostly, people tell me what they think. That is the problem. People think too much."

"They won't be blatant." I am preoccupied with ATF again as Anna and I sit across from each other. "Their attack will be covert, like the FBI.

And in truth, the FBI ran her off for the same reason. She was their rising star, a computer wizard, a helicopter pilot, the first female member of the Hostage Rescue Team." I rush through Lucy's resume as Anna's expression turns increasingly skeptical. We both know it is unnecessary for me to recite all this. She has known Lucy since Lucy was a child. "Then the gay card was played." I can't stop. "Well, she left them for ATF and here we go again. On and on, history repeated. Why are you looking at me like that?"

"Because you are consuming yourself with Lucy's problems when your own loom larger than Mont Blanc."

My attention wanders out the window. A blue jay helps himself to the bird feeder, feathers ruffling, sunflower seeds falling and peppering the snowy earth like lead shot. Pale fingers of sunlight probe the overcast morning. I nervously turn my coffee cup in small circles on the table. My elbow throbs slowly and deeply as we eat. Whatever my problems are, I resist talking about them, as if to voice them will somehow give them life—as if they don't have life already. Anna doesn't push. We are quiet. Silverware clinks against plates and snow drifts down more thickly, frosting shrubbery and trees and hovering foggily over the river. I return to my room and take a long, hot bath, my cast propped on the side of the tub. I am dressing with difficulty, realizing that I am not likely to ever master tying shoes with one hand, when the doorbell rings. Moments later, Anna knocks and asks me if I am decent.

Thoughts bloom darkly and roll like storms. I am not expecting company. "Who is it?" I call out.

"Buford Righter," she says.

CHAPTER 4

EHIND HIS BACK, THE CITY
commonwealth's attorney is called many
things: Easy Righter (he is weak), Righter
Wrong (wishy-washy), Fighter Righter (anything
but), Booford (scared of his own shadow). Always
proper, always appropriate, Righter is always the
Virginia gentleman he was trained to be in the
Caroline County horse country of his roots. No
one loves him. No one hates him. He is neither
feared nor respected. Righter has no fire. I can't
recall ever seeing him emotional, no matter how
cruel or heart-wrenching the case. Worse, he is
squeamish when it comes to the details I bring to
the forum, preferring to focus on points of law
and not the appalling human messiness left by its
violations.

His avoidance of the morgue has resulted in his
not being as well versed in forensic science and
medicine as he ought to be. In fact, he is the only

seasoned prosecutor I know who doesn't seem to mind stipulating cause of death. In other words, he allows the paper record to speak for the medical examiner in the courtroom. This is a travesty. To me it constitutes malpractice. When the medical examiner isn't in the courtroom, then, in a sense, neither is the body, and jurors don't envision the victim or what he went through during the process of dying violently. Clinical words on protocols simply don't evoke the terror or the suffering, and for this reason, it is usually the defense, not the prosecution, who wants to stipulate cause of death.

"Buford, how are you?" I hold out my hand and he glances at my cast and my sling, and down at my untied shoelaces and my shirttail hanging out. He has never seen me in anything less than a suit and in a setting that befits my professional rank, and his brow knits into an expression that is supposed to evince genteel compassion and understanding, the humility and caring of those handpicked by God to rule the rest of us lesser creatures. His type abounds among the first families of Virginia, a privileged, dusty people who have refined the skill of disguising their elitism and arrogance beneath a heavy aura of burden, as if it is so damn hard to be them.

"The question is, how are you?" he says, sitting

back down in Anna's handsome oval living room with its vaulted ceiling and view of the river.

"I really don't know how to answer that, Buford." I choose a rocking chair. "Every time someone asks, my mind reboots." Anna must have just gotten the fire going and has vanished, and I have the uneasy sensation that her absence is about more than her being politely unobtrusive.

"No small wonder. Don't even know how you're able to function after what you've been through." Righter speaks with a syrupy Virginia drawl. "Sure am sorry to barge in like this, Kay, but something's come up, something unexpected. Nice place, isn't it?" He continues to survey his surroundings. "She build or was it already here?"

I don't know or care.

"You two are pretty close, I gather," he adds.

I am not sure if he is making small talk or fishing. "She's been a good friend," I reply.

"I know she thinks the world of you. All of which is to say," he goes on, "that you couldn't be in better hands right now, in my opinion."

I resent his implying that I am in anybody's hands, as if I am a patient on a ward, and I say so.

"Oh, I see." He continues his scan of oil paintings on pale rose walls, of art glass and sculptures and European furniture. "Then you don't have a professional relationship? Never have?"

"Not literally," I reply testily. "I have never had an appointment."

"She ever prescribe medications for you?" he blandly goes on.

"Not that I recall."

"Well, can't believe it's almost Christmas." Righter sighs, his attention wandering back in from the river, back to me.

To use a Lucy term, he looks *dorky* in Bavarian button-up heavy green wool pants tucked into fleece-lined rubber boots with big tread. He wears a plaid Burberry-type wool sweater buttoned up to his chin, as if he can't decide whether he will climb a mountain or play golf in Scotland this day.

"Well," he says, "let me tell you why I'm here. Marino called a couple hours ago. There's been an unanticipated development in the Chandonne case."

The stab of betrayal is instant. Marino has told me nothing. He hasn't even bothered to see how I am doing this morning.

"I'll give you a summation as best I can." Righter crosses his legs and demurely places his hands in his lap, a thin wedding band and University of Virginia class ring glinting in lamplight. "Kay, I'm sure you're aware the news of what happened at your house and the subsequent apprehension of Chandonne has been broadcast all over. I mean *all over*. I'm sure you've followed it and can appreciate the magnitude of what I'm about to say."

Fear is a fascinating emotion. I have studied it endlessly and often tell people the best example of how it works is to recall the reaction of another driver you have pulled in front of and almost hit. Panic instantly turns to rage and the other person lays on the horn, makes obscene gestures or, these days, shoots you. I go through the progression completely, flawlessly, shrill fear turning to fury. "I've not followed the news deliberately and certainly won't appreciate the magnitude of it," I reply. "I never appreciate having my privacy violated."

"The murders of Kim Luong and Diane Bray created a lot of attention, but nothing like this—the murder attempt on you," he continues. "I'm supposing, then, you didn't see *The Washington Post* this morning?"

I just stare at him, seething.

"Front-page photo of Chandonne in the stretcher being carried into the E.R., his hairy shoulders sticking out of the sheets like some sort of long-haired dog. Of course, his face was covered by bandages, but you certainly could get the sense of how grotesque he is. And the tabloids. You can imagine. Werewolf in Richmond, Beauty and the Beast, that sort of thing." Disdain creeps around the edges of his voice, as if sensationalism is obscene, and I am subjected to an un-wanted image of him making love to his wife. I can envision him fucking with his socks on. I sus-pect he would consider sex an indignity, the prim-itive judge of biology overruling his higher self. I have heard rumors. In the men's room, he won't use the urinals or toilets in front of anybody. He is a compulsive hand-washer. All of this is buzzing through my mind as he continues to sit so prop-erly and disclose the wilting public exposure Chandonne has caused me.

"Do you know if photographs of my house have shown up anywhere?" I have to ask. "There were photographers when I came out of my driveway last night."

"Well, I do know there have been some heli-copters flying over this morning. Someone told me that," he replies, making me instantly suspi-cious that he has been back at my house again and witnessed this for himself. "Taking aerial shots." He stares out at snow drifting down. "I guess the weather's put a stop to it. The guard gate's been turning away quite a few cars. The press, the cu-rious. In an unexpected way, a damn good thing you're staying with Dr. Zenner. Funny how things work out." He pauses, staring off toward the river again. A flock of Canada geese circles, as if wait-ing for instructions from the tower. "Normally, what I'd recommend is you don't return to your house until after the trial. . . ."

"Until after the trial?" I interrupt.

"That would be if the trial were here," he leads up to his next revelation, which I automatically assume is a reference to a change of venue.

"You're saying, the trial will probably be moved out of Richmond," I interpolate. "And what do you mean by *normally?*"

"That's what I'm getting to. Marino got a call from the Manhattan D.A.'s office."

"This morning? This is the new development?" I am baffled. "What does New York have to do with anything?"

"This was a few hours ago," he goes on. "The head of the sex crimes division, a woman named Jaime Berger—a weird name, spelled J-A-I-M-E but pronounced *Jamie.* You may have heard of her. In fact, I wouldn't be surprised if you two know each other."

"We've never met," I reply. "But I've heard of her."

"Friday, December fifth, two years ago," Righter goes on, "the body of a twenty-eight-year-old black female was found in New York, an apartment in the area of Second Avenue and Seventy-seventh Street, Upper East Side. Apparently a woman who was a television meteorologist, uh, did the weather, on CNBC. Don't know if you heard about the case?"

I begin to make connections against my will.

"When she didn't show up at the studio early that morning, the morning of the fifth, and didn't answer the phone, someone checked on her. The victim"—Righter pulls a tiny leather notebook out of his back pants pocket and flips through pages—"name of Susan Pless. Well, her body's back in her bedroom on the rug by the bed. Clothes ripped off from the waist up, face and head so badly beaten it looks like she was in a plane crash." He glances up at me. "And that's a quote, the plane crash part—supposedly how Berger described it to Marino. What was the word you used to use? Remember that case where the drunk teenagers were racing in a pickup truck and one of them decides to hang halfway out his window and has the misfortune of encountering a tree?"

"Bogging," I dully reply as I take in what he is saying. "Face caved in from severe impact, such as you might find in plane crashes or in cases where people have jumped or fallen from high places and hit face first. Two years ago?" My thoughts spin. "How can that be?"

"I won't go into all the gory detail." He is flipping more pages in his notebook. "But there were bite marks, including on the hands and feet, and a lot of strange, long pale hairs adhering to blood that at first were presumed to be animal hairs. Maybe a long-haired Angora cat or something." He looks up at me. "You're getting the drift."

All along we have assumed Chandonne's trip to Richmond was his first to the United States. We have no logical reason for this assumption beyond our painting him as a Quasimodo of sorts who spent his life hidden in the basement of his powerful family's Paris home. We also assumed he sailed to Richmond from Antwerp at the same time his brother's dead body was headed our way. Are we wrong about that, too? I toss this out to Righter.

"You know what Interpol conjectured, at any rate," he comments.

"That he was aboard the *Sirius* under an alias," I recall, "a man named Pascal who was immediately taken to the airport when the ship came to port here in Richmond in early December. Supposedly a family emergency required him to fly back to Europe." I repeat information Jay Talley presented while I was in Lyon at Interpol last week. "But no one ever actually saw him board the plane, so it's been assumed Pascal was really Chandonne and he never flew anywhere but stayed here and started killing. But if this guy readily travels in and out of the U.S., no telling how long he's been in the States or when he got here or anything. So much for theories."

"Well, I suppose a lot of them may end up revised before it's all over. No disrespect to Interpol or anyone else intended." Righter recrosses his legs and seems strangely pleased.

"Has he been located? This Pascal person?"

Righter doesn't know, but he speculates that whoever the real Pascal is—assuming he exists— he is probably just one more rotten apple involved with the Chandonne family's criminal cartel. "Another guy with an alias, possibly even an associate of the dead guy in the cargo container," Righter speculates. "The brother, I guess. Thomas Chandonne, who we certainly know was involved in the family business."

"I'm assuming Berger heard the news about Chandonne's being caught, heard about his murders and called us," I say.

"Recognized the MO, that's right. Says the case of Susan Pless has always haunted her. Berger's in a hellfire hurry to compare DNA. Apparently got seminal fluid and they've got a profile on it, have had it for two years now."

"So the seminal fluid in Susan's case was analyzed." I ponder this, somewhat surprised because typically overworked, financially stressed labs do not analyze DNA evidence until there is a suspect for comparison—especially if there isn't an extensive databank to run the profile through in hopes of a cold hit. In 1997, New York's databank wasn't even in existence yet. "Does this mean they had a suspect originally?" I ask.

"I think they had one guy in mind who didn't pan out," Righter replies. "All I know is they did get a profile and we're getting Chandonne's DNA up there to the M.E.'s office immediately—in fact, the sample's on its way, even as we speak. To state the obvious, we've got to know if it's a match *before* Chandonne's arraigned here in Richmond. Got to cut that off at the pass, and the good news is we're given the gift of at least a few extra days because of his medical condition, because of the chemical burns to his eyes." He says this as if I had nothing to do with it. "Kind of like the golden hour you always talk about, that brief period of time you've got to save someone who's been in an awful accident or whatever. This is our golden hour. We'll get the DNA compared and see if Chandonne is in fact the person who killed the woman in New York two years ago."

Righter has an annoying habit of repeating things I have said, as if being anecdotal somehow lets him off the hook for remaining ignorant about matters that count. "What about bite marks?" I ask. "Was there any information on those? Chandonne has very unusual dentition."

"You know, Kay," he says, "I really didn't get into those sorts of details."

Of course, he would not have. I push for the

truth, for the real reason he has come to see me this morning. "And what if the DNA points to Chandonne? You want to know before the arraignment here? Why?" It is a rhetorical question. I think I know why. "You don't want him arraigned here. You intend to turn him over to New York and let him be tried up there first."

He avoids my eyes.

"Why in the world would you do that, Buford?" I go on as I become convinced that this is exactly what he has decided. "So you can wash your hands of him? Ship him up to Riker's Island and be rid of him? And bring no justice to the cases here? Let's just be honest, Buford, if they get a first-degree murder conviction in Manhattan, you won't bother to try him here, now will you?"

He gives me one of his sincere looks. "Everyone in the community has always respected you so much," he startles me by saying.

"Has always?" Alarm shoots through me like cold water. "As in not anymore?"

"I'm just telling you I understand how you feel—that you and these other poor women deserve him punished to the full extent of the . . ."

"So I guess the bastard just gets away with what he tried to do to me," I hotly cut him off. Beneath all this is pain. The pain of rejection. The pain of abandonment. "I guess he just gets away with what he did to these other poor women, as you put it. Am I right?"

"They have the death penalty in New York," he replies.

"Oh for God's sake," I exclaim in disgust. I fix on him intensely, hotly, like the focus of the magnifying glass I used in childhood experiments to burn holes in paper and dead leaves. "And when have they ever imposed it?" He knows the answer is *never*. No one ever gets the needle in Manhattan.

"And there's no guarantee it would be imposed in Virginia, either," Righter reasonably answers. "The defendant isn't an American citizen. He has a bizarre disease or deformity or whatever it is. We're not even certain he speaks English."

"He certainly spoke English when he came to my house."

"He might get off on insanity, for all we know."

"I guess that depends on the skill of the prosecutor, Buford."

Righter blinks. His jaw muscles bunch. He looks like a Hollywood parody of an accountant—all buttoned up tight and in tiny glasses—who has just been subjected to an offensive smell.

"Have you talked to Berger?" I ask him. "You must have. You couldn't have come up with this on your own. You two have made a deal."

"We've conferred. There's pressure, Kay. Certainly you've got to appreciate that. For one thing, he's French. You got any idea how the French would react if we tried to execute one of their native sons here in Virginia?"

"Good God," I blurt out. "This isn't about capital punishment. This is about punishment, period. You know how I feel about capital punishment, Buford. I'm against it. I'm more against it the older I get. But he should be held responsible for what he did here in Virginia, damn it."

Righter says nothing, looking out the window again.

"So you and Berger agreed if the DNA matches, Manhattan can have Chandonne," I offer my summation.

"Think about it. This is the best we could hope for in terms of change of venue, so to speak." Righter gives me his eyes again. "And you know damn well the case could never be tried here in Richmond with all the publicity and whatnot. We'd probably all get sent out to some rural courthouse a million miles from here, and how would you like to be put through that for weeks, possibly months, on end?"

"That's right." I get up and jab logs with the poker, heat pressing against my face, sparks exploding up the chimney like a flock of spooked starlings. "God forbid that we should be incon-

venienced." I jab hard with my good arm, as if I
am trying to kill the fire. I sit back down, flushed
and suddenly on the verge of tears. I know all
about post-traumatic stress syndrome and accept
that I am suffering from it. I am anxious and star-
tle easily. A little while ago I turned on a local clas-
sical music station and Pachelbel overwhelmed
me with grief and I began to sob. I know the
symptoms. I swallow hard and steady myself.
Righter watches me in silence, with a tired look
of sad nobility, as if he is Robert E. Lee remembering a painful battle.

"What will happen to me?" I ask. "Or do I just
go on with my life now as if I never worked these
God-awful murders—as if I never autopsied his
victims or escaped with my life when he forced
his way into my house? What will my role in this
be, Buford, supposing he's tried in New York?"

"That will be up to Ms. Berger," he replies.

"Free lunches." It is a term I use when referring to victims who never see justice. In the scenario Righter is suggesting, I, for example, would
be a free lunch because Chandonne will never go
to trial in New York for what he intended to do
to me in Richmond. More unconscionably, he
will not be given so much as a slap on the hand
for the murders he committed here, either.
"You've just thrown this entire city to the
wolves," I tell him.

He realizes the double entendre the same moment I do. I see it in his eyes. Richmond has already been thrown to one wolf, Chandonne, whose modus operandi when he began killing in France was to leave notes signed *Le Loup-Garou,* the werewolf. Now justice for this city's victims will be in the hands of strangers, or more to the point, there will be no justice. Anything can happen. Anything will.

"What if France wants to extradite him?" I challenge Righter. "What if New York allows it?"

"We could cite *what ifs* until the moon turns blue," he says.

I stare at him with open disdain.

"Don't take this personally, Kay." Righter gives me that pious, sad look again. "Don't turn this into your personal war. We just want the bastard out of commission. Doesn't matter who accomplishes that."

I get up from my chair. "Well, it does matter. It sure as hell does," I tell him. "You're a coward, Buford." I turn my back on him and walk out of the room.

Minutes later, from behind the shut door in my wing of the house, I hear Anna showing Righter out. Obviously, he lingered long enough to talk to her, and I wonder what he might have said about me. I sit on the edge of my bed, utterly lost. I can't remember ever feeling this lonely, this frightened, and am relieved when I hear Anna coming down the hall. She knocks lightly on my door.

"Come in," I say in an unsteady voice.

She stands in the doorway looking at me. I feel like a child, powerless, hopeless, foolish. "I insulted Righter," I tell her. "Doesn't matter if what I said was true. I called him a coward."

"He thinks you are unstable right now," she replies. "He is concerned. He is also *ein Mann ohne Rückgrat*. A man without backbone, as we say where I come from." She smiles a little.

"Anna, I'm not unstable."

"Why are we in here when we can be enjoying the fire?" she says.

She intends to talk to me. "Okay," I concede, "you win."

CHAPTER 5

I HAVE NEVER BEEN ANNA'S PA-
tient. For that matter, I have never had psy-
chotherapy of any sort, which is not to say I
have never needed it. Certainly I have. I don't
know anybody who can't benefit from good
counsel. It is simply that I am so private and don't
trust people easily and for good reason. There is
no such thing as absolute discretion. I am a doctor. I know other doctors. Doctors talk to each
other and to their family and friends. They tell secrets that they swear upon Hippocrates they will
never utter to another soul. Anna switches off
lamps. The late morning is overcast and as dark as
dusk, and rose-painted walls catch firelight and
make the living room irresistibly cozy. I am suddenly self-conscious. Anna has set the stage for my
unveiling. I pick the rocker and she pulls an ottoman close and perches on the edge of it, facing
me like a great bird hunched over its nest.

"You will not get through this if you remain silent." She is brutally direct.

Grief rises in my throat and I try to swallow it.

"You are traumatized," Anna goes on. "Kay, you are not made of steel. Not even you can endure so much and just keep going as if nothing has happened. So many times I called you after Benton was killed, and you would not find time for me. Why? Because you did not want to talk."

I can't hide my emotions this time. Tears slide down my face and drop in my lap like blood.

"I have always told my patients when they do not face their problems, they are headed for a day of reckoning." Anna sits forward, intensely leaning into the words she fires straight at my heart. "This is your day of reckoning." She points at me, staring. "Now you will talk to me, Kay Scarpetta."

I blearily look down at my lap. My slacks are speckled with tears and I make the inane connection that the drops are perfectly round because they fell at a ninety-degree angle. "I can never get away from it," I say in despair under my breath.

"Get away from what?" This has snagged Anna's interest.

"What I do. Everything reminds me of something from my work. I don't talk about it."

"I want you to talk about it now," she tells me.

"It's foolish."

She waits, the patient fisherman, knowing I am nudging the hook. Then I take it. I give Anna examples I find embarrassing, if not ridiculous. I tell her I never drink tomato juice or V8 or Bloody Marys on the rocks because when the ice begins to melt, it looks like coagulating blood separating from serum. I stopped eating liver in medical school, and the idea of considering any sort of organ as something for my palate is impossible. I recall a morning on Hilton Head Island when Benton and I were walking on the beach, and the receding surf had left areas of crinkled gray sand that looked remarkably like the lining of the stomach. My thoughts twist and turn where they will, and a trip to France unfolds for the first time in years. On one of the rare occasions when Benton and I ever really got away from our work, we toured the Grands Vins de Bourgogne and were received by the revered domains of Drouhin and Dugat, and tasted from casks of Chambertin, Montrachet, Musigny and Vosne-Romanée. "I remember being moved in ways I can't say," I share memories I did not know I still had. "The light of early spring changing on the slopes and the gnarled reach of cut-back winter vines, all holding up their hands in the same way, offering the best they have, their essence, to us. And so often we don't touch their character, don't take the time to find the harmony in subtle tones, the symphony fine wines play on your tongue if you let them." My voice drifts off. Anna silently waits for me to come back. "Like my being asked only about my cases," I go on. "Only asked about the horrors I see, when there is so much else to me. I am not some god-damn cheap thrill with a screw cap."

"You feel lonely," Anna softly observes. "And misunderstood. Perhaps as dehumanized as your dead patients."

I do not answer her but continue my analogies, describing when Benton and I traveled by train across France for several weeks, ending in Bordeaux, and the rooftops got redder toward the south. The first touch of spring shimmered an unreal green on trees, and veins of water and the bigger arteries aspired toward the sea, just as all blood vessels in the body begin and end at the heart. "I'm constantly struck by the symmetry in nature, the way creeks and tributaries from the air look like the circulatory system, and rocks remind me of old scattered bones," I say. "And the brain starts out smooth and becomes convoluted and crevassed with time, much as mountains develop distinction over thousands of years. We are subjected to the same laws of physics. Yet we aren't. The brain, for example, doesn't look like what it does. On gross examination, it's about as exciting as a mushroom."

Anna is nodding. She asks if I shared any of these reflections with Benton. I say, no. She wants to know why I didn't feel inclined to share what seem like harmless perceptions with him, my lover, and I tell her I need to think about this for a minute. I am not sure of the answer.

"No." She prods me. "Do not think. Feel it."

I ponder.

"No. Feel it, Kay. *Feel it.*" She touches her hand over her heart.

"I have to think. I've gotten where I am in life by thinking," I reply defensively, snapping to, coming out of uncommon space I have just been in. I am back in her living room now and understand everything that has happened to me.

"You have gotten where you are in life by knowing," she says. "And knowing is perceiving. Thinking is how we process what we perceive, and thinking often masks the truth. Why did you not wish to share your more poetic side with Benton?"

"Because I don't really acknowledge that side. It's a useless side. To compare the brain to a mushroom in court would get you nowhere, for example," I reply.

"Ah." Anna nods again. "You make analogies in court all the time. That is why you are such an effective witness. You evoke images so the common person can understand. Why did you not tell

Benton the associations you are just now telling me?"

I stop rocking and reposition my broken arm, resting the cast in my lap. I turn away from Anna and look out at the river, feeling suddenly evasive like Buford Righter. Dozens of Canada geese have congregated around an old sycamore tree. They sit in the grass like dark, long-necked gourds, and puff and flap and peck for food. "I don't want to go through that looking glass," I tell her. "It isn't just that I didn't want to tell Benton. I don't want to tell anyone. I don't want to tell it at all. And by not repeating involuntary images and associations, I don't, well, I don't . . ."

Anna nods again, deeply this time. "By not acknowledging them, you don't invite your imagination into your work," she finishes my thought.

"I have to be clinical, objective. You of all people should understand."

She studies me before replying. "Is it that? Or might it be that you are avoiding the unbearable suffering you most certainly would invite if you allowed your imagination to get involved in your cases?" She leans closer, resting her elbows on her knees, gesturing. "What if, for example"—she pauses dramatically—"you could take the facts of science and medicine and use your imagination to reconstruct in detail the last minutes of Diane Bray's life? What if you could conjure it up like the footage of a film and watch—watch her being attacked, watch her hemorrhage, watch her being bitten and beaten? Watch her die?"

"That would be unspeakably awful," I barely reply.

"How powerful if a jury could see a film like that," she says.

Nervous impulses boil beneath my skin like thousands of minnows.

"But if you went through that looking glass, as you refer to it," she goes on, "then where might it end?" She throws her hands up. "Ah. Maybe it would not end, and you would be forced to watch the footage of Benton's murder."

I shut my eyes. I resist her. No. Please, Lord, don't make me see that. A flash of Benton in the dark, a gun trained on him and the ratcheting sound, the snap of steel as they handcuff him. Taunts. They would taunt him, *Mister FBI, you're so smart, what are we gonna do next, Mister Profiler? Can you read our minds, figure us out, predict? Huh?* He wouldn't answer them. He would ask them nothing as they forced him into a small neighborhood grocery store on the western fringes of the University of Pennsylvania that had closed at five in the afternoon. Benton was going to die. They would torment and torture him, and that was the part he would center on—how to short-circuit the pain and degradation he knew they would inflict if they had time. Darkness and the spurt of a match. His face wavering in the light of a small flame that trembles with each stir of air as those two psychopathic assholes move about in the plenum of a shitty little Pakistani grocery store they torched after he was dead.

My eyelids fly open. Anna is talking to me. Cold sweat crawls down my sides like insects. "I'm sorry. What did you say?"

"Very, very painful." Her face melts with compassion. "I cannot imagine."

Benton walks into my mind. He wears his favorite khakis, and his running shoes, Saucony running shoes. Sauconys were the only brand he would wear and I used to call him a fussbudget because he was so particular if he really liked something. And he has on the old UVA sweatshirt Lucy gave him, dark blue with bright orange letters, and over the years it has gotten very faded and soft. He cut off the sleeves because they were too short, and I have always liked how he looks in that old, worn-out sweatshirt, with his silver hair, his clean profile, the mysteries behind his intense, dark eyes. His hands lightly curl around the armrests of his chair. He has the fingers of a pianist, long and slender and expressive when he talks, and always gentle when they touch me, which is less and less with time. I am saying all this out loud to Anna, speaking in the present tense about a man who has been dead for more than a year.

"What secrets do you think he kept from you?" Anna asks. "What mysteries did you see in his eyes?"

"Oh God. Mostly about work." My breath trembles, my heart flying away in fear. "He kept many details to himself. Details about what he saw in certain cases, things he felt were so awful no one else should be subjected to them."

"Even you? Is there anything you have not seen?"

"Their pain," I speak quietly. "I don't have to see their terror. I don't have to hear their screams."

"But you reconstruct it."

"Not the same thing. No, not the same. Many of the killers Benton dealt with liked to photograph, audiotape and in some instances videotape what they did to their victims. Benton had to watch. He had to listen. I always knew. He'd come home looking gray. He wouldn't talk much during dinner, wouldn't eat much, and on those nights he drank more than usual."

"But he wouldn't tell you . . ."

"Never," I interrupt with feeling. "Never. That was his Indian Burial Ground and no one was allowed to step there. I taught at a death investigation school in Saint Louis. This was early in my career, before I moved here, when I was still a deputy chief in Miami. I was doing a class on drowning and decided since I was already there, I'd go ahead and attend the entire weeklong school. One afternoon, a forensic psychiatrist taught a class on sexual homicide. He showed slides of living victims. A woman was bound to a chair and her assailant had tightly tied rope around one of her breasts and inserted needles in the nipple. I can still see her eyes. They were dark pools filled with hell, and her mouth was wide open as she screamed. And I saw videotapes," I go on in a monotone. "A woman, abducted, bound, tortured and about to be shot in the head. She keeps whimpering for her mother. Begging, crying. I think she was in a basement, the footage dark, grainy. The sound of the gun going off. And silence."

Anna says nothing. The fire snaps and pops.

"I was the only woman in a room of about sixty cops," I add.

"Even worse, then, because the victims were women and you were the only woman," Anna says.

Anger touches me as I remember the way some of the men stared at the slides, at the videotapes. "The sexual mutilation was arousing to some of them," I say. "I could see it in their faces, sense it.

Same thing with some of the profilers, Benton's colleagues in the unit. They'd describe the way Bundy would rape a woman from the rear as he strangled her. Eyes bulging, tongue protruding. He would climax as she died. And these men Benton worked with enjoyed the telling a bit too much. Do you have any idea what that's like?" I fix a stare on her that is as sharp as nails. "To see a dead body, to see photographs, videos, of someone brutalized, of someone suffering and terrified and realize that the people around you are secretly enjoying it? That they find it sexy?"

"Do you think Benton found it sexy?" Anna asks.

"No. He witnessed such things weekly, maybe even daily. Sexy, never. He had to hear their screams." I have begun to ramble. "Had to hear them crying and begging. Those poor people didn't know. Even if they had, they couldn't have helped it."

"Didn't know? What didn't these poor people know?"

"That sexual sadists are only more aroused by crying. By begging. By fear," I reply.

"Do you think Benton cried or begged when his killers abducted him and took him to that dark building?" Anna is about to score.

"I've seen his autopsy report." I slip into my clinical hiding place. "There's really nothing in it to tell me definitively what happened before death. He was badly burned in the fire. So much tissue burned away, it wasn't possible to see, for example, if he still had a blood pressure when they cut him."

"He had a gunshot wound to his head, too, did he not?" Anna asks.

"Yes."

"Which do you think came first?"

I stare mutely at her. I have not reconstructed what led up to his death. I have never been able to bring myself to do that.

"Envision it, Kay," Anna tells me. "You *know*, do you not? You have worked too many deaths not to know what happened."

My mind is dark, as dark as the inside of that grocery store in Philadelphia.

"He did something, didn't he?" She pushes, leaning into me, on the very edge of the ottoman. "He won, didn't he?"

"Won?" I clear my throat. "Won!" I exclaim. "They cut his face off and burned him up and you say he *won?*"

She waits for me to make the connection. When I offer her nothing further, she gets up and walks to the fire, lightly touching my shoulder as she passes. She tosses on another log and looks at me and says, "Kay, let me ask you. Why would they shoot him *after the fact?*"

I rub my eyes and sigh.

"Cutting off the face was part of the MO," she goes on. "What Newton Joyce liked to do to his victims." She refers to the evil male partner of the evil Carrie Grethen—a psychopathic pair that made Bonnie and Clyde seem like a Saturday morning cartoon from my youth. "Excise their faces and store them in the freezer as souvenirs, and because Joyce's face was so homely, so scarred by acne," Anna goes on, "he stole what he envied, beauty. Yes?"

"Yes, I suppose. As much we can go with any such theory about why people do what they do."

"And it was important that Joyce do the excisions carefully and not damage the faces. Which is why he did not shoot his victims, certainly not in the head. He did not want to risk causing damage to the face, the scalp. And shooting is too easy." Anna shrugs. "Quick. Maybe merciful. Far better to be shot than to have your throat cut. So why did Newton Joyce and Carrie Grethen shoot Benton?"

Anna stands over me. I look up at her. "He said something," I answer slowly, finally. "He must have."

"Yes." Anna sits back down. "Yes, yes." She encourages me with her hands, as if directing traffic to move across the next intersection. "What, what? Tell me, Kay."

I reply that I don't know what Benton said to Newton Joyce and Carrie Grethen. But he said something or did something that caused one or the other to lose control of the game. It was an impulse, an involuntary reaction when one of them pushed the gun to Benton's head and pulled the trigger. Boom. And the fun was over. Benton felt nothing, was cognizant of nothing after that. No matter what they did to him after that, it didn't matter. He was dead or dying. Unconscious. He never felt the knife. Maybe he never saw it.

"You knew Benton so well," Anna says. "You knew his killers, or at least you knew Carrie Grethen—you'd had experiences with her in the past. What do you think Benton said and to whom did he say it? Who shot him?"

"I can't . . ."

"You can."

I look at her.

"*Who* lost control?" She pushes me farther than I ever thought I could go.

"*She* did." I pull this up from the deep. "Carrie did. Because it was personal. She'd been around Benton from the old days, from the start, when she was at Quantico, at the Engineering Research Facility."

"Where she also met Lucy long years ago, maybe ten years ago."

"Yes, Benton knew her, knew Carrie, knew her probably as well as you can know any reptilian mind like hers," I add.

"What did he say to her?" Anna's eyes are riveted to me.

"Something about Lucy, probably," I say. "Something about Lucy that would insult Carrie. He insulted Carrie, taunted her about Lucy, that's what I believe." I have a direct shunt from my subconscious to my tongue. I don't even have to think.

"Carrie and Lucy were lovers at Quantico," Anna adds another piece. "Both working on the artificial intelligence computer in the Engineering Research Facility."

"Lucy was an intern, just a teenager, a kid, and Carrie seduced her. They were working on the computer system together. I got Lucy that internship," I bitterly add. "I did. Me, her influential, powerful aunt."

"Didn't lead to quite what you intended, did it?" Anna suggests.

"Carrie used her. . . ."

"Made Lucy gay?"

"No, I wouldn't go that far," I say. "You don't make people gay."

"Made Benton dead? Can you go that far?"

"I don't know, Anna."

"A volatile past, a personal history. Yes. Benton said something about Lucy, and Carrie lost control and shot him just like that," Anna summarizes. "He did not die the way they planned." She sounds triumphant. "He did not."

I rock quietly, looking out at a gray morning that has become full of bluster. The wind exerts itself in fierce gusts that fling dead branches and vines across Anna's backyard, reminding me of the angry tree hurling apples at Dorothy in *The Wizard of Oz*. Then Anna gets up with no announcement, as if an appointment is up. She leaves me to go about other business in her house. We have talked enough for now. I decide to retreat to the kitchen, and that is where Lucy finds me around noon after her workout. I am opening a can of whole tomatoes when she walks in, the early stages of a marinara sauce simmering on the stove.

"Need some help?" She looks at sweet onions, peppers and mushrooms on the cutting board. "Kind of hard getting around with only one hand."

"Pull up a stool," I tell her. "You can be impressed with my fending for myself." I exaggerate bravado as I finish opening the can with no help, and she smiles as she moves a bar stool from the other side of the counter and sits. She is still in her running clothes and has a look in her eye, a secret light, reminding me of the river catching the sun very early in the morning. I steady an onion with two fingers of my immobilized left hand and begin to slice.

"Remember our game?" I lay the onion slices flat and begin to chop. "When you were ten? Or can't you remember back that far? I certainly will never forget," I say in a tone meant to remind Lucy what an impossible brat she was as a child. "Bet you have no idea how many times I would have put you on admin leave, given the choice." I dare to push that painful truth. Maybe I am feeling bold because of my naked talk with Anna, which has left me unnerved and at the same time exhilarated.

"I wasn't that bad." Lucy's eyes dance because she loves to hear what a little terror she was when she was a child and would come stay with me.

I drop handfuls of chopped sweet onions in the sauce and stir. "Truth Serum. Remember that game?" I ask her. "I'd come home, usually from work, and I could tell by the look on your face that you'd been up to something. So I'd sit you in that big red chair in the living room, remember? It was by the fireplace in my old house in Windsor Farms. And I'd bring you a glass of juice and tell you it was truth serum. And you'd drink it and confess."

"Like the time I formatted your computer while you were gone." She is laughing hard.

"Ten damn years old and you format my hard drive. I about had a heart attack," I recall.

"Hey, but I did back up all your files first. I just wanted to give you a bad moment." She is really enjoying this.

"Well, I almost sent you home." I wipe the fingertips of my left hand with a dishtowel, careful that my cast doesn't smell like onions as I experience a wave of sweet sadness. I don't really remember why Lucy came to stay with me on her first visit to Richmond, but I was not the child-rearing type and was new in the job and under tremendous pressure. There was some sort of crisis with Dorothy. Maybe she ran off and got married again, or maybe I was a sucker. Lucy adored me and I wasn't accustomed to being adored. Whenever I would visit her in Miami, she would follow me all over the house, everywhere I went, tenaciously moving with my feet like a soccer ball.

"You weren't going to send me home." Lucy is challenging me, but I catch the doubt in her eyes. The fear of not being wanted is based on fact in her life.

"Only because I felt inadequate to take care of you," I reply, leaning against the sink. "Not because I wasn't crazy about you, little rat fink that you were." She laughs again. "But no, I wouldn't have sent you home. Both of us would have been devastated. I couldn't." I shake my head. "Thank God for our little game. It was about the only way I could get to what was going on inside of you or what mischief you had engaged in while I was off somewhere, at work, whatever. So do I need to pour you juice or a glass of wine, or are you going to just go on and tell me what's happening with you? I wasn't born yesterday, Lucy. You aren't staying in a hotel for the heck of it. You're up to something."

"I'm not the first woman they've run off," she starts in.

"You would be the best woman they've run off," I answer.

"Remember Teun McGovern?"

"I'll remember her for the rest of my life." Teun—pronounced Tee-Un—McGovern was Lucy's ATF supervisor in Philadelphia, an extraordinary woman who was wonderful to me when Benton was killed. "Please don't tell me something's happened to Teun," I worry.

"She quit about six months ago," Lucy replies. "Seems ATF wanted her to move to L.A. and be the SAC of that field division. The worst assignment on God's earth. Nobody wants L.A."

A SAC is a special agent in charge, and very few women in federal law enforcement end up running entire field divisions. Lucy goes on to tell me

McGovern's answer was to resign and start a private investigative business of sorts. "The Last Precinct," she says, getting more animated by the moment. "Pretty cool name, right? Based in New York. Teun's rounding up arson investigators, bomb guys, cops, lawyers, all kinds of people to help out, and in less than six months she's already got clients. It's sort of turned into a secret society. There's a real buzz on the street. When shit hits, call The Last Precinct—where you go when there's nowhere left."

I stir the simmering tomato sauce and taste a little. "Obviously you've been keeping up with Teun since you left Philadelphia." I drip in a few teaspoons of olive oil. "Darn. I guess this will be all right, but not for the salad dressing." I hold up the bottle and frown. "You press olive oil with the pits still in, it's like squeezing oranges with the rind still on and you get what you deserve."

"Why is it I don't assume Anna is an aficionado of things Italian?" Lucy dryly comments.

"We'll just have to educate her. Grocery list." I nod at a notepad and pen by the phone. "First item, extra virgin olive oil Italian integrate style—pitted before pressed. Mission Olives Supremo is a nice one, if you can find it. Not a trace of bitterness."

Lucy makes notes. "Teun and I have stayed in touch," she informs me.

"You're somehow involved in what she's doing?" I know this is where the conversation is headed.

"You could say that."

"Crushed garlic. In the refrigerated section, in little jars. I'm going to be lazy." I pick up a bowl of lean ground beef that I have thoroughly cooked and patted free of grease. "Not a good time for me to crush garlic myself." I stir the beef into the sauce. "How involved?" I go into the refrigerator and open drawers. Anna doesn't have fresh herbs, of course.

Lucy sighs. "God, Aunt Kay. I'm not sure you want to hear it."

Until very recently, my niece and I have talked little and not in depth. We have seen each other seldom over the past year. She moved to Miami, and both of us retreated behind bunkers after Benton's death. I try to read the stories hiding in Lucy's eyes and instantly begin to entertain possibilities. I am suspicious about her relationship with McGovern and was last year when all of us were called out to a catastrophic arson scene in Warrenton, Virginia, a homicide disguised by fire that turned out to be the first of several master-minded by Carrie Grethen.

"Fresh oregano, basil and parsley," I dictate the grocery list. "And a small wedge of Parmesan Reggiano. Lucy, just tell me the truth." I look for spices. McGovern is about my age and single—or at least she was single last time I saw her. I shut a cupboard door and face my niece. "Are you and Teun involved?"

"We weren't that way."

"Weren't?"

"Actually, you're one to talk," Lucy says without rancor. "What about you and Jay?"

"He doesn't work for me," I reply. "I certainly don't work for him. I don't want to talk about him, either. We're talking about you."

"I hate it when you dismiss me, Aunt Kay," she quietly says.

"I'm not dismissing you," I offer as an apology. "I just worry when people who work together get too personal. I believe in boundaries."

"You worked with Benton." She points out another of my exceptions to my own rules.

I tap the spoon on the side of the pot. "I've done a lot of things in life that I tell you not to do. I tell you not to do them because I made the mistake first."

"Did you ever moonlight?" Lucy stretches her lower back and rolls her shoulders.

I frown. "Moonlight? Not that I recall."

"Okay. Truth serum time. I'm a felonious moonlighter and Teun's biggest backer—the major stockholder for The Last Precinct. There. The whole truth. You're going to hear it."

"Let's go sit." I direct us to the table and we pull out chairs.

"It all began accidentally," Lucy begins. "A couple years ago, I created a search engine for my own use. Meanwhile, all I was hearing about was the fortunes people were making on Internet technology. So I said what the hell and sold the search engine for three quarters of a million dollars."

I am not shocked. Lucy's earning possibilities have been limited only by the profession she chose.

"Then I got another idea when we seized a bunch of computers during a raid," she continues. "I was helping restore deleted e-mail and it got me thinking about how vulnerable all of us are to having the ghosts of our electronic communications conjured up to haunt us. So I figured out a way to scramble e-mail. Shred it, figuratively speaking. Now there are a number of software packages for that sort of thing. I made a hell of a lot of money off that brainstorm."

There is nothing diplomatic about my next question. Does ATF know she invented technology that might foil law enforcement efforts to restore the e-mail of the bad guys? Lucy replies that someone was going to come up with the technology, and the privacy of law-abiding people needs to be protected, too. ATF doesn't know about her entrepreneurial activities or that she has been investing in Internet inventions and stocks. Until this moment, only her financial adviser and Teun McGovern are privy to the fact that Lucy is a multimillionaire who has her own helicopter on order.

"So that's how Teun was able to start up her own business in a prohibitively expensive city like New York," I figure.

"Exactly," Lucy says. "And it's why I'm not going to fight ATF, or at least one good reason. If I do battle with them, then the truth about what I've been up to on my own time would probably come out. Internal Affairs, the Inspector General's Office, everyone would dig. They'd find more nails to drive into my reputation as they hang me on their bureaucratic, bullshit cross. Why the hell would I want to do that to myself?"

"If you don't fight injustice, others will suffer from it, Lucy. And maybe those people won't have millions of dollars, a helicopter and a company in New York to fall back on as they try to start a new life."

"That's exactly what The Last Precinct is all about," she replies. "Fighting injustice. I'll fight it in my own way."

"Legally, your moonlighting is not within the scope of the case it appears ATF is making against you, Lucy," the lawyer in me speaks.

"Making money on the side speaks to my veracity, supposedly, though, doesn't it?" she plays the other side.

"Has ATF accused you of lacking veracity? Have they called you dishonest?"

"Well, no. That won't be in any letter from them. For sure. But truth is, Aunt Kay, I broke the rules. You aren't supposed to make money from another source while you're employed by ATF, the FBI or any other federal law enforcement agency. I don't agree with that prohibition. It's not fair. Cops get to moonlight. We don't. Maybe I've always known my days with the feds are numbered." She gets up from the table. "So I took care of my future. Maybe I was just sick of everything. I don't want to spend the rest of my life taking orders from other people."

"If you want to leave ATF, make it your choice, not theirs."

"It *is* my choice," she says with a trace of anger. "Guess I'd better get to the store."

I walk her to the door, arm in arm. "Thank you," I tell her. "It means everything to me that you let me know."

"I'm going to teach you how to fly helicopters." She puts on her coat.

"May as well," I say. "I've been in a lot of unfamiliar airspace today. I guess a little more isn't going to matter."

CHAPTER 6

THE RUDE JOKE FOR YEARS has been that Virginians go to New York for art and New York comes to Virginia for garbage. Mayor Giuliani almost started another civil war when he made that snipe during his much-publicized war with Jim Gilmore, Virginia's governor at the time, over Manhattan's right to ship megatons of northern trash to our southern landfills. I can only imagine the reaction when word gets out that now we have to go to New York for justice, too.

As long as I have been the chief medical examiner of Virginia, Jaime Berger has been the head of the sex crimes unit for the district attorney's office in Manhattan. Although we have never met, we are often mentioned together. It is said that I am the most famous female forensic pathologist in the country and she is the most famous female prosecutor. Until now, the only reaction I might have had to such a claim is that I don't want to be famous and don't trust people who are, and *female* should not be an adjective. Nobody talks about successful men in terms of a male doctor or male president or male CEO.

Over the past few days, I have spent hours on Anna's computer researching Berger on the Internet. I resisted being impressed but can't help it. I didn't know, for example, that she is a Rhodes scholar or that after Clinton was elected she was short-listed for attorney general and, according to *Time* magazine, was privately relieved when Janet Reno was appointed instead. Berger didn't want to give up prosecuting cases. Supposedly, she has turned down judgeships and staggering offers from private law firms for the same reason, and is so admired by her peers that they established a public service scholarship in her name at Harvard, where she spent her undergraduate years. Strangely, very little is said about her personal life except that she plays tennis—extremely well, of course. She works out with a trainer three mornings a week at a New York athletic club and runs three or four miles a day. Her favorite restaurant is Primola. I take some comfort in the fact that she likes Italian food.

It is now Wednesday, early evening, and Lucy and I are Christmas shopping. I have browsed and purchased as much as I can stomach, my mind poisoned by worries, my arm itching like mad inside its plaster cocoon, my craving for tobacco akin to lust. Lucy is somewhere inside Regency Mall taking care of her own list, and I search for a spot where I might evade the churning herd. Thousands of people have waited until three days before Christmas to find thoughtful, special gifts for those significant people in their lives. Voices and constant motion combine in a steady roar that shorts out thoughts and normal conversation, and piped-in holiday music jars my already vibrating nerves out of phase. I face plate glass in front of Sea Dream Leather, my back to discordant people who, like unskilled fingers on a piano, rush and stop and force without joy. Pressing my cell phone tight against my ear, I yield to a new addiction. I check my voice mail for what must be the tenth time today. It has become my slender, secret connection to my former existence. Tapping into my messages is the only way I can go home.

There are four calls. Rose, my secretary, checked in to see how I am holding up. My mother left a long complaint about life. AT&T customer service tried to reach me about a billing question, and my deputy chief, Jack Fielding, needs to talk to me. I call him right away.

"I can hardly hear you," his scratchy voice sounds in one ear, my hand covering the other. In the background, one of his children is crying.

"I'm not in a good place to talk," I tell him.

"Me, either. My ex is here. Joy to the world."

"What's up?" I say to him.

"Some New York prosecutor just called me."

Jolted, I will myself to sound calm, almost indifferent, when I ask him this person's name. He tells me Jaime Berger reached him at home several hours ago. She wanted to know if he assisted in the autopsies I performed on Kim Luong and Diane Bray. "That's interesting," I comment. "Isn't your number unlisted?"

"Righter gave it to her," he informs me.

Paranoia heats up. The wound of betrayal flares. Righter gave her Jack's number and not mine? "Why didn't he tell her to call me?" I ask.

Jack pauses as another child adds to the upset chorus in his house. "I don't know. I told her I didn't officially assist. You did the posts. I'm not listed on the protocols as a witness. Said she really needs to speak to you."

"What was her response when you told her that?" I ask.

"Started asking me questions, obviously has copies of the reports."

Righter again. Copies of the medical examiner's initial report of investigation and the autopsy protocols go to the commonwealth's attorney's office. I feel dizzy. It now seems that two prosecutors have spurned me, and fear and bewilderment gather like an army of fiery ants, teaming over my interior world, stinging my very psyche. What is happening is uncanny and cruel. It is beyond anything I have ever imagined in my most unsettled moments. Jack's voice sounds distant through static that seems a projection of the chaos in my mind. I make out that Berger was a very cool customer and sounded as if she was on a car phone, and then something about special prosecutors. "I thought they were only brought in for the president or Waco or whatever," he says as the cell suddenly clears and he yells—to his ex-wife, I assume—"Can you take them in the other room? I'm on the phone! Jesus," he blurts out to me, "don't ever have kids."

"What do you mean, *special prosecutor*?" I inquire. "What special prosecutor?"

Jack pauses. "I guess I'm assuming they're bringing her here to try the case because Fighter-Righter doesn't want to," he replies with sudden nervousness. In fact, he sounds evasive.

"It appears they had a case in New York." I am careful what I say. "That's why she's involved, or so I'm told."

"You mean a case like ours?"

"Two years ago."

"No shit? News to me. Okay. She didn't say anything about that. Just wants to know about the ones here," Jack tells me.

"How many for the morning, so far?" I inquire about our case load for tomorrow.

"Five so far. Including a weirdo one that's going to be a pain in the butt. Young white male— maybe Hispanic—found inside a motel room. Looks like the room was torched. No ID. A needle stuck in his arm, so we don't know if he's a drug OD or smoke inhalation."

"Let's not talk about it over a cell phone," I cut him off, looking around me. "We'll talk about it in the morning. I'll take care of him."

A long, surprised pause is followed by, "You sure? Because I . . ."

"I'm sure, Jack." I have not been to the office at all this week. "See you then."

I am supposed to meet Lucy in front of Waldenbooks at seven-thirty, and I venture back out into the churning herd. I have no sooner parked myself at the appointed spot when I notice a familiar, big, sour-looking man riding up the escalator. Marino bites into a soft pretzel and licks his fingers as he stares at the teenage girl one step above him. Her tight jeans and sweater leave no mysteries about her curves, dips and elevations, and even from this distance, I can tell Marino is mapping her routes and imagining what it would be like to travel them.

I watch him carried along crowded steps of

steel, heavily involved with the pretzel, chewing with his mouth open, lusting. Faded, baggy blue jeans ride below his swollen gut, and his big hands look like baseball mitts protruding from the sleeves of a red NASCAR windbreaker. A NASCAR cap covers his balding head and he wears ridiculous Elvis-size wire-rim glasses. His fleshy face is furrowed by discontent and has the slack, flushed look of chronic dissipation, and I am startled by an awareness of how miserable he is in his own body, of how much he wars against flesh that by now fails him with a vengeance. Marino reminds me of someone who has taken terrible care of his car, driving it hard, letting it rust and fall apart, and then violently hating it. I imagine Marino slamming down the hood and kicking the tires.

We worked our first case together shortly after I moved here from Miami, and he was surly and condescending and positively boorish from the start. I was certain that by accepting the chief medical examiner's position in Virginia I had made the biggest mistake of my life. In Miami, I had earned the respect of law enforcement and the medical and scientific community. The press treated me reasonably well and I enjoyed a rise to minor stardom that gave me confidence and reassurance. Gender did not seem an issue until I met Peter

Rocco Marino, begotten of hardworking Italian stock in New Jersey, a former New York cop, now divorced from his childhood sweetheart, father of a son he never talks about.

He is like the harsh lighting in dressing rooms. I was relatively comfortable with myself until I saw my reflection in him. This minute, I am unsettled enough to accept that the flaws he holds up to me are probably true. He notices me against the glass storefront, tucking my phone back into my satchel, shopping bags at my feet, and I wave at him. He takes his time maneuvering his bulk through prepossessed people who right now aren't thinking about murderers or trials or New York prosecutors.

"What are you doing here?" he asks me as if I am trespassing.

"Buying your Christmas present," I say. He takes another bite of pretzel. It appears he has purchased nothing but the pretzel. "And you?" I inquire.

"Came to sit on Santa's lap and get my picture took."

"Don't let me stop you."

"I paged Lucy. She told me where in this zoo you was probably at. I thought you might need someone to carry your bags, being that you're a little shorthanded at the moment. How you gonna do autopsies with that thing on?" He indicates my cast.

I know why he is here. I detect the distant roar of information headed my way like an avalanche. I sigh. Slowly but surely I am surrendering to the fact that my life is only going to get worse. "Okay, Marino, now what?" I ask him. "What's happened now?"

"Doc, it's going to be in the paper tomorrow." He bends over to pick up my bags. "Righter called me a little while ago. The DNA matches. Looks like Wolfman whacked that weather lady in New York two years ago, and apparently the asshole's decided he's feeling up to leaving MCV and ain't fighting extradition to the Big Apple— just happy as a clam to get the hell out of Virginia. Kind of a weird coincidence the son of a bitch decides to leave town the same day as Bray's memorial service."

"What memorial service?" Thoughts crash into each other from all directions.

"At Saint Bridget's."

I also didn't know Bray was Catholic and just happened to attend the church where I am a member. An eerie feeling tickles up my spine. No matter what world I occupy, it seemed her mission was to break into it and eclipse me. That she might even have attempted this at my own unassuming church reminds me of how utterly ruthless and arrogant she was.

"So Chandonne is transported out of Richmond on the same day we're supposed to say good-bye to the last woman he snuffed," Marino talks on, scanning every shopper bobbing past. "Don't think for a minute the timing's a coincidence. Every move he makes, the press will be there in droves. So he'll outshine Bray, steal her thunder, 'cause the media's gonna be a hell of a lot more interested in what he's doing than in who shows up to pay their respects to one of his victims. *If* anybody shows up to pay respects. I know I ain't, not after all the shit she did to make my life happy. And oh yeah, Berger's on her way here even as we speak. I guess with a name like that she probably ain't into Christmas," he adds.

We spot Lucy at the same moment a gang of loud, turbulent boys do. They have the latest funky hair and cargo jeans falling off their tiny loins and do exaggerated double-takes, lusting after my niece, who is wearing black tights, scuffed Army boots and an antique flight jacket she rescued from a vintage clothing shop somewhere. Marino gives her admirers a look that would kill if glaring with hatred in one's heart could penetrate skin and perforate vital organs. The boys weave and bounce, shuffling in huge leather basketball shoes, reminding me of puppies that haven't grown into their paws yet.

"What'd you buy me?" Marino asks Lucy.

"A year's supply of maca root."

"What the hell's maca root?"

"Next time you go bowling with some really hot woman, you'll appreciate my little gift," she says.

"You didn't really get him that." I halfway believe her.

Marino snorts. Lucy laughs, seeming much too jovial for someone about to be fired, millionaire or not. Outside in the parking lot, the air is damp and very cold. Headlights dazzle the dark, and everywhere I look I find cars and people in a hurry. Silver wreaths shimmer from light posts, and drivers circle like sharks, looking for spaces close to mall entrances, as if walking several hundred feet is the worst thing that can happen to a person.

"I hate this time of year. I wish I were Jewish," Lucy comments, ironically as if she were privy to Marino's earlier allusion to Berger's ethnicity.

"Was Berger a D.A. when you started out in New York?" I ask him as he places my packages inside Lucy's ancient green Suburban.

"Just getting started." He shuts the tailgate. "I never met her."

"What did you hear about her?" I ask.

"Really hot-looking with big tits."

"Marino, you're so highly evolved," Lucy says.

"Hey." He jerks his head in parting. "Don't ask me something if you don't want to know the answer."

I watch his shadowy bulk move through a confusion of headlights and shoppers and shadows. The sky is milky in the light of an imperfect moon, and snow drifts down in slow, small flakes. Lucy backs out of her parking place and eases into a line of cars. Dangling from her key chain is a silver medallion engraved with the logo for Whirly-Girls, a seemingly frivolous name for a very serious international association of female helicopter pilots. Lucy, who joins nothing, is an ardent member, and I am grateful that in spite of everything else gone wrong, at least her Christmas present is safely tucked inside one of my bags. Months ago, I conspired with Schwarzchild's Jewelers to have a Whirly-Girls necklace made for Lucy in gold. The timing is perfect, especially in light of late-breaking revelations about her plans in life. "Just what exactly will you do with your own helicopter? You're really getting one?" I ask. In part, I want to steer the conversation away from New York and Berger. I am still chafed by what Jack had to say over the phone, and a shadow has fallen across my psyche. Something else bothers me and I am not quite sure what.

"A Bell four-oh-seven, yup, I'm getting it." Lucy dips into an endless stream of red taillights flowing sluggishly along Parham Road. "What do I plan to do with it? Fly it, that's what. And use it in the business."

"About this new business, what's next?"

"Well, Teun's living in New York. So that's where my new headquarters will be."

"Tell me more about Teun," I prompt her. "Does she have family? Where will she spend Christmas?"

Lucy stares straight ahead as she drives, always the serious pilot. "Let me go back, give you a little history, Aunt Kay. When she heard about the shootout in Miami, she contacted me. Then I went to New York the other week and had a rather bad time."

How well I remember. Lucy vanished, sending me into a panic. I tracked her down by phone in Greenwich Village, where she was at Rubyfruit on Hudson, a favorite hangout in the Village. Lucy was upset. She was drinking. I thought she was angry and hurt because of problems with Jo. Now the story is changing right before my eyes. Lucy has been financially involved with Teun McGovern since last summer, but it wasn't until this incident in New York last week that Lucy made the decision to change her entire life. "Ann asks me if there's someone she can call," Lucy explains.

"I wasn't exactly in a frame of mind to get myself back to my hotel."

"Ann?"

"A former cop. She owns the bar."

"Oh, that's right."

"I admit I was pretty whacked, and I told Ann to try Teun," Lucy says. "Next thing I know, Teun's walking into the bar. She pumped me full of coffee and we stayed up all night talking. Mostly about my personal situation with Jo, with ATF, with everything. I haven't been happy." Lucy glances over at me. "I think I've been ready for a change for a long, long time. That night I made a decision. The decision had already been made even before this other thing happened." This other meaning Chandonne's trying to kill me. "Thank God Teun was there for me." Lucy doesn't mean at the bar. She is talking about Mc-Govern's being there for her in general, and I feel happiness radiating from some space deep within Lucy's core. Common psychology dictates that other people and jobs can't make you happy. You have to make yourself happy. This is not entirely true. McGovern and The Last Precinct seem to make Lucy happy.

"And you had already been involved in The Last Precinct for some time?" I encourage her to continue the story. "Since last summer? Is that when the idea first came up?"

"It started out as a joke in the old days, in Philly, when Teun and I were driven nuts by bureaucrats with lobotomies, by people getting in the way, by watching how innocent victims get ground up in the system. We came up with this fantasy organization which I dubbed The Last Precinct. We'd say, *Where do you go when there's nowhere to go?*" Her smile is forced and I sense that all of her upbeat news is about to get questionable shadings. Lucy is going to tell me something I don't want to hear. "You realize this means I need to move to New York," she says. "Soon."

Righter has surrendered the case to New York and now Lucy is moving to New York. I turn up the heat and pull my coat more tightly around me.

"I think Teun's found me an apartment on the Upper East Side. Maybe a five-minute jog from the park. On Sixty-seventh and Lexington," she says.

"That was quick," I comment. "And close to where Susan Pless was murdered," I add, as if this is an ominous sign. "Why that part of town? Is Teun's office near there?"

"A few blocks. She's just a couple doors down from the nineteenth precinct, apparently knows a bunch of NYPD guys who work that tour."

"And Teun had never heard of Susan Pless, of that murder? How strange to think she ended up just several streets from there." Negativity carries me along. I can't help it.

"She knows about the murder because we've discussed what's going on with you," Lucy replies. "Before that, she'd never heard of the case. Neither had I. I guess the preoccupation of our neighborhood is the East Side Rapist, which is something we've gotten involved in, as a matter of fact. They've had these rapes going on for some five years, same guy, likes blondes in their thirties to early forties, usually they've had a few drinks, have just left a bar and he grabs them as they're going into their apartments. New York's first John Doe DNA. We got his DNA but not an identity." All roads seem to lead back to Jaime Berger. The East Side Rapist would most certainly be a high-priority case for her office. "I'm going to dye my hair blond and start walking home from bars late," Lucy wryly says, and I believe she would do that.

I want to tell Lucy that the direction she has chosen is exciting and I am thrilled for her, but the words won't come. She has lived many places that aren't close to Richmond, but for some reason, this time it feels as if she is finally leaving home for good, that she is grown. Suddenly, I become my mother criticizing, pointing out the downside, the deficits, lifting up the rug to look for that one spot I missed when I cleaned the

house, reviewing my report card of straight A's
and commenting what a shame it is I have no
friends, tasting what I cook and finding it lacking.

"What will you do with your helicopter? Will
you keep it up there?" I hear myself say to my
niece. "Seems like that will be a problem."

"Probably Teterboro."

"So you'll have to go all the way into New Jersey when you want to fly?"

"It's not that far."

"The cost of living up there, too. And you and
Teun . . ." I hammer away.

"What about me and Teun?" The lift has left
Lucy's voice. "Why do you keep picking on that?"
Anger rolls in. "I don't work for her anymore.
She's not ATF or my supervisor anymore. There's
nothing wrong with us being friends."

My fingerprints are all over the crime scene of
her disappointment, her hurt. Even worse, the
echoes of Dorothy are in my voice. I am ashamed
of myself, deeply ashamed. "Lucy, I'm sorry." I
reach over and take her hand in the fingertips of
my plaster-confined one. "I don't want you to
leave. I'm feeling selfish. I'm being selfish. I'm
sorry."

"I'm not leaving you. I'll be in and out. Only
two hours away by chopper. It's all right." She
looks at me. "Why don't you come work with us,

Aunt Kay?" She is out with what I can tell is not a new thought. Obviously, she and McGovern have discussed quite a lot about me, including my possible role in their company. This realization gives me a peculiar sensation. I have resisted contemplating my future and suddenly it rises before me like a great blank screen. While I know in my mind that the way I have lived my life is in the past, I have yet to accept this truth in my heart. "Why don't you go into business for yourself instead of the state telling you what to do?" Lucy goes on. "Have you ever given serious thought to that?"

"It's always been the plan for later on," I reply.

"Well, later on is here," she tells me. "The twentieth century ends in exactly nine days."

CHAPTER 7

IT IS ALMOST MIDNIGHT. I SIT before the fire in the hand-carved rocker that is the only hint of rusticity in Anna's house. She has set her chair at a deliberate angle so she can look at me but I don't have to look at her if I find myself in sensitive discovery of my own psychological evidence. I have learned of late that I never know what I might find during my conversations with Anna, as if I am a crime scene I am searching for the first time. The lights are switched off in the living room, the fire in its agonal stages of going out. Incandescence spreads along smoldering coals that breathe shades of orange as I tell Anna about a Sunday night in November a little over a year ago, when Benton got uncharacteristically hateful toward me.

"When you say uncharacteristically, you mean what?" Anna asks in her strong, quiet tone.

"He was accustomed to my peregrinations late

at night when I couldn't settle down, when I would stay up late and work. On the night in question he fell asleep while reading in bed. Not unusual, and it was my cue that I could have my own time now. I crave the silence, the absolute aloneness when the rest of the world is unconscious and not needing something from me."

"You always have felt this need?"

"Always," I tell her. "It's when I come alive. I come into myself when I'm absolutely alone. I need the time. I must have it."

"What happened on the night you mention?" she asks.

"I got up and took the book out of his lap, turned out the light," I reply.

"What was he reading?"

Her question catches me by surprise. I have to think. I don't remember clearly, but I seem to recall Benton was reading about Jamestown, the first permanent English settlement in American that is less than an hour's drive east of Richmond. He was very interested in history and had double-majored in it and psychology in college, and then his curiosity about Jamestown was ignited when archaeologists began excavating out there and discovered the original fort. It slowly comes back to me: The book Benton was reading in bed was a collection of narratives, many of them written by John Smith. I don't recall the title, I tell Anna. I suppose the book is still in my house somewhere, and the idea of happening upon it one of these days pains me. I go on with my story.

"I left the bedroom and quietly shut the door and went down the hall to my office," I say. "As you know, when I do autopsies, I take sections of every organ and sometimes of wounds, as well. The tissue goes to the histology lab where it's made into slides I must review. I can never keep up with micro-dictations and routinely take slide folders home, and of course the police asked me all about this. It's funny, but my normal activities seem mundane and beyond question until they are inspected by others. That's when I realize I don't live like other people."

"Why do you think the police wanted to know about slides you might have in your house?" Anna asks.

"Because they wanted to know about everything." I go back to my story about Benton, describing being in my office, bent over my microscope, lost in heavy metal-stained neurons that looked like a swarm of one-eyed purple and gold creatures with tentacles. I felt a presence behind me and turned to find Benton standing in my open doorway, his face filled with an eerie, ominous glow, like St. Elmo's fire before lightning strikes.

Can't sleep? he asked me in a mean, sarcastic

tone that didn't sound like him. I pushed my chair back from my powerful Nikon microscope. *If you could teach that thing to fuck, you wouldn't need me at all,* he said, and his eyes flew at me with the bright fury of the cells I was looking at. Dressed in pajama bottoms, Benton was pale in the partial light spreading out from the lamp on my desk, his chest heaving and shiny with sweat, veins roping in his arms, his silver hair plastered to his forehead. I asked him what in the world was the matter, and he ordered me back to bed, jabbing his finger at me.

At this point, Anna interrupts me. "Nothing else might have preceded this? No forewarning whatsoever?" She knew Benton, too. This wasn't Benton. This was an alien who had invaded Benton's body.

"Nothing," I answer her. "No warning." I rock slowly, nonstop. Smoldering wood pops. "The last place I wanted to be with him that moment was in bed. He may have been the FBI's star psychological profiler, but for all of his prowess at reading others, he could be as cold and uncommunicative as a stone. I had no intention of staring up at the dark all night while he lay with his back to me, mute, hardly breathing. But what he wasn't was violent or cruel. He had never talked to me in such a demeaning, abusive way. If we had nothing else, Anna, we had respect. We always treated each other with respect."

"And did he tell you what was wrong?" She presses me on this.

I smile bitterly. "When he made the crude comment about teaching my microscope to fuck, that told me." Benton and I had grown comfortable living in my house, yet he never stopped feeling like a guest. It is my house and everything about it is me. The last year of his life, he was disillusioned with his career, and as I look back on it now, he was tired and without purpose and feared getting old. All of it eroded our intimacy. The sexual part of our relationship became an abandoned airport that looked normal from a distance but had no one in the tower. No landings, no takeoffs, only an occasional touch-and-go because we thought we should, because of the accessibility and old habit, I guess.

"When you did have sex, who usually initiated it?" Anna asks.

"Eventually, just him. More out of desperation than desire. Maybe even frustration. Yes, frustration," I decide.

Anna watches me, her face in shadows that deepen as the fire dies. Her elbow is propped on the armrest, her chin resting on her index finger in what has become the pose I associate with our intense time together these past few nights. Her living room has become a dark confessional booth where I can be emotionally newborn and naked and feel no shame. I don't see our sessions as therapy, but rather as a priesthood of friendship that is sacred and safe. I have begun to tell another human being what it is like to be me.

"Let's go back to the night he got so angry," Anna navigates. "Can you remember when this was, exactly?"

"Just weeks before his murder." I talk calmly, mesmerized by coals that look like glowing alligator skin. "Benton knew my space needs. Even on nights when we made love, it wasn't unusual for me to wait until he fell asleep and get up with the stealth of an adulterer to slip inside my office down the hall. He was understanding about my infidelities." I feel Anna smile in the dark. "He rarely complained when he reached for me and felt an empty space on my side of the bed," I explain. "He accepted my need to be alone, or seemed to. I never knew how much my nocturnal habits hurt him until that night when he came into my office."

"Was it really your nocturnal habits?" Anna inquires. "Or your aloofness?"

"I don't think of myself as aloof."

"Do you think of yourself as someone who connects with others?"

I analyze, searching everywhere inside me for a truth I have always feared.

"Did you connect with Benton?" Anna goes on. "Let's start with him. He was your most significant relationship. Certainly, he was the longest."

"Did I connect with him?" I hold up the question like a ball I am about to serve, not sure of the angle or spin or how hard. "Yes and no. Benton was one of the finest, kindest men I've ever known. Sensitive. Deep and intelligent. I could talk to him about anything."

"But did you? I get the impression you didn't." Anna, of course, is on to me.

I sigh. "I'm not sure I've ever talked to anybody about absolutely anything."

"Perhaps Benton was safe," she suggests.

"Perhaps," I reply. "I do know there were deep places in me he never reached. I also never wanted him to, didn't want to get that intense, that close. I suppose starting out as we did may be part of the explanation. He was married. He always went home to his wife, to Connie. It went on for years. We were on opposite sides of a wall, separated, only touching when we could sneak. God, I would never do that again with anybody, I don't care who."

"Guilt?"

"Of course," I answer. "Every good Catholic

feels guilt. In the beginning, I felt terribly guilty. I've never been the type to break rules. I'm not like Lucy, or should I say she's not like me. If rules are mindless and ignorant, she breaks them right and left. Hell, I don't even get speeding tickets, Anna."

It is here that she leans forward and holds up a hand. This is her signal. I have said something important. "Rules," she says. "What are rules?"

"A definition? You want a definition of rules?"

"What are rules to you? Your definition, yes."

"Right and wrong," I reply. "What is legal versus illegal. Moral versus immoral. Humane versus inhumane."

"Sleeping with a married person is immoral, wrong, inhumane?"

"If nothing else, it's stupid. But yes, it's wrong. Not a fatal error or unforgivable sin or illegal, but dishonest. Yes, definitely dishonest. A broken rule, yes."

"Then you admit you are capable of dishonesty."

"I admit I'm capable of being stupid."

"But dishonest?" She won't let me evade the question.

"Everyone is capable of anything. My affair with Benton was dishonest. I indirectly lied because I hid what I was doing. I presented a front to others, including Connie, that was false. Simply false. So am I capable of deception, of lying? Clearly I am." The confession depresses me deeply.

"What about homicide? What is the rule about homicide? Wrong? Immoral? Is it always wrong to kill? You have killed," Anna says.

"In self-defense." On this point I feel strong and certain. "Only when I had no choice because the person was going to kill me or someone else."

"Did you commit a sin? *Thou shalt not kill.*"

"Absolutely not." Now I am getting frustrated. "It's easy to make judgments about matters one looks at from the distant vantage point of morality and idealism. It's different when you're confronted by a killer who's holding a knife to another person's throat or reaching for a pistol to shoot you. The sin would be to do nothing, to allow an innocent person to die, to allow yourself to die. I feel no remorse," I tell Anna.

"What do you feel?"

I close my eyes for a moment, firelight moving across my lids. "Sick. I can't think about those deaths without feeling sick. What I did wasn't wrong. I had no choice. But I wouldn't call it right, either, if you understand the difference. When Temple Gault was hemorrhaging to death in front of me and begging me to help, there are really no words for how that felt and how it feels now to remember it."

"This was in the subway tunnel in New York. Four or five years ago?" she asks, and I answer with a nod. "Carrie Grethen's former partner in crime. Gault was her mentor, in a sense. Isn't that right?" Again, I nod. "Interesting," she says. "You killed Carrie's partner and then she killed yours. A connection, perhaps?"

"I have no idea. I have never looked at it like that." I am jolted by the thought. It has never occurred to me and seems so obvious now.

"Did Gault deserve to die, in your opinion?" Anna then asks.

"Some people would say he forfeited his right to be in this world and we're all better off now that he's gone. But my God, I wouldn't have chosen to be the one who carried out the sentence, Anna. Never, never. Blood was spurting through his fingers. I saw fear in his eyes, terror, panic, the evil in him gone. He was just a human being dying. And I'd caused it. And he was crying and begging me to make his bleeding stop." I have stopped rocking. I feel Anna's full attention on me. "Yes," I finally say. "Yes, it was awful. Just awful. Sometimes I dream about him. Because I killed him, he will forever be part of me. That's the price I pay."

"And Jean-Baptiste Chandonne?"

"I don't want to hurt anybody anymore." I stare at the dying fire.

"At least he is alive?"

"I take no comfort in that. How can I? People like him don't stop hurting others, even after they're locked up. The evil lives on. That is my conundrum. I don't want them killed, but I know the damage they do while they're alive. Lose-lose, any way you look at it," I tell Anna.

Anna says nothing. It is her method to offer silences more than opinions. Grief throbs in my chest and my heart beats in a staccato of fear. "I suppose I'd be punished if I'd killed Chandonne," I add. "Without question I'll be punished because I didn't."

"You could not save Benton's life." Anna's voice fills the space between us. I shake my head as tears fill my eyes. "Do you feel you should have been able to defend him, too?" she asks. I swallow and spasms of that agonizing loss rob me of my ability to speak. "Did you fail him, Kay? And now it is your penance to eradicate other monsters, perhaps? To do it for Benton, because you let monsters murder him? You did not save him?"

My helplessness, my outrage boil over. "He didn't save himself, goddamn it. Benton wandered into his murder like a dog or cat wandering off to die, because it was time. Jesus!" I am out with it. "Jesus. Benton was always complaining about wrinkles and sagging and aches and pains, even during the early years of our relationship. As you know, he was older than I. Maybe aging threatened him more for that reason. I don't know. But when he reached his mid-forties, he couldn't look in the mirror without shaking his head and griping. 'I don't want to get old, Kay.' That's what he would say.

"I remember late one afternoon we were taking a bath together and he was complaining about his body. 'Nobody wants to get old,' I finally said to him. 'But *I really* don't—don't to the point that I don't think I can survive it,' was his reply. 'We have to survive it. It's selfish not to, Benton,' I said. 'And besides, we survived being young, didn't we?' Ha! He thought I was being ironic. I wasn't. I asked him how many days of your youth were spent waiting for tomorrow? Because somehow tomorrow is going to be better? He thought about this for a moment as he pulled me closer in the tub, touching and fondling me beneath the steamy cover of hot water scented with lavender. He knew exactly how to play me back in those days when our cells came alive instantly on contact. Back then, when it was good. 'Yeah,' he considered, 'it's true. I've always waited for tomorrow, thinking tomorrow's going to be better. That's survival, Kay. If you don't think tomorrow or next year or the year after that will be better, why bother?' "

I stop for a moment, rocking. I tell Anna,

"Well, he stopped bothering. Benton died because he no longer believed what was ahead was better than what was past. It doesn't matter that it was another person who took his life. Benton was the one who decided." My tears have dried and I feel hollow inside, defeated and furious. Feeble light touches my face as I stare into the afterglow of fire. "Fuck you, Benton," I mutter to smoking coals. "Fuck you for giving up."

"Is that why you had sex with Jay Talley?" Anna asks. "To fuck Benton? To pay him back for leaving you, for dying?"

"If so, it wasn't conscious."

"What do you feel?"

I try to feel. "Dead. After Benton was murdered . . . ?" I consider this. "Dead," I decide. "I felt dead. I couldn't feel anything. I think I had sex with Jay . . ."

"Not what you think. What you feel," she gently reminds me.

"Yes. That was the whole thing. Wanting to feel, desperate to feel something, anything," I tell her.

"Did making love with Jay help you feel something, anything?"

"I think it made me feel cheap," I reply.

"Not what you think," she reminds me again.

"I felt hunger, lust, anger, ego, freedom. Oh yes, freedom."

"Freedom from Benton's death, or perhaps from Benton? He was somewhat repressed, wasn't he? He was safe. He had a very powerful super-ego. Benton Wesley was a man who did things properly. What was sex like with him? Was it proper?" Anna wants to know.

"Thoughtful," I say. "Gentle and sensitive."

"Ah. Thoughtful. Well, there is something to be said for that," Anna says with a hint of irony that draws attention to what I have just revealed.

"It was never hungry enough, never purely erotic." I am more open about it. "I have to admit that many times I was *thinking* while we were having sex. It's bad enough to think while talking to you, Anna, but one shouldn't think while making love. There should be no thoughts, just unbearable pleasure."

"Do you like sex?"

I laugh in surprise. No one has ever asked me such a thing. "Oh yes, but it varies. I've had very good sex, good sex, okay sex, boring sex, bad sex. Sex is a strange creature. I'm not even sure what I think of sex. But I hope I've not had the *premier grand cru* of sex." I allude to superior Bordeaux. Sex is very much like wine, and if the truth be told, my encounters with lovers usually end up in the *village* section of the vineyard: low on the slope, fairly common and modestly priced—nothing special, really. "I don't believe I've had my best sex yet, my deepest, most erotic sexual harmony with another person. I haven't, not yet, not at all." I am rambling, speaking in stops and starts as I try to figure it out and argue with myself about whether I even want to figure it out. "I don't know. Well, I guess I wonder how important it should be, how important it is."

"Considering what you do for a living, Kay, you should know how important sex is. It is power. It is life and death," Anna states. "Of course, in what you see, mainly we are talking about power that has been terribly abused. Chandonne is a good example. He gets sexual gratification from overpowering, from causing suffering, from playing God and deciding who lives and who dies and how."

"Of course."

"Power sexually excites him. It does most people," Anna says.

"The greatest aphrodisiac," I agree. "If people are honest about it."

"Diane Bray is another example. A beautiful, provocative woman who used her sex appeal to overpower, to control others. At least this is the impression I have," Anna says.

"It's the impression she gave," I reply.

"Do you think she was sexually attracted to you?" Anna asks me.

I evaluate this clinically. Uncomfortable with

the idea, I hold it away from me and study it like an organ I am dissecting. "That never entered my mind," I decide. "So it probably wasn't there or I would have picked up the signals." Anna doesn't answer me. "Possibly," I equivocate.

Anna isn't buying it. "Didn't you tell me she had tried to use Marino to get to know you?" she reminds me. "That she wanted to have lunch with you, socialize, get to know you, and tried to arrange this through him?"

"That's what Marino told me," I reply.

"Because she was sexually attracted to you, possibly? That would have been the ultimate overpowering of you, wouldn't it? If she not only ruined your career, but helped herself to your body in the process and therefore appropriated every aspect of your existence? Isn't that what Chandonne and others of his type do? They must feel attraction, too. It is simply that they act it out differently from the rest of us. And we know what you did to him when he tried to act out his attraction to you. His big mistake, no? He looked at you with lust and you blinded him. At least temporarily." She pauses, her chin resting on her finger, her eyes steady on me.

I am looking directly at her now. I have that feeling again. I would almost describe it as a warning. I just can't put a name to it.

"What might you have done had Diane Bray

tried to act out her sexual attraction to you, saying it was there? If she had hit on you?"Anna keeps digging.

"I have ways of deflecting unwanted advances," I reply.

"From women, too?"

"From anyone."

"Then women *have* made advances."

"Now and then, over the years." It is an obvious question with an obvious answer. I don't live in a cave. "Yes, I've certainly been around women who show interest I can't reciprocate," I say.

"Can't or won't?"

"Either."

"And how does it make you feel when it is a woman who desires you? Any different than if it is a man?"

"Are you trying to find out if I'm homophobic, Anna?"

"Are you?"

I consider this. I reach as deep as I can to see if I am uncomfortable with homosexuality. I have always been quick to assure Lucy that I have no problem with same-sex relationships beyond the hardships they bring. "I'm okay with it," I answer Anna. "Really and truly. It simply isn't my preference. It's not my choice."

"People choose?"

"In a sense." Of this I am certain. "And I say so

because I believe people feel many attractions that aren't what they would be most comfortable with, and so they don't act on them. I can understand Lucy. I have seen her with her lovers and in a way envy their closeness, because although they have the difficulty of going against the majority, they also have the advantage of the special friendships women are capable of having with each other. It's harder for men and women to be soul mates, deep friends. I'll admit that much. But I think the significant difference between Lucy and me is I don't expect to be a man's soul mate, and men make her feel overpowered. And true intimacy can't occur without a balance of power between the individuals. So because I don't feel overpowered by men, I choose them physically." Anna says nothing. "That's probably as much as I'll ever figure it out," I add. "Not everything can be explained. Lucy and her attractions and needs can't be completely explained. Nor can mine."

"You really don't think you can be a man's soul mate? Then maybe your expectations are too low? Possible?"

"Very possible." I almost laugh. "If anyone has low expectations, I deserve to after all of the relationships I've fucked up," I add.

"Have you ever felt attracted to a woman?" Anna finally gets to this. I figured she would.

"I have found some women very compelling,"

I admit. "I remember getting crushes on teachers when I was growing up."

"By crushes, you mean sexual feelings."

"Crushes include sexual feelings. Innocent and naïve as they may be. A lot of girls get crushes on their female teachers, especially if you're in a parochial school and are taught exclusively by women."

"Nuns."

I smile. "Yes, imagine getting a crush on a nun."

"I imagine some of those nuns got crushes on each other, too," Anna remarks.

A spreading dark cloud of uncertainty and un-easiness encroaches on me and a warning taps at the back of my awareness. I don't know why Anna is so focused on sex, particularly homosexual sex, and I entertain the possibility that she is a lesbian and this is why she never married, or maybe she is testing me to see how I might react if she finally, after all these years, tells me the truth about herself. It hurts to think she might have, out of fear, withheld such an important detail from me.

"You told me you moved to Richmond for love." It is my turn to probe. "And the person proved a waste of time. Why didn't you go back to Germany? Why did you stay in Richmond, Anna?"

"I went to medical school in Vienna and am from Austria, not Germany," she tells me. "I grew up in a *Schloss,* a castle, that had been in the family for hundreds of years, near Linz on the Danube River, and during the war the Nazis lived in the house with us. My mother, my father, two older sisters and my younger brother. And from the windows I could see the smoke from the crematorium some ten miles away, at Mauthausen, a very notorious concentration camp, a huge quarry where prisoners were forced to mine the granite, carrying huge blocks of it up hundreds of steps, and if they faltered, they were beaten or pushed into the abyss. Jews, Spanish Republicans, Russians, homosexuals.

"Day in and day out, dark clouds of death stained the horizon, and I would catch my father staring off and sighing when he thought no one was looking. I could feel his deep pain and shame. Because we could do nothing about what was happening, it was easy to slip into denial. Most Austrians were into denial about what was happening in our beautiful little country. This was unforgivable to me but could not be helped. My father had much wealth and influence, but to go against the Nazis was to end up in a camp or to be shot on the spot. I can still hear laughter and the clink of glasses in my house, as if those monsters were our best friends. One of them started coming into my bedroom at night. I was seventeen. This went on for two years. I never said a word because I knew my father could do nothing, and I suspect he was aware of what was going on. Oh yes, I am sure of it. I worried the same thing was happening to my sisters, and am quite certain it was. After the war, I finished my education and met an American music student in Vienna. He was a very fine violinist, very dashing and witty, and I came back to the States with him. Mainly, because I could not live in Austria anymore. I could not live with what my family had averted its conscience from, and even now, when I see the countryside of my homeland, the image is stained with that dark, ominous smoke. I see it in my mind always. Always."

Anna's living room is chilled, and fire-scattered embers look like dozens of irregular eyes glowing in the dark. "What happened with the American musician?" I ask her.

"I suppose reality introduced itself." Her voice is touched by sadness. "It was one thing for him to fall in love with a young female Austrian psychiatrist in one of the most beautiful, romantic cities in the world. Quite another to bring her back to Virginia, to the former capital of the Confederacy where people still have Confederate flags all over the place. I began my residency at MCV, and James played with the Richmond symphony for several years. Then he moved to Washington and we parted. I am grateful we never married. At least I did not have that complication, that or children."

"And your family?" I ask.

"My sisters are dead. I have a brother in Vienna. Like my father, he is involved in banking. We should get some sleep," Anna says.

I shiver when I first slide beneath the covers, and I draw up my legs and tuck a pillow beneath my broken arm. Talking to Anna has begun to unsettle me around the edges, like the earth about to cave in. I feel phantom pains in parts of me that are past, gone, and my spirit is heavy from the added burden of the story she has told about her own life. Of course, she would not volunteer her past to most people. A Nazi association is a terrible stigma, even now, and to consider that fact causes me to paint her demeanor and her privileged lifestyle on a very different canvas. It doesn't matter that Anna no more had a choice about who stayed in her family home than she had a say about whom she had sex with when she was seventeen. She would not be forgiven if others knew. "My God," I mutter, staring up at the ceiling in Anna's dark guest room. "Dear God."

I get back up and make my way down the dark hallway, passing through the living room again and into the east wing of the house. The master bedroom is at the end the hallway, and Anna's door is open, thin moonlight seeping through windows and softly outlining her shape beneath the covers. "Anna?" I speak quietly. "Are you awake?"

She stirs, then sits up. I can barely make out her face as I come closer. Her white hair is down around her shoulders. She looks a hundred years old. "Is everything all right?" she asks groggily and with a trace of alarm.

"I'm sorry," I tell her. "I can't tell you enough how sorry I am. Anna, I've been a terrible friend."

"You have been my most trusted friend." She reaches for my hand and squeezes it, and her bones feel small and fragile beneath soft, loose skin, as if she has suddenly become ancient and vulnerable, not the titan I have always envisioned. Perhaps it is because I now know her story.

"You've suffered so much, carried so much all alone," I whisper. "I'm sorry I've not been there for you. I'm just so sorry," I tell her again. I bend over and hug her awkwardly, cast and all, and kiss her cheek.

CHAPTER 8

EVEN DURING MY MOST BUR-
dened, distracted moments, I appreciate
where I work. I am always aware that the
medical examiner system I head is probably the
finest in the country, if not the world, and that I
co-direct the Virginia Institute of Forensic Science and Medicine, the first training academy of
its kind. I am able to do all of this in one of the
most advanced forensic facilities I have ever seen.

Our new thirty-million-dollar, one-hundred-
and-thirty-thousand-square-foot building is called
Biotech II and is the center of the Biotechnology
Research Park, which has stunningly transformed
downtown Richmond by relentlessly replacing
abandoned department stores and other boarded-
up shells with elegant buildings of brick masonry
and glass. Biotech has reclaimed a city that continued to be bullied long after those Northern ag-
gressors fired their last shot.

When I moved here in the late eighties, Richmond consistently topped the list of cities with the highest homicide rate per capita in the United States. Businesses fled to neighboring counties. Virtually no one went downtown after hours. That can be said no more. Remarkably, Richmond is on its way to becoming a city of science and enlightenment, and I confess I never thought it possible. I confess, I hated Richmond when I first moved here for reasons that reach far deeper than Marino's nastiness to me or what I missed about Miami.

I believe cities have personalities; they take on the energy of the people who occupy and rule them. During its worst era, Richmond was stubborn and small-minded, and bore itself with the wounded arrogance of a has-been now ordered about by the very people it once dominated, or in some instances owned. There was a maddening exclusivity that caused people like me to feel looked down on and alone. Through it all, I detected the traces of old injuries and indignities as surely as I find them on bodies. I found a spiritual sadness in the mournful haze that during summer months clings like battle smoke over swamps and endless stands of scrawny pines and drifts along the river, swathing the wounds of brick pilings and foundries and prison camps left from that awful war. I felt compassion. I did not give up on

Richmond. This morning, I struggle with my growing belief that it has given up on me.

The tops of buildings in the downtown skyline have vanished in clouds, the air thick with snow. I stare out my office window, distracted by big flakes drifting past as phones ring and people move along the corridor. I worry that state and city government will shut down. This can't happen on my first day back.

"Rose?" I call out to my secretary in the adjoining office. "Are you keeping up with the weather?"

"Snow," her voice sails back.

"I can see that. They aren't closing anything yet, are they?" I reach for my coffee and silently marvel over the unrelenting white storm that has seized our city. Winter wonderlands typically grace the commonwealth west of Charlottesville and north of Fredericksburg, and Richmond is left out. The explanation I have always heard is that the James River in our immediate area warms up the air just enough to replace snow with freezing rains that sweep in like Grant's troops to paralyze the earth.

"Accumulation of possibly eight inches. Tapering off by later afternoon with lows in the twenties." Rose must have logged on to an Internet weather update. "Highs not to get above freezing for the next three days. It looks like we'll have a white Christmas. Isn't that something?"

"Rose, what are you doing for Christmas?"

"Nothing much," her response comes back.

I scan stacks of case files and death certificates and push around phone message slips, mail and inter-office memos. I can't see the top of my desk and don't know where to start. "Eight inches? They'll declare a national emergency," I comment. "We need to find out if anything's closing besides schools. What's on my schedule that hasn't already been canceled?"

Rose is tired of yelling through the wall at me. She walks into my office, looking sharp in a gray pants suit and white turtleneck sweater, her gray hair pinned up in a French twist. She is rarely without my big calendar and opens it. She runs her finger over what is written in it for today, peering through half-moon reading glasses. "The obvious is we now have six cases and it's not even eight o'clock yet," she lets me know. "You're on call for court, but I have a feeling that's not going to happen."

"Which case?"

"Let's see. Mayo Brown. Don't believe I remember him."

"An exhumation," I remember. "A homicidal poisoning, a rather shaky one." The case is on my desk, somewhere. I start looking for it as muscles tense in my neck and shoulders. The last time I saw Buford Righter in my office it was over this very case, which was destined to create nothing but confusion in court even after I spent four hours explaining to him the dilution effect on drug levels when the body has been embalmed, that there is no satisfactory method to quantitate the rate of degradation in embalmed tissue. I went over the toxicology reports and prepared Righter for the defense of dilution. Embalming fluid displaces blood and dilutes drug levels, I drilled into him. So if the decedent's codeine level is at the low end of the acutely lethal dose range, then prior to embalming, the level could only have been higher. I meticulously explained that this is what he needs to focus on because the defense is going to muddy the waters with heroin versus codeine.

We were seated at the oval table in my private conference room, paperwork spread before us. Righter tends to blow out a lot when he is confused, frustrated or just pissed off. He continued to pluck up reports and frown at them, and then put them back down, all the while blowing like a whale breaking surface. "Greek," he kept saying. "How the hell do you make the jury understand things like 6-mono-acetylmorphine is a marker for heroin, and since it wasn't detected, then it doesn't necessarily mean heroin wasn't present, but if it was present, then that would mean heroin was too? Versus telling if codeine is medicinal?" I told him that was my point, the very thing he didn't want to focus on. Stick to the dilution offense—that the level had to have been higher before the person was embalmed, I coached him. Morphine is a metabolite of heroin. Morphine is also a metabolite of codeine, and when codeine is metabolized in the blood we get very low levels of morphine. We can't tell anything definitively here, except we have no marker for heroin, and we do have levels of codeine and morphine, indicating the man took something—willingly or unwillingly—before he died, I painted the scenario for him. And it was a much higher dose than is indicated now because of the embalming, I stressed again. But do these results prove the man's wife poisoned him with Tylenol Three, for example? No. Don't get gummed up in the tar baby of 6-mono-acetylmorphine, I told Righter repeatedly.

I realize I am obsessing. I am sitting at my desk, angrily going through stacks of backed-up work as I anguish over how much trouble I went to preparing Righter for yet another case, promising I would be there for him, just as I always have been. It is a shame he does not seem inclined to return the favor. I am a free lunch. All of Chandonne's Virginia victims are free lunches. I just can't accept it and am beginning to resent the hell out of Jaime Berger, too. "Well, check with the courts," I say to Rose. "And by the way, he's being released from MCV this morning." I resist saying Jean-Baptiste Chandonne's name. "Expect the usual phone calls from the media."

"I heard on the news this New York prosecutor's in town." Rose flips through my date book. She doesn't look up at me. "Wouldn't that be something if she gets snowed in?"

I get up from my desk, take off my lab coat and hang it on the back of my chair. "I don't guess we've heard from her."

"She hasn't called here, not for you." My secretary hints she knows that Berger did track down Jack or at least someone besides me.

I am very skilled at becoming prepossessed with business and deflecting any effort on another person's part to probe an area I choose to avoid. "To expedite things," I say before Rose can give me one of her pregnant looks, "we'll skip staff meeting. We need to get these bodies out of here before the weather gets any worse."

Rose has been my secretary for ten years. She is my office mother. She knows me better than anyone but doesn't abuse her position by pushing me in directions I don't want to go in. Curiosity about Jaime Berger fizzes on the surface of Rose's thoughts. I can see questions rising in her eyes.

But she won't ask. She knows damn well how I feel about trying the case in New York instead of here, and that I don't want to talk about it. "I think Dr. Chong and Dr. Fielding are already in the morgue," she is saying. "I haven't seen Dr. Forbes yet."

It occurs to me that even if the Mayo Brown case goes forward today—even if the courts don't close because of snow—Righter isn't going to call me. He will stipulate my report and resort to putting the toxicologist on the stand, at best. There is no way in hell Righter is going to face me after I called him a coward, especially since the accusation is true and a part of him must know it. He will probably figure out a way to avoid me the rest of his life, and that unpleasant thought leads to another one as I cross the hallway. What does all this bode for me?

I push through the ladies' room door and make the transition from civilized paneling and carpeting, through a series of changing rooms, into a world of biological hazards, starkness and violent attacks on the senses. Along the way, one sheds shoes and outer clothing, stowing them safely in teal-green lockers. I keep a special pair of Nikes parked near the door that leads inside the autopsy suite. The shoes are not destined to walk through the land of the living ever again, and when it is time to get rid of them, I will burn them. I clumsily arrange my suit jacket, slacks and white silk blouse on hangers, my left elbow throbbing. I struggle into a full-length Mega Shield gown that has viral-resistant front panels and sleeves, sealed seams and a gripper neck, which is a snug stand-up collar. I pull on shoe covers, then an O.R. cap and surgical mask. The final touch of my fluid-proofing is a face shield to protect my eyes from splashes that might carry such frights as hepatitis or HIV.

Stainless steel doors automatically open, and my feet make paper sounds over the tan vinyl floor of the biohazard epoxy-finished autopsy suite. Doctors in blue hover over five shiny stainless steel tables fastened to steel sinks, water running, hoses sucking, X rays on light boxes a black-and-white gallery of organ-shaped shadows and opaque bones and tiny, bright bullet fragments that, like loose metal chips in flying machines, break things and cause leaks and vital gears to seize. Hanging from clips inside safety cabinets are DNA specimen cards that have been stained with blood. They look oddly like a bunting of tiny Japanese flags as they air-dry beneath a hood. From closed-circuit television monitors mounted in corners a car engine rumbles loudly in the bay, a funeral home here to deliver or take away. This is my theater. It is where I perform. As unwelcome as the average person might find the morbid odors, sights and sounds that rush to greet me, I am suddenly and immensely relieved. My heart lifts as doctors glance up at me and nod good morning. I am in my element. I am home.

A sour, smoky stench taints the long, high-ceilinged room, and I spot the slender, naked, sooty body on a sheet-covered gurney that has been rolled out of the way of traffic. Alone, cold and silent, the dead man waits his turn. He waits for me. I am the last person he will ever talk to in a language that matters. The name on the toe tag scrawled in permanent Magic Marker, pitifully, is John Do. Someone couldn't spell Doe right. I tear open a packet of latex gloves and am gratified I can stretch one over my cast, which is further protected by the fluidproof sleeve. I am not wearing the sling and will have to resort to doing autopsies with my right hand for a while. Although being left-handed in a right-handed world has its difficulties, it is not without advantages. Many of us are ambidextrous or at least reasonably functional on both sides. My aching fractured bones radiate reminders that all isn't right in my world, no matter how tenaciously I go about my business, no matter how intensely I focus on my work.

I slowly circle my patient, leaning close, looking. A syringe is still embedded in the crook of his right arm, and second-degree burns blister his upper body. They have bright red margins, and his skin is streaked black with soot that is thick inside his nose and mouth. He is telling me he was alive when the fire started. He had to be breathing to inhale smoke. He had to have a blood pressure for fluid to be pumped into his burns, causing them to blister and have a bright red margin. The circumstances of a set fire and the needle in his arm certainly could suggest suicide. But on his right upper thigh, he has a contusion that is swollen to the size of a tangerine and crimson. I palpate it. Indurated, hard as a rock. It appears recent. How did it happen? The needle is in his right arm, suggesting that if he injected himself, he most likely is left-handed, yet his right arm is more muscular than his left one, hinting he is right-handed. Why is he nude?

"We still don't have an ID on him?" I raise my voice to Jack Fielding.

"No further info." He snaps a new blade into a scalpel. "The detective's supposed to be here."

"Found unclothed?"

"Yup."

I run my gloved fingers through the dead man's thick, carbon-dusted hair to see what color it is. I won't be certain until I wash him, but his body and pubic hair are dark. He is clean-shaven with high cheekbones, a sharp nose and square jaw. Burns on his forehead and chin will need to be covered up with funeral home makeup before we can circulate a photograph of him for identification purposes, if it comes to that. He is fully rigorous, arms straight by his sides, fingers slightly curled. Livor mortis, or the blood settling to dependent regions of the body due to gravity, is also fixed, causing the sides of his legs and buttocks to be a deep red, the backs of them blanched wherever they rested against the wall or the floor after death. I hold him tilted on his side to check for injuries to his back and find parallel linear abrasions over the scapula. Drag marks. There is a burn between his shoulder blades and another one at the base of the back of his neck. Clinging to one of the burns is a fragment of a plastic-like material, narrow, about two inches long, white with small blue type on it, such as you might see on the back of a food product's packaging. I remove the fragment with forceps and hold it up to the surgical lamp. The paper is more like thin, pliable plastic, a material I associate with candy or snack wrappers. I make out the words *this product,* and *9–4 EST* and a toll-free number and part of a website address. The fragment goes inside an evidence bag.

"Jack?" I summon him and begin collecting blank forms and body diagrams, attaching them to a clipboard.

"I can't believe you're going to work with that

damn cast on." He walks across the autopsy suite, his bulging biceps straining against the short sleeves of his scrubs. My deputy chief may be famous for his body, but no amount of weightlifting or chocolate cream Myoplex high-protein meals in a glass can stop him from losing his hair. It is eerie, but in recent weeks his light brown hair has started falling out before our very eyes, clinging to his clothing, drifting through the air like down, as if he is molting.

He frowns at the misspelling on the toe tag. "The guy from the removal service must be Asian. John Dooo."

"Who's the detective?" I ask.

"Stanfield. Don't know him. Just don't get a puncture in your glove or you'll be wearing a biological hazard for the next few weeks." He indicates my latex-coated cast. "Actually, what would you do, now that I think of it?"

"Cut it off and put on a new one."

"So maybe we should have disposable casts down here."

"I feel like cutting it off anyway. This guy's burn pattern isn't making sense to me," I tell him. "Do we know how far the body was from the fire?"

"About ten feet from the bed. I was told the bed's the only thing that burned and only partially. He was nude, sitting on the floor, back against the wall."

"I wonder why only his upper body got burned." I point out discrete burns the size and shape of silver dollars. "Arms, chest. One here on his left shoulder. And these on his face. And he has several on his back, which should have been spared if he was leaning against the wall. What about the drag marks?"

"As I understand it, when the fire department got there, they dragged his body out into the parking lot. One thing's for sure, he must've been unconscious or incapacitated when the fire started," Jack says. "Sure as hell don't know why else someone would just sit there getting burned and breathing in smoke. Obviously that happy-holiday time of year." My second-in-command is cloaked in a hung-over weariness that causes me to suspect he had a very bad night. I wonder if he and his ex-wife had another one of their explosions. "Everybody killing themselves. That woman over there." He points to the body on table 1, where Dr. Chong is busy taking photographs from a stepladder. "Dead on the kitchen floor, a pillow, a blanket. The neighbor heard one shot. Mother found her. There's a note. And behind door number two"—Jack stares at table 2—"a motor vehicle death the state police are suspicious is a suicide. She has extensive injuries. Plowed right into a tree."

"Did her clothes come in?"

"Yup."

"Let's x-ray her feet and get the labs to check the bottom of her shoes to see if she was braking or accelerating when she hit the tree." I shade areas of a body diagram, indicating soot.

"And we got a known diabetic with a history of overdose," Jack recites our guest list of the morning. "Was found outside in the yard. Question is drugs, alcohol or exposure."

"Or a combination of the above."

"Right. I see what you mean about the burns, though." He leans closer to look, blinking often, reminding me he wears contact lenses. "And it's weird they're all about the same size and shape. You want me to help with this?"

"Thanks. I'll manage. How are you?" I glance up from my clipboard.

His eyes are tired, his boyish good looks strained. "Maybe we can grab some coffee sometime," he says. "One of these days. And I should be asking about you."

I pat his shoulder to let him know I am okay. "As well as can be expected, Jack," I add.

I begin the external examination of John Doe with a PERK. This is a physical evidence recovery kit, a decided unpleasantness that includes swabbing orifices, clipping fingernails and plucking head, body and pubic hair. We PERK all bodies when there is any reason to suspect something other than a natural death, and I will always PERK a body that is nude, unless there is an acceptable reason for the person's not being clothed when he died—in the bathtub or on the operating table, for example. For the most part, I don't spare my patients indignities. I can't. Sometimes the most important evidence lurks in the darkest, most delicate hollows, and clings underneath nails and in hair. During my violation of this man's most private places I discover healing tears of his anal ring. He has abrasions at the angles of his mouth. Fibers adhere to his tongue and the inside of his cheeks.

I go over every inch of him with a lens and the story he tells grows more suspicious. His elbows and knees are slightly abraded and covered with dirt and fibers, which I mundanely collect by pressing them with the adhesive backs of Post-its, which I seal inside plastic bags. Over the bony prominences of both wrists are incomplete circumferential dry, reddish-brown abrasions and minute skin tags. I draw blood from the iliac veins and vitreous fluid from the eyes, and test tubes ride up on the dumbwaiter to the third-floor toxicology lab for STAT alcohol and carbon monoxide tests. At half past ten, I am reflecting back tissue from the Y incision when I notice a tall, older man heading toward my station. He has a wide, tired face and maintains a safe distance from my table, gripping a grocery-size brown paper bag, the top folded over and sealed with red evidence tape. I have a flash of my bagged clothing on my red Jarrah Wood dining room table.

"Detective Stanfield, I hope?" I hold up a flap of skin and free it from ribs with small, quick strokes of the scalpel.

"Good morning." He catches himself as he stares at the body. "Well, I guess not for him."

Stanfield hasn't bothered with protective clothing over his ill-fitting herringbone suit. He wears no gloves or shoe covers. He glances at my bulky left arm and refrains from asking me how I broke it, telling me he already knows. I am reminded that my life has been all over the news, which I am adamant in my refusal to follow. Anna has halfway accused me of being chicken, as much as a psychiatrist is allowed to accuse, and she would never actually use the word "chicken." "Denial" is her word. I don't care. I am staying away from newspapers. I don't watch or listen to a goddamn thing that is said about me.

"Sorry it took so long, but the roads out there are bad on their way to awful, ma'am," Stanfield says. "Hope you got chains on your tires, 'cause I didn't and got stuck. Had to get the tow truck and then get the chains put on, so that's why I wasn't here earlier. You found out anything?"

"His CO's seventy-two percent." Vernacular

for carbon monoxide. "Notice how cherry-red the blood is? Typical in high levels of CO." I pick up rib shears from the surgical cart. "STAT alcohol's zero."

"So it was the fire that got him, for sure?"

"We know he had a needle in his arm, but carbon monoxide poisoning is his cause of death. Doesn't tell us much, I'm afraid." I cut through ribs. "He's got anal tunneling—evidence of homosexual activity, in other words—and his wrists were bound at some point prior to his death. It appears he was gagged." I point out the abrasions on the wrists and the corners of the mouth. Stanfield's eyes pop open. "The abrasions on his wrists aren't crusty," I go on. "They don't look old, in other words. And because he has fibers in his mouth, you can be pretty certain he was gagged at or around the time of death." I hold a lens over the anticubital fossa, or crook of the arm, and show Stanfield two tiny blood spots. "Fresh injection sites," I explain. "But what's interesting is he has no old needle tracks to suggest a history of drug abuse. I'll put a block of liver through to check for triaditis—mild inflammation of the structural support system of bile duct, artery and vein. And we'll see what comes back on his tox."

"Guess he could have AIDS." This is foremost on Detective Stanfield's mind.

"We'll do an HIV on him," I reply.

Stanfield backs up another step as I remove the triangular-shaped breastplate of ribs. This a stage cue for Laura Turkel, on loan to us from the graves registration unit at the Fort Lee Army Base in Petersburg. She is so attentive and officious and almost salutes me when she suddenly appears at the end of the table. Turk, as everyone knows her, always refers to me as "Chief." I suppose for her Chief is a rank and doctor isn't.

"Ready for me to open up the skull, Chief?" Her question is an announcement that requires no answer. Turk is like a lot of the military women we get in here—tough, eager, quick to eclipse the men, who often, truthfully, are the squeamish ones. "That lady Dr. Chong's working on," Turk says as she plugs the Stryker saw into the overhead cord reel, "she's got a living will and even wrote her own obituary. Got all her insurance papers in order, everything. Put 'em all in a binder and left it and her wedding band on the kitchen table before she laid herself down on the blanket and shot herself in the head. Can you imagine? Really, really sad."

"It's very sad." The organs are a shimmering bloc as I lift them out en masse and set them on a cutting board. "If you're going to be in here, you really should cover up." I direct this at Stanfield. "Did anybody show you where things are in the locker room?"

He blankly stares at the cuffs of my blood-soaked sleeves, at the blood splashed on the front of my gown. "Ma'am, if you don't mind, I'd like to go over what I got," he says. "If we could maybe sit down for a minute? Then I need to head on back before the weather gets any worse. Pretty soon, you're gonna need Santa's sleigh to get anywhere."

Turk picks up a scalpel and makes an incision around the back of the head, ear to ear. She reflects back the scalp and pulls it forward, and the face goes slack, collapsing into tragic protest before it is inside out like a folded-down sock. The exposed dome of the skull glistens pristinely white, and I take a good look at it. No hematomas. No indentations or fractures. The whir of the electric saw sounds like a hybrid of a table saw and a dentist's drill as I pull off my gloves and drop them in a red biohazard trash can. I motion Stanfield to follow me to the long countertop that runs the length of the wall opposite the autopsy stations. We pull out chairs.

"I gotta be honest with you, ma'am," Stanfield begins with a slow, negative shake of his head. "We don't got a clue where to start on this one. All I can tell you right now is this man"—he indicates the body on the table—"checked into The Fort James Motel and Camp Ground yesterday at three P.M."

"Where exactly is The Fort James Motel and Camp Ground?"

"On Route Five West, no more than ten minutes from William and Mary."

"You talked to the clerk at this motel, The Fort James Motel?"

"The lady in the office, yes ma'am, I did." He opens a large manila envelope and scoops out a handful of Polaroid photographs. "Her name's Bev Kiffin." He spells it for me, slipping reading glasses out of an inner jacket pocket, hands trembling slightly as he flips through a notepad. "She said the young man come in and said he wants the sixteen-oh-seven special."

"I'm sorry. The what?" I rest my ballpoint pen on the notes I am making.

"One hundred and sixty dollars and seventy cents Monday through Friday. That's five nights. Sixteen-oh-seven. The usual rate's forty-six dollars a night, which is mighty high for a place like that, you ask me. But you know tourist traps."

"Sixteen-oh-seven? As in the date Jamestown was founded?" It seems odd to hear a reference to Jamestown. I just mentioned Jamestown to Anna last night when I was talking about Benton.

Stanfield nods deeply. "As in Jamestown. Sixteen-oh-seven. That's the business rate, or so they call it. The amount for the business week, and let me add, ma'am, this isn't a very nice motel, not at all, no ma'am. A fleabag is what I would call it."

"Does it have a history of crime?"

"Oh no. No ma'am. No history of crime I'm aware of, not at all."

"Just seedy."

"Just seedy." He nods deeply.

Detective Stanfield has a distinct way of speaking with emphasis, as if he is used to teaching a slow child who needs important words repeated or emphasized. He neatly arranges photographs in a lineup on the countertop and I look at them. "You took these?" I assume.

"Yes ma'am, I sure did."

Like him, what he has captured on film is emphatic and to the point: the motel door with the number 14 on it, the view of the room through the open doorway, the scorched bed, the smoke damage to the curtains and walls. There is a single chest of drawers and an area to hang clothes that is nothing more than a rod in a recessed area just inside the door. I note that the mattress on the bed has remnants of a cover and white sheets but nothing else. I ask Stanfield if perhaps he submitted the bedcovers to the labs to test for accelerants. He replies that there was nothing on the bed, nothing to submit except burned areas of the mattress, which he placed inside a tightly sealed aluminum paint can—"according to procedure" are his exact words, the words of someone very new at detective work. But he does agree it is odd that the bedcovers were missing.

"They were on the bed when he checked in?" I ask.

"Mrs. Kiffin says she didn't accompany him to the room, but is sure the bed was properly made because she cleaned it up herself after the last guest checked out several days ago," he replies, so that is good. At least he thought to ask her about it.

"What about luggage?" I ask next. "Did the victim have luggage?"

"Didn't find any luggage."

"And the fire department got there when?"

"They were called at five-twenty-two P.M."

"Who called?" I am making notes.

"Someone anonymous driving by. Saw smoke and called from his car phone. This time of year, the motel doesn't do a lot of business, according to Mrs. Kiffin. She says about three fourths of the rooms was empty yesterday, being as how it's almost Christmas and the weather and all the rest. You can see by looking at the bed, the fire wasn't going nowhere." He touches several of the photographs with a thick, rough finger. "It pretty much had put itself out by the time the fire trucks got there. All they needed was fire extinguishers, didn't need to hose things down, which is a good thing for us. This here's his clothes."

He shows me a photograph of a dark pile of clothing on the floor just beyond the open bathroom door. I make out pants, a T-shirt, a jacket and shoes. Next I look at photographs taken inside the bathroom. On the sink is a coppertone plastic ice bucket, plastic glasses covered with cellophane and a small bar of soap still in its wrapper. Stanfield fishes in a pocket for a small knife, opens a blade and slits the evidence tape sealing the paper bag he brought with him. "His clothes," he explains. "Or at least I assume they're his."

"Hold on," I tell him. I get up and cover a gurney with a clean sheet, and put on fresh gloves and ask him if a wallet or any other personal effects were recovered. He tells me no. I smell urine as I pull out clothing from the bag, careful that if any trace evidence is dislodged, it will fall on the sheet. I examine black bikini briefs and black Giorgio Armani cashmere trousers, both soaked with urine.

"He wet his pants," I tell Stanfield.

He just shakes his head and shrugs, and doubt crosses his eyes—maybe doubt tainted by fear. None of this is making much sense, but the feeling I have is clear. This man may have checked in alone, but at some point, another person entered the picture, and I am wondering if the victim lost control of his bladder because he was terrified. "Does the lady in the office, Mrs. Kiffin, remember him dressed like this when he checked in?" I ask as I pull pockets inside out to see if there is anything in them. There isn't.

"Didn't ask her that," Stanfield responds. "So he's got nothing in his pockets. That's kind of unusual."

"No one checked them at the scene?"

"Well, I didn't bag the clothes, to tell you the truth. Another officer did that, but I'm sure nobody dug in the pockets, or at least no personal effects was found or I would know and have them with me," he says.

"Well, how about you call Mrs. Kiffin right now and see if she remembers him wearing this clothing when he checked in?" I politely tell Stanfield to do his job. "And what about a car? Do we know how he got to the motel?"

"No vehicle's turned up so far."

"The way he was dressed is certainly inconsistent with a low-budget motel, Detective Stanfield." I am drawing pants on a clothing diagram form.

The black jacket and black T-shirt as well as the belt, shoes and socks are expensive designer labels, and this makes me think about Jean-Baptiste Chandonne, whose unique baby-fine hair was found all over Thomas's decomposing body when it showed up in the Richmond Port earlier this month. I comment on the similarity of the clothes to Stanfield. The prevailing theory, I go on to explain to him, is that Jean-Baptiste murdered his brother, Thomas, probably in Antwerp, Belgium, and switched clothing with him before sealing the body inside a cargo container bound for Richmond.

"Because you found all those hairs I been reading about in the paper?" Stanfield is trying to understand what would be difficult for even the most experienced investigator who has seen it all.

"That and microscopic findings that relate to diatoms—algae—consistent with an area of the Seine near the Chandonne house in Île Saint-Louis, in Paris." I talk on. Stanfield is completely lost. "Look, all I can tell you, Detective Stanfield, is this man"—I refer to Jean-Baptiste Chandonne—"has a very rare congenital disorder and allegedly has been known to bathe in the Seine, maybe thinking it might cure him. We have reason to believe the clothing on his brother's body was originally Jean-Baptiste's. Make sense?" I am drawing a belt and noting from the indentation in the leather which notch was used the most.

"Well, to tell you the truth," Stanfield replies, "I been hearing about nothing but this weird case and this Werewolf fellow. I mean, ma'am, that really is all you hear when you turn on TV or pick up the paper, and I guess you know that, and by the way, I'm really sorry for what you been through and to tell you the truth, can't figure how you can even be in here or thinking straight. Godalmighty!" He shakes his head. "The wife said if something like that showed up at our door, he wouldn't have to do a thing to her. She'd die right off of a heart attack."

I catch a spark of his misgivings about me. He is wondering if I am completely rational right now, if I might just be projecting—if somehow everything I experience becomes tainted by Jean-Baptiste Chandonne. I slip the clothing diagram off the clipboard and place it with John Doe's paperwork as Stanfield dials a number he reads from his notepad. I watch him insert a finger in his free ear, squinting as if Turk's sawing open another skull hurts his eyes. I can't hear what Stanfield is saying. He hangs up and comes back over to me as he reads the video display of his pager.

"Well, we got good news and bad news," he announces. "The lady, Mrs. Kiffin, remembers him dressed real nice in a dark suit. That's the good news. The bad news is, she also remembers he had a key in his hand, one of those remote kinds that a lot of new, expensive cars have."

"But there's no car," I reply.

"No ma'am, no car. No key, either," he says. "Sure looks like whatever happened to him, he had some help. You think maybe somebody drugged him and then tried to burn him up to hide the evidence?"

"I think we'd better seriously consider homicide." I state the obvious. "We need to get him printed and see if he matches up with anybody in AFIS."

The Automated Fingerprint Identification System allows us to scan fingerprints into a computer and compare them with those in a database that can be linked state to state. If this dead man has a criminal record in this country, or if his prints are in the database for some other reason, we most likely will get a hit. I work my hands into a pair of fresh gloves, doing my best to cover the plaster looped around my left lower palm and thumb. Fingerprinting dead bodies requires a simple tool called a spoon. It is nothing more than a curved metal implement shaped much like a hollow tube cut in half lengthwise. A strip of white paper is threaded through slits in the spoon so that the paper's surface is curved to accommodate the contours of fingers no longer flexible or compliant to their owner's will. With each print, the strip is advanced ahead to the next clean square. The procedure isn't hard. It doesn't require great intelligence. But when I tell Stanfield where the spoons are, he frowns as if I have just spoken to him in a foreign language. I ask him if he has ever printed a dead body before. He admits he has not.

"Hold on," I say, and I go to the phone and dial the extension for the fingerprints lab. No one answers. I try the switchboard. Everyone is gone for the day because of the weather, I am told. I get a spoon and ink pad from a drawer. Turk wipes off the dead man's hands and I ink his fingers, pressing them one at a time against the curved paper strip. "What I can do if you have no objection," I tell Stanfield, "is see if Richmond City will pop these into AFIS so we can get that going." I press a thumb inside the spoon while Stanfield watches with an unpleasant expression on his face. He is one of these people who hates the morgue and can't get out of it fast enough. "Doesn't look like there's anyone in the labs to help us right now, and the sooner we can figure out who this guy is, the better," I explain. "And I'd like to get the prints and other information to Interpol in the event this man has international connections."

"Okay," Stanfield says with another nod as he glances at his watch.

"Have you ever dealt with Interpol?" I ask him.

"Can't say I have, ma'am. They're sort of like spies, aren't they?"

I page Marino to see if he can help. He drops by forty-five minutes later, by which time Stanfield is long gone and Turk is tucking John Doe's sectioned organs inside a heavy plastic bag that she will place in the body cavity before she sews up the Y incision.

"Yo Turk," Marino hails her when he passes

through opening steel doors. "Freezing leftovers again?"

She glances up at him with one raised eyebrow and a cocked smile. Marino likes Turk. He likes her so much he is rude to her at every opportunity. Turk doesn't look like what one might conjure up from her nickname. She is petite, with a clean prettiness and creamy complexion, her long blond hair tied back and clipped up high like a show horse's tail. She threads heavy white waxed twine into a twelve-gauge suture needle as Marino continues to pick on her. "I tell ya," he says, "I ever get cut, I ain't coming to you for stitches, Turk." She smiles, dipping the big, angled needle into flesh and tugging twine through.

Marino looks hung over, his eyes bloodshot and puffy. Despite his quips, he is in a foul mood. "You forget to go to bed last night?" I ask him.

"More or less. It's a long story." He tries to ignore me, watching Turk and oddly distracted and ill at ease. I untie my gown and take off my face shield, mask and O.R. cap. "See how quickly you guys can get these into the computer," I tell him, all business and not especially friendly. He is keeping secrets from me and I am pissed off by his peacock display of adolescent behavior. "We've got a bad situation here, Marino."

His attention lifts off Turk and lights on me. He gets serious. He drops the childish act. "How 'bout you tell me what's going on while I smoke," he says to me, meeting my eyes for the first time in days.

Mine is a nonsmoking building, which has not stopped various people high in the pecking order from lighting up inside their offices if they are surrounded by people who won't snitch on them. In the morgue, I don't care who asks. I don't allow smoking, period. It isn't that our clientele need to worry about inhaling secondhand smoke, but my concern is for the living who should do nothing in the morgue that requires them to have hand-to-mouth contact. No eating, drinking or smoking, and I discourage chewing gum or sucking on candies or lozenges. Our designated smoking area is two chairs by an upright ash can near the soda machines in the bay. This time of year, this is not a warm, cozy place to sit, but it is private. The James City County case isn't Marino's jurisdiction, but I need to tell him about the clothes. "It's a feeling I have," I sum it up.

He flicks an ash toward the can, his legs splayed in the plastic chair. We can see our breath.

"Yeah, well I don't like it, either," he replies. "Fact is, it may be coincidence, Doc. But another fact is, the Chandonne family's scary shit. What we don't know is what the hell the fallout's going to be now that their ugly duckling son's locked up in the U.S. for murder—now that he's managed to draw so much attention to his Godfather daddy and all the rest. These are bad people capable of anything, you ask me. Believe me, I'm just beginning to see how really, really bad they are," he cryptically adds. "I don't like the mob, Doc. No sir. When I was coming along, they ran everything." His eyes get hard as he says this. "Fuck, they probably still do, only difference is, there ain't any rules, any respect anymore. I don't know what the hell this guy was doing out near Jamestown, but it wasn't to sightsee, that's for sure. And Chandonne's just sixty miles away in the hospital. Something's going on."

"Marino, let's get Interpol on this immediately," I say.

It is up to the police to report individuals to Interpol, and to do this Marino will have to contact the liaison at State Police, who will pass on the case information to Interpol's U.S. National Central Bureau in Washington. What we will be asking Interpol to do is to issue an international advisory notice for our case and to search their massive criminal intelligence database at their General Secretariat in Lyon. Notices are color-coded: Red is for immediate arrest with probable extradition; blue is for someone who is wanted but his identity isn't absolutely clear; green is a warning about someone who is likely to commit crimes, such as habitual offenders like child molesters and pornographers; yellow is for missing people; and black is for unidentified dead bodies, those who most likely are fugitives and are also coded red. My case will be my second black notice this year, following the first one just weeks ago when the badly decomposed body of Thomas Chandonne was discovered in a cargo container at the Richmond Port.

"Okay, we'll get Interpol a mug shot, prints and your autopsy info," Marino makes a mental note. "I'll do that soon as I leave here. Just hope Stanfield don't feel I'm stepping on his toes." He says this as more of a warning. Marino doesn't care if he steps on Stanfield's toes but he doesn't want a hassle.

"He's clueless, Marino."

"A shame, too, because James City County has real good cops," Marino replies. "Problem is, Stanfield's brother-in-law is Representative Matthew Dinwiddie, so Stanfield's always gotten extra good treatment down there and has about as much business working homicides as Winnie-the-Pooh. But I guess he had that on his wish list and Dimwit, as I call him, must have sweet-talked the chief."

"See what you can do," I tell Marino.

He lights another cigarette, his eyes roving around the bay, thoughts palpable. I resist smoking. The craving is awful and I hate myself for ever resuming the habit. Somehow I always think I can have just one cigarette, and I am always wrong. Marino and I share an awkward silence. Finally, I bring up the subject of the Chandonne case and what Righter told me on Sunday.

"Are you going to tell me what's going on?" I quietly say to Marino. "I assume he was released from the hospital early this morning, and I assume you were there. And I guess you've met Berger."

He sucks on the cigarette, taking his time. "Yeah, Doc, I was there. Fucking zoo." His words drift out on smoke. "They even had reporters from Europe." He glances at me, and I sense there is much he isn't going to tell me, and this depresses me deeply. "You ask me, they ought to stick assholes like him in the Bermuda Triangle and not let nobody talk to them or take their picture," Marino goes on. "It ain't right, except at least in this case, the guy's so ugly, he probably gave everybody technical problems, broke a bunch of expensive cameras. They brought him out in enough chains to anchor a damn battleship, leading him along like he was stone-blind. He had bandages over his eyes, faking like he's in pain, the whole nine yards."

"Did you talk to him?" This is what I really want to know.

"It wasn't my show," he oddly replies, staring off across the bay, clenching his jaw muscles.

"They're saying they might have to do cornea transplants. Fuck. Here we got all these people in the world who can't even afford glasses, and this piece of furry shit's gonna get new corneas. And I guess the taxpayers will bankroll his corrective surgery, just like we're paying all these doctors and nurses and God knows who to take care of his ass." He crushes out the cigarette in the ash can. "Guess I'd better get cracking." He reluctantly gets up. He wants to talk to me but for some reason won't. "The Luce and I are grabbing a beer later on. Says she's got some big news for me."

"I'll let her tell you herself," I reply.

He gives me a sidelong glance. "So you're gonna just leave me hanging, huh?"

I start to say that he is one to talk.

"Not even a hint? I mean, is it good news or bad? Don't tell me she's pregnant," he adds ironically as he holds the door for me and we leave the bay.

Inside the autopsy suite, Turk is hosing off my workstation, water slapping and steel grates clanking loudly as she sponges off the table. When she spots me, she shouts above the clamor that Rose is trying to reach me. I go to the phone. "Courts are closed," Rose tells me. "But Righter's office says he plans to stipulate your testimony anyway. So not to worry."

"What a shock." What was it Anna called him? *Ein Mann* something. No backbone.

"And your bank called. A man named Greenwood wants you to call." My secretary gives me a number.

Whenever my bank tries to reach me, I am paranoid. Either investments have taken a dive or I am overdrawn because the computer is screwed up or there is a problem of one sort or another. I get hold of Mr. Greenwood in the private banking division. "I'm very sorry," he says coolly. "The message was a mistake. A misunderstanding, Dr. Scarpetta. I'm very sorry you were bothered."

"So no one needs to talk to me. No problems?" I am perplexed. I have dealt with Greenwood for years and he is acting as if he has never met me.

"It was a mistake," he repeats in the same distant tone. "Again, I apologize. Have a good day."

CHAPTER 9

I SPEND THE NEXT FEW HOURS at my desk, dictating the autopsy report of John Doe and returning phone calls and initialing paperwork, and leave the office late afternoon, heading west.

Sunlight filters through broken clouds and gusts of wind send brown leaves fluttering to the earth like lazy birds. It has stopped snowing and the temperature is rising, the world dripping and sizzling with the wet sounds of traffic.

I drive Anna's silver Lincoln Navigator toward Three Chopt Road while news on the radio endlessly goes on about Jean-Baptiste Chandonne's transport out of the city. There is much made over his bandaged eyes and chemical burns. The story of my maiming him to save my life has taken on an energy. Reporters have found their angle. Justice is blind. Dr. Scarpetta has rendered the classic corporeal punishment. "Blinding somebody, hey take that," a host says on the air. "Who was the guy in Shakespeare? Remember, they gouged his eyes out? King Lear? You see that movie? The old king had to put raw eggs in his eye sockets or something so it wouldn't hurt so much. Really gross."

The sidewalk leading to St. Bridget's brown double front doors is slushy with salt and melted snow, and there are at most twenty cars in the parking lot. It is as Marino predicted: The police are not out in force, nor is the press. The weather may be what has kept the crowds away from the old Gothic brick church, or more likely it is the deceased herself. I, for one, am not here out of respect or affection or even a sense of loss. I un-button my coat and step inside the narthex as I try to evade the uncomfortable truth: I could not stand Diane Bray and have come here only out of duty. She was a police official. I was acquainted with her. She was my patient.

There is a large photograph of her on a table, just inside the narthex, and I am startled to see her haughty self-absorbed beauty, the icy cruel glint in her eyes that no camera could disguise, no mat-ter the angle, the lighting or skills of the photog-rapher. Diane Bray hated me for reasons I still fail to completely grasp. By all accounts, she was ob-sessed with me and my power and focused on my every dimension in ways I never have. I suppose

I do not see myself the way she did, and I was slow to catch on when she began her aggressions, her unbelievably intense war against me which culminated in her aspiring to be appointed to a cabinet position in the commonwealth.

Bray had it all figured out. She would help mastermind transferring the medical examiner's division from the health department to public safety so she could then, if all went according to plan, somehow maneuver the governor into appointing her secretary of public safety. That done, I would politically answer to her, and she could even have the pleasure of firing me. Why? I continue to search for reasonable motivations and fail to find any that completely satisfy me. I had never even heard of her before she signed on with the Richmond P.D. last year. But she certainly knew about me and moved to my fair city with plots and schemes in the works to undo me sadistically, slowly, through a series of shocking disruptions, slanders and professional obstructions and humiliations before she ultimately ruined my career, my life. I suppose in her fantasies, the climax to her cold-blooded machinations would have been for me to give up my position in disgrace, commit suicide and leave a note saying it was her fault. Instead, I am still here. She is not. That I should have been the one who tended to her brutalized remains is an irony beyond description.

A cluster of police officers in dress uniform are talking to each other, and near the sanctuary door, Chief Rodney Harris is with Father O'Connor. There are civilians, too, people in fine clothes who don't look familiar, and I sense from the lost, vacant way they are casting about that they aren't local. I pick up a service bulletin and wait to speak to Chief Harris and my priest. "Yes, yes, I understand," Father O'Connor is saying. He is serene in a long, creamy robe, his fingers laced at his waist. I realize with a twinge of guilt that I have not seen him since Easter.

"Well, Father, I just can't. That's the part I can't accept," Harris replies, his thinning red hair plastered back from his flabby, unattractive face. He is a short man with a soft body that is genetically coded to be fat, a Pillsbury Dough Boy in dress blues. Harris is not a nice man and he resents powerful women. I have never understood why he hired Diane Bray and can only assume it wasn't for the right reasons.

"God's will is not always for us to understand," says Father O'Connor, and then he sees me. "Dr. Scarpetta." He smiles and takes my hand in both of his. "So good of you to come. You've been in my thoughts and prayers." The pressure of his fingers and the light in his eyes convey that he understands what has happened to me and cares. "How's your arm? I wish you would come by to see me sometime."

"Thank you, Father." I offer my hand to Chief Harris. "I know this is a difficult time for your department," I tell him. "And for you personally."

"Very, very sad," he says, staring off at other people as he gives me a perfunctory, brusque handshake.

The last time I saw Harris was at Bray's house when he walked in and was confronted by the appalling sight of her body. That moment will forever lodge between him and me. He should never have come to the scene. There was no good reason for him to see his deputy chief so completely degraded, and I will always resent him for it. I have a special distaste for people who treat crime scenes callously and with disrespect, and Harris's showing up at Bray's scene was a power play and an indulgence in voyeurism, and he knows I know it. I move on into the sanctuary and feel his eyes on my back. "Amazing Grace" swells from the organ, and people are finding pews midway up the aisle. Saints and crucifixion scenes glow in rich stained glass, and marble and brass crosses gleam. I sit on the aisle, and moments later the processional begins, and the smartly dressed strangers I noticed earlier walk in with the priest. A young crucifer carries the cross, while a man in a black suit bears the gold-and-red enamel urn containing Diane Bray's cremated remains. An elderly couple holds hands, dabbing tears.

Father O'Connor greets all of us and I learn that Bray's parents and two brothers are here. They have come from upstate New York, Delaware and Washington, D.C., and loved Diane very much. The service is simple. It isn't long. Father O'Connor sprinkles the waters of baptism on the urn. No one but Chief Harris offers any reflections or eulogies, and what he has to say is stilted and generic. "She gladly enlisted in a profession that is all about rendering help to others." He stands stiffly behind the pulpit and reads from his notes. "Knowing every day that she was placing herself at risk, for that is the life of the police. We learn to stare death in the face and fear not. We know what it is to be alone and even to be hated, and yet we fear not. We know what it is to be a lightning rod for evil, for those who are on this planet to take from others."

Wood creaks as people shift in their pews. Father O'Connor smiles kindly, his head tilted at an angle as he listens. I tune out Harris. I have never attended such a sterile, hollow service and I shrink inside with dismay. The liturgy, the gospel acclamations, the singing and prayers carry no music or passion, because Diane Bray did not love anyone, including herself. Her rapacious, overreaching life has scarcely left a ripple. All of us leave silently, venturing out into the raw, dark night to find our cars and escape. I walk briskly with head bent, the way I do when I wish to avoid others. I am aware of sounds, of a presence, and I turn around as I unlock my car door. Someone has stepped up behind me.

"Dr. Scarpetta?" The woman's refined features are accentuated by the uneven glare of street-lights, her eyes deeply set in shadows, and she wears a full-length shorn mink coat. A hint of recognition sparks somewhere in the deep. "I didn't know you were going to be here, but sure am glad," she adds. I am aware of her New York accent, and shock rocks me before I comprehend. "I'm Jaime Berger," she says, offering a kid-gloved hand. "We need to talk."

"YOU WERE AT THE SERVICE?" THESE are the first words out of my mouth. I didn't see her there. I am paranoid enough to consider that Jaime Berger never stepped inside the church at all but has been waiting in the parking lot for me. "Did you know Diane Bray?" I ask her.

"I'm getting to know her now." Berger turns up her coat collar, her breath smoking out. She glances at her watch and pushes the winding stem.

The luminescent dial glows pale green. "I don't suppose you're going back to your office."

"I wasn't planning on it, but I can," I say without enthusiasm. She wants to talk about the murders of Kim Luong and Diane Bray. Of course, she's interested in the unidentified body from the port, too—the one we all assume is Chandonne's brother, Thomas. But if his case ever sees a courtroom at all, she adds, it isn't going to be in this country. This is her way of telling me Thomas Chandonne is another free lunch. Jean-Baptiste murdered his brother and got away with it. I climb up into the driver's seat of the Navigator.

"How do you like your car?" she asks what seems an inane, inappropriate question at a time like this. Already I am feeling probed. I sense instantly that Berger does nothing, asks nothing, without a reason. She surveys the luxurious sport utility vehicle that Anna is letting me use while my sedan remains strangely off limits.

"It's borrowed. Maybe you'd better follow me, Ms. Berger," I say. "There are some parts of town you wouldn't want to get lost in after dark."

"I'm wondering if you could track down Pete Marino." She points a remote key at her own sport utility vehicle, a white Mercedes ML430 with New York plates, and headlights flash as the doors unlock. "Maybe it would be a good thing for all of us to talk."

I start the engine and shiver in the dark. The night is soggy and icy water drips from trees. The cold seeps inside my cast and finds its way into the cracks of my fractured elbow, seizing exquisitely tender spaces where nerve endings and marrow live, and they begin to complain in deep rolling throbs. I page Marino and realize I don't know the number of Anna's car phone. I fumble to dig my cell phone out of my satchel while steering with the fingertips of my broken arm and keeping an eye on Berger's headlights in my rearview mirror. Marino calls me back long minutes later. I tell him what has happened and he reacts with typical cynicism, but beneath it is an excited current, maybe anger, maybe something else. "Yeah, well, I don't believe in coincidences," he says sharply. "You just happen to go to Bray's memorial service and Berger just happens to be there? Why the hell did she go, in the first place?"

"I don't know why," I reply. "But if I were new to the town and to the characters involved, I'd want to see who cared enough about Bray to show up. I'd also want to see who didn't." I try to be logical. "She didn't tell you she was going? What about when you met with her last night?" I am out with it. I want to know what went on in that meeting.

"Didn't say nothing about it," he replies. "She had other things on her mind."

"Such as? Or are we keeping secrets?" I add pointedly.

He is silent for a long moment. "Look, Doc," he finally says, "this ain't my case. It's New York's case and I'm just doing what I'm told. You want to know stuff, ask her, 'cause that's the way she fucking wants it." Resentment hardens his tone. "And I'm in the middle of lovely Mosby Court and have other things to do besides jump every time she snaps her fancy big-city fingers."

Mosby Court is not the princely residential neighborhood the name suggests, but one of seven low-rent housing projects in the city. All are called courts, and four are named for outstanding Virginians: an actor, an educator, a prosperous tobacconist, a Civil War hero. I hope Marino isn't in Mosby Court because there has been another shooting. "You're not bringing me more business, are you?" I ask him.

"Another misdemeanor murder."

I don't laugh at this bigoted code—this cynical label for a young, black male shot multiple times, probably on the street, probably over drugs, probably dressed in expensive athletic clothes and basketball shoes, and nobody saw a thing.

"Meet you in the bay," Marino sullenly says. "Five, ten minutes."

The snow has completely stopped and the temperature remains warm enough to keep the city

from locking up with freezing slush again. Downtown is dressed for the holidays, the skyline bor-
dered in white lights, some of them burned out.
In front of the James Center, people have pulled
over to explore a blaze of reindeer sculpted of
light, and on 9th Street, the capitol glows like an
egg through the bare branches of ancient trees, the
pale yellow mansion next to it elegant with candles in every window. I catch a glimpse of cou-
ples in evening clothes getting out of cars in the
parking lot and remember with panic that tonight
is the governor's Christmas party for top state of-
ficials. I sent in my RSVP more than a month ago,
confirming I would attend. Oh God. It will not
be lost on Governor Mike Mitchell and his wife,
Edith, that I am a no-show, and the impulse to
swerve onto the capitol grounds is so strong that
I flip on my turn signal. I just as quickly flip it off.
I can't possibly go, not even for fifteen minutes.
What would I do with Jaime Berger? Take her
along? Introduce her to everyone? I smile ruefully
and shake my head inside my dark cockpit as I
imagine the looks I would get, as I fantasize about
what would happen if the press found out.

Having worked for government my entire career, I never underestimate the potential for the
mundane. The telephone number for the governor's mansion is listed, and directory assistance
can automatically dial it for an additional fifty

cents. Momentarily, I have an executive protection unit officer on the line, and before I can explain that I simply want to pass on a message, the trooper puts me on hold. A tone sounds at measured intervals, as if my call is being timed, and I wonder if calls to the mansion are taped. Across Broad Street, an older, drearier part of town gives way to the new brick and glass empire of Biotech, where my office is the anchor. I check the rearview mirror for Berger's SUV. She doggedly follows, her lips moving in my rearview mirror. She is on the phone, and it gives me an uneasy feeling as I watch her say words I can't hear.

"Kay?" Governor Mitchell's voice suddenly sounds over Anna's hands-free car phone.

My own voice catches in surprise as I rush to tell him I wasn't expecting to disturb him, that I am terribly sorry to miss his party tonight. He doesn't answer right away, his hesitation his way of saying I am making a mistake by not coming to his party. Mitchell is a man who understands opportunity and knows how to appropriate it. In his way of thinking, for me to pass up a chance for even a moment with him and other powerful leaders of the commonwealth is foolish, especially now. Yes, now of all times.

"The New York prosecutor's in town." I don't have to say for which cases. "I'm on my way to meet her right now, Governor. I hope you understand."

"I think it would be a good idea for you and me to meet, too." He is firm. "I was going to take you aside at the party."

I have the sensation of stepping on broken glass, afraid to look because I might find I am bleeding. "Whenever it's convenient for you, Governor Mitchell," I respectfully answer.

"Why don't you stop by the mansion on your way home?"

"I can probably be free in about two hours," I tell him.

"I'll see you then, Kay. Say hello to Ms. Berger," he goes on. "When I was attorney general, we had a case that involved her office. I'll tell you about it sometime."

Off 4th Street, the enclosed bay where bodies are received looks like a square, gray igloo appended to the side of my building. I drive up the ramp and stop at the massive garage door, realizing with intense frustration that I have no way to get in. The remote opener is in my car, which is inside my garage at the house I have been banished from. I dial the number for the after-hours morgue attendant. "Arnold?" I say when he answers on the sixth ring. "Could you please open the bay door?"

"Oh, yes ma'am." He sounds groggy and confused, as if I just woke him up. "Doing it right now, ma'am. Your opener not working?"

I try to be patient with him. Arnold is one of those people who is overwhelmed by inertia. He battles gravity. Gravity wins. I am constantly having to remind myself that there is no point in getting angry with him. Highly motivated people aren't fighting for his job. Berger has pulled up behind me and Marino is behind her, all of us waiting for the door to rise, granting us entrance into the kingdom of the dead. My portable phone rings.

"Well, ain't this cozy," Marino says in my ear.

"Apparently she and the governor are acquainted." I watch a dark van turn into the ramp behind Marino's midnight blue Crown Victoria. The bay door begins to lurch up with screeching complaints.

"Well, well. You don't think he has something to do with Wolfman leaving us for the Big Apple, do you?"

"I don't know what to think anymore," I confess. The bay is large enough to hold all of us, and we get out at the same time, the rumbling of engines and shutting of doors amplified by concrete. Cold, raw air jars my fractured elbow again, and I am baffled to see Marino in a suit and tie. "You look nice," I dryly comment. He lights a cigarette, his eyes fastened to Berger's mink-draped figure

as she leans inside her Mercedes to collect belongings from the backseat. Two men in long,
dark coats open the tailgate of the van, revealing
the stretcher inside and its ominous, shrouded
cargo.

"Believe it or not," Marino says to me, "I was
going to stop by the memorial service for the hell
of it, then he decides to get whacked." He indicates the dead body in the back of the van. "It's
turning out to be a little more complicated than
we thought at first. Maybe more than a case of
urban renewal." Berger heads toward us, loaded
down with books, accordion files and a sturdy
leather briefcase. "You came prepared." Marino
stares at her with a flat expression on his face.
Aluminum clacks as stretcher legs open. The tailgate slams shut.

"I really appreciate both of you seeing me on
such short notice," Berger says.

In the glare of the lighted bay, I note the fine
lines on her face and neck, the faint hollows in her
cheeks that tattle on her age. At a glance, or when
she's made up for the camera, she could pass for
thirty-five. I suspect she is a few years older than
I am, closer to fifty. Her angular features, short
dark hair and perfect teeth coalesce into a portrait
of the familiar, and I connect her with the expert
I have seen on Court TV. She begins to resemble
the photographs I pulled up on the Internet when

I released search engines to find her in cyberspace so I could prepare myself for this invasion from what seems an alien galaxy.

Marino doesn't offer to help her carry anything. He ignores her the same way he does me when he is stung or resentful or jealous. I unlock the door leading inside as the attendants wheel the stretcher in our direction, and I recognize the two men but can't recall their names. One of them stares at Berger with starstruck eyes. "You're the lady on TV," he pipes up. "Holy smoke. That lady judge."

" 'Fraid not. I'm no judge." Berger looks them in the eye and smiles.

"You ain't the lady judge? You swear?" The stretcher clatters through the doorway. "I guess you want him in the cooler," one of the men says to me.

"Yes," I reply. "You know where to sign him in. Arnold's around here somewhere."

"Yes ma'am, I know what to do." Neither attendant makes any indication that I might have ended up in their van last weekend as another delivery had my destiny turned out differently. It is my observation that people who work for funeral homes and removal services aren't shocked or even moved by much. It is not lost on me that these two guys are more impressed with Berger's celebrity than with the fact that their local chief

medical examiner is lucky to be alive and is far-
ing rather poorly in the public eye these days.
"You ready for Christmas?" one of them asks me.

"Never am," I reply. "You gentlemen have a
happy one."

"Lot happier than he's gonna have." Indicating
the pouched body, they roll off in the direction
of the morgue office, where they will fill out a toe
tag and sign in the newest patient. I push buttons
to open several sets of stainless steel doors as we
walk over disinfected floors, passing coolers and
the rooms where autopsies are done. Industrial-
strength deodorizers are heavy-handed in their
presence, and Marino talks about the case from
Mosby Court. Berger asks him nothing about it,
but he seems to think she wants to know. Or
maybe he is showing off now.

"First, it looked like a drive-by since he was in
the street and his head was bloody. But I gotta tell
you, now I'm wondering if maybe he got hit by
a car," he informs us. I open doors leading into
the dim silence of the administrative wing while
he goes on to tell Berger every detail of a case he
hasn't even discussed with me yet. I show them
into my private conference room and we take off
our coats. Berger is dressed in dark wool slacks and
a heavy black sweater that does not accentuate but
certainly can't hide her ample bosom. She has the

slender, firm build of an athlete, and her scuffed Vibram boots hint that she will go anywhere and do anything if work requires it. She pulls out a chair and begins arranging briefcase, files and books on the round wooden table.

"See, he's got burns here and here." Marino points to his left cheek and neck and pulls out Polaroid photographs from the inside pocket of his suit jacket. He makes the smart choice of handing them to me first.

"Why would a hit-and-run have burns?" My question is a rebuttal, and I am getting an uneasy feeling.

"If he was pushed out while the car was moving, or if he got toasted by the exhaust pipe," Marino suggests, not sure, not really caring. He has other matters on his mind.

"Not likely," I reply in an ominous tone.

"Shit," Marino says, and it begins to dawn on him as he meets my eyes. "I never looked at him, was already in a bag by the time I got there. Goddamn, I just went by what I was told by the guys at the scene. Shit," he says again, glancing at Berger, his face darkening with gathering embarrassment and irritation. "They'd already bagged the body by the time I got there. Dumb as a bag of hammers, all of 'em."

The man in the Polaroids is light-skinned with

handsome features and short, tightly curled hair dyed egg-yolk yellow. A small gold loop pierces his left ear. I know instantly that his burns were not made by an exhaust pipe, which would leave elliptical burns and not these, which are perfectly round and the size of silver dollars and blistered. He was alive when he got them. I give Marino a long look. He makes the connection and blows out, shaking his head. "We have an ID?" I say to him.

"We don't got a clue." He smooths back hair that at this stage in his life is nothing more than gray fringe gelled to the top of his broad bald pate. He would look much better if he would just shave his head. "Nobody in the area says they've ever seen him before, either, and none of my guys think he looks like anybody we're used to seeing out there on the street."

"I need to look at the body now." I get up from the table.

Marino pushes back his chair. Berger watches me with penetrating blue eyes. She has stopped spreading out her paperwork. "Do you mind if I come along?" she asks.

I do, but she is here. She is a professional. It would be unthinkably rude for me to imply she might not act like one or to suggest I don't trust her. I step next door to fetch my lab coat from my office. "I guess you've got no way of knowing whether it's possible this guy might have been gay. I guess it's not an area where gays might cruise or hang out." I quiz Marino as we head out of the conference room. "What about male prostitutes in Mosby Court?"

"He has that look, now that you mention it," Marino replies. "One of the cops said he was sort of a pretty boy, that buffed kind of workout build. He was wearing an earring. Like I said, though, I ain't seen the body."

"I do believe you win the prize for stereotypes," Berger comments to him. "And I thought my guys were bad."

"Oh yeah? What guys?" Marino is a millimeter from being snide to her.

"At my office," she says in a blasé way. "The investigative squad."

"Oh yeah? You got your own personal NYPD cops? Ain't that sweet. How big?"

"About fifty."

"They work in your building?" I can hear it in his tone. Berger threatens the hell out of him.

"Yes." She does not relay this with any sort of condescension or arrogance, but simply reports the facts.

Marino walks ahead of her and tosses back, "Well, ain't that something."

The removal service attendants are in the office chatting with Arnold. He looks stricken when I appear, as if I have caught him in the middle of something he shouldn't be doing, but then, this is simply Arnold. He is a timid, quiet man. Like a moth that has begun to turn the color of his environment, he is wan with an unhealthy gray tint to his skin, and chronic allergies keep his eyes red-rimmed and runny. The second John Doe of the day is in the middle of the hallway, zipped up inside a burgundy, deep-pile pouch that is embroidered with the name of the removal service, *Whitkin Brothers.* I suddenly remember the names of the attendants. Of course, they are the Whitkin brothers. "I'll take care of him." I let the brothers know they don't have to roll the body into the cooler or transfer him onto a gurney.

"We don't mind," they are quick to nervously offer, as if I am implying they are lollygagging.

"That's all right. I need to spend a little time with him first," I say, and I push the stretcher through double steel doors and hand out shoe covers and gloves. It takes a few moments for me to do the necessary housekeeping of signing John Doe into the autopsy log, assigning him a number and photographing him. I smell urine.

THE AUTOPSY SUITE GLEAMS BRIGHT and clean, devoid of the usual sights and sounds.

The quiet is a relief. After all these years, the constant clamor of water running into steel sinks, of Stryker saws, of steel clacking against steel still makes me tense and tired. The morgue can be surprisingly noisy. The dead are loud in their demands and gory colors, and this new patient is going to resist me. I can already tell. He is completely rigorous and not about to allow me to undress him or open his jaws to look at his tongue or teeth, not without a struggle. I unzip the pouch and smell urine. I pull a surgical lamp close and palpate his head, feeling no fractures. Blood smeared on his jaw and drops on the front of his jacket indicate he was upright when he was bleeding. I direct the light up his nostrils. "He's had a nosebleed," I report to Marino and Berger. "So far, I'm not seeing any injuries to his head."

I begin examining the burns through a lens while Berger moves near me to observe. I note fibers and dirt adhering to blistered skin, and I find abrasions at the corners of his mouth and on the inside of his cheeks. I push up the sleeves of his red warm-up jacket and look at his wrists. Sharply angled ligature marks have left pronounced indentations in the skin, and when I unzip his jacket, I find two burns directly centered on the navel and left nipple. Berger is leaning so close, her gown brushes me. "Rather cold to be out with

just a warm-up suit and no T-shirt or anything beneath it," I point out to Marino. "Were his pockets checked at the scene?"

"Better to wait and do it here where you can
see worth a damn," he answers.

I slide my hands into the pockets of the warm-
up pants and jacket, finding nothing. I pull the
pants down and blue running shorts underneath
are soaked with urine, and the ammonia smell
sends an alert through my psyche, and tiny hairs
all over my flesh stand up like sentries. The dead
rarely frighten me. This man does. I check the
pocket inside the waistband and pull out a steel
key etched with *Do Not Duplicate,* and written on
it in permanent Magic Marker is the number 233.
"A hotel or house, maybe?" I wonder out loud as
I place the key inside a transparent plastic bag and
am pricked by more paranoid feelings. "Maybe a
locker." Two-thirty-three was my family's post
office box number when I was a child in Miami.
I wouldn't go so far as to say that 233 is my lucky
number, but it is one I have frequently used for
pass codes and lock combinations, because the
number isn't obvious and I can remember it.

"Anything so far that might suggest what killed
him?" Berger asks me.

"Not so far. I don't guess we've had any luck
with AFIS or Interpol yet?" I say to Marino.

"Didn't get a cold hit, so whoever your motel

guy is, he ain't in AFIS. Nothing from Interpol yet, which ain't necessarily good, either. If it's obvious, you usually know in an hour," he says.

"Let's print this guy and get him into AFIS as fast as we can." I try not to sound anxious. With a lens I check the hands, front and back, for any obvious trace evidence that might be dislodged by my getting fingerprints. I clip fingernails and place them in an envelope that I label and leave on a countertop with the beginnings of the paperwork, then I ink the fingertips and Marino helps me with the spoon. I take two sets of prints. Berger is silent and keenly curious during all this, her scrutiny like the warmth of a bright lamp. She watches my every move, listens to my every question and instruction. I don't focus on her but am aware of her attention, and in the far reaches of my consciousness, I know this woman is making assessments that I may or may not like. I gather the sheet around the body and zip up the pouch, motioning to Marino and Berger to follow me as I roll the gurney to the cooler against one wall and open the stainless steel door. The stench of death blasts out in a frigid front. Our residents are few this night, only six, and I check the tags on pouch zippers, looking for the John Doe from the motel. When I find him, I uncover his face and point out his burns, and the abrasions at the corners of his mouth and around his wrists.

"Jesus," Marino says. "What the hell is this? Some serial killer going around tying up people and torturing them with a blow-dryer?"

"We need to let Stanfield know about this right away," I answer him, because it is apparent that the death of John Doe from the motel may be connected to the body dumped in Mosby Court. I glance at Marino, reading his thoughts. "I know." He makes no effort to disguise his disdain at telling Stanfield anything. "We've got to tell him, Marino," I add.

We walk out of the cooler and he goes to the "clean hands" wall phone. "Can you find your way back to the conference room?" I ask Berger.

"Sure." She looks almost glazed, maybe puzzled as distant thoughts show in her eyes.

"I'll be right there," I say to her. "I'm sorry for the interruption."

She hovers in the doorway, untying her surgical gown in back. "Strange. But I had a case a couple months back, a woman tortured with a heat gun. Burns looked a lot like the ones in these two cases." She bends over to pull off her booties and drop them in the trash. "Gagged, tied up and had these round burns on her face, her breasts."

"Did they catch who did it?" I am quick to ask, not happy about the parallel.

"A construction guy working in her apartment building," she says with a small frown. "The heat gun was for burning off paint. A real dumb shit, loser—broke into her apartment about three o'clock in the morning, raped, strangled her and all the rest, and when he went out several hours later, his truck had been stolen. Welcome to New York. So hello, he calls the cops and next thing is in a patrol car, a duffel bag in his lap, giving a statement about his stolen truck at the same time the victim's housekeeper shows up, finds the body, starts screaming hysterically and calls nine-one-one. The killer's sitting right there in the cop car when the detectives roar up, and he tries to run. A clue. Turns out the asshole has clothesline and a heat gun inside the duffel bag."

"Was there a lot about the case in the news?" I ask.

"Locally. The *Times,* the tabloids."

"Let's hope it didn't give someone else the idea," I reply.

CHAPTER 10

I AM SUPPOSED TO HANDLE ANY sight, any image, any smell, any sound without flinching. I am not allowed to react to horror the way normal people do. It is my job to reconstruct pain without feeling it vicariously, to conjure up terror and not allow it to follow me home. I am supposed to submerge myself in Jean-Baptiste Chandonne's sadistic art without imagining that his next mutilated work was supposed to be me.

He is one of the few killers I have seen who looks like what he does, the classic monster. But he didn't step from the pages of Mary Shelley. Chandonne is real. He is hideous, his face formed of two halves set together unevenly, one eye lower than the other, teeth widely spaced, small and pointed like an animal's. His entire body is covered with long, unpigmented, baby-fine hair, but it is his eyes that disturb me most. I saw hell in that stare, a lust that seemed to light up the air when he pushed his way into my house and back-kicked the door shut behind him. His evil intuition and intelligence are palpable, and although I resist feeling even a breath of mercy for him, I know the suffering Chandonne causes others is a projection of his own wretchedness, a transient re-creation of the nightmare he endures with every beat of his hateful heart.

I found Berger in my conference room and now she accompanies me down a corridor as I explain that Chandonne suffers from a rare disorder called congenital hypertrichosis. It afflicts only one in a billion people, if such statistics are to be trusted. Before him, I had encountered only one other case of this cruel genetic disorder, when I was a resident physician in Miami, rotating through pediatrics, and a Mexican woman gave birth to one of the ghastliest deformities of human life I have ever seen. The infant girl was covered with long, gray hair that spared only her mucous membranes, her palms and the soles of her feet. Long tufts protruded from her nostrils and ears, and she had three nipples. Hypertrichotic people can be overly sensitive to light and suffer anomalies of their teeth and genitalia. They might have extra fingers and toes. In earlier centuries these wretched people were sold to carnivals or royal courts. Some were accused of being werewolves.

"Then do you think there's significance to his biting his victims' palms and feet?" Berger asks. She has a strong, modulated voice. I would almost call it a television voice: Low-pitched and refined, it gets your attention. "Maybe because those are the only areas of his own body that aren't covered with hair? Well, I don't know," she reconsiders. "But I would have to suppose there's some sort of sexual association, like people, for example, who have foot fetishes. But I've never seen a case where someone bites hands and feet."

I turn on lights in the front office and pass an electronic key over the lock of the fireproof vault we call the evidence room, where the door and walls are reinforced with steel, and a computer system logs the code of whoever enters and when and how long he stays. We rarely have much in the way of personal effects locked up in here. Generally, the police take such items to the property room or we return them to the families. My reason for having this room built is I face the reality that no office is immune from leaks and I need a secure place to store extremely sensitive cases. Against a back wall are heavy steel cabinets, and I unlock one of them and pull out two thick files sealed with heavy tape that I have initialed so no one can snoop without my knowing. I enter Kim Luong's and Diane Bray's case numbers in the log book beside the printer that has just hammered out my code and the time. Berger and I continue talking as we follow the hallway back to the conference room where Marino awaits us, impatiently, tensely.

"Why haven't you had a profiler look at these cases?" Berger asks me as we pass through the doorway.

I set the files on the table and give Marino a look. He can take this one. It is not my responsibility to send cases to profilers.

"A profiler? What for?" he answers Berger in a manner that can only be described as confrontational. "The point of profiling is to figure out what sort of squirrel did it. We already know what sort of squirrel did it."

"But the why? The meaning, the emotion, the symbolism? Those sorts of analyses. I would like to hear what a profiler has to say." She pays no attention to him. "Especially about the hands and feet. Weird." She is still focused on that detail.

"You ask me, most profiling is smoke and mirrors," Marino holds forth. "Not that I don't think there are some guys who really got the gift, but most of it's bullshit. You get some squirrel like Chandonne who's into biting hands and feet and it don't take no FBI profiler to consider that maybe those body parts have some significance to him. Like maybe he's got something oddball with his own hands and feet—or in this case, it's the opposite. Those are the *only* places he ain't got hair, except inside his friggin' mouth and maybe his asshole."

"I can understand him destroying what he hates in himself, mutilating those areas of his victims' bodies, such as their faces." She will not be bullied by Marino. "But I don't know. The hands and feet. There's something more to that." Berger rebuffs him by her every gesture and inflection.

"Yeah, but his favorite part of the chicken's the white meat," Marino pushes. He and Berger treat each other like lovers who have turned on each other. "That's his thing. Women with big tits. He's got some mother-thing going when he selects victims with certain body types. Don't take no FBI profiler to connect them dots, either."

I say nothing but give Marino a look that tells him plenty. He is acting like an insensitive ass, apparently so intent on battling this woman that he fails to realize what he is saying in front of me. He knows damn well that Benton had a genuine gift based on science and a significant database the Bureau has been building by studying and interviewing thousands of violent offenders. And I don't appreciate references to the victims' body types since mine was selected by Chandonne, too.

"You know, I don't like the word 'tit.' " Berger says this matter-of-factly, as if she is telling a waiter to hold the béarnaise sauce. She looks levelly at Marino. "Do you even know what a tit is, Captain?"

Marino, for once, is without words.

"A small bird, maybe," she goes on, shuffling through her paperwork, the energy of her hands betraying her anger. "A blow. Tit for tat, blow for blow. Etymology. And I don't mean the study of bugs. That would be with an N—Entomology. I'm talking about words. Which can offend. And can offend back. Balls, for example, can be something used in games—tennis, soccer. Or refer to the very limited brains between the legs of males who talk about tits." She glances at him with a weighty pause. "Now that we've crossed our language barrier, shall we proceed?" She turns expectantly to me.

Marino's face is the color of a radish.

"You have copies of the autopsy reports already?" I know the answer, but ask her anyway.

"I've been through them numerous times," she responds.

I peel tape off the cases and push them in her direction while Marino pops his knuckles and avoids our eyes. Berger slides color photographs out of an envelope. "What can you tell me?" she asks us.

"Kim Luong," Marino begins in a workmanlike tone, reminding me of M. I. Calloway after he persisted in humiliating her. Marino is seething. "Thirty-year-old Asian, worked part-time in a West End convenience store called Quik Cary. It appears Chandonne waited until there was no one there but her. This was at night."

"Thursday, December ninth," Berger says as she looks at a scene photo of Luong's mutilated, semi-nude body.

"Yeah. The burglar alarm went off at nineteen-sixteen," he says as I puzzle. What did Marino and Berger talk about last night, if not this? I assumed she met with him to go over the investigative aspects of the cases, but it seems clear the two of them have not discussed the murders of Luong or Bray.

Berger frowns, looking at another photograph. "Sixteen past seven P.M.? That's when he came into the store or when he left after the fact?"

"When he left. Went out a back door that was always armed, on a separate alarm system. So he came into the store sometime earlier than that, through the front door, probably right after dark. He had a gun, walked in, shot her as she was sitting behind the counter. Then he put up the closed sign, locked the door, and dragged her back into the storeroom so he could do his thing with her." Marino is laconic and on good behavior, but beneath all this is a volatile concoction of chemistry that I am beginning to recognize. He wants to impress, belittle and bed Jaime Berger, and all of it is about his aching wounds of loneliness and insecurity, and his frustrations with me. As I watch him struggle to hide his embarrassment behind a wall of nonchalance, I am touched by sorrow. If only Marino wouldn't force misery upon himself. If only he wouldn't invite bad moments like these.

"Was she alive when he began beating and biting her?" Berger directs this at me as she slowly goes through more photographs.

"Yes," I reply.

"Based on?"

"There was sufficient tissue response to the injuries of her face to suggest she was alive when he began beating her. What we can't know is whether she was conscious. Or better put, how long she was conscious," I say.

"I got videotapes of the scenes," Marino offers in a voice meant to suggest he is bored.

"I want everything." Berger makes that patently clear.

"At least I filmed the Luong and Diane Bray scenes. Not brother Thomas. We didn't videotape him in the cargo container, which is probably a damn lucky thing." Marino stifles a yawn, his act becoming more ridiculous and annoying.

"You went to all the scenes?" Berger asks me.

"I did."

She looks at another photograph.

"No way I'd ever eat blue cheese again, not after spending quality time with ol' Thomas." Hostility bristles closer to the surface of Marino's skin.

"You know, I was going to put on coffee," I say to him. "Would you mind?"

"Mind what?" Stubbornness holds him in his chair.

"Mind putting on a pot." I look at him in a way that strongly suggests he leave me alone with Berger for a few minutes.

"I'm not sure I know how to work your machine here." He makes a stupid excuse.

"I have complete faith you'll figure it out," I reply.

"I can see you two have a nice rhythm going," I ironically observe when Marino is down the hall and can't hear us.

"We had plenty of opportunity to get acquainted this morning, very early this morning, I might add." Berger glances up at me. "At the hospital, before Chandonne was sent along his merry way."

"Might I suggest, Ms. Berger, that if you're going to spend some time around here, you might want to start by telling him to keep his mind on the mission. He seems to have some battle going with you that overshadows everything else, and it simply isn't helpful."

She continues studying photographs with no expression on her face. "God, it's like an animal tore into them. Just like Susan Pless, my case. These could just as easily be photos of her body. I'm halfway ready to believe in werewolves. Of course, there's the theory in folklore that the notion of werewolves might have been based on real people who suffered from hypertrichosis." I am not sure if she is trying to show me how much research she has done, or if she is deflecting what I just said about Marino. She meets my eyes. "I appreciate your words of advice about him. I know you've worked with him forever, so he can't be all bad."

"He's not. You won't find a better detective."

"And let me guess. He was obnoxious when you first met him."

"He's still obnoxious," I reply.

Berger smiles. "Marino and I have a few issues that we still haven't worked out. Clearly, he isn't used to prosecutors who tell him how a case is going to work. It's a little different in New York," she reminds me. "For example, cops can't arrest a defendant in a homicide case without the D.A.'s approval. We run the cases up there, and frankly"—she picks up lab reports—"it works a whole lot better, as a result. Marino feels it excruciatingly necessary to be in charge, and he's overly protective of you. And jealous of anyone who comes into your life," she sums it up, skimming the reports. "No alcohol on board, except Diane Bray. Point-zero-three. Isn't the thought that she'd had a beer or two and pizza before the killer showed up at her door?" She pushes photographs around on the table. "I don't think I've ever seen anybody beaten this badly. Rage, unbelievable rage. And lust. If you can call something like this lust. I don't think there's a word for whatever he was feeling."

"The word is 'evil.' "

"I guess we won't know about other drugs for a while."

"We'll test for the usual suspects. But it will be weeks," I tell her.

She spreads out more photographs, sorting them as if she is playing Solitaire. "How does it make you feel, knowing this might have been you?"

"I don't think about that," I answer.

"What do you think about?"

"What the injuries are saying to me."

"Which is?"

I pick up a photograph of Kim Luong—a bright, wonderful young woman by all reports, who was working to put herself through nursing school. "The blood pattern," I describe. "Almost every inch of her exposed skin is smeared with bloody swirls, part of his ritual. He fingerpainted."

"After they were dead."

"Presumably. In this photo"—I show her—"you can plainly see the gunshot wound to the front of her neck. It hit her carotid and her spinal cord. She would have been paralyzed from the neck down when he dragged her into the storeroom."

"And hemorrhaging. Because of the severed carotid."

"Absolutely. You can see the arterial spatter pattern on the shelves he dragged her past." I lean closer to her and show her in several photographs. "Big sweeps of blood that start getting lower and weaker the farther he dragged her through the store."

"Conscious?" Berger is fascinated and grim.

"The injury to her spinal cord wasn't immediately fatal."

"How long could she have survived, bleeding like that?"

"Minutes." I find an autopsy photograph that shows the spinal cord after it has been removed from the body and centered on a green towel, along with a white plastic ruler for a scale. The smooth creamy cord is contused a violent purple-blue and partly severed in an area correlating with the gunshot wound that penetrated Luong's neck between the fifth and sixth cervical disks. "She would have been instantly paralyzed," I explain, "but the contusion means she had a blood pressure, her heart was still pumping, and we know that anyway from the arterial blood spatter at the scene. So yes. She was probably conscious as he dragged her by her feet along the aisle, back to the storeroom. What I can't say is how long she was conscious."

"She would have been able to see what he was doing and watch her own blood spurting out of her neck as she bled to death?" Berger's face is keen, her energy at a higher wattage that burns brightly in her eyes.

"Again, it depends on how long she was conscious," I tell her.

"But it's in the realm of possibility she might have been conscious the entire time he was dragging her down the aisle, back to the storeroom?"

"Absolutely."

"Could she talk or scream?"

"She might not have been able to do anything."

"But saying no one heard her scream, that wouldn't mean she was unconscious?"

"No, it wouldn't mean that necessarily," I reply. "If you've been shot in the neck and are hemorrhaging and being dragged . . ."

"Especially dragged by someone who looks like him."

"Yes. You might be too terrified to scream. He might have told her to shut up, for that matter."

"Good." Berger seems pleased. "How do you know he dragged her by the feet?"

"Bloody drag pattern made by her long hair, and trails of blood from her fingers above her head," I describe. "If you're paralyzed and being dragged by your ankles, for example, your arms are going to spread. Like making angels in the snow."

"Wouldn't the human impulse be to grab your neck and try to stop the bleeding?" Berger asks. "And she can't. She's paralyzed and awake, watching herself die and anticipating what the hell he's going to do to her next." She pauses for impact. Berger has the jury in mind, and I can tell already that she didn't earn her incredible reputation accidentally. "These women really suffered," she quietly adds.

"They most certainly did." My blouse is damp and I am cold again.

"Did you anticipate the same treatment?" She looks at me, a challenge in her eyes, as if daring me to explore everything that went through my mind when Chandonne forced his way through my front door and tried to throw his coat over my head. "Can you remember anything you thought?" she prods. "What did you feel? Or did it all happen so fast . . ."

"Fast," I cut in. "Yes, it happened fast," I go back. "Fast. And forever. Our internal clocks quit working when we are panicking, fighting for our lives. That's not a medical fact, just a personal observation," I add, groping, feeling my way through memories that aren't complete.

"Then minutes might have seemed like hours to Kim Luong," Berger decides. "Chandonne was with you probably only minutes as he chased you through your great room. How long did it seem?" She is completely focused on this, riveted to me.

"It seemed . . ." I struggle to describe it. There is no basis for comparison. "Like a flutter . . ." My voice trails off as I stare at nothing, unblinking, sweating and chilled.

"Like a flutter?" Berger sounds faintly incredulous. "Can you explain what you mean by that, by flutter?"

"Like reality distorts, ripples, like wind ruffling water, the way a puddle looks when wind blows across it, all of your senses suddenly so acute as the animal's survival instinct overrides the brain. You hear air move. You see air move. Everything seems in slow motion, collapsing in on itself, and endless. You see everything, every detail of what is happening, and notice . . ."

"Notice?" Berger prods.

"Yes, *notice*," I talk on. "Notice the hair on his hands catching light like monofilament, like fishing line, almost translucent. Notice that he looks almost happy."

"Happy? What do you mean?" Berger quietly asks me. "Was he smiling?"

"I would describe it differently. Not a smile so much as the primitive joy, lust, raging hunger you see in the eyes of an animal about to be fed fresh raw meat." I take a deep breath, focusing on the wall inside my conference room, on a calendar with a Christmas snow scene. Berger sits rigidly, her hands motionless on top of the table. "The problem is not what you observe, it's what you remember," I go on more lucidly. "I think the shock of it all causes a disk error and you can't remember with the same degree of intense attention to detail. Maybe that's survival, too. Maybe we need to forget some things so we don't keep reliving them. Forgetting is part of healing. Like the Central Park jogger dragged off by a gang, raped, beaten, left for dead. Why would she want to remember? And I know you are well acquainted with that case," I add with irony. It was Berger's case, of course.

Assistant District Attorney Berger shifts in her chair. "But you do remember," she quietly points out. "And you had seen what Chandonne does to his victims. 'Severe lacerations to the face.' " She begins skimming Luong's autopsy report out loud. " 'Massive comminuted fractures of right parietal bone . . . fracture of right frontal bone . . . extending down the midline . . . bilateral subdural hematoma . . . disruption of cerebral tissue beneath with accompanying subarachnoid hemorrhaging . . . depressed fractures that drove the inner table of the skull into the underlying brain . . . eggshell-like fractures . . . clotting . . .' "

"Clotting suggests a survival time of at least six minutes from the time the injury was inflicted." I return to my role of interpreter for the dead.

"A hell of a long time," Berger observes, and I can imagine her making a jury sit in silence for six minutes to show them just how long.

"The crushed facial bones, and here"—I touch areas of a photograph—"the splits and tears to skin made by some sort of tool that left a pattern of round and linear wounds."

"Pistol whipping."

"In this case, the Luong case, yes. In Bray's case, he used an unusual type of hammer."

"A chipping hammer."

"I can see you've done your homework."

"A funny habit of mine," she says.

"Premeditation," I go on. "He brought his weapons to the scenes versus using something he found when he got there. And this photo here"— I pick out another horror—"shows knuckle bruises from punching. So he also used his fists to beat her, and from this angle we can see her sweater and bra over there on the floor. It appears he tore them off with his bare hands."

"Based on what?"

"Under the scope you can see that the fibers are torn instead of cut," I reply.

Berger is staring at a body diagram. "Don't think I've ever seen so many bite marks inflicted by a human. Frenzied. Any reason to suspect he might have been under the influence of drugs when he committed these murders?"

"I wouldn't have a way to know."

"What about when you encountered him?" she asks. "When he attacked you on Saturday, shortly after midnight. And by the way, he had the same odd type of hammer, as I understand? A chipping hammer?"

" 'Frenzied' is a good word for it. But I would have no reason to know whether he was on drugs." I pause. "Yes, he had a chipping hammer with him when he tried to attack me."

"Tried? Let's state the facts." She gives me her eyes. "He attacked you. Not tried. He attacked you and you escaped. You got a good look at the hammer?"

"Good point, if we're stating facts. It was a tool of some sort. I know what a chipping hammer looks like."

"What do you remember? The flutter," she refers back to my strange rendition. "Those endless minutes, the hair on his hands catching light like monofilament."

I envision a black coil handle. "I saw the coil," I tell her as best I can. "I remember that. It's so unusual. A chipping hammer has a handle that looks like a thick, black spring."

"You sure? That's what you saw when he came after you?" She pushes me.

"I am vaguely sure."

"It would be helpful if you are more than vaguely sure," she responds.

"I saw the tip of it. Like a big black beak. When he raised it to hit me. Yes, I'm sure. He had a chipping hammer." I become defiant. "That's exactly what he had."

"They took Chandonne's blood in the E.R.," Berger informs me. "Negative for drugs and alcohol."

She is testing me. She already knew Chandonne was negative for drugs and alcohol, yet she withheld that detail long enough to hear my impressions. She wants to see if I can be objective when talking about my own case. She wants to see if I can stick to the facts. I hear Marino down the hall. He walks in with three steaming Styrofoam cups and sets them on the table, sliding a black coffee my way. "I don't know what you take, but you got cream," he rudely tells Berger. "And yours truly takes it fully loaded with cream and sugar because I sure as hell wouldn't want to do anything that might deprive me of my nourishment."

"How seriously messed up would someone be if he got formalin in his eyes?" Berger says to me.

"Depends on how quickly the person rinsed," I objectively answer, as if her inquiry is theoretical and not an allusion to my maiming another human being.

"Must hurt like living hell. An acid, right? I've seen what it does to tissue—turns it into rubber," she comments.

"Not literally."

"Of course not literally," she agrees with a trace of a smile that suggests I ought to lighten up a little, as if that is possible.

"If you suspend tissue in formalin for a long period of time, or inject it—in embalming, for example," I explain, "then yes, it fixes tissue, preserves it indefinitely."

But Berger has little interest in the science of

formalin. I am not even sure how interested she is in the extent of any permanent damage the chemical may have caused Chandonne. I have the sensation she is more focused on how I feel about causing him pain and possible disability. She does not ask me. She just looks at me. I am beginning to feel the weight of those looks. Her eyes are like experienced palpating hands feeling for any anomaly or tenderness.

"We got any idea who he's going to get for a lawyer?" Marino reminds us he is present.

Berger sips her coffee. "The six-million-dollar question."

"So you don't got a clue," Marino says with suspicion.

"Oh, I have a clue. It will be someone you definitely won't like."

"Huh," he retorts. "That's easy to predict. I've never met a defense attorney I liked."

"At least it will be my problem," she says. "Not yours." She puts him in his place again.

I bristle at this, too. "Look," I tell her, "trying him in New York isn't something that makes me happy."

"I understand how you feel."

"I seriously doubt it."

"Well, I've talked to your friend Mr. Righter—enough to tell you exactly how it would go if you put Monsieur Chandonne on trial here in Virginia." She is cool now, the expert, just a little sardonic. "The court would null pross the impersonating-an-officer charge and reduce attempted murder to entering a dwelling with intent to commit murder." She pauses, looking for my reaction. "He never actually touched you. That's the problem."

"Actually, it would have been more of a problem if he had," I answer, refusing to show that she is really beginning to piss me off.

"He may have raised that hammer to strike you, but he never did." Her eyes are steady on mine. "For which we're all grateful."

"You know what they say, your rights are honored only in the breach." I lift my coffee.

"Righter would have filed a motion to have all of the charges combined into one trial, Dr. Scarpetta. And then what would have been your role? Expert witness? Fact witness? Or victim? The conflict is glaringly apparent. Either you testify as the medical examiner and the attack on you is completely left out, or you're simply a victim who survived and someone else testifies to your record. Or worse"—she pauses for effect—"Righter stipulates your reports. He seems to have a habit of that, from what I understand."

"The guy's got the guts of an empty sock," Marino says. "But the Doc's right. Chandonne ought to pay for what he tried to do to her. And he sure as hell should pay for what he did to the other two women. And he ought to get the death penalty. At least down here, we'd fry him."

"Not if Dr. Scarpetta were somehow discredited as a witness, Captain. A good defense attorney would be quick to paint her as conflicted and squirt a lot of ink into the water."

"Don't matter. It's all moot, right?" Marino says. "He ain't being tried here and I wasn't born yesterday. He won't ever be tried here. You guys will lock him up and us small-timers down here will never get our day in court."

"What was he doing in New York two years ago?" I ask. "Do you have any ideas about that?"

"Huh," Marino says as if he knows details that have not been shared with me yet. "That's a story."

"Could it be his family has cartel connections in my fair city?" Berger lightly suggests.

"Hell, they probably have a damn penthouse apartment," Marino retorts.

"And Richmond?" Berger goes on. "Isn't Richmond a stopping-off point between New York and Miami along the I-95 drug corridor?"

"Oh yeah," Marino answers. "Before Project Exile got going and slapped these drones with time in federal prison if they were caught with guns, drugs. Yeah, Richmond used to be a real

popular place to do your business. So if the Chandonne cartel's in Miami—and we already know
that, based on the undercover stuff Lucy was
doing down there—and if there's a big New York
connection, then no big surprise that cartel guns
and drugs were ending up in Richmond, too."

"Were?" she queries. "Maybe still are."

"I guess all this will keep ATF busy for a while,"
I say.

"Huh," Marino snorts again.

A weighty pause, then Berger says, "Well, now
that you've brought that up." Her demeanor tells
me she is about to give me news I will not appreciate. "ATF has a little problem, it appears. As do
the FBI and the French police. The hope, obviously, was to use Chandonne's arrest as an opportunity to get warrants to search his family's Paris
home and maybe during the course of it find evidence that might help bring down the cartel. But
we're having a little difficulty placing Jean-Baptiste
inside the family house. In fact, we have nothing
to prove who he is. No driver's license. No passport or birth certificate. No record this bizarre
man even exists. Only his DNA, which is so close
to the DNA of the man found in your port we can
assume they are probably related, probably brothers. But I need something more tangible than that
if I'm going to get a jury on my side."

"And no way in hell his family's going to come forward and claim the Loup-Garou," Marino says in awful French. "That's the whole reason there's no record of him to begin with, right? The mighty Chandonnes don't want the world to know they got a son who's a hairy-ass serial-killing freak."

"Wait a minute," I stop them. "Didn't he identify himself when he was arrested? Where did we get the name Jean-Baptiste Chandonne, if not from him?"

"We got it from him." Marino rubs his face in his hands. "Shit. Show her the videotape," he suddenly blurts out to Berger. I have no idea what videotape he is talking about, and Berger isn't at all happy he mentioned it. "The Doc has a right to know," he says.

"What we have here is a new spin on a defendant who has a DNA profile but no identity." Berger sidesteps the subject Marino has just tried to force.

What tape? I think, as paranoia heats up. What tape?

"You got it with you?" Marino regards Berger with open hostility, the two of them squaring off in a stony angry tableau, staring across the table at each other. His face darkens. He outrageously grabs her briefcase and slides it toward him as if he plans to help himself to whatever is inside it.

Berger places her hand on top of it with an arresting look. "Captain!" she warns in a tone that bodes the worst trouble he has ever seen. Marino withdraws his hand, his face a furious red. Berger opens her briefcase and gives me her full attention. "I have every intention of showing the tape to you," she measures her words. "I just wasn't going to do it right this minute, but we can." She is very controlled but I can tell she is very angry as she slides a videotape out of a manila envelope. She gets up and inserts it into the VCR. "Someone know how to work this thing?"

CHAPTER 11

I TURN ON THE TELEVISION AND hand Berger the remote control.

"Dr. Scarpetta"—she completely ignores Marino—"before we get into this, let me give you a little background on how the district attorney's office works in Manhattan. As I've already mentioned, we do a number of things very differently from what you're accustomed to here in Virginia. I was hoping to explain all that to you before you were subjected to what you are about to see. Are you familiar with our system of homicide call?"

"No," I reply as my nerves tighten and begin to hum.

"Twenty-four hours a day, seven days a week, an assistant D.A. is on call should a homicide go down or the cops locate a defendant. In Manhattan, the cops can't arrest a defendant without the D.A.'s office giving them the go-ahead, as I've already explained. This is to ensure that every-thing—search warrants, for example—are exe-cuted properly. It's common for the prosecutor, the assistant, to go to the crime scene, and in a situa-tion where a defendant is arrested, if he's willing to be interviewed by the assistant, we jump all over it. Captain Marino," she says, giving him her cool attention, "you started out in NYPD, but that may have been before all this was implemented."

"Never heard of it before today," he mumbles, face still dangerously red.

"What about vertical prosecution?"

"Sounds like a sex act," Marino replies.

Berger pretends she didn't hear that. "Morgen-thau's idea," she says to me.

Robert Morgenthau has been the district at-torney in Manhattan for nearly twenty-five years. He is a legend. It is obvious Berger loves work-ing for him. Something stirs deep inside me. Envy? No, maybe wistfulness. I am tired. I expe-rience a growing feeling of powerlessness. I have no one but Marino, who is anything but innova-tive or enlightened. Marino is not a legend and right now I don't love working with him or even want him around.

"The prosecutor has the case from intake on," Berger begins to explain vertical prosecution. "Then we don't have to fool with three or four people who have already interviewed our witnesses or the victim. If a case is mine, for example, I might literally start out at the crime scene and end up in court. A purity you absolutely can't argue with. If I'm lucky, I interrogate the defendant before he retains counsel—obviously, no defense attorney's going to agree to his client talking to me." She hits the play button on the remote control. "Fortunately, I caught Chandonne before he got counsel. I interviewed him several times in the hospital beginning at the rather inhumane hour of three o'clock this morning."

To say I am shocked would be a gross trivialization of my reaction to what she has just revealed. It can't be possible that Jean-Baptiste Chandonne would talk to anyone.

"Clearly, you're a bit taken aback." Berger's comment to me seems rhetorical, as if she has some point to make.

"You might say that," I answer her.

"Maybe it hasn't really occurred to you that your assailant can walk, talk, chew gum, drink Pepsi? Maybe he doesn't seem fully human to you?" she suggests. "Maybe you think he really is a werewolf."

I never actually saw him when he spoke cogently on the other side of my front door. *Police. Is everything all right in there?* After that, he was a monster. Yes, a monster. Yes, a monster coming after me with a black iron tool that looked like something from the Tower of London. Then he was grunting and screaming and sounded very much the way he looks, which is hideous, unearthly. A beast.

Berger smiles a bit wearily. "Now you're about to see our challenge, Dr. Scarpetta. Chandonne isn't crazy. He isn't supernatural. And we don't want jurors holding him to a different standard just because he has an unfortunate medical condition. But I also want them to see him now, before he's cleaned up and wearing a three-piece suit. I think the jurors need to fully appreciate the terror his victims felt, don't you?" Her eyes touch mine. "Might help them get the drift that no one in her right mind would have invited him into her home."

"Why? Is he saying he was invited in?" My mouth has gone dry.

"He's saying quite a lot of things," Berger replies.

"Biggest bunch of fucking bullshit you ever heard," Marino says in disgust. "But then I knew that right off the bat. I go to his room late last night, right? Tell him Ms. Berger wants to interview him and so he asks me what she looks like. I don't say a word, play the asshole along. I tell him, 'Well, let's just put it this way, John. A lotta guys have a real hard time—no pun intended—concentrating when she's around, know what I mean?' "

John, I numbly think. Marino calls him John.

"Testing, one, two, three, four, five, one, two, three, four, five," a voice sounds on the tape, and a cinder-block wall fills the screen. The camera begins to focus on a bare table and a chair. In the background a telephone rings.

"He wants to know if she has a good body, and Ms. Berger, I hope you'll excuse me for making reference to it." Marino oozes sarcasm, still furious with her for reasons I don't yet fully understand. "But I'm just repeating what the piece of shit said. And so I tell him, 'Geez, it wouldn't be right for me to comment, but like I said, the guys can't think straight when she's around. At least straight guys can't think straight.' "

I know damn well this is not what Marino said. In fact, I doubt Chandonne asked about Berger's appearance at all. More likely, the suggestion of her sexy good looks came from Marino, to bait Chandonne into talking to her, and as I recall the crude comment Marino made about Berger when we were walking out to Lucy's car last night, I feel a rush of resentment, of anger. I am fed up with him and his machismo. I am sick of his male chauvinism and crudity.

"What the hell is this?" I feel like hosing him off with cold water. "Do female body parts have to enter every goddamn conversation? Do you think it's possible, Marino, that you might focus on this case without obsessing over how big a woman's breasts are?"

"Testing, one, two, three, four, five," the cameraman's voice sounds again on tape. The telephone stops ringing. Feet shuffle. Voices murmur. "We're gonna sit you at this table and chair right here." I recognize Marino's voice on tape, and in the background someone knocks on a door.

"The point is, Chandonne talked." Berger is looking at me, palpating me with her eyes again, finding my weaknesses, my inflamed spots. "He talked to me quite a lot."

"For whatever that's worth." Marino angrily stares at the TV screen. So that's it. Marino might have helped induce Chandonne into talking to Berger, but the truth is, Marino wanted Chandonne to talk to him.

The camera is fixed and I see only what is directly in its view. Marino's big gut comes into the picture as he pulls out a wooden chair, and someone in a dark blue suit and deep red tie helps Marino steer Jean-Baptiste Chandonne into the chair. Chandonne wears short-sleeved blue hospital scrubs and long pale hair hangs from his arms in tangles of wavy, soft fur the color of pale honey. Hair splays over his v-necked collar and climbs up his neck in repulsive, long swirls. He sits and his head enters the frame, swathed in gauze from mid-forehead to the tip of his nose. Directly around the bandages, the flesh has been shaven and is as white as milk, as if it has never seen the sun.

"Can I have my Pepsi, please?" Chandonne asks. He wears no restraints, not even handcuffs.

"You want it topped off?" Marino says to him.

No answer. Berger moves past the camera and I note that she is wearing a chocolate brown suit with padded shoulders. She sits across from Chandonne. I see only the back of her head and shoulders.

"You want a refill, John?" Marino asks the man who tried to murder me.

"In a minute. Can I smoke?" Chandonne says.

His voice is soft and heavily French. He is polite and calm. I stare at the television screen, my concentration flickering. I experience electrical disturbances again, post-traumatic stress, my nerves jump like water hitting hot grease, and I am getting another bad headache. The dark blue—sleeved arm with the white cuff reaches into the picture, setting a drink and a pack of Camel cigarettes in front of Chandonne, and I recognize the blue-and-white tall paper cup as coming from the hospital cafeteria. A chair scrapes back and the blue-sleeved arm lights a cigarette for Chandonne.

"Mr. Chandonne." Berger's voice sounds at ease and in charge, as if she talks to mutant serial killers every day. "I'm going to start with introducing myself. I'm Jaime Berger, a prosecutor with the New York County district attorney's office. In Manhattan."

Chandonne raises a hand to lightly touch his bandages. The backs of his fingers are covered with downy pale hair, almost albino, colorless hair. It is maybe half an inch long, as if until recently he shaved the backs of his hands. I have flashbacks of those hands coming after me. His fingernails are long and filthy and for the first time, I catch the contours of powerful muscles, not thick and bulging like men who obsessively work out in the gym, but ropey and hard, the physical habitat of one who, like a wild animal, uses his body to feed, to fight and flee, to survive. His strength seems to contradict our assumption that he has lived a rather sedentary and useless life, hiding inside his family's *hôtel particulier*, as the elegant private houses on Île Saint-Louis are called.

"You've already met Captain Marino," Berger says to Chandonne. "Also present is Officer Escudero from my office—he's the cameraman. And Special Agent Jay Talley with the Bureau of Alcohol, Tobacco and Firearms."

I feel Berger's eyes touch me. I avoid looking.

I refrain from interrupting to ask, *Why? Why was Jay there?* It streaks through my mind that she is exactly the sort of woman he would be attracted to—intensely. I slip a tissue out of a jacket pocket and blot cold sweat off my brow.

"You know this is being videotaped, don't you, and you have no objection to that," Berger is saying on tape.

"Yes." Chandonne takes a drag on the cigarette and picks a piece of tobacco off the tip of his tongue.

"Sir, I'm going to ask you some questions about the death of Susan Pless on December fifth, nineteen-ninety-seven."

Chandonne has no reaction. He reaches for his Pepsi, finding the straw with his pink, uneven lips as Berger goes on to give him the victim's address in New York's Upper East Side. She tells him that before they can go any further, she wants to advise him of his rights, even though he has already been advised of them God knows how many times. Chandonne listens. Maybe it is my imagination, but he seems to be enjoying himself. He does not seem in pain or the least bit intimidated. He is quiet and courteous, his hairy, awful hands resting on top of the table or touching his bandages, as if to remind us of what we—what I—did to him.

"Anything you say can be used against you in court," Berger goes on. "Do you understand? And it would be helpful if you would say *yes* or *no* instead of nodding."

"I understand." He cooperates almost sweetly.

"You have a right to consult a lawyer now before any questioning or to have a lawyer present during any questioning. Do you understand?"

"Yes."

"And if you don't have a lawyer or can't afford one, a lawyer will be provided to you free of charge. Do you understand?"

At this, Chandonne reaches for his Pepsi again. Berger relentlessly goes on making sure that he and all the world know this process is legal and fair and that Chandonne is completely informed and is talking to her of his own volition, freely, without any pressure of any sort. "Now that you have been advised of your rights," she concludes her forceful, self-assured opening, "are you going to tell the truth about what happened?"

"I always tell the truth," Chandonne replies softly.

"And you've been read these rights in front of Officer Escudero, Captain Marino and Special Agent Talley, and you understood these rights?"

"Yes."

"Why don't you just tell me in your own words what happened to Susan Pless?" Berger says.

"She was very nice," Chandonne replies, to my amazement. "I am still made sick by it."

"Yeah, I just bet you are," Marino sardonically mutters inside my conference room.

Berger instantly hits the pause button. "Captain," she fires at him, "no editorializing. Please."

Marino's sullenness is like a poisonous vapor. Berger points the remote control and on tape she is asking Chandonne how he and Susan Pless met. He replies that they met in a restaurant called Lumi on 70th Street, between Third and Lexington.

"You were what? Eating there, working there?" Berger pushes ahead.

"Eating there by myself. She walked in, also by herself. I had a very nice bottle of Italian wine. A nineteen-ninety-three Massolino Barolo. She was very beautiful."

Barolo is my favorite Italian wine. The bottle he mentions is pricey. Chandonne goes on to tell his story. He was eating antipasto—"*Crostini di polenta con funghi trifolati e olio tartufato*," he says in perfect Italian—when he noticed a stunning African-American woman enter the restaurant alone. The maître d' treated her as if she was important and a regular customer, and seated her at a corner table. "She was well-dressed," Chandonne says. "She obviously was not a prostitute." He asked the maître d' to see if she would like to come to his table and join him, and she was *very easy*.

"What do you mean, *very easy*?" Berger inquires.

Chandonne gives a slight shrug and reaches for his Pepsi again. He takes his time sucking on the straw. "I think I would like another." He holds up the cup and the dark blue–sleeved arm—Jay Talley's arm—takes it from him. Chandonne blindly feels for the pack of cigarettes, his hairy hand groping over the top of the table.

"What do you mean when you say Susan was *very easy*?" Berger asks again.

"She needed no coaxing to join me. She came over to my table and sat. And we had a very nice conversation."

I don't recognize his voice.

"What did you talk about?" Berger asks him.

Chandonne touches his bandages again and I am imagining this hideous man with his long body hair, sitting in a public place, eating fine food and drinking fine wine and picking up women. It weirdly darts through my thoughts that Chandonne might have suspected Berger would show me this videotape. Is the Italian food and wine something he mentions for my benefit? Is he taunting me? What does he know about me? Nothing, I answer myself. There is no reason he would know anything about me. Now he is telling Berger that he and Susan Pless discussed politics and music over dinner. When Berger asks him if he was aware of what Pless did for a living, he answers that she told him she worked for a television station.

"I said to her, 'So you're famous,' and she laughed," Chandonne says.

"Had you ever seen her on television?" Berger asks him.

"I don't watch much television." He slowly blows out smoke. "Now, of course, I don't watch anything. I can't see."

"Just answer the question, sir. I didn't ask how much television you watch but if you had ever seen Susan Pless on television."

I strain to recognize his voice as fear tickles over my flesh and my hands begin to shake. His voice is completely unfamiliar. It sounds nothing like the voice outside my door. *Police. Ma'am, we've gotten a call about a suspicious person on your property.*

"I don't remember seeing her on television," Chandonne replies.

"What happened next?" Berger asks him.

"We ate. We drank the wine, and I asked her if she would like to go somewhere and have a little champagne."

"Somewhere? Where were you staying?"

"In the Barbizon Hotel, but not under my real name. I had just gotten in from Paris and was only in New York a few days."

"What was the name you signed in under?"

"I don't remember."

"How did you pay?"

"Cash."

"And you'd come to New York for what reason?"

"I was very frightened."

Inside my conference room, Marino shifts in his chair and blows out in disgust. He editorializes again. "Hold on to your hats, folks. Here comes the good part."

"Frightened?" Berger's voice sounds on the tape. "What were you frightened of?"

"These people who are after me. Your government. That's what this whole thing is about." Chandonne touches his bandages again, this time with one hand, then with the one holding the Camel cigarette. Smokes curls around his head. "Because they are using me—have been using me—to get to my family. Because of untrue rumors about my family . . ."

"Hold on. Hold on a minute," Berger interrupts.

Out of the corner of my eye I see Marino angrily shaking his head. He leans back in his chair and crosses his arms over his swollen gut. "You get what you ask for," he mutters, and I can only assume he means that Berger should never have interviewed Chandonne. It was a mistake. The tape is going to hurt more than it will help.

"Captain, please," the real Berger in this room says to Marino in a tone that means business, while her voice on tape asks Chandonne, "Sir, who is using you?"

"FBI, Interpol. Maybe even CIA. I don't know exactly."

"Yeah," Marino sarcastically pipes up from the table. "He don't mention ATF 'cause no one's ever heard of ATF. It's not even in spellcheck."

His hatred for Talley in addition to what is happening to Lucy's career has metastasized into Marino's hating all of ATF. Berger says nothing this time. She ignores him. On tape she confronts Chandonne, her no-nonsense nature marching forth, "Sir, I need you to understand how important it is for you to tell the truth now. Do you understand how important it is that you are absolutely truthful with me?"

"I tell the truth," he softly, earnestly says. "I know it sounds unbelievable. It seems incredible, but it all has to do with my powerful family. Everyone in France knows of them. They have lived for hundreds of years on Île Saint-Louis and it's rumored they are connected with organized crime, like the Mafia, which isn't true at all. This is where the confusion comes. I've never lived with them."

"You're part of this powerful family, though. Their son?"

"Yes."

"Do you have brothers and sisters?"

"I had a brother. Thomas."

"Had?"

"He's dead. You know that. He's why I'm here."

"I would like to get back to that. But let's talk about your family in Paris. Are you telling me you don't live with your family and have never lived with them?"

"Never."

"Why is that? Why have you never lived with your family?"

"They've never wanted me. When I was very young they paid a childless couple to take care of me so no one would know."

"Know what?"

"That I am Monsieur Thierry Chandonne's son."

"Why wouldn't your father want people to know you're his son?"

"You look at me and ask such a question?" Anger tightens his mouth.

"I'm asking you the question. Why wouldn't your father want people to know you're his son?"

"Oh, all right. I will pretend you don't notice my appearance. You are very kind to pretend you don't notice." A sneer creeps into his voice. "I have a severe medical condition. Shame, my family is ashamed of me."

"Where does the couple live? These people who you say took care of you?"

"Quai de l'Horloge, very near the Conciergerie."

"The prison? Where Marie Antoinette was detained during the French Revolution?"

"The Conciergerie is very famous, of course. A tourist place. People seem so preoccupied with prisons, torture chambers and beheadings. Especially Americans. I've never understood it. And you will kill me. The United States will kill me easily. You people kill everyone. It is all part of the big plan, the conspiracy."

"Where exactly on the Quai de l'Horloge? I thought that entire huge block was the Palais de Justice and the Conciergerie." Berger pronounces French like one who speaks it. "Yes, there are some apartments, very expensive ones. You're saying your foster home was there?"

"Very near there."

"What is the name of this couple?"

"Olivier and Christine Chabaud. Sadly, they are both dead, for many years."

"What did they do? Their occupations?"

"He was a *boucher*. She was a *coiffeureuse*."

"A butcher and a hairdresser?" Berger's tone hints that she doesn't believe him and knows damn well he is mocking her and all of us. Jean-Baptiste Chandonne is a butcher. He is dressed in hair.

"A butcher and a hairdresser, yes," Chandonne affirms.

"Did you ever see your family, the Chandonnes, while you were living with these other people near the prison?"

"Now and then I would show up at the house. Always after dark so people wouldn't see me."

"So people wouldn't see you? Why didn't you want people to see you?"

"It's as I've said." He taps an ash blindly. "My family didn't want people to know I am their son. There would have been much made of it. He's very, very well known. I can't really blame him. So I would go late at night when it was dark and the streets on Île Saint-Louis were deserted, and I would sometimes get money from them or other things."

"Would they let you into the house?" Berger is desperate to place him inside the family house so authorities can have probable cause for a search warrant. I can see already that Chandonne is a master of the game. He knows damn well why she wants to place him inside the incredible Chandonne *hôtel particulier* on Île Saint-Louis, a house I actually saw with my own eyes when I was recently in Paris. There will be no search warrant in my lifetime.

"Yes. But I wouldn't stay long, and I didn't go into all the rooms," he is telling Berger as he calmly smokes. "There are many rooms in my family's house that I have never been in. Only the kitchen, and, let me see, the kitchen and the servants' quarters and just inside the door. For the most part, you see, I have taken care of myself."

"Sir, when was the last time you visited your family's home?"

"Oh, no time recently. Two years, at least. I really don't remember."

"You don't remember? If you don't know, just say you don't know. I'm not asking you to guess."

"I don't know. But not recently, of that I'm sure."

Berger points the remote control and the picture freezes. "You see his game, of course," she says to me. "First, he gives us information we can't trace. People who are dead. Cash in a hotel where he signed in under an assumed name he can't remember. And now, no basis for a warrant to search his family's home because he's saying he never lived there and has scarcely been inside it. And certainly not recently. No probable cause that's fresh."

"Hell! No probable cause, period," Marino adds. "Not unless we can find witnesses who've seen him in and out of the family house."

CHAPTER 12

BERGER RESUMES THE VIDEO-tape. She is asking Chandonne, "Are you employed or have you ever been?"

"This and that," he mildly replies. "Whatever I can find."

"Yet you could afford to stay in a nice hotel and eat at an expensive New York restaurant? And buy a good bottle of Italian wine? Where did you get the money for all that, sir?"

At this, Chandonne hesitates. He yawns, giving us a startling view of his grotesque teeth. Small and pointed, they are widely spaced and gray. "Sorry. I am very tired. I don't have much strength." He touches his bandages again.

At this, Berger reminds him that he is talking of his own volition. No one is forcing him. She offers to stop but he says he will continue a little longer, maybe just a few minutes longer. "I've been on the street much of my life when I can find no work," he tells her. "Sometimes I beg, but most times I find any job I can. Washing dishes, sweeping. Once I even drove a *moto-crottes*."

"And what is that?"

"A *trottin'net*. One of those green motorcycles in Paris that cleans sidewalks, you know, with the vacuum that picks up dog shit."

"Do you have a driver's license?"

"No."

"Then how did you drive a *trottin'net*?"

"If it's under one hundred and twenty-five CCs you don't need a driver's license, and the *moto-crottes* only go maybe twenty kilometers an hour."

This is all bullshit. Again, he is mocking us. Marino shifts in his chair inside my conference room. "The asshole's got an answer to everything, don't he?"

"Any other ways you get money?" Berger is asking Chandonne.

"Well, from women sometimes."

"And how do you get money from women?"

"If they give money to me. I admit women are my weakness. I love women—the way they look, smell, feel, taste." He who sinks his teeth into women he brutalizes and murders says all this in a gentle tone. He feigns perfect innocence. He has begun flexing his fingers on the table as if they are stiff, splaying his fingers in and out, slowly, hair shining.

"You like the way they taste?" Berger is getting more aggressive. "Is that why you bite them?"

"I don't bite them."

"You didn't bite Susan Pless?"

"No."

"Sir, she was covered with bite marks."

"I didn't do that. They did it. I'm followed and it's they who kill. They kill my lovers."

"They?"

"I told you. Government agents. FBI, Interpol. So they can get to my family."

"If your family has been so careful to hide you from the world, then how do these people—FBI, Interpol, whatever—know you are a Chandonne?"

"They must have seen me come out of the house at times, followed me. Or maybe someone told them."

"And you think it's been at least two years since you were in your family home?" She tries again.

"At least."

"How long do you believe you have been followed?"

"Many years. Maybe five years. It's hard to know. They're very clever."

"And how might you help these people, quote, *get to your family*?" Berger asks him.

"If they can frame me as if I'm a terrible killer, then the police might get into my family's house.

They would find nothing. My family is innocent. It's all politics. My father is very powerful politically. Beyond that, I don't know. I only can say what has been happening to me, to my life, and it's all a conspiracy to get me into this country and be arrested and then put to death. Because you Americans kill people even when they are innocent. It is well known." His claim seems to make him weary, as if he is tired of pointing it out.

"Sir, where did you learn to speak English?" Berger then asks.

"I picked it up myself. And when I was younger, my father would give me books when I would show up at the house. I read a lot of books."

"In English?"

"Yes. I wanted to learn English very well. My father speaks many languages because he is in international shipping and deals with many foreign countries."

"Including this country? The United States?"

"Yes."

Talley's arm enters the picture again as he sets down another Pepsi. Chandonne greedily plunges the straw between his lips and makes loud sucking sounds.

"What kind of books did you read?" Berger continues.

"A lot of histories and other books to educate

myself, because I had to teach myself, you see. I never went to school."

"Where are these books now?"

"Oh, I wouldn't know. Gone. Because I am homeless sometimes or move around a lot. Always on the move, looking over my shoulder because of these people after me."

"Do you know any other languages besides French and English?" Berger asks.

"Italian. A little German." He belches quietly.

"And you picked those up yourself, too?"

"I find newspapers in many languages in Paris and have learned that way, also. Sometimes I have slept on newspapers, you see. When I have no shelter."

"He's breaking my heart." Marino can't restrain himself as Berger says to Chandonne on tape, "Let's get back to Susan, to her death on December fifth, two years ago in New York. Tell me about that night, the night you say you met her in Lumi. What exactly happened?"

Chandonne sighs as if he is getting more tired by the second. He touches his bandages frequently and I notice that his hands tremble. "I need something to eat," he says. "I'm feeling faint, very weak."

Berger points the remote control and the picture freezes and blurs. "We broke for about an hour," she tells me. "Long enough for him to eat something and rest."

"Yeah, the guy sure as hell knows the system," Marino tells me, as if I haven't yet figured that out. "And the stuff about this couple who raised him is bullshit. He's just protecting his Mafia family."

Berger says to me, "I'm wondering if you're familiar with the restaurant Lumi?"

"Not off the top of my head," I reply.

"Well, it's interesting. When we began investigating Susan Pless's murder two years ago, we knew then that she had eaten at Lumi the night she was killed because the person who waited on her called the police the minute he heard the news. The medical examiner even found traces of the meal in her stomach contents, indicating she had probably eaten several hours, at most, before death."

"Was she alone at the restaurant?" I inquire.

"Came in alone and joined a man who was also alone, only he wasn't a freak—not hardly. Was described as tall, broad-shouldered, well dressed, good-looking. Clearly someone for whom money wasn't a problem, or at least he gave that impression."

"Do you know what he ordered?" I ask.

Berger runs her fingers through her hair. It is the first time I have seen her uncertain. In fact, the word *spooked* comes to mind. "He paid cash, but the waiter remembered what he served her and her companion. He got the polenta and mushrooms and a bottle of Barolo, exactly what Chandonne described on the tape. Susan had an antipasto of grilled vegetables and olive oil, and lamb, which is, by the way, consistent with her stomach contents."

"Jesus," Marino says. Clearly, this part is news to him. "How the hell can that be? It would take Holly-fuckin'-wood special effects to turn that ugly hairball into some good-looking ladies' man."

"Unless it wasn't him," I say. "Might it have been his brother, Thomas? And Jean-Baptiste was following him?" I catch myself by surprise. I called the monster by name.

"A very logical first thought," Berger says. "But there's another monkey wrench thrown into the scenario. The doorman of Susan's apartment re- members her coming in with a man who fits the description of the one in Lumi. This was around nine o'clock that night. The doorman was on duty until seven the next morning, so he was there when the man left around three-thirty A.M., the time Susan would normally be up and on her way to work. She was due at the television sta- tion around four or four-thirty because the broad- cast begins at five. Her body was found around seven A.M., and according to the medical examiner, Susan had been dead for several hours. The main suspect has always been the stranger she met in the restaurant. In fact, I just can't see how it could have been anybody but this guy. He kills her. Spends some time mutilating the body. Leaves at three-thirty, and no trace of him ever again. And if he's not guilty, why didn't he contact the police when he heard about her murder? God knows the news was blasted all the hell over the place."

It gives me a strange feeling to realize that I heard about this case when it happened. Suddenly, I am vaguely remembering details that were part of huge, sensational stories at the time. It is numbing to consider that when I heard about Susan Pless two years ago, I had no idea that eventually I would be involved in her case, especially like this.

"Unless he's not local or even from this country," Marino is suggesting.

Berger shrugs a question mark, hands palm up. I am trying to add up the evidence she has presented and am not getting an answer that even begins to make sense. "If she ate between seven and nine P.M., her food should have been largely digested by as early as eleven P.M.," I point out. "Assuming the medical examiner is correct in his estimated time of death, if she died several hours before her body was found—let's just say, by one or two A.M.—then her food should have cleared her stomach before that."

"The explanation was stress. She was frightened and her digestion may have slowed down," Berger says.

"That makes sense when you talk about a stranger hiding in your closet and jumping out at you when you get home. But she was apparently comfortable enough with this man to invite him into her apartment," I offer. "And he was comfortable enough not to care if the doorman saw him come in and then leave much later. What about vaginal swabs?"

"Positive for seminal fluid."

"This guy"—I indicate Chandonne—"isn't into vaginal penetration and there's no evidence he ejaculates," I remind Berger. "Not in the Paris murders, certainly not in the ones here. The victims are always clothed from the waist down. They have no injuries from the waist down. He doesn't seem remotely interested in them from the waist down, except for their feet. I was under the impression Susan Pless was clothed from the waist down, too."

"She was, had pajama bottoms on. But she had seminal fluid—possibly suggesting consensual sex, at least at first. Certainly not after that, not when you see what he did to her," Berger replies. "The DNA from the seminal fluid matches up with

Chandonne. Then we've got the weird long hairs that sure as hell look like his." She nods at the television. "And you guys tested brother Thomas, right? And his DNA isn't identical to Jean-Baptiste's, so it doesn't appear Thomas left the seminal fluid."

"Their DNA profiles are very close, but not identical," I agree. "And wouldn't be unless the brothers were identical twins, which clearly they aren't."

"How do you know that for sure?" Marino frowns.

"If Thomas and Jean-Baptiste were identical twins," I explain, "both of them would have congenital hypertrichosis. Not just one of them."

"So how do you explain it?" Berger asks me. "A genetic match in all cases, yet the descriptions of the killers seem to indicate they can't be the same person."

"If the DNA in Susan Pless's case matches Jean-Baptiste Chandonne's DNA, then I can only explain it by concluding that the man who left her apartment at three-thirty in the morning isn't the man who killed her," I reply. "Chandonne killed her. But the man people saw her with isn't Chandonne."

"So maybe Wolfman screws 'em now and then, after all," Marino adds. "Or tries to and we just don't know it because he usually don't leave any juice."

"And then what?" Berger challenges him. "Puts their pants back on? Dresses them from the waist down after the fact?"

"Hey, it ain't like we're talking about somebody who does things the normal way. Oh, almost forgot to tell you." He looks at me. "One of the nurses got a peek at what he's packing. Unclipped." Marino's jargon for uncircumcised. "And smaller than a damn Vienna sausage." He shows us by holding his thumb and index finger about an inch apart. "No wonder the squirrel's in such a bad mood all the time."

CHAPTER 13

WITH A CLICK OF THE RE-mote control, I am returned to the cinder block interview room inside the forensic ward of MCV. I am returned to Jean-Baptiste Chandonne, who wants us to believe he is capable of somehow transforming his uniquely hideous appearance into elegant good looks when he is in the mood to dine out and pick up a woman. Impossible. His torso with its swirling coat of immature hair fills the television screen as he is helped back into his chair, and when his head enters the picture I am startled to discover that his bandages have been removed, his eyes now masked by dark plastic Solar Shield glasses, the flesh around them an irritated raw pink. His eyebrows are long and confluent, as if someone has taken a strip of downy fur and glued it on his brow. The same downy pale hair covers his forehead and temples.

Berger and I sit in my conference room. It is not quite seven-thirty and Marino has left for two reasons: He was paged about a possible identification of the body found dumped on the street in Mosby Court, and Berger encouraged him not to rejoin us. She said she needed to have some private time with me. I think she also was just plain sick of him, not that I blame her. Marino has made it abundantly clear that he is intensely critical of the way she interviewed Chandonne and that she did it in the first place. Part of this—no, all of this—is jealousy. There isn't an investigator on this planet who wouldn't want to interview such a notorious, freakish killer. It just so happens that the beast picked the beauty, and Marino is seething.

As I listen to Berger remind Chandonne on camera that he understands his rights and has agreed to talk to her further, I am gripped more convincingly by a certain reality. I am a small creature caught in a web, an evil web spun of threads that seem to wrap around the entire globe like lines of latitude and longitude. Chandonne's attempt to murder me was incidental to what he is all about. I was an amusement. If he figures I am watching his taped interview, then I am still an amusement. Nothing more. It occurs to me that if he had succeeded in ripping me to shreds, he would have already been focused on someone new and I would be nothing but a brief bloody moment, a past wet dream in his hateful, hellish life.

"And the detective got you something to eat and drink, sir, isn't that right?" Berger is asking Chandonne.

"Yes."

"And what was that?"

"A hamburger and a Pepsi."

"And fries?"

"*Mais oui.* Fries." He seems to think this is funny.

"So you've been given whatever you need, isn't that right?" she asks him.

"Yes."

"And the hospital staff removed your bandages and gave you special glasses to wear. You're comfortable?"

"I hurt a little bit."

"Were you given any pain medication?"

"Yes."

"Tylenol. Isn't that right?"

"Yes, I suppose. Two tablets."

"Nothing more than that. Nothing that might interfere with your thinking."

"No, nothing." His black glasses are fixed on her.

"And nobody is forcing you to talk to me or made you any promises, isn't that right?" Her shoulders move as she flips a page in what I assume is a legal pad.

"Yes."

"Sir, have I made any threats or promises to get you to talk to me?"

This goes on and on as Berger runs through her checklist. She is making sure that Chandonne's eventual representation won't have any opportunity to say that Chandonne was intimidated, badgered, abused or treated unfairly in any way. He sits straight in his chair, his arms folded on top of each other in a tangle of hair that splays over the top of the table and hangs in repulsive clumps, like dirty cornsilk, from the short sleeves of his hospital-issue shirt. Nothing about the way his anatomy has been put together computes. He reminds me of old campy movies where silly boys on the beach bury each other in sand and paint eyes on their foreheads and make beards look like head hair or wear sunglasses on the backs of their heads or kneel with shoes on their knees to turn themselves into dwarfs—people turning themselves into freakish caricatures, because they think it is amusing. There is nothing amusing about Chandonne. I can't even find him pitiful. My anger stirs like a great shark deep beneath the surface of my stoical demeanor.

"Let's get back to the night you say you met Susan Pless," Berger says to him on the tape. "In

Lumi. That's on the corner of Seventieth and Lexington?"

"Yes, yes."

"You were saying you had dinner together and
then you asked her if she would like to drink
champagne with you somewhere. Sir, are you
aware that the description of the gentleman Susan
met and dined with that night doesn't fit yours in
the least?"

"I have no way to know."

"But you must be aware that you have a serious medical condition that causes you to look
very different from other people, and it's hard to
imagine, therefore, that you could be confused
with someone who absolutely doesn't have your
condition. Hypertrichosis. Isn't that what you
have?"

I catch the barely perceptible flicker of Chandonne blinking behind the dark glasses. Berger has
touched a nerve. The muscles in his face tense. He
begins flexing his fingers again.

"Is that the name of your medical condition? Or
do you know what it's called?" Berger says to
him.

"I know what it is," Chandonne replies in a
tone that is tighter.

"And you have lived with it all your life?"

He stares at her.

"Please answer the question, sir."

"Of course. That is a stupid question. What do you think? You come down with it like a cold?"

"My point is, you don't look like other people, and therefore I'm having a hard time imagining you might be mistaken for a man described as clean-cut and handsome with no facial hair." She pauses. She is picking at him. She wants him to lose control. "Someone well groomed in an expensive suit." Another pause. "Didn't you just finish telling me you've virtually lived like a homeless person? How could that man in Lumi have been you, sir?"

"I had on a black suit, a shirt and tie." Hate. Chandonne's true nature has begun to shine through his mantle of dark deceit like a distant cold star. I expect him to dive over the table any moment and crush Berger's throat or bash her head against the wall before Marino or anyone else can stop him. I have almost quit breathing. I remind myself that Berger is alive and well, sitting at the table with me inside my conference room. It is Thursday night. In four hours, it will have been exactly five days since Chandonne kicked his way into my house and tried to beat me to death with a chipping hammer.

"I have gone through periods where my condition isn't as bad as it is now." Chandonne has steadied himself. His politeness returns. "Stress makes it worse. I've been under so much stress. Because of them."

"And who is *them*?"

"The American agents who've set me up. When I began to realize what was happening, that they were setting me up to look like a murderer, I became a fugitive. My health deteriorated to the worst it has ever been, and the worse I got, the more I had to hide. I haven't always looked like this." His dark glasses point slightly away from the camera as he stares at Berger. "When I met Susan, I was nothing like this. I could shave. I could get odd jobs and manage and even look good. And I had clothes and money sometimes because my brother would help me."

Berger stops the tape and says to me, "Possible the bit about stress could be true?"

"Stress tends to make everything worse," I reply. "But this man has never looked good. I don't care what he says."

"You're talking about Thomas," Berger's voice resumes on the videotape. "Thomas would give you clothes, money, maybe other things?"

"Yes."

"You say you were wearing a black suit in Lumi that night. Did Thomas give you the suit?"

"Yes. He liked very fine clothes. We were about the same size."

"And you dined with Susan. Then what? What happened when you were finished eating? You paid the check?"

"Of course. I'm a gentleman."

"How much was the bill?"

"Two hundred and twenty-one dollars, not including the gratuity."

Berger corroborates what he says as she stares straight ahead at the TV screen, "And that's exactly what the bill was. The man paid in cash and left two twenty-dollar bills on the table."

I quiz Berger closely on how much about the restaurant, the bill, the tip was publicly disclosed. "Was any of this ever in the news?" I ask her.

"No. So if it wasn't him, how the hell did he know what the damn bill was?" Frustration seeps into her voice.

On the videotape she asks Chandonne about the tip. He claims he left forty dollars. "Two twenties, I believe," he says.

"And then what? You left the restaurant?"

"We decided to have a drink at her apartment," he says.

CHAPTER 14

CHANDONNE GOES INTO great detail at this point. He claims he left Lumi with Susan Pless. It was very cold, but they decided to walk because her apartment was only a few blocks from the restaurant. He describes the moon and the clouds in sensitive, almost poetic detail. The sky was streaked with great swipes of bluish-white chalk and the moon was partially obscured and full. A full moon has always excited him sexually, he says, because it reminds him of a pregnant belly, of buttocks, of breasts. Gusts of wind kicked up around tall apartment buildings and at one point, he took off his scarf and put it around Susan to keep her warm. He claims to have been wearing a long, dark cashmere coat, and I remember the chief medical examiner of France, Dr. Ruth Stvan, telling me about her encounter with the man we believe was Chandonne.

I visited Dr. Stvan at the Institut Médico-Légal not even two weeks ago because Interpol asked me to review the Paris cases with her, and during our conversation she recounted to me a night when a man came to her home, feigning car trouble. He asked to use her phone, and she recalled he was wearing a long dark coat and seemed very much a gentleman. But Dr. Stvan said something else when I was with her. It was her recollection that the man had a strange, most unpleasant body odor. He smelled like a dirty, wet animal. And he made her uneasy, very uneasy. She sensed evil. All the same, she might have let him in or, more likely, he would have forced his way in except for one miraculous happenstance.

Dr. Stvan's husband is a chef at a famous Paris restaurant called Le Dome. He happened to be home sick that night and called out from another room, wanting to know who was at the door. The stranger in the dark coat fled. The next day a note was delivered to Dr. Stvan. It was written in block printing on a bit of bloody, torn brown paper and signed *Le Loup-Garou*. I have yet to really face my denial of what should have been obvious. Dr. Stvan autopsied Chandonne's French victims and then he went after her. I autopsied his American victims and didn't take serious measures to prevent him from coming after me. A great common denominator underlies this denial, and it is this:

People tend to believe that bad things happen only to others.

"Can you describe what the doorman looked like?" Berger asks Chandonne on the videotape.

"A thin mustache. In a uniform," Chandonne says. "She called him Juan."

"Wait a minute," I speak up.

Berger stops the tape again.

"Did he have a body odor?" I ask her. "When you sat in the room with him early this morning." I indicate the television. "When you interviewed him, did he have . . ."

"No kidding," she interrupts. "Smelled like a filthy dog. Kind of a strange mix of wet fur and bad body odor. It was all I could do not to gag. I guess the hospital didn't give him a bath."

It is a misconception that people are automatically bathed in the hospital. Usually, only the injuries are scrubbed unless the person is a long-term patient. "When Susan's murder was investigated two years ago, did anyone in Lumi mention a body odor? That the man she was with smelled bad?" I ask.

"No," Berger replies. "Not at all. Again, I just don't see how that person could have been Chandonne. But listen. It gets stranger."

For the next ten minutes I watch Chandonne suck down more Pepsi as he smokes and tells the incredible account of his alleged visit with Susan

Pless in her apartment. He describes where she lived in amazing detail, from the rugs on the hardwood floor to the floral upholstered furniture to the faux Tiffany lamps. He says he was not impressed with her taste in art, that she had a lot of rather pedestrian museum exhibit posters and some prints of seascapes and horses. She liked horses, he said. She told him she grew up with horses and missed them terribly. Berger taps the table inside my conference room whenever she verifies what he is saying. Yes, his description of the inside of Susan's apartment certainly leads one to believe he was there at some point. Yes, Susan did grow up with horses. Yes, yes, to everything.

"Jesus." I shake my head as fear coils tightly in my gut. I am afraid of where this is going. I resist thinking about it. But a part of me can't stop thinking about it. Chandonne is going to say that I invited him into my house.

"And it's what time now?" Berger asks him on the tape. "You said Susan opened a bottle of white wine. What time was it when she did that?"

"Maybe ten or eleven. I don't remember. It was not good wine."

"How much had you had to drink at this point?"

"Oh, maybe half a bottle of wine at the restaurant. I didn't drink much of the wine she poured for me later. Cheap California wine."

"Then you weren't drunk."

"I am never drunk."

"You were thinking clearly."

"Of course."

"In your opinion, was Susan drunk?"

"Only maybe a little. I would say happy, she was happy. So we sat on the sofa in her living room. It has a very nice view, a southwest view. From the living room you can see the red sign for the Essex House hotel on the park."

"All true," Berger says to me as she taps the table again. "And her blood alcohol was point-one-one. She'd had a few," she adds details from Susan Pless's postmortem examination.

"Then what happened?" she is asking Chandonne.

"We hold hands. She puts my fingers in her mouth, one after the other, very sexy. We started kissing."

"Do you know what time it was at this point?"

"I had no reason to be looking at my watch."

"You were wearing a watch?"

"Yes."

"Do you still have that watch?"

"No. My life got worse because of *them*." He spits the word *them*. Saliva sprays through the air every time he says "them" with a loathing that seems genuine. "I no longer had money. I pawned the watch maybe a year ago."

"Them? These same people you keep referring to? Law enforcement agents?"

"American federal agents."

"Back to Susan," Berger directs him.

"I am a shy person. I don't know how much detail you will want me to go into at this point." He lifts his Pepsi and his lips curl around the straw like grayish worms.

I can't imagine anyone wanting to kiss those lips. I can't imagine anyone wanting to touch this man.

"I want you to tell me everything you remember," Berger says to him. "The truth, sir."

Chandonne sets down the Pepsi and I am slightly jarred when Talley's sleeved arm enters the picture again. He lights another Camel for Chandonne. I wonder if it occurs to Chandonne that Talley is a federal agent, that he is one of the very people who Chandonne says have been following him and ruining his life. "Yes then, I will tell you. I don't want to, but I'm trying to be cooperative." Chandonne blows out smoke.

"Please go on. In as much detail as you can remember."

"We kissed for a while and it quickly progressed." He says nothing more.

"What do you mean, *it quickly progressed*?"

Ordinarily, it is enough for someone to say he had sex and leave it at that. Ordinarily, the officer or attorney conducting the interview or the direct or cross-examination doesn't find it relevant to ask for explicit details. But the sexual violence done to Susan and to all of the women we believe Chandonne murdered makes it important to know the details, all the details of what his idea of sex might be.

"I am reluctant," Chandonne says, playing with Berger again. He wants coaxing.

"Why?" Berger asks him.

"I don't talk about such things, certainly not with a woman present."

"It would be better for all of us if you would think of me as a prosecutor and not a woman," Berger tells him.

"I can't talk to you and not think *woman*," he says softly. He smiles a little. "You are very pretty."

"You can see me?"

"I can barely see, not really. But I can tell you are pretty. I've heard you are."

"Sir, I'll ask you to make no further personal references to me. Are we clear on that?"

He stares at her and nods.

"Sir, what exactly did you do after you began kissing Susan? What next? You touched her, fondled her, undressed her? Did she touch you, fondle you, undress you? What? Do you remember what she was wearing that night?"

"Brown leather pants. I would describe them

as the color of Belgian chocolate. They were tight but not in a way that was cheap. She had on boots, brown leather half boots. She had on a black top, sort of a leotard. Long-sleeved." He looks up at the ceiling. "A scoop neck, rather low scooped neck. The kind of top that snaps between the legs." He makes a snapping motion. His fingers with their short, pale hair remind me of cacti, of bottle brushes.

"A bodysuit," Berger helps him out.

"Yes. I was a bit confused at first when I tried to touch her and couldn't pull out her top."

"You were trying to put your hands under her top but couldn't because it was a bodysuit that snapped between her legs?"

"Yes, that's it."

"And what was her response when you tried to untuck her top?"

"She laughed at my confusion and made fun of me."

"She made fun of you?"

"Oh, not in a mean way. She thought I was funny. She made a joke. She said something about Frenchmen. We are supposed to be such skilled lovers, you know."

"Then she knew you're from France."

"But of course," Chandonne blandly answers.

"Did she speak French?"

"No."

"She told you that or did you just assume it?"

"I asked her at dinner if she knew French."

"So she teased you, then, about her bodysuit."

"Yes. Teased. She slid my hand down her pants and helped me undo the snaps. I remember she was aroused and I was a little surprised that she had gotten aroused so quickly."

"And you know she was aroused because . . . ?"

"Wet," Chandonne says. "She was very wet. I really don't like saying all this." His face is animated. He loves saying all this. "Is it really necessary for me to continue in such detail?"

"Please, sir. Everything you can remember." Berger is firm and unemotional. Chandonne may as well be telling her about a clock he took apart.

"I begin to touch her breasts and unhook her bra."

"Do you remember what her bra looked like?"

"It was black."

"Were the lights on?"

"No. But the bra was a dark color, I think black. I could be mistaken. But it wasn't a light color."

"How did you unhook it?"

Chandonne pauses, his dark glasses boring into the camera. "I just unhooked it in back." He makes an unhooking motion with his fingers.

"You didn't rip her bra off?"

"Of course not."

"Sir, her bra was ripped in front. Ripped off from the front. Literally torn in half."

"I didn't. Someone else must have done that after I left."

"All right, let's get back to your taking her bra off. Are her pants undone at this time?"

"Undone but still on. I pull up her top. I am very oral, you see. She liked that quite a bit. It was difficult to slow her down."

"Please explain what you mean by, 'It was difficult to slow her down.'"

"She began to grab for me. Between my legs, trying to get my pants off, and I wasn't ready. I still had much to do."

"Much to do? What else did you have to do, sir?"

"I wasn't ready for it to end."

"What do you mean by end? For sex to end? For what to end?"

For her life to end, I think.

"For making love to end," he replies.

I hate this. I can't stomach listening to his fantasies, especially when I consider that he might know I am listening to them, that he is subjecting me to them just as he is subjecting Berger to them, and that Talley is listening, sitting right there, watching. Talley isn't so different from

Chandonne. Both of them secretly hate women, no matter how much they lust for them. I didn't realize the truth about Talley until it was too late, until he was in my bed in my hotel room in Paris. I imagine him close to Berger in the small interview room at the hospital. I can almost see what is in his mind as Chandonne gives us an account of an erotic night he has probably never lived even once in his entire existence.

"She had a very lovely body and I wanted to enjoy it for a while, but she was most insistent. She couldn't wait." Chandonne relishes each word. "So we went back to the bedroom. We got on her bed and took our clothes off and made love."

"Did she take her own clothes off or did you do all of it? Beyond helping with the snaps?" she asks with a hint of her underlying and overwhelming disbelief of his veracity.

"I took all her clothes off. And she took mine off," he says.

"Did she make any comment about your body?" Berger asks. "Had you shaved your entire body?"

"Yes."

"And she didn't notice?"

"I was very smooth. She didn't notice. You must understand, a lot has happened to me since then, because of *them*."

"What has happened?"

"I have been pursued and persecuted and beaten. I was jumped by some men months after the night with Susan. They beat my face very badly. Split my lip, crushed bones in my face here." He touches his glasses, indicating his orbits. "I had many dental problems as a child because of my condition and had much work done as a result. Crowns on my front teeth so they would look more normal."

"This couple you say you stayed with paid for cosmetic dental work?"

"My family helped them with money."

"Did you shave before you went to the dentist?"

"I would shave those areas that would show. Such as my face. Always, if I was going out during the day. When I was beaten, my front teeth were broken, my crowns were broken, and eventually, well, you can see what my teeth look like now."

"Where did this beating occur?"

"I was still in New York."

"Did you receive medical treatment or report this assault to the police?" Berger asks him.

"Oh, that would have been impossible. The top law enforcement people are all in this together, of course. They are the ones who did it to me. I could report nothing. I received no medical treatment. I became a nomad, always hiding. Ruined."

"What about the name of your dentist?"

"Oh, that was very long ago. I doubt he's still alive. His name was Corps. Maurice Corps. His office was on rue Cabanis, I believe."

"*Corps* as in corpse?" I comment to Berger. "And is *Cabanis* a play on cannabis, or marijuana?" I am shaking my head in disgust and amazement.

"So you and Susan had sex in her bedroom." Berger gets back to that on the tape. "Please continue. How long were the two of you in bed?"

"I would say until three o'clock in the morning. Then she told me I had to leave because she needed to get ready for work. So I got dressed and we made arrangements to see each other that night again. We said we would meet at seven at L'Absinthe, a nice French bistro in the neighborhood."

"You say you got dressed. What about her? Was she dressed when you left her?"

"She had a pair of black satin pajamas. She put those on and kissed me at the door."

"So you went downstairs? Did you see anyone?"

"Juan, the doorman. I went out and walked for a while. I found a cafe and had breakfast. I was

very hungry." He pauses. "Neil's. That's the name.
It is right across the street from Lumi."

"Do you remember what you ate?"

"Espresso."

"You were very hungry but all you had was
espresso?" Berger lets him know she picks up on
the word "hunger" and realizes he is mocking her,
jerking her around, fucking with her. Chandonne's hunger wasn't for breakfast. He was enjoying the afterglow of violence, of destroying
flesh and blood because he had just left behind a
woman he had beaten to death and bitten. No
matter what he says, that is what he did. The bastard. The goddamn lying bastard.

"Sir, when did you first learn that Susan was
murdered?" Berger asks him.

"She didn't show up for dinner that night."

"Well, I guess not."

"Then the next day . . ."

"Would this be December fifth or the sixth?"
Berger asks, and she is stepping up the tempo, indicating to him that she's had it with his games.

"The sixth," he says. "I read about her in the
paper the morning after she was supposed to meet
me at L'Absinthe." He now puts on the act of
feeling sad about it. "I was shocked." He sniffs.

"Obviously, she didn't show up at L'Absinthe
the night before. But you're saying you did?"

"I had a glass of wine in the bar and waited. Finally, I left."

"Did you mention to anyone in the restaurant that you were waiting for her?"

"Yes. I asked the maître d' if she had been by and perhaps left a message for me. They knew who she was because of her being on TV."

Berger questions him closely about the maître d', asking his name, what Chandonne was wearing that night, how much he had paid for the wine and was it in cash, and when he inquired after Susan, did he give his name. Of course not. She spends five minutes on all this. She mentions to me that the police had been contacted by the bistro and were told that a man had come in and said he was waiting for Susan Pless. All of it was painstakingly checked out back then. It is true. The description of the way the man was dressed is identical to Chandonne's description of how he was dressed that night. This man did order a glass of red wine at the bar and ask if Susan had been by or had left a message, and he did not give his name. This man also fit the description of the man who had been in Lumi with Susan the night before.

"And did you tell anyone you had been with her the night of her murder?" Berger says on tape.

"No. Once I knew what happened, I could say nothing."

"And what was it that you knew had happened?"

"*They* did it. *They* did that to her. To set me up again."

"Again?"

"I had women in Paris before all this. *They* did it to them, too."

"These women were before Susan's death?"

"Maybe one or two before. Then some afterwards, as well. The same thing happened to all of them because I was followed. This is why I went more and more into hiding, and the stress and hardships made my condition so much worse. It has been a nightmare and I've said nothing. Who would believe me?"

"Good question," Berger says sharply. "Because you know what? I, for one, don't believe you, sir. You murdered Susan, didn't you, sir?"

"No."

"You raped her, didn't you, sir?"

"No."

"You beat her and bit her, didn't you, sir?"

"No. This is why I've told nothing to anybody. Who would believe me? Who would believe people are trying to destroy me all because they think my father is a criminal, a godfather?"

"You never told the police or anyone that you may have been the last person to see Susan alive because you murdered her, didn't you, sir?"

"I told no one. If I had, I would have been blamed for her death, just as you are blaming me. I returned to Paris. I wandered. I hoped they would forget me, but they haven't. You can see they haven't."

"Sir, are you aware that Susan was covered with bite marks and that your saliva was found on those bite marks and the DNA testing on them and on the seminal fluid found in her vagina matches your DNA?"

He just fixes those black glasses on Berger.

"You know what DNA is, don't you?"

"I would expect my DNA to come up."

"Because you bit her."

"I never bit her. But I am very oral. I . . ." He stops.

"You what? What did you do that might explain your saliva being on bite marks you say you didn't inflict?"

"I'm very oral," he says again. "I suck and lick. All over the body."

"Where specifically? Do you literally mean every inch of the body?"

"Yes. All of it. I love a woman's body. Every inch of it. Perhaps because I don't have . . . Perhaps because it is so beautiful, and beauty is something I can never have for myself, you see. So I worship them. My women. Their flesh."

"You lick and kiss their feet, for example?"

"Yes."

"The bottoms of their feet?"

"Everywhere."

"Have you ever bitten a woman's breasts?"

"No. She had very beautiful breasts."

"But you sucked them, licked them?"

"Obsessively."

"Are breasts important to you?"

"Oh yes. Very much—I am honest about it."

"You seek out big-breasted women?"

"I have a type I like."

"What exactly is your type?"

"Very full." He cups his hands at his chest and sexual tension shines in his face as he describes the type of woman who arouses him. Maybe it is my imagination, but his eyes gleam behind the black Solar Shields. "But not fat. I don't like fat women, no, no. Slender through the waist and hips, but very full." He cups his hands again, as if he is gripping volleyballs, and veins rope through his arms and his muscles flex.

"And Susan was your type?" Berger is completely unflappable.

"The instant I spotted her in the restaurant, I was attracted," he replies.

"In Lumi?"

"Yes."

"Hairs were also found on her body," Berger then says. "Are you aware that unusual long, baby-fine hair consistent with your unusual baby-fine hair was found on her body? How can that be if you'd shaved? Didn't you just tell me you shaved your entire body?"

"*They* plant things. I'm sure of it."

"These same people who are out to get you?"

"Yes."

"And where would they get your hair?"

"There was a period, in Paris some five years ago, when I started getting the sense someone was after me," he says. "I had a feeling I was being watched, being followed. I had no idea why. But when I was younger I didn't shave my body always. My back, you can imagine. It is very hard to reach, hard to shave my back, impossible really, so sometimes many, many months would go by, and you see, when I was younger, I was more shy with women and rarely approached them. So I didn't think about shaving as much, would just hide beneath long pants and sleeves and only shave my hands and neck and face." He touches his cheek. "One day I came home to the apartment where my foster parents lived . . ."

"Your foster parents are still alive at this point? The couple you've mentioned? Who lived near the prison?" she adds with a trace of irony.

"No. But I still was able to live there for a while. It was not expensive and I had work, odd jobs. I come home and I can tell someone has been inside. It was strange. Nothing was missing except the covers on my bed. I think, well, that's not so bad. At least whoever it was took only that. Then it happened again several more times. I realize now it was them. They wanted my hair. That's why they took my bedcovers. Because I lose a lot of hair, you see?" He touches tangles of hair on top of his head. "It is always falling out if I don't shave. It gets caught on things when it's so long." He holds out an arm to show her, and long hair wafts weightlessly on the air.

"Then you're saying you didn't have long hair when you met Susan? Not even on your back?"

"Not at all. If you found long hairs on her body, then they were put there, you see what I am saying? All the same, I accept that her murder is my fault."

CHAPTER 15

"WHY IS IT YOUR FAULT?" Berger asks Chandonne. "Why would you say that Susan's murder is your fault?"

"Because *they* followed me," he answers her. "They must have come in just after I left, and then they did that to her."

"And did they follow you to Richmond, too, sir? Why did you come here?"

"I came because of my brother."

"Explain that to me," Berger replies.

"I heard about the body at the port, and I was convinced it was my brother, Thomas."

"What did your brother do for a living?"

"He was in the shipping business with my father. He was a few years older. Thomas was good to me. I didn't see him much, but he would give me his clothes when he no longer wanted them, and other things, as I've told you. And money. I know the last time I saw him, maybe two months ago in Paris, he was frightened something bad was going to happen to him."

"Where in Paris was this meeting with Thomas?"

"Faubourg Saint Antoine. He loved to go where the young artists and nightclubs are, and we met in a stone alleyway. Cour des Trois Frères, where the artisans are, you know, not too far from Sans Sanz and the Balanjo and, of course, the Bar Américain, where girls can be paid to keep you company. He gave me money and said he was going to Belgium, to Antwerp, and then on to this country. I never heard from him again, and next the news came out about the body."

"And where did you hear this news?"

"I told you I get many newspapers. I pick up what people throw away. And many tourists who don't speak French read the international version of *USA Today*. There was a small story in it about the body found here, and I knew right away it was my brother. I was sure. For this reason, I came to Richmond. I had to know."

"How did you get here?"

Chandonne sighs. He looks fatigued again. He touches the inflamed, raw skin around his nose. "I don't want to say," he replies.

"Why don't you want to say?"

"I'm afraid you'll use it against me."

"Sir, I need you to be truthful with me."

"I'm a pickpocket. I took a wallet from a man who had his coat draped over a monument in Père-Lachaise, the most famous cemetery in Paris, where some of my family is buried. A *concession à perpétuité*," he says proudly. "Stupid man. An American. It was a big wallet, the sort people keep passports and plane tickets in. I've done this many times, I regret to tell you. It's part of living on the street, and I've lived on the street more and more since they started after me."

"These same people again. Federal agents."

"Yes, yes. Agents, magistrates, everyone. I immediately took the plane because I didn't want to give the man time to report his wallet missing and then have someone stop me at the gate in the airport. It was a return ticket, coach, to New York."

"You flew out of what airport and when?"

"De Gaulle. That would have been last Thursday."

"December sixteenth?"

"Yes. I got in early that morning and took a train to Richmond. I had seven hundred dollars because of what I took from the man."

"Do you still have the wallet and passport?"

"No, never. That would be stupid. I threw them in the trash."

"Where in the trash?"

"At the train station in New York. I can't tell you exactly where. I got on the train. . . ."

"And during your travels, nobody looked at you? You weren't shaven, sir? No one stared at you or reacted to you?"

"I had my hair in a net under a hat. I wore long sleeves and a high collar." He hesitates. "I have another thing I do when I look like this, when I have not cleaned off the hair. I wear a mask. The type of mask people put over their nose and mouth if they have severe allergies. And I wear black cotton gloves and large tinted glasses."

"This is what you wore on the plane and the train?"

"Yes. It works very well. People move away from me and I, in this instance, had an entire row of seats to myself. So I slept."

"Do you still have the mask, hat, gloves and glasses?"

He stops to think before answering. She has thrown him a curveball and he is uncertain. "I can possibly find them," he hedges.

"What did you do when you got to Richmond?" Berger asks him.

"I got off the train."

She questions him about this for several minutes. Where is the train station? Did he take a taxi next? How did he get around? Just what did he think he would do about his brother? His answers are lucid. Everything he describes makes it seem plausible that he might have been where he claims to have been, such as the Amtrak station on Staples Mill Road and in a blue taxicab that let him off at a dump of a motel on Chamberlayne Avenue, where he paid twenty dollars for a room, again using an assumed name and paying cash. From here, he states that he called my office to get information about the unidentified body he says is his brother. "I asked to speak to the doctor but no one would help me," he is telling Berger.

"Who did you talk to?" she asks him.

"It was a woman. Maybe a clerk."

"Did this clerk tell you who the doctor is?"

"Yes. A Dr. Scarpetta. So then I asked to speak to him, and the clerk tells me Dr. Scarpetta is a woman. So I say, okay. May I speak to *her*? And she is busy. I don't leave my name and number, of course, because I must continue to be careful. Maybe I'm followed again. How do I know? And then I get a newspaper and read about a murder here, a lady in a store killed a week earlier, and I'm shocked—frightened. *They* are here."

"These same people? The ones you say are after you?"

"*They* are here, don't you see? They killed my brother and knew I would come to find him."

"They certainly are amazing, aren't they, sir? How amazing they are to know you would come all the way to Richmond, Virginia, because you just happen to read a discarded *USA Today* and learn that a body has turned up here, and that you would assume it's Thomas, and that you would steal a passport and wallet and off you'd go."

"They would know I would come. I love my brother. My brother is all I have in life. He is the only one ever good to me. And I need to find out for Papa. Poor Papa."

"What about your mother? She wouldn't be upset to find out Thomas is dead?"

"She is drunk so much."

"Your mother's an alcoholic?"

"She's always drinking."

"Every day?"

"Every day, all day. And then she gets angry or cries a lot."

"You don't live with her, yet you know she drinks every day and all day long?"

"Thomas would tell me. It's been her life ever since I can remember. I've always been told she is drunk. The few times I would go to the house, she was drunk. It was mentioned to me once that my condition might have happened because she was drunk when she was pregnant with me."

Berger looks at me. "Possible?"

"Fetal alcohol syndrome?" I consider. "Not

likely. Generally severe mental and physical retardation would result if the mother were a chronic alcoholic, and cutaneous changes such as hypertrichosis would be the least of the child's problems."

"Doesn't mean he doesn't believe she caused his condition."

"He certainly might believe it," I agree with her.

"Helping to explain his extreme hatred of women."

"As much as anything can explain his kind of hate," I reply.

On tape, Berger has returned Chandonne to the subject of his allegedly calling the morgue here in Richmond. "So you tried to get through to Dr. Scarpetta on the phone but couldn't. Then what?"

"Then the next day, Friday, I hear on the TV in my motel room that another woman has been murdered. This time a policewoman. They do a newsbreak, you know, and I'm watching it as it is happening and next thing the cameras focus on a big black car pulling up to the scene and they say it is the medical examiner. It is her, Scarpetta. So I get the idea to go there immediately. I will wait until she is leaving the scene and then I will approach her. I will tell her I must talk to her. So I get a taxi."

His remarkable memory fails him here. He recalls nothing about the taxi company, not even
the color of the car, only that the driver was a
"black man." Probably eighty percent of the taxi
drivers in Richmond are black. Chandonne
claims that while he is being driven to the
scene—and he knows the address because it was
on the news—he hears another newsbreak. This
time, the public is being warned about the killer,
that he may have a strange medical condition
which causes him to have a very unusual appearance. The hypertrichotic description fits
Chandonne. "I know now, for sure," he goes on.
"They have set the trap and the world thinks I
have killed these women in Richmond. So I
panic in the back of the taxi, trying to figure out
what to do. I say to the taxi driver, 'Do you
know this lady they speak of? Scarpetta?' He says
that everyone in the city knows her. I ask where
she lives and say I'm a tourist. He takes me to her
neighborhood but we don't go in because there
are guards and a gate. But I know enough to find
her. I get out of the taxi several blocks from
there. I'm determined I will find her before it's
too late."

"Too late for what?" Berger asks.

"Before anybody else is killed. I must come
back later that night and somehow get her to open

the door so I can talk to her. You know, of course, I'm worried they will kill her next. It's their pattern, you see. They did that in Paris, you know. They tried to murder the medical examiner there, a woman. She was very lucky."

"Sir, let's keep on the subject of what happened here in Richmond. Tell me what happened next. It's what, midmorning on Friday, December seventeenth, last Friday? What did you do after the taxi dropped you off? What did you do the rest of the day?"

"Wandered. Found an abandoned house on the river and went in it just to get out of the weather."

"Do you know where that house is?"

"I can't tell you, but not far from her neighborhood."

"From Dr. Scarpetta's neighborhood?"

"Yes."

"You could find that house again, the one you stayed in, couldn't you, sir?"

"It's under construction. Very big. A mansion no one lives in right now. I know where it is."

Berger says to me, "The one where they think he was staying the entire time he was here?"

I nod. I am familiar with the house. I think of the poor people it belongs to and can't imagine them ever wanting to live there again. Chandonne says he hid in the abandoned mansion until dark. Several times that night he ventured out, avoiding the guard gate in my neighborhood by simply following the river and railroad tracks that run behind it. He claims to have knocked on my door early evening and got no answer. At this point, Berger asks me when I got home that night. I tell her it was after eight. I had stopped off at Pleasants Hardware store after leaving the office. I wanted to look at tools because I was perplexed by the strange wounds I had found on Diane Bray's body and by bloody transfers made to the mattress when the killer had set down the bloody tool he had beaten her with. It was during this foraging at Pleasants Hardware that I came across a chipping hammer, and I purchased one and went on home, I tell Berger.

Chandonne goes on to claim he began to get fearful about coming to see me. He claims there were a lot of police cars cruising the neighborhood, and that at one point when he came to my house late, there were two police cruisers parked in front. This was because my alarm had gone off—when Chandonne forced open my garage door so the police would come. Of course, he tells Berger that it wasn't him who set off the alarm. It was *them*—it must have been them, he says. By now, it is getting close to midnight. It is snowing hard. He hides behind trees near my house and waits until the police leave. He says it is his last chance, he has to see me. He believes *they* are in the area and will kill me. So he goes to my front door and knocks.

"What did you knock with?" Berger asks him.

"I recall there was a door knocker. I believe I used that." He drains the last of his Pepsi and Marino on tape asks him if he wants another one. Chandonne shakes his head and yawns. He is talking about coming into my house to bash my brains out and the bastard is yawning.

"Why didn't you ring the bell?" Berger wants to know. This is important. My doorbell activates the camera system. Had Chandonne rung the bell, I would have been able to see him on a video screen inside the house.

"I don't know," he replies. "I saw the knocker and used it."

"Did you say anything?"

"Not at first. Then I heard a woman ask, 'Who is it?' "

"And what did you say?"

"I told her my name. I said I have information about the body she's trying to identify, and to please let me talk to her."

"You told her your name? You identified yourself as Jean-Baptiste Chandonne?"

"Yes. I said I was here from Paris and had been trying to get her at her office." He yawns again. "The most amazing thing happens," he goes on. "The door suddenly opens and she is there. She tells me to come in, and the minute I do, she slams the door shut behind me and I can't believe it. She suddenly has this hammer and is trying to hit me."

"Suddenly has a hammer? Where did she get it? Did it just appear out of thin air?"

"I believe she grabbed it off a table just inside the doorway. I don't know. It happened so fast. And I try to get away from her. I run into the living room, yelling for her to stop, and that's when the terrible thing happened. It was fast. I only remember I was on the other side of the sofa, and then something was flying in my face. It felt like liquid fire in my eyes. I have never felt anything so, so . . ." He sniffs again. "The pain. I was screaming and trying to get it out of my eyes. I was trying to get out of the house. I knew she was going to kill me and suddenly it went into my mind that she is one of them. *Them.* They have got me at last. I walked right into their trap! It was planned all along that she would get my brother's body because she is *them*. Now I would be arrested and they would finally get the opportunity they want, finally, finally."

"And they want what?" Berger asks him. "Tell me again, because I'm having a very hard time understanding, much less believing, this part."

"They want my father!" he says with the first emotion I have seen. "To get Papa! To find a reason to go after him and bring him down, destroy him. To make it look like my father has a son who is a killer so they can get to my family. All this for years! And I am Chandonne and look at me! *Look at me!!*"

He stretches out his arms in a pose of crucifixion, hair floating out from his body. I watch in shock as he rips off his dark glasses and light pierces his tender, burned eyes. I stare into those bright red, chemically burned eyes. They don't seem to focus and tears stream down his face.

"I am ruined!" he cries out. "I am ugly and blind and accused of crimes I didn't do! You Americans want to execute a Frenchman! Isn't that it! To make an example!" Chairs scrape loudly and Marino and Talley are all over him, holding him in his chair. "I killed no one! She tried to kill me! *Look what she did to me!*"

And Berger is calmly saying to him, "We've been at this an hour. We're going to stop now. That's enough. Calm down, calm down."

Frames flicker and bars fill the screen before it turns the bright blue of a perfect afternoon. Berger turns off the VCR. I sit in stunned silence.

"Hate to tell you." She breaks the appalling spell Chandonne has cast over my small, private conference room. "There are some anti-government, paranoid idiots in the world who are going to find this guy believable. Let's hope none of them end up on the jury. It only takes one."

CHAPTER 16

"JAY TALLEY," BERGER STARTLES me by saying.

Now that Chandonne has vanished from our midst with a simple pointing of a remote control, this New York prosecutor wastes no time shifting her intense focus to me. We are returned to a small, bland reality—a conference room with a round wooden table and wooden built-in bookcases and a vacant television screen. Case files and gory photographs are spread out before us, forgotten, ignored, because Chandonne has preempted everything and everyone for the past two hours.

"Do you want to volunteer, or should I start with telling you what I know?" Berger confronts me.

"I'm not sure what you want me to volunteer." I am taken aback, then offended, then furious all over again as I think of Talley's presence at Chandonne's interview. I imagine Berger talking to Talley before and after her interrogation of Chandonne and during his break for rest and fast food. Berger had hours with Talley and Marino. "And more to the point," I add, "what does this have to do with your New York case?"

"Dr. Scarpetta." She leans back in her chair. I feel as if I have been inside this room with her for half my life, and I am late. I am hopelessly late for meeting the governor. "As hard as it's going to be for you," Berger says, "I'm asking you to trust me. Can you do that?"

"I don't know who to trust anymore," I reply truthfully.

She smiles a little and sighs. "That's honest. Fair enough. You have no reason to trust me. Maybe you have no reason to trust anyone. But you really have no factual reason not to trust me as a professional whose singular intent is to make Chandonne pay for his crimes—if he murdered these women."

"If?" I ask her.

"We have to prove it. And absolutely anything I can learn from what has happened here in these Richmond cases is invaluable to me. I promise you, I'm not trying to be a voyeur or to violate your privacy. But I must have the full context. Frankly, I need to know what the hell I'm dealing with, and my difficulty lies in that I don't know who all the characters are or what they are or if any of them might in any way overlap my case in New York. For example, could Diane Bray's prescription drug habit in fact be a marker for other illegal activity possibly connected to organized crime, to the Chandonne family? Or possibly even connected to why brother Thomas's body ended up in Richmond?"

"By the way." I am stuck on another matter, namely, my credibility. "How does Chandonne explain that there were two chipping hammers at my house? Yes, I bought one at the hardware store, as I have told you. So where did the other one come from if he didn't bring it with him? And if I wanted to kill him, why didn't I use the pistol? My Glock was right there on the dining-room table."

Berger hesitates and completely dodges my questions. "If I don't know the whole truth, then it makes it very difficult to sort out what's relevant to my case and what isn't."

"I understand that much."

"Can we start with the status of your relationship with Jay now?"

"He drove me to the hospital." I give up. I am clearly not the one who is going to be asking the questions in this situation. "When I broke my arm. He showed up with the police, with ATF, and I spoke briefly to him Saturday afternoon while the police were still at my home."

"Do you have any idea why he thought it necessary to fly here from France to assist in the manhunt for Chandonne?"

"I can only assume it's because he's so familiar with the case."

"Or an excuse to see you?"

"He'd have to answer that."

"Are you seeing him?"

"Not since Saturday afternoon, as I've said."

"Why not? Do you consider the relationship over?"

"I don't consider it ever began."

"But you slept with him." She raises an eyebrow.

"So I'm guilty of poor judgment."

"He's handsome, bright. And young. Some might be more likely to convict you of good taste. He's single. So are you. It's not as if you committed adultery." She drags out a pause. Is she alluding to Benton, to the fact that I have been guilty of adultery in the past? "Jay Talley has a lot of money, doesn't he?" She taps her felt-tip pen on the legal pad, a metronome measuring what a bad time I am having. "From his family, supposedly. I'll check into that. And by the way, you should know I've talked to him, to Jay. At length."

"I just assume you've talked to the entire world. What I haven't yet figured out is how you've had time."

"There was a little downtime at MCV, the medical college hospital."

I imagine her drinking coffee with Talley. I can picture the look on his face, his demeanor. I wonder if she is attracted to him.

"I talked to both Talley and Marino while Chandonne had his various rest periods and whatnot." Her hands are folded on top of a notepad that has the letterhead of her office on it. She has not taken a single note, not one word the entire time we have been inside this room. Already, she is planning for the defense to huff and puff about Rosario this and that. Whatever is in writing, the defense is entitled to see it. So don't write anything down. Now and then she doodles. She has filled two pages with doodles since she entered my conference room. A red flag is raised in the back of my mind. She is treating me like a witness. I shouldn't be a witness, not in her New York case.

"I'm getting the impression that you're wondering if Jay is somehow involved. . . ." I start to say.

Berger interrupts me with a shrug. "No stone unturned," she says. "Is it possible? By this point, I'm about to believe anything is possible. What a wonderful position Talley would be in if he were in collusion with the Chandonnes, true? Interpol, ah, that's handy for a crime cartel. He calls you and brings you to France, perhaps for the purpose of seeing what you know about the loose cannon Jean-Baptiste. Suddenly, Talley's in Richmond for the manhunt." She crosses her arms and penetrates me with that gaze again. "I don't like him. I'm surprised you did."

"Look," I say with a hint of defeat in my voice, "Jay and I were intimate in Paris over a twenty-four-hour period, at most."

"You initiated sex. Quarreled in a restaurant that evening and you stormed out, jealous because he was looking at another woman. . . ."

"What?" I blurt out. "He said *that*?"

She regards me silently. Her tone is no different from the one she was using with Chandonne, a terrible monster. Now she is interviewing me, a terrible person. That is how I feel. "It had nothing to do with another woman," I answer her. "What other woman? I certainly wasn't jealous. He was coming on too strong and acting petulant and I'd had enough."

"The Café Runtz on rue Favard. You made quite a scene." She continues my story, or at least Talley's version of it.

"I didn't make a scene. I got up from the table and walked out, period."

"From there you returned to the hotel, got

into a cab and went to Île Saint-Louis, where the Chandonne family lives. You walked around after dark, staring up at the Chandonne home, then got a water sample from the Seine."

What she has just said sends electrical shocks through my every cell. Sweat rolls in cold tickles beneath my blouse. I never told Jay what I did after I left him in the restaurant. How does Berger know all this? How did Jay know if he is the one who told her? Marino. How much has Marino volunteered to her?

"What was your real purpose in finding the Chandonne house? What did you think that might tell you?" Berger asks.

"If I knew what something would tell me, I wouldn't need to investigate," I reply. "As for the water sample, as you must know from the lab reports, we found diatoms, or microscopic algae, on the clothing of the unidentified body from the Richmond port—from Thomas's body. I wanted a water sample from near the Chandonne home to see if there was any chance the same type of diatom might be present in that area of the Seine. And it was. Freshwater diatoms were consistent with those I found on the inside of the clothing on the body, Thomas's body, and none of this matters. You aren't trying Jean-Baptiste for the murder of his alleged brother, since that probably happened in Belgium. You've already made that clear."

"But the water sample is important."

"Why?"

"Anything that happened reveals more to me about the defendant and possibly leads to motive. More importantly, to identity and intent."

Identity and *intent*. Those words roar through my mind like a train. I am a lawyer. I know what those words mean.

"Why did you take the water sample? Do you routinely go around collecting evidence that isn't directly associated with a body? Collecting water samples really isn't your jurisdiction, in other words, especially in a foreign country. Why did you go to France to begin with? Isn't that a little out of the ordinary for a medical examiner?"

"Interpol summoned me. You just pointed that out yourself."

"Jay Talley summoned you, more specifically."

"He represents Interpol. He's the ATF liaison."

"I'm wondering why he really orchestrated your going there." She pauses to allow that chilly fear to touch my brain. It occurs to me that Jay may have manipulated me for reasons I am not sure I can bear to entertain. "Talley has many layers," Berger adds cryptically. "If Jean–Baptiste was tried here, I fear Talley would more likely be used by the defense than by the prosecution. Possibly to discredit you as a witness."

Heat crawls up my neck. My face burns. Fear rips through me like shrapnel, tearing apart any hope I have had that something like this would not happen. "Let me ask you something." My outrage is complete. It is all I can do to steady my voice. "Is there anything you don't know about my life?"

"Quite a bit."

"Why is it I feel that I'm the one about to get indicted, Ms. Berger?"

"I don't know. Why do you feel that way?"

"I'm trying not to take any of this personally. But it's getting harder by the minute."

Berger doesn't smile. Resolve turns her eyes to flint and hardens her tone. "It's going to get very personal. I highly recommend you don't take it that way. You of all people know how it works. The actual commission of a crime is incidental to the real damage its ripples do. Jean-Baptiste Chandonne didn't inflict a single blow on you at the time he broke into your house. It's now he begins to hurt you. He *has* hurt you. He *will* hurt you. Even though he's locked up, he will inflict blows on you daily. He has started a deadly, cruel process, the violation of Kay Scarpetta. It's begun. I'm sorry. It's a fact of life that you know all too well."

I silently return her stare. My mouth is dry. My heart seems to beat out of rhythm.

"It isn't fair, is it?" she says with the sharp edge of a prosecutor who knows how to dismantle human beings as completely as I do. "But then, I'm sure your patients wouldn't enjoy being naked on your table and under your knife, to have their pockets and orifices explored, if they knew. And yes, there's a hell of a lot I don't know about your life. And yes, you aren't going to like my probing. And yes, you will cooperate if you're the person I've heard you are. And yes, goddamn it, I desperately need your help or this case is fucked to the moon."

"Because you're going to try to drag in his other bad acts, aren't you?" I am out with it. "A Molineux application."

She hesitates. Her eyes linger on me and light up for an instant, as if I have just said something that fills her with happiness or maybe a new respect. Then just as quickly, those eyes shut me out again, and she says, "I'm not sure what I'll do yet."

I don't believe her. I am the only living witness. The only one. She fully intends to suck me into it—to put every one of Chandonne's crimes on trial, all magnificently showcased within the small context of one poor woman he murdered in Manhattan two years ago. Chandonne is smart.

But he may have made a fatal mistake on video-tape. He gave Berger the two weapons she needs to shoot for a Molineux: identity and intent. I can identify Chandonne. I know goddamn well what his intent was when he forced his way into my house. I am the only living person who can counter his lies.

"So now we hammer at my credibility." The tasteless pun is deliberate. She is swinging at me just as Chandonne did, but for a very different reason, of course. She doesn't want to destroy me. She wants to make sure I am not destroyed.

"Why did you sleep with Jay Talley?" She is at it again.

"Because he was there, damn it," I retort.

She erupts in a sudden salvo of laughter, deep throaty laughs that push her back in her chair.

I am not trying to be funny. I am disgusted, if anything. "That's the banal truth, Ms. Berger," I add.

"Please call me Jaime." She sighs.

"I don't always know the answers even to things I should. Such as why I had my moment with Jay. But I'm ashamed of it. Up until a few minutes ago, I felt guilty about it, so afraid I used him, hurt him. But at least I didn't kiss and tell."

To this she has no response.

"I should have known he's still in the locker

room," I go on as my indignation unfurls brightly before our eyes. "No better than those teenaged boys gawking at my niece in the mall the other night. Walking hormones. So Jay has bragged about it, I'm sure, told everyone, including you. And let me add . . ." I pause. I swallow. Anger is a lump in my throat. "Let me add that some details aren't your business and will never be your business. I ask you, Ms. Berger, as a matter of professional courtesy, not to go places where you don't belong."

"If only others would abide by that."

I make a point of looking at my watch again. But I can't leave, not before I ask her the most important question. "You believe he attacked me?" She knows I am referring to Chandonne this time.

"Is there any reason why I shouldn't believe that?"

"Obviously, my eyewitness account turns everything else he's said to the bullshit it is," I reply. "It wasn't *them*. There was no *them*. Only that goddamn son of a bitch pretending to be the police and coming after me with a hammer. I'd like to know how the hell he can explain that. Did you ask him why there were two chipping hammers at my house? I can prove from the hardware store receipt that I bought only one." I push that point again. "So where did the other one come from?"

"Let me ask you a question instead." She avoids answering me again. "Is there any possibility you only assumed he was attacking you? That you saw him and panicked? You're positive he had a chipping hammer and was coming after you with it?"

I stare at her. "*Assumed* he was attacking me? What possible explanation could there be for him being inside my house?"

"Well, you opened the door. That much we know, right?"

"You aren't asking me if he was an invited guest, are you?" I stare defiantly at her, the inside of my mouth sticky. My hands are trembling. I push back my chair when she doesn't answer me. "I don't have to sit here and take this. It's gone from the ridiculous to the sublimely ridiculous!"

"Dr. Scarpetta, how would it make you feel if it was publicly suggested that you, in fact, did invite Chandonne into your home and assaulted him? For no reason, except perhaps you panicked? Or worse. That you are part of his conspiracy as he has stated on tape—you and Jay Talley. Which also helps explain why you went to Paris and slept with Talley and then met Dr. Stvan and took evidence from the morgue."

"How would that make me feel? I don't know what else to say."

"You're the only witness, the only living person who knows that what Chandonne is saying is lies and more lies. If you're telling the truth, then this case is completely up to you."

"I'm not a witness in your case," I remind her. "I had nothing to do with the Susan Pless murder investigation."

"I need your help. It's going to be very, very time-consuming."

"I won't help you. Not if you're going to start questioning my veracity or state of mind."

"Actually, I don't question either. But the defense will. Seriously. Excruciatingly." She is cautiously working her way around the edges of a reality she has yet to share with me. Opposing counsel. I suspect she knows who. She knows exactly who is going to finish what Chandonne started: the dismantling, the humiliation of me for all the world to see. My heart beats in sick thuds. I feel dead. My life has just ended right before my eyes.

"I will need you to come to New York at some point," Berger is saying. "Sooner rather than later. And by the way, let me caution you to be very, very careful who you talk to right now. I don't recommend, for example, that you talk to anyone about these cases without conferring with me first." She begins packing up her paperwork and books. "I caution you about having any contact with Jay Talley." Her eyes flick mine as she snaps shut her briefcase. "Unfortunately, I think we're all going to get a Christmas present we're not going to like." We get up from our chairs and face each other.

"Who?" I go ahead and ask her in a tired voice. "You know who's going to represent him, don't you? That's why you stayed up all night with him. You wanted to get to him before his counsel slams the door shut."

"All true," she replies with a hint of irritation. "The question is whether I was suckered into it." We look at each other across the shiny expanse of the wooden table. "I find it a little too coincidental that within an hour of my last interview with Chandonne, I get word that he's retained counsel," she adds. "I suspect he already knew who his counsel was and may, in fact, have already retained him. But Chandonne and the dirtbag he's hooked up with would believe that this tape"—she pats her briefcase—"would only hurt us and help him."

"Because jurors either believe him or think he's paranoid and crazy," I summarize.

She nods. "Oh sure. They'll go for insanity, if all else fails. And we don't want Mister Chandonne at Kirby, now do we?"

Kirby is a notorious forensic psychiatric hospital in New York. It is where Carrie Grethen was incarcerated before she escaped and murdered Benton. Berger has just touched another part of my painful history. "You know about Carrie Grethen, then," I say in a defeated way as we walk out of a conference room that I will never feel the same about again. It, too, has become a crime scene. My entire world is turning into one.

"I've done some research on you," Berger says almost apologetically. "And you're right, I do know who's going to represent Chandonne, and it's not good news. In fact, it's pretty damn awful." She puts on her mink coat as we walk out into the hallway. "Have you ever met Marino's son?"

I stop and stare at her, dumbfounded. "I don't know anyone who has ever met his son," I reply.

"Come on, let's get you to your party. I'll explain as we walk out." Berger cradles her books and files, walking slowly over quiet carpet. "Rocco Marino, affectionately known as 'Rocky,' is an exceptionally sleazy criminal defense attorney who has an affinity for representing the mob and others who make it worth his while to get them off the hook by any means. He's flashy. Loves publicity." She glances over at me. "Most of all, he loves to hurt people. That's his power trip."

I flip off the hallway lights, throwing us briefly into darkness as we approach the first set of stainless steel doors.

"Some years ago—in law school, I'm told," she continues, "Rocky changed his last name to

Caggiano. A final rejection of the father he despises, I suppose."

I hesitate, facing her in deep shadows. I don't want her to see the expression on my face, to detect my sense of utter undoing. I have always known that Marino hates his son. I have entertained many theories about why. Maybe Rocky is gay or a drug addict or simply a loser. Certainly it has been clear that Rocky is *something* of an anathema to his father, and now I know. I am struck by the bitter irony, the shame of it all. My God. "Rocky so-called Caggiano heard about the case and volunteered?" I ask.

"Could be. Could also be that the Chandonne family's organized crime ties have led him to their son, or hell, maybe Rocky is already connected to them. It may be a combination—personal and Rocky's own connections. But it does smack a little of throwing father and son into the Colosseum. Patricide in front of the world, albeit indirectly. Marino won't necessarily be testifying in Chandonne's trial in New York, but it could happen, depending on how this all unfolds."

I know how it will unfold. It is all so clear to me. Berger came to Richmond fully intending to insert these cases into the one in New York. I wouldn't be surprised if she doesn't somehow manage to get the Paris cases included, as well.

"But regardless," she says, "Chandonne will always feel like Marino's case. Cops like him care what happens. And Rocky's representing Chandonne puts me in an unfortunate position. If the case were in Richmond, I would go marching up to the judge *ex parte* and point out the very obvious conflict of interest. Probably get thrown out of his chambers and reprimanded. But at the very least, I might be able to get the His or Her Honor to request a co-counselor on the defendant's legal team so son doesn't actually cross-examine father."

I push a button and more steel doors open.

"But I would create a storm of protest," she goes on. "And maybe the court would rule in my favor, or if nothing else, I'd use the situation to get sympathy from the jury, show what bad guys Chandonne and his counsel are."

"No matter how your case unfolds in New York, Marino won't be a fact witness." I see where she is going with this. "Not in the Susan Pless murder. So you aren't going to have any luck getting rid of Rocky."

"Exactly right. No conflict. Nothing I can do about it. And Rocky's poison."

Our conversation continues into the bay, where we stand in the cold by our cars. The starkness of the bare concrete around us seems a symbol of the realities I now face. Life has turned hard and unforgiving. There is no view, no way out. I can't imagine how Marino will feel when he finds out that the very monster he has helped apprehend will be defended by Marino's estranged son. "Clearly, Marino doesn't know," I say.

"Maybe I've been remiss in not telling him yet," she replies. "But he's a big enough pain in the ass already. I thought I'd wait and drop this bomb tomorrow or the next day. You know he wasn't happy about my interviewing Chandonne." She adds this with a glint of triumph.

"I could tell."

"I had a case with Rocky several years ago." Berger unlocks her car door. She leans inside to start it and get the heat going. "A wealthy man on business in New York is accosted by a kid with a knife." She straightens up and faces me. "The man struggles and manages to wrestle the kid to the ground, bangs the kid's head on the pavement, knocking him out, but not before he stabs the man in the chest. The man dies. The kid is hospitalized for a while but recovers. Rocky tried to turn the case on self-defense but fortunately the jury didn't buy it."

"I'm sure that made Mr. Caggiano a fan of yours for life."

"What I couldn't prevent was him then representing the kid in a civil suit, asking ten million for alleged permanent emotional damage, yada,

yada, yada. The murdered man's family finally settled. Why? Because they just couldn't take it anymore. There was a lot of shit happening behind the scenes—harassment, weird events. They were burglarized. One of their cars was stolen. Their Jack Russell puppy was poisoned. On and on, and all of it I'm convinced was orchestrated by Rocky Marino Caggiano. I just could never prove it." She climbs up into her Mercedes sport utility vehicle. "His modus operandi is pretty simple. He gets away with anything he can and puts everybody on trial except the defendant. He is also a very poor loser."

I remember Marino telling me years ago he wished Rocky were dead. "Might that be part of his motivation then?" I ask. "Revenge. Not just getting the father, but getting you? And doing so very publicly."

"Might be," Berger says to me from the high perch of her SUV. "Whatever his motive, I do want you to know I plan to protest anyway. Just can't tell you how much good it will do since this really doesn't constitute an ethical violation. It's up to the judge." She reaches for her seat belt and pulls it across her chest. "How are you spending Christmas Eve, Kay?"

So now I am Kay. I have to think for a minute. Christmas Eve is tomorrow. "I need to follow up on these cases, the ones with the burns," I reply.

She nods. "It's important we go back to Chandonne's crime scenes while they still exist."

Including my house, I think.

"Might you find some time tomorrow afternoon?" she asks. "Any time you can give me. I'm working through the holidays. I don't mean to ruin yours."

I have to smile at the irony. The holidays. Yes, Merry Christmas. Berger has given me a gift and doesn't even know it. She has helped me make a decision, an important decision, maybe even the most important decision of my life. I am going to quit my job and the governor will be the first to know. "I'll call you when I'm finished in James City County," I tell Berger. "We can try for two o'clock."

"I'll pick you up," she says.

CHAPTER 17

IT IS ALMOST TEN WHEN I turn off 9th street into Capitol Square, cruising past the up-lit statue of George Washington astride his horse, and winding around the south portico of the building Thomas Jefferson designed, where a thirty-foot lighted tree decorated with glass balls rises behind thick white columns. I recall that the governor's party was a drop-in and not a dinner and am relieved at signs that his guests have left. I find not a single car in spaces designated for legislators and visitors.

The early-nineteenth-century executive mansion is pale yellow stucco with white trim and columns. According to legend, it was saved by a bucket brigade when Richmonders burned their own city at the end of the Civil War. In the understated tradition of Virginia Christmases, candles glow and fresh wreaths hang in every window, and evergreen swags decorate black iron gates. I roll down my window as a capitol police officer steps up to my car.

"May I help you?" he asks with an air of suspicion.

"I'm here to see Governor Mitchell." I have been to the mansion a number of times, but not at this hour or in a big Lincoln SUV. "I'm Dr. Scarpetta. I'm a little late. If it's too late, I'll understand. Please tell him I'm sorry. "

The officer brightens. "Didn't recognize you in that car. You get rid of your Mercedes? If you could just wait right here for a minute."

He gets on the phone inside his booth as I look out at Capitol Square and am touched by ambivalence, then sadness. I have lost this city. I can't go back. I can blame it on Chandonne, but that isn't all of it, if I am honest with myself. It is time to do the harder thing. Change. Lucy has inspired courage, or maybe she has made me see myself for what I have become, which is entrenched, static, institutionalized. I have been the chief medical examiner of Virginia for more than a decade. I am edging close to fifty. I don't like my only sister. My mother is difficult and her health is bad. Lucy is moving to New York. Benton is dead. I am alone.

"Merry Christmas, Dr. Scarpetta." The capitol police officer leans close to my window and lowers his voice. The name on his brass tag is Renquist. "Just want you to know I hate what happened, but I'm glad you got that S.O.B. That was real quick thinking on your part."

"I appreciate that, Officer Renquist."

"You won't be seeing me down here anymore after the first of the year," he goes on. "They've switched me to plainclothes investigations."

"I hope that's good."

"Oh, yes ma'am."

"We'll miss you."

"Maybe I'll see you on a case."

I hope not. If he sees me on a case, that means someone else is dead. He gives me a crisp wave, directing me through the gates. "You can park right in front."

Change. Yes, change. Suddenly, I am surrounded by it. In thirteen months, Governor Mitchell will be gone, too, and that is unsettling. I like him. I especially like his wife, Edith. In Virginia, governors have a one-term limit, and every four years the world gets turned on end. Hundreds of employees are moved, fired and hired. Phone numbers are changed. Computers get formatted. Job descriptions no longer apply even if the jobs themselves do. Files disappear or are destroyed. Mansion menus are redone or shredded. The only constancy is the mansion staff itself. The same prison inmates do the gardening and small outside tasks, and the same people cook and clean, or at least if they are rotated, it has nothing to do with politics. Aaron, for example, has been the butler for as long as I have lived in Virginia. He is a tall, handsome African American, lean and graceful in a long, spotless white coat and snappy black bow tie.

"Aaron, how are you?" I inquire as I step inside an entry hall that is dazzling with crystal lighting that passes its torch, chandelier to chandelier, through sweeping archways all the way to the back of the house. Between the two ballrooms is the Christmas tree decorated in red balls and white lights. Walls and plaster friezes and trim have been recently restored to their original gray and white and look like Wedgwood. Aaron takes my coat. He indicates he is fine and pleased to see me, using few words because he has mastered the art of being gracious with little noise.

Just off the entry hall, on either side, are two rather stiff parlors of Brussels carpet and formidable antiques. Wallpaper in the men's parlor has a Greco-Roman border. A floral border is in the women's. The psychology of these sitting areas is simple. They allow the governor to receive guests without ever really letting them inside the mansion. People are granted an audience at the front door and are not destined to stay long. Aaron guides me past these impersonal historic rooms and up a stairway carpeted in a Federal design of black stars against deep red that leads to the first family's personal quarters. I emerge in a sitting area of fir hardwood floors and accessible chairs and couches, where Edith Mitchell waits for me in a flowing red silk pants suit. She smells faintly exotic as she gives me a hug.

"When are we playing tennis again?" she asks dryly, staring at my cast.

"It's a very unforgiving sport if you haven't done it in a year, have a fractured arm and are doing battle with cigarettes again," I say.

My reference to the past year is not lost on her. Those who know me are aware that after Benton's murder, I vanished into a dark vortex of frantic, perpetual motion. I stopped seeing friends. I didn't go out or have people in. I rarely exercised. All I did was work. I saw nothing that went on around me. I didn't hear what people said to me. I didn't feel. Food had no taste. I scarcely noticed the weather. In Anna's words, I became sensory deprived. Somehow through it all, I didn't make mistakes in my cases. If anything, I was more obsessive about them. But my absenteeism as a human being was detrimental in the office. I wasn't a good administrator and it began to show. Certainly, I have been a shitty friend to everyone I know.

"How are you?" she asks, kindly.

"About as well as can be expected."

"Please sit. Mike's getting off the phone," Edith tells me. "I guess he didn't talk to enough people at the party." She smiles and rolls her eyes as if she is talking about a naughty boy.

Edith has never really assumed the role of first lady, not in any tradition the Commonwealth of Virginia has ever seen, and although she may have her detractors, she has also become celebrated as a strong, modern woman. She is a historical archaeologist who didn't give up her career when her husband took office and avoids official events she considers frivolous or a poor use of her time. Yet she is her husband's devoted partner and has raised three children, now grown or in college. In her late forties, she has deep brown hair that she wears one length, at her collar and brushed straight back. Her eyes are almost amber, and in them thoughts and questions stir. She has something on her mind. "I was going to take you aside at the party. Kay, I'm glad you called. Thank you for dropping by. You know it's not like me to pry into your cases," she goes on, "but I have to say I'm really unsettled by the one I just read about in the paper—the man found in that awful motel near Jamestown. Mike and I are both very concerned, well, obviously, because of the Jamestown connection."

"I'm not aware of a Jamestown connection." I am puzzled, and my first thought is that information has come in that she knows and I don't. "No connection to the archaeological excavation. Not that I'm aware of."

"Perceptions," she says simply. "If nothing else."

Jamestown is Edith Mitchell's passion. Her own profession drew her to the site years ago, and then she became an advocate for it in her present political position. She has unearthed postholes and human bones and tirelessly courted the interest of potential financial backers and the media. "I've driven past that motel just about every time I go down there because it's closer to downtown to take Route Five instead of Sixty-four." A shadow passes over her face. "A real dump. Can't say it would surprise me if something bad happened there. Looks like the sort of place drug dealers and hookers would hang out. Did you go to the scene?"

"Not yet."

"Can I get you anything to drink, Kay? I have some very good whisky I bootlegged back from Ireland last month. I know you like Irish whisky."

"Only if you're having some."

She reaches for the phone and asks Aaron to bring up the bottle of Black Bush and three glasses.

"What's going on at Jamestown these days?" The air is tainted by a patina of cigar smoke that awakens my frustrating hunger for cigarettes. "I think the last time I was there was three or four years ago," I tell her.

"When we found JR," she recalls.

"Yes."

"It's been that long since you were there?"

"Nineteen ninety-six, I think."

"Well, you must come see what we're doing. It's amazing how the footprint of the fort has changed, and the artifacts, hundreds of thousands of them, as you probably know from the news. We've been doing isotopic studies on some of the bones, which I should think you would find interesting, Kay. JR continues to be our biggest mystery. His isotopic profile wasn't at all consistent with a diet of either corn or wheat, so we didn't know what to make of that, except that maybe he wasn't English. So we sent one of his teeth to a lab in England, for DNA."

JR stands for Jamestown Rediscovery. It is the prefix given every feature discovered at the excavation site, but in this instance, Edith refers specifically to the one-hundred-and-second feature unearthed in the third or C layer of soil. JR102C is a grave. It has become the most celebrated grave of the excavation because the skeleton inside it is thought to be that of a young man who arrived at Jamestown with John Smith in May 1607 and was shot to death that fall. At the first hint of violence inside the coffin-stained clay,

Edith and the chief archaeologist called me to the site, where together we brushed back dirt from a sixty-caliber musket ball and twenty-one shot that had fractured the tibia and rotated it one hundred and eighty degrees, so that the foot was pointing backward. The injury would have torn if not severed the popliteal artery behind the knee, and JR, as he has since become affectionately known, would have bled to death quickly.

Of course, there was acute interest in what was immediately dubbed the first murder in America, a rather presumptuous claim since we can't say for a fact it is a murder or the first one and the New World was hardly America yet. We did prove from forensic testing that JR was shot with a combat load fired from a European weapon called a matchlock musket and that, based on the spread of the shot, the gun was fired from a distance of approximately fifteen feet. He could not possibly have shot himself accidentally. One might deduce that a fellow settler was to blame, leading to the not so far-fetched notion that America's karma, sadly, seems to be for us to kill each other.

"Everything's moved indoors for the winter." Edith slips out of her jacket and drapes it over the back of the sofa. "Cataloging artifacts, writing up the findings, all the things we can't get around to while we're working on the site. And of course, fund-raising. That awful part of life that tends to fall in my lap more and more these days. Bringing me to my point. I got a rather disturbing phone call from one of our legislators who read about the motel death. He's in an uproar, which is unfortunate, because he's only going to end up doing the very thing he says he doesn't want, which is to draw attention to the case."

"Uproar over what?" I frown. "There was very little information in the newspaper."

Edith's expression stiffens. Whoever this legislator is, she obviously has no use for him. "He's from the Jamestown area," she tells me. "He seems to think the case might be a hate crime, that the victim was gay."

Footsteps sound softly on the carpeted stairs and Aaron appears with a tray, a bottle and three tumblers etched with the seal of the commonwealth.

"Needless to say, such a thing could severely compromise what we're doing out there." She chooses her words carefully as Aaron pours Black Bush. A door off the sitting area opens and the governor emerges from his private office in a draft of cigar smoke, his tuxedo jacket and tie off.

"Kay, I'm sorry to keep you waiting," he says to me with a hug. "Brushfires. Maybe Edith has given you the hint."

"She was just getting around to it," I reply.

CHAPTER 18

GOVERNOR MITCHELL IS VISibly disturbed. His wife gets up to allow us a private conversation and the two of them have a quick exchange about a call that needs to be made to one of their daughters, then Edith tells me good night and leaves. The governor lights another cigar. He is a rugged, good-looking man with a former football player's strong body and hair as white as Caribbean sand. "I was going to try to get you tomorrow but didn't know if you might be off somewhere for the holidays," he begins. "Thanks for coming over."

Whisky heats up my throat with each swallow as we engage in a polite exchange about Christmas plans and how things are going at the Virginia Institute of Forensic Science and Medicine. With every breath, I think of Detective Stanfield. The fool. He obviously divulged sensitive case information, and of all people, to a goddamn politician, his brother-in-law, Representative Dinwiddie. The governor is an astute man. More importantly, he began his career as a prosecutor. He knows I am furious and why.

"Representative Dinwiddie has a tendency to stir up a hornet's nest," the governor confirms who the troublemaker is. Dinwiddie is a militant pain in the ass who never lets the world forget his lineage can be traced back, albeit very indirectly, to Chief Powhatan, the father of Pocahontas.

"The detective was wrong to have told Dinwiddie anything," I reply, "and Dinwiddie was wrong to have told you or anyone else. This is a criminal case. This is not about the four-hundredth anniversary of Jamestown. It's not about tourism or politics. This is about a man who was most likely tortured and left to burn up in a motel room."

"No question about it," Mitchell replies. "But there are certain realities we have to consider. A hate crime that might in any shape or fashion seem connected to Jamestown would be catastrophic."

"I'm not aware of any Jamestown connection, beyond the fact that the victim checked into a Jamestown area motel that offers a business special called the sixteen-oh-seven." I am getting exasperated.

"With all the publicity Jamestown has already gotten, that information alone is enough to make the media's antennae go up." He rolls the cigar in his fingertips and slowly raises it to his lips. "It's projected that the two-thousand-seven celebration could eventually generate a billion dollars in revenue for the commonwealth. It's our World's Fair, Kay. Next year Jamestown is being commemorated on a coin, a quarter. News crews have been coming to the excavation site in droves."

He gets up to stir the fire and I am taken back in time to his former rumpled suits and harried demeanor, to his cramped office overwhelmed by files and books in the District Courts Building. We tried many cases together, some of them the most painful landmarks in my history, those sorts of random, cruel crimes whose victims still haunt my mind: the newspaper carrier abducted from her route and raped and left to slowly die; the old woman shot to death for the hell of it while she was hanging up clothes; the multiple people executed by the Briley brothers. Mitchell and I anguished over so many awful acts of violence, and I missed him when he moved on to a higher calling. Success separates friends. Politics, especially, is ruinous to relationships, because the very nature of politics is to re-create the person. The Mike Mitchell I knew has been replaced by a statesman who has learned to process his fiery beliefs through safe and meticulously calculated subroutines. He has a plan. He has one for me.

"I don't like media feeding frenzies any more than you do," I say to him.

He replaces the poker on its brass stand and smokes with his back to the fire, his face flushed from heat. Wood pops and hisses. "What can we do about it, Kay?"

"Tell Dinwiddie to keep his mouth shut."

"Mister Headline News?" He smiles wryly. "Who has been very vocal in pointing out that there are those who think Jamestown was the original hate crime—against the Native Americans?"

"Well, I think it's also rather hateful to kill, scalp and starve people to death. Seems there's always been plenty of hate to go around since the beginning of time. It won't be me using the term 'hate crime,' Governor. It's not on any form I fill out, not a box to check on a death certificate. As you very well know, such a label is up to the prosecution, the investigators, not the medical examiner."

"What about your opinion?"

I tell him about the second body found in Richmond late this afternoon. I worry the deaths are related.

"Based on?" His cigar smolders in an ashtray.

He rubs his face and massages his temples as if he has a headache.

"Bondage," I reply. "Burns."

"Burns? But the first guy was in a fire. Why does the second guy have burns?"

"I suspect torture."

"Gay?"

"No obvious evidence of it in the second victim. But we can't rule it out."

"Do we know who he is or if he's local?"

"So far, no. Neither victim has personal effects."

"Suggesting someone involved doesn't want them identified. Or robbery. Or both."

"Possibly."

"Tell me more about the burns," the governor says.

I describe them. I mention the case Berger had in New York, and the governor's anxieties become more palpable. Anger flashes across his face. "This sort of speculation needs to stay in this room," he says. "Last thing we need is another New York connection. Jesus God."

"There's no evidence of a connection, unless someone simply got the idea from the news," I reply. "I can't say for a fact a heat gun was used in the cases here, for that matter."

"Do you find it a little strange that Chandonne's murders have a New York connection? So the trial moves up there. Now we suddenly have two murders here that are similar to yet another New York murder?"

"Strange, yes. Very strange. Governor, all I can tell you with certainty is I've no intention of making the autopsy reports a major element in fueling other people's political agendas. I will, as always, stick to the facts and avoid speculating. I suggest we think in terms of managing rather than suppressing."

"Goddamn. All hell's going to break loose," he mutters in a cloud of smoke.

"I hope not," I tell him.

"And your case? The French Werewolf, as some people are calling him?" Mitchell finally gets around to that. "What's all that going to do to you, hmmm?" He sits down again and gives me one of his earnest looks.

I sip my whisky, wondering how to tell him. There really is no graceful way to launch it. "What's that going to do to me?" I smile ruefully.

"Has to be awful. I'm just glad you nailed the son of a bitch." Tears brighten his eyes and he quickly looks away. Mitchell is the prosecutor again. We are comfortable. We are old colleagues, old friends. I am touched, very touched, and at the same time, depressed. The past is past. Mitchell is the governor. He will probably land in Washington next. I am the chief medical examiner of

Virginia and he is my boss. I am about to tell him I have to give up my position as chief.

"I don't think it's in my best interest or the best interest of the commonwealth for me to continue to serve in my position." I am out with it.

He just stares at me.

"I'll submit this more formally, of course, in writing. But I've made my decision. I am resigning as of January first. Of course I'll stay on as long as you need me, while you search for my replacement." I wonder if he was expecting this. Maybe he is relieved. Maybe he is angry.

"You're not a quitter, Kay," he says. "That's one thing you've never been. Don't let assholes run you off, goddammit."

"I'm not quitting my profession. Just changing the boundaries. No one's running me off."

"Oh yes, boundaries," the governor observes, leaning back against the cushions and studying me. "Sounds like you're becoming a hired gun."

"Please." We both share the same contempt for experts whose choice of which side to represent is based on money, not justice.

"You know what I mean." He relights his cigar and stares off, already forming a new plan. I can see his mind working.

"I'll go to work as a private contractor," I say. "But I will never be a hired gun. Actually, what I've got to do first won't earn me a dime, Mike.

The case. New York. I've got to help and it's going to take a lot of my time."

"All right. Then it's simple. You go to work as a private contractor, Kay, and the commonwealth will be your first client. We'll hire you as acting chief until there's a better solution for Virginia. I hope your rates are reasonable," he drolly adds.

This isn't at all what I expected to hear.

"You look surprised," he observes.

"I am."

"Why?"

"Maybe Buford Righter could explain," I start to say, and indignation rises again. "We have two women horrendously murdered in this city, and no matter what, I don't feel it's right that their killer is now in New York. I can't help it, Mike. I feel it's my fault. I feel I've compromised the cases here because Chandonne came after me. I feel as if I've turned into a liability."

"Ah, Buford," Mitchell blandly comments. "Well, he's a good enough guy but a lousy commonwealth's attorney, Kay. And I don't think letting New York have the first crack at Chandonne is all that bad an idea in light of the circumstances." His words have the weight of many considerations, not the least of which, I suspect, is the way Europeans would react if Virginia executed a French native, and Virginia is known for the number of people it puts to death every year. I autopsy every one of them. I know the statistics all too well. "Even I would be a little at odds as to how to handle this case," Mitchell adds with a drawn-out pause.

I have the sensation that the sky is about to fall. Secrets crackle like static electricity, but there is no point in my prying. Governor Mitchell will not be coaxed into relaying any information he isn't ready to give. "Try not to take all this too personally, Kay," he gives me advice. "I support you. I'll continue to do so. I've worked with you a long time and know you."

"Everybody tells me not to take any of this personally." I smile a little. The ominous feeling strengthens. He will continue to support me, as if to imply there are reasons he shouldn't.

"Edith, my kids, staff, all tell me the same thing," he is saying. "And I still take things personally. I just don't let on that I do."

"Then you had nothing to do with Berger—with this rather remarkable change of venue, so to speak?" I have to ask.

He sharpens his ash to a point, slowly rolling the cigar, puffing, buying time. He did have something to do with it. He had everything to do with it, I am convinced. "She's really good, Kay." His non-answer is an answer.

I accept this. I resist prying. I simply ask him exactly how he is acquainted with her.

"Well, you know we both went to UVA law school," he says. "Then when I was AG, I had a case. You should remember since it had to do with your office. The socialite from New York who took out a huge life insurance policy on her husband one month before she murdered him in a Fairfax hotel. She tried to pass it off as a suicidal shooting."

I remember all too well. She later named my office and me in a lawsuit, accusing us of racketeering, among other things, for allegedly colluding with the insurance company to falsify records so no claim was paid to her.

"Berger got involved because it turns out the woman's first husband had died under suspicious circumstances in New York some years earlier," Mitchell says. "Seems he was an older man, frail, and drowned in the bathtub just one month after the wife had taken out a huge life insurance policy. The medical examiner found bruises that might have indicated a struggle, and pended the case for a very long time, hoping the investigation would turn up something conclusive. It didn't. The D.A.'s office just couldn't make the case. Then the woman sues the medical examiner there, too. For slander, emotional duress, baloney like that. I had numerous conversations with the people up there, mostly Bob Morgenthau, the D.A., but also with Jaime, comparing notes."

"Guess I'm wondering if the feds might try to make Chandonne flip and snitch on his cartel family. Let's make a deal," I say. "And then what?"

"I think you can bank on that," Mitchell replies solemnly.

"So that's it." Now I know. "He is guaranteed not to get the death penalty? That's the deal."

"Morgenthau's not known for putting people to death," he says. "But I am. I'm a tough old bird."

The governor has just clued me in on the negotiations that have gone on. The feds get to work on Chandonne. In exchange, Chandonne is tried in New York, where he is assured he will not get the death penalty. No matter what happens, Governor Mitchell doesn't look bad. It is no longer his problem. It is no longer Virginia's problem. We won't incite an international incident by sticking a needle in Chandonne's arm.

"That's a shame," I sum it up. "Not that I believe in capital punishment, Mike, but it's a shame that politics have gotten into the mix. I just listened to several hours of Chandonne's lies. He's not going to help anyone take down his family. Never. And I'll tell you something else, if he ends up in Kirby or Bellevue, he'll somehow get out. He'll kill again. So on the one hand, I'm glad there's an excellent prosecutor on the case and not Righter. Righter's a coward. But on the other hand, I'm sorry we've lost control of Chandonne."

Mitchell leans forward and places his hands on his knees, a ready position signaling our conversation has ended. He isn't going to discuss the matter further with me, and that also speaks volumes. "Good of you to come, Kay," he says. He holds my stare. This is his way of saying, "Don't ask."

CHAPTER 19

ARON LEADS ME BACK DOWN the stairs and gives me a slight smile as he opens the front door. The trooper waves at me as I drive through the gates. There is a sense of closure, of finality as I wind through Capitol Square, the mansion disappearing in my rearview mirror. I have left something. I have just walked away from my life as I have known it, and I have discovered a wrinkle of distrust for a man I have always admired so much. No, I don't think Mitchell has done anything wrong. But I know he hasn't been forthright with me, not totally. He is directly responsible for Chandonne's leaving our jurisdiction, and the reason is politics, not justice. I sense it. I am sure of it. Mike Mitchell is not the prosecutor anymore. He is the governor. Why should I be surprised? What the hell did I expect?

Downtown seems unfriendly and foreign as I

follow 8th Street to get on the expressway. I watch the faces of people driving past and marvel that virtually none of them is present in the moment they occupy. They drive and look in the mirror and reach for something on the seat or fool with the radio or talk on the phone or to their passengers. They don't notice the stranger watching them. I see faces so clearly that I can determine if they are handsome or pretty or have scars from acne or good teeth. I realize that at least one big difference between killers and their victims is killers are present. They live entirely in the moment, taking in their surroundings, intensely aware of every detail and how it might benefit or compromise them. They watch strangers. They fix on a face and decide to follow the person home. I wonder if this is how the two young men, my latest patients, were selected. I wonder what sort of predator I am dealing with here. I wonder what the governor's real agenda is for wanting to see me tonight and why he and the first lady questioned me about the James City County case. Something is going on. Something bad.

I call my home phone and have seven messages. Three of them are from Lucy. She doesn't tell me what she wants, only that she is trying to reach me. I try her on her mobile phone and when she answers, I feel tension. I sense she is not alone. "Is everything all right?" I ask her.

She hesitates. "Aunt Kay, I'd like to bring Teun by."

"McGovern's in Richmond?" I say in surprise.

"We can be at Anna's house in about fifteen minutes," Lucy tells me.

Signals are coming fast and strong. I can't identify what it is that taps my subconscious, trying to make me recognize a very important truth. What is it, damn it? I am so unsettled I am jumpy and confused. A motorist behind me blares his horn and my heart jerks. I gasp. I realize the light has turned green. The moon is incomplete and shrouded by clouds, the James River a plain of darkness below the Huguenot Bridge as I pass into the south side of the city. I park in front of Anna's house behind Lucy's Suburban, and instantly Anna's front door opens. It appears that Lucy and McGovern have arrived only a moment before me. Both of them and Anna are in the foyer beneath the sparkling crystal chandelier. McGovern's eyes meet mine and she smiles reassuringly, as if to let me know I will be all right. She has cut her hair short and is still a very attractive woman, slender and boyish in black leggings and a long leather jacket. We hug and I am reminded she is firm and in charge, but gentle. I am glad to see her, immensely glad.

"Come in, come in," Anna says. "Merry Christmas Eve, almost. Isn't this fun!" But her expression is anything but fun. Her face is drawn, her eyes bruised by worry and fatigue. She catches me staring and tries to smile. All of us head toward the kitchen at the same time. Anna is asking about drinks and snacks. Has everyone eaten? Do Lucy and McGovern want to stay here for the night? No one should be in a hotel on Christmas Eve—that is criminal. On and on she talks, and her hands are unsteady as she pulls out bottles from a cabinet, lining up whiskies and liquors. The signals are firing so rapidly now I barely hear what anyone is saying. Then, the moment of recognition thunders in my psyche. I get it. The truth runs through me in a jolting current as Anna pours me a Scotch.

I told Berger I have no deep, dark secrets. What I meant was I have always been private. I don't tell people anything that could be used against me. I am by nature cautious. But lately I have talked to Anna. We have spent hours exploring the deepest crevices of my life. I have told her things I am not sure I even knew, and I have never paid her for these sessions. They are not protected by doctor-patient confidentiality. Rocky Caggiano could subpoena Anna, and as I look at her now, I assume this is what has occurred. I take the tumbler of Scotch from her, our eyes locked.

"Something's happened," I say.

She glances away. I play out the scenario. Berger

will get the subpoena quashed. It is ridiculous. Caggiano is harassing me, trying to intimidate me, plain and simple, and it won't work. Fuck him. I have everything figured out and resolved, just that fast, because I am a pro at ducking any truth that directly impacts my inner self, my well being, my feelings. "Tell me, Anna," I say.

Silence fills the kitchen. Lucy and McGovern have stopped talking. Lucy comes over and hugs me. "We're here for you," she says.

"You bet." McGovern gives me a thumbs up.

Their efforts to reassure me leave a wake of foreboding as they disappear into the living room. Anna looks at me and it is the first time I have ever seen even a hint of tears in my stoical, Austrian friend. "I have done a terrible thing, Kay." She clears her throat and woodenly fills another tumbler with ice from the refrigerator icemaker. She drops an ice cube on the floor and it slides out of reach behind the trash can. "This sheriff's deputy. I could not believe it when the buzzer sounded at my gate this morning. And here is a deputy with a subpoena. To do this to me at home is bad enough. Always I get subpoenas at my office. That is not so unusual, I do get called in as an expert witness from time to time, as you know. I cannot believe he did this to me. I trusted him."

Doubt. Denial quakes. The first breath of fear

touches my central nervous system. "Who did this to you?" I say. "Rocky?"

"Who?" She looks bewildered.

"Oh God," I mutter. "Oh God." I lean against the countertop. This isn't about Chandonne. It can't be. If Caggiano didn't subpoena Anna, then that leaves only one other possibility, and it isn't Berger. Of course, the prosecution would have no reason to talk to Anna. I think of the odd phone call from my bank, the message from AT&T and of Righter's behavior and the look on his face when he saw me in Marino's truck last Saturday night. I play through the governor's sudden need to see me, his evasiveness, even Marino's sour moods and the way he has been avoiding me, and I take another look at Jack's sudden loss of hair and fears about being the chief. Everything slips into place and forms an unbelievable composite. I am in trouble. Dear God, I am in serious trouble. My hands begin to shake.

Anna is rambling, stuttering, tripping over her words as if she has involuntarily resorted to what she learned first in life, which is not English. She struggles. She confirms what I now am forced to suspect. Anna has been subpoenaed by a special grand jury. A Richmond special grand jury is investigating me to see if there is sufficient evidence to indict me in the murder of Diane Bray. Anna has been used, she says. She has been set up.

"Who set you up? Righter? Buford's behind this?" I ask.

Anna nods affirmatively. "I never will forgive him. I told him," she swears.

We go into the living room, where I reach for a cordless phone on an elegant yew wood stand. "You realize, you don't have to be telling me all this, Anna." I try Marino's home number. I will myself to be remarkably calm. "I'm sure Buford wouldn't appreciate it. So maybe you shouldn't talk to me."

"I do not care what I should or should not do. The moment I got the subpoena, Buford called and explained what he needed from me. I called Lucy right away." Anna continues speaking in fractured English as she stares blankly at McGovern. It seems to occur to Anna that she has no idea who McGovern is or why she is in her house.

"What time did the deputy show up at your house with the subpoena?" I ask Anna. Marino's phone cuts straight into his voice mail. "Dammit," I mutter. He is on the line. I leave him the message to call me. It is urgent.

"About ten o'clock this morning," Anna answers my question.

"Interesting," I reply. "About the same time Chandonne was transported out of here to New York. And then Bray's memorial service and when I first met Berger."

"In your mind, how does all of this connect?" McGovern is listening carefully with her astute, experienced eyes fastened on me. She was one of ATF's most gifted certified fire investigators before she got promoted to supervision by the very people who would eventually cause her to quit.

"I'm not sure," I reply. "Except Berger was interested in seeing who showed up at Bray's service. I'm now wondering if she wanted to see if I would, and if that might indicate she knows I'm being investigated and is checking me out on her own." Anna's phone rings. "Zenner residence," I answer.

"What's going on?" Marino says loudly over his television.

"I'm just beginning to figure that out," I reply.

He knows instantly by my tone not to ask questions but to get in his truck and drive over here right now. It is time for truth. No games and no secrets, I tell him. We wait for him in front of the fire in Anna's living room, where a tree is wrapped in white lights and garlands and decorated with glass animals and wooden fruit, with presents underneath. I am silently going through every word I have said to Anna, trying to remember what she surely will when Righter asks her under oath about me in front of jurors who have been seated and sworn to decide if I should go on trial for murder.

My heart is seized by frigid fingers of raw fear, yet I sound reasonable when I speak. I am outwardly steady as Anna goes into detail about how she has been set up. It began when Righter contacted her on Tuesday, December 14. She spends a good fifteen minutes explaining that Righter called as a *friend*, a *concerned friend*. People were talking about me. He was hearing *things* that he felt he must check out and he knew Anna and I are close.

"This isn't making any sense," Lucy says. "Diane Bray hadn't even been murdered yet. Why was Righter talking to Anna that early on?"

"I don't get it," McGovern agrees. "Something really stinks about this."

She and Lucy sit on the floor in front of the fire. I am in my usual rocking chair and Anna is on the ottoman, sitting rigidly.

"When Righter called on the fourteenth, what exactly did he say to you?" I ask Anna. "How did he introduce the conversation?"

She meets my eyes. "There was concern about your mental health. That is what he said right off."

I simply nod. I am not offended. Although it is true I wobbled badly after Benton was murdered, I have never been mentally ill. I am secure in my sanity and my ability to reason and think. I have been guilty only of running from pain. "I know I didn't handle Benton's death well," I admit.

"How do you handle something like that *well*?" Lucy replies.

"No, no. That is not what Buford meant," Anna says. "He wasn't calling about how you've managed grief, Kay. He was calling about Diane Bray, about your relationship with her."

"What relationship?" I instantly wonder if Bray called Righter—yet one more trap she set for me. "I hardly knew her."

Anna's eyes are steady on mine, the shadow from the fire wavering on her face. I am startled again by how old she looks, as if she has aged ten years in a day. "You'd had a series of confrontations with her. You told me so," she replies.

"Instigated by her," I am quick to say. "We didn't have a personal relationship. Not even a social one."

"I think when you go to war against someone, that is personal. Even people who hate each other have a personal relationship, if you see what I am saying. Certainly, she had gotten very personal with you, Kay. Starting rumors. Lying about you. Creating a bogus medical column on the Internet that made it appear you were the one writing it, making a fool out of you and getting you into trouble with the secretary of public safety, even with the governor."

"I was just with the governor. I don't feel I'm

in trouble with him at all." I say this and at the same time find it curious. If Mitchell knows I am being investigated by a special grand jury, and I know he must, then why didn't he accept my resignation and thank God to be rid of me and my messy life?

"She also put Marino's career in jeopardy because he is your sidekick," Anna goes on.

The only thought that flashes is Marino would not appreciate being called my sidekick. As if on cue, the intercom blares, announcing that he is at the front gates.

"Sabotaging your career, in other words." Anna gets up. "Correct? Isn't that what you have told me?" She pushes a button on a console on the wall, suddenly energized. Anger burns off her depression. "Yes? Who is it?" she snaps into the speaker.

"Me, baby." The rude sounds of Marino and his truck fill the living room.

"Oh, he calls me *baby* again I will kill him." Anna throws her hands up in the air.

She goes to the door, and then Marino is walking into the living room. He left his house in such a hurry he didn't bother with a coat, only a gray sweat suit and tennis shoes. He is dumbstruck when he sees McGovern sitting by the fire, looking up at him from her Indian-style position on the floor.

"Well, I'll be damned," Marino says. "Look what the cat drug in."

"Great to see you, too, Marino," McGovern replies.

"Someone want to tell me what the hell's going on?" He moves a wing chair closer to the fire and sits, going from one face to the other, trying to read the situation, acting obtuse, as if he doesn't already know. I believe he knows. Oh yes, now it is clear why he has been acting so strange.

We get into it. Anna continues to unravel what happened in the days preceding Jaime Berger's coming to Richmond. Berger continues to dominate, as if she is sitting in our midst. I don't trust her. And at the same time, I feel my life may very well be in her hands. I try to remember where I was on December fourteenth, moving backward from today, December 23, until I land on that Tuesday. I was in Lyon, France, at Interpol's headquarters, where I met Jay Talley for the first time. I run through that encounter, reconstructing the two of us alone at a table in Interpol's cafeteria. Marino took an instant dislike to Jay and stalked off. During lunch, I told Jay about Diane Bray, about my problems with her and that she was doing all she could to persecute Marino, including throwing him back into uniform and on midnight shift. What was it Jay called her? *Toxic waste in tight clothes*. Apparently, the two of them had run-ins when she was with the D.C. police and he was briefly assigned to ATF headquarters. He seemed to know all about her. Can it be coincidence that the very day I discussed her with him, Righter called Anna and questioned her about my relationship with Bray and made implications about my mental health?

"I wasn't going to tell you this," Anna continues in a hard voice. "I shouldn't tell you this, but now that I am clearly going to be used against you . . ."

"What do you mean, *used against her*?" Marino butts in.

"Originally, I was hoping to guide you, to help allay these allegations about your mental health," Anna says to me. "I did not believe it. And if I had any doubt, and maybe there was just a slight doubt because I had not seen you in so long, then I wanted to talk to you anyway, out of concern. You are my friend. Buford assured me that anything I could find out was not something he planned to do anything with. Our conversations were supposed to be private, his and mine. He said nothing, absolutely nothing, about accusing you."

"Righter?" Marino scowls. "He ask you to be some kind of fucking snitch?"

Anna shakes her head. "A guide," she uses that word again.

"That fucking figures. The loser." Marino's anger springs forth.

"He had to know if Kay was mentally stable. Certainly you can see why he needs to know that if she was going to be his star witness. I always thought this was about your being a star witness, not a suspect!"

"Suspect my ass." Marino scowls. He makes no pretenses now. He knows exactly what is going on.

"Marino, I know you're not supposed to tell me I'm being investigated by a special grand jury for the murder of Diane Bray," I say to him, evenly. "But out of curiosity, I'm wondering, how long have you known? For example, when you ushered me out of my house on Saturday night, you knew then, didn't you? That's why you watched me like a hawk inside my own house. So I didn't do something sneaky like dispose of evidence, or God knows what? That's why you wouldn't let me drive my car, right? Because you guys needed to see if there might be evidence in it, maybe Diane Bray's blood? Fibers? Hair? Something that would put me at her house the night she was killed?" My tone is cool but searing.

"Jesus fucking Christ!" Marino erupts. "I know you didn't do nothing. Righter's the biggest fuckhead, and I told him that. I've been telling him that every day. What'd you ever do to him, huh? You want to tell me why the hell he's doing this to you?"

"You know what?" I stare hard at him. "I'm not going to hear one more time that everything is my fault. I didn't do a damn thing to Righter. I don't know what's gotten him on this ridiculous kick unless it's Jay planting stuff."

"And I guess that ain't your fault, either. Sleeping with him."

"He's not doing this because I slept with him," I fire back. "If he's doing anything, it's because I only slept with him once."

McGovern is frowning, leaning against the hearth. She says, "Dear ol' Jay. Mister Squeaky Clean, pretty boy. Funny, I've never had a good feeling about him."

"I told Buford that you are definitely not mentally ill." Anna sets her jaw squarely and looks at me fiercely. "He wanted to know if I thought you were competent to assist him, if I think you are stable. See, he lied. This was supposed to be about our assisting him in the trial of Chandonne. I never imagined. I cannot believe Buford would slither out from under a rock and subpoena me like this." She places a hand on her breast as if her heart is bothering her and briefly shuts her eyes.

"Are you all right, Anna?" I start to get up.

She shakes her head from side to side. "I will never be all right again. I would never have talked to you, Kay, if I thought such a thing would happen."

"Did you tape her, take notes?" McGovern asks.

"Of course not."

"Good."

"But if I am asked . . ." she starts to say.

"I understand," I reply. "Anna, I understand. What's done is done." It is now that I must tell Marino the other news. While we are on such dreadful subjects, he may as well hear it all. "Your son, Rocky," I say his name and nothing more. Maybe I am trying to see if Marino already knows this, too.

He turns to stone. "What about him?"

"It appears he is representing Chandonne," I reply.

Marino's face darkens to a deep, scary red. For a moment, no one speaks. He doesn't know. Then Marino says in a flat, hard tone, "He would do something like that. Probably has something to do with what's happening to you, too, if that's possible. Funny thing about it, I halfway wondered if he had something to do with Chandonne's ending up here."

"Why would you wonder that?" McGovern asks in amazement.

"He's a mob boy, that's why. Probably knows Big Papa Chandonne over there in Paris and would like nothing better than causing me trouble here."

"I think it's time you talk about Rocky," I tell him.

"You got any bourbon in this house?" Marino asks Anna.

She gets up and leaves the room.

"Aunt Kay, you can't stay here anymore," Lucy says to me in a quiet, urgent voice.

"You can't talk to her anymore, Kay," McGovern adds.

I don't answer. Of course, they are right. Now, on top of it all, I have lost my friend.

"So, did you tell her anything?" Marino says to me in an accusing tone that has become all too familiar.

"I told her the world was better off without Diane Bray," I reply. "In other words, I basically said I'm glad she's dead."

"So's everybody who knew her," Marino retorts. "And I'll be glad to tell the fucking special grand jury that."

"Not a helpful statement, but doesn't mean you murdered anybody," McGovern says to me.

"*Not helpful* is right," Marino mutters. "Damn, I hope Anna don't tell Righter you're glad Bray was whacked," he says to me.

"This is so absurd," is my response.

"Well," Marino replies, "yes and no, Doc."

"You don't have to talk to me about this," I tell him. "Don't put yourself in a bad spot, Marino."

"Oh fuck it!" He waves me off. "I know you didn't kill that damn bitch. But you gotta look at it from the other side. You had problems with her. She was trying to get you fired. You've been acting a little hinky ever since Benton died, or at least that's what people have been saying, right? You have a confrontation with Bray in a parking lot. The theory is you was jealous of this new big-shot police lady. She was making you look bad and complaining about you. So you killed her and disguised it to look like it was the same guy who whacked Kim Luong, and who better to do that than you, right? Who more capable of the perfect murder than you, right? And you had access—first dibs on all the evidence. You could have beaten her to death and planted Wolfman's hairs on her body, even switched swabs so they come up with his DNA. And it don't look good that you took that evidence from the Paris morgue and brought it over here, either. Or took that water sample. Righter thinks you're a nut case, I hate to tell you. And I gotta add that he don't like you personally and never has because he's got the balls of a soprano and don't like powerful women. He don't even like Anna, if the truth be known. The Berger thing's kind of the best revenge. He really hates her."

Silence.

"I wonder if they're going to subpoena me," Lucy says.

CHAPTER 20

IGHTER THINKS YOU'RE A
nut case, too," Marino tells my niece.
"The only point we're in agreement on."

"Any chance Rocky's been involved with the
Chandonne family?" McGovern looks at Marino.
"In the past? You're serious when you say you
wondered it?"

"Huh." Marino snorts. "Rocky's been involved
with criminals most of his goddamn life. But do
I know details about what he does with his fucking time, day to day, month to month? No. I can't
honestly swear to that. I just know what he is.
Scum. He was born bad. Bad seed. As far as I'm
concerned, he ain't my son."

"Well, he *is* your son," I tell him.

"Not in my book. He took after the wrong side
of my family," Marino insists. "In New Jersey, we
had good Marinos and bad Marinos. I had an
uncle who was with the mob, another uncle who

was a cop. Two brothers different as night and day. And then when I turned fourteen, Uncle Asshole Louie had my other uncle whacked—my other uncle being the cop, also named Pete. I was named after Uncle Pete. Shot down when he was in his own front yard picking up his fucking newspaper. We never could prove Uncle Louie had it done, but everyone in the family believed it. I still believe it."

"Where's your Uncle Louie now?" Lucy asks as Anna returns with Marino's drink.

"I heard he died a couple years back. I didn't keep up with him. Never had nothing to do with him." He takes the glass from Anna. "But Rocky's his spittin' image. Even looked like him when he was growing up, and from day one was bent, warped, just a piece of living shit. Why do you think he took the name Caggiano? Because that's my mother's maiden name, and Rocky knew it would really piss me off if he crapped on my mother's name. There's some people who can't be fixed. There's some just born bad. Don't ask me to explain it, because Doris and I did everything we could for that boy. Even tried sending him off to military school, which was a mistake. He ended up liking it, liked the hazing part, doing really crappy things to the other boys. Nobody picked on him, not even on the first damn day. He was big like me and just so goddamn mean the other kids didn't dare touch a hair on his head."

"This is not right," Anna mutters as she sits back down on the ottoman.

"What's Rocky's motive for taking this case?" I know what Berger said. But I want to hear Marino's slant. "To spite you?"

"He'll get off on the attention. A case like this will create a circus." Marino doesn't want to say the obvious, that just maybe Rocky wants to humiliate, to best his father.

"Does he hate you?" McGovern asks him.

Marino snorts again and his pager vibrates.

"What eventually happened to him?" I ask. "You sent him off to military school, then what?"

"I kicked his ass out. Told him if he couldn't follow the rules of the house, he wasn't living under my roof. That was after his freshman year at the military school. So you know what the little psycho did?" Marino reads the display on his pager and gets up. "He moves up to Jersey, moves in with Uncle Louie, the fucking Mafia. Then has the balls to come back here for school, including law school, William and Mary, so yeah, he's smart as shit."

"He passed the bar in Virginia?" I ask.

"Here, practices all the hell over the place. I ain't seen Rocky in seventeen years. Anna, you mind if I make a call? Don't look like I want to be using the cell phone on this one." He glances at me as he walks out of the living room. "It's Stanfield."

"What about the ID he called you about earlier?" I ask.

"Hopefully what this is about," Marino says. "Another real strange one, if it's true."

While he is on the phone, Anna vanishes from her own living room. I supposed she was going to the bathroom, but she does not come back and I can only imagine how she feels. In many ways, I am more worried about her than about me. I now know enough about her life to appreciate her intense vulnerability and realize the terribly barren, scarred spots on her emotional landscape. "This isn't fair," I begin to lose my composure. "It's not fair to anyone." Everything that has piled up on me begins to unsettle and slide downhill. "Someone please tell me how this happened? Did I do something wrong in a former life? I don't deserve this. None of us do."

Lucy and McGovern listen to me ventilate. They seem to have their own ideas and plans but are not inclined to offer them right away.

"Well, say something," I tell them. "Go ahead and let it out." Mostly, I say this for my niece's benefit. "My life is wrecked. I haven't handled anything the way I should. I'm sorry." Tears threaten. "Right now I want a cigarette. Does anybody have a cigarette?" Marino does, but he is in the kitchen on the phone, and I'll be damned if I am going to creep in there and interrupt him for a cigarette, as if I need one to begin with. "You know, what hurts me most is to be accused of the very thing I'm so against. I don't abuse power, goddamn it. I would never murder somebody in cold blood." I talk on and on. "I hate death. I hate killing. I hate every goddamn thing I see every goddamn day. And now the world thinks I did something like this? A special grand jury thinks maybe I might have?" I let the questions hang. Neither Lucy nor McGovern responds.

Marino is loud. His voice is muscular and big like he is and tends to shove rather than guide, confront rather than fall in stride. "You sure she's his girlfriend?" he is saying over the telephone. I presume he is speaking to Detective Stanfield. "Versus just friends. Tell me how you know that for a fact. Yeah, yeah. Uh huh. What? Do I get it? Hell no, I don't get it. It don't make a shit's worth of sense, Stanfield." Marino is walking around the kitchen as he talks. He is on the verge of snapping Stanfield's head off. "You know what I tell people like you, Stanfield?" Marino snaps. "I tell them to get out of my fucking way. I don't give a rat's ass who your fucking brother-in-law is, got it? He can kiss my butt and tuck it in bed, tell it a beddy-bye story." Stanfield is obviously trying to get in a word or two, but Marino won't let him.

"Oh boy," McGovern mutters, returning my attention to the living room, to my own mess. "He's the investigator for these two men who were probably tortured and killed? Whoever Marino's talking to?" McGovern inquires.

I give her a strange look as an even stranger sensation ripples through me. "How do you know about the two men who were killed?" I grope for an answer that I must be missing. McGovern has been in New York. I haven't even autopsied the second John Doe yet. Why does everybody seem to be omniscient all of a sudden? I think of Jaime Berger. I think of Governor Mitchell and Representative Dinwiddie and Anna. A strong breath of fear seems to foul the air like Chandonne's body odor, and I imagine I smell him again and my central nervous system has an involuntary reaction. I begin to tremble as if I have drunk a pot of strong coffee or half a dozen of those heavily sugared Cuban espressos called *coladas.* I realize I am more afraid than I have ever been in my life and begin to entertain the unthinkable: Maybe Chandonne was offering a hint of truth when he persisted in his seemingly absurd claim that he is the victim of some huge political conspiracy. I am paranoid, justifiably. I try to reason with myself. I am, after all, being investigated for the murder of a corrupt policewoman who probably was involved with organized crime.

I realize Lucy is talking to me. She has gotten up from her spot before the fire and is pulling a chair close to me. She sits and leans over, touching my good arm, as if trying to wake me up. "Aunt Kay?" she says. "You with us, Aunt Kay? Are you listening?"

I focus on her. Marino is telling Stanfield over the phone that they will meet in the morning. It sounds like a threat. "He and I rendezvoused at Phil's for a beer." She glances toward the kitchen and I remember Marino telling me late this morning that he and Lucy were getting together this afternoon because she had news for him. "We know about the guy from the motel." Now she refers to McGovern, who sits very still by the fire, looking at me, waiting to see how I will react when Lucy tells me the rest. "Teun's been here since Saturday," Lucy then says. "When I called you from the Jefferson, remember? Teun was with me. I asked her to get here right away."

"Oh," is all I can think to say. "Well, that's good. It bothered me to think of you alone in a hotel." Tears flood my eyes. I am embarrassed and look away from Lucy and McGovern. I am supposed to be strong. I am the one who has always rescued my niece from trouble, most of it of her own

making. I have always been the torchbearer who
guided her along the right path. I put her through
college. I bought her books, her first computer,
sent her to any special course she wanted to attend anywhere in the country. I took her to London with me one summer. I have stood up to
anyone who tried to interfere with Lucy, including her mother, who has rewarded my efforts
with nothing but abuse. "You're supposed to respect me," I say to my niece as I wipe tears with
my palm. "How can you anymore?"

She stands up again and looks down at me.
"That's total bullshit," she says with feeling, and
now Marino is returning to the living room, another bourbon in hand. "This isn't about my not
respecting you," Lucy says. "Jesus Christ. Nobody
in the room has any less respect for you, Aunt Kay.
But you need help. For once, you've got to let
other people help you. You sure as hell can't deal
with this all by yourself, and maybe you need to
sit on your pride a little and let us help, you know?
It's not like I'm still ten years old. I'm twenty-
eight, okay? I'm not a virgin. I've been an FBI
agent, an ATF agent and am fucking rich. I could
be any kind of fucking agent I want." Her wounds
inflame before my eyes. She does care about being
put on administrative leave; of course she cares.
"And now I'm being my own agent, doing things
my own way," she goes on.

"I resigned tonight," I tell her. A stunned silence follows.

"What did you say?" Marino asks me, standing in front of the fire, drinking. "You did what?"

"I told the governor," I reply, and an inexplicable calm begins to settle over me. It feels good to consider that I did something instead of everything being done to me. Maybe quitting my job makes me less a victim, if I am willing to finally admit that I am a victim. I suppose I am one, and the only comeback is to finish what Chandonne started: end my life as I have known it and start all over. What a weird and stunning thought. I tell Marino, McGovern and Lucy all about my conversation with Mike Mitchell.

"Hold on." Marino is sitting on the hearth. It is getting close to midnight and Anna is so quiet I forgot for a moment that she was in the house. Maybe she has gone to bed. "This mean you can't work cases no more?" Marino says to me.

"Not at all," I reply. "I'll be acting chief until the governor decides otherwise." No one asks me what I plan to do with the rest of my life. It really doesn't make sense to worry about some distant future when the present is shot. I am grateful not to be asked and probably am sending out my usual signals that I don't want to be asked. People sense when to remain silent, or if nothing else, I deflect their interest and they don't even realize I have just manipulated them into not probing for information that I prefer to keep to myself. I became an expert at this maneuver at a very young age when I didn't want my classmates asking me about my father and if he was still sick or would ever get better or what it is like to have your father die. I was conditioned not to tell, and I was conditioned not to ask, either. The last three years of my father's life were spent in absolute avoidance by my entire family, including him, especially him. He was a lot like Marino, both of them macho Italian men who seem to assume their bodies will never part company with them, no matter how ill or out of shape. I envision my father as Lucy, Marino and McGovern talk about all they plan to do and are already doing to help me, including background checks already in the works and all sorts of things The Last Precinct has to offer me.

I really am not listening. Their voices may as well be the chatter of crows as I remember the thick Miami grass of my childhood, and dried-out chinch bug husks and the key lime tree in my small backyard. My father taught me how to crack coconuts on the driveway with a hammer and a screwdriver, and I would spend an inordinate amount of time prying the fleshy, sweet white meat from the hard, hairy shell, and he got a lot of amusement from observing my obsessive labors. The coconut meat would go in the squat white refrigerator, and no one, including me, ever ate it. During blistering summer Saturdays, my father would surprise Dorothy and me now and then by bringing home two big blocks of ice from his neighborhood grocery store. We had a small, inflatable pool we filled with the hose, and my sister and I would sit on the ice, getting scorched by the sun while we froze our asses off. We would jump in and out of the pool to thaw, then perch on our frigid, slick thrones again like princesses while my father laughed at us through the living room window, laughed hilariously and tapped on the glass, playing Fats Waller full blast on the hi–fi.

My father was a good man. When he felt halfway decent he was generous, thoughtful and full of humor and fun. He was handsome, of medium height, blond and broad-shouldered when he wasn't wasted by cancer. His full name was Kay Marcellus Scarpetta III, and he insisted that his firstborn take this name, which has been in the family since Verona. It didn't matter that I happened to arrive first, a girl. Kay is one of those names that can be assigned to either gender, but my mother has always called me Katie. In part, according to her, it was confusing to have two Kays in the house. Later, when that was no longer an issue because I was the only Kay left, she still called me Katie, refusing to accept my father's death, to get over it, and she still isn't over it. She won't let him go. My father died more than thirty years ago, when I was twelve, and my mother has never gone out with another man. She still wears her wedding band. She still calls me Katie.

LUCY AND MCGOVERN GO OVER plans until past midnight. They have given up trying to include me in their conversations and no longer even seem to notice that I have slipped away to the Old Country in my mind, staring into the fire, absently massaging my stiff left hand and worming a finger under plaster to scratch my miserable, air-starved flesh. Finally, Marino yawns like a bear and pulls himself to his feet. He is made slightly unsteady by bourbon and smells like stale cigarettes, and regards me with a softness in his eyes that I might call sad love if I were willing to accept his true feelings for me. "Come on," he says to me. "Walk me out to my truck, Doc." This is his way of calling for a treaty between us. Marino is not a brute. He is feeling bad about the way he has been treating me since I was almost murdered, and he has never seen me so distant and strangely quiet.

The night is cold and still, and stars are shy behind vague clouds. From Anna's driveway, I take in the glow of her many candles in the windows and am reminded that tomorrow is Christmas Eve, the last Christmas Eve of the twentieth century. Keys disturb the peace as Marino unlocks his truck and hesitates awkwardly before opening the driver's door. "We got a lot to do. I'll meet you at the morgue early." This is not what he really wants to say. He stares up at the dark sky and sighs. "Shit, Doc. Look, I've known for a while, okay? By now you've figured that out. I've known what that son of a bitch Righter was up to and I had to let it run its course."

"When were you going to tell me?" I don't ask this accusingly, simply curiously.

He shrugs. "I'm glad Anna brought it up first. I know you didn't kill Diane Bray, for God's sake. But I wouldn't blame you if you had, truth be told. She was the biggest fucking bitch ever born. In my book, if you'd done her in, it would have been damn self-defense."

"Well, it wouldn't have been." I address the possibility seriously. "It wouldn't have been, Marino. And I didn't kill her." I look closely at his hulking shape in the castoffs of carriage lamps and holiday lights in trees. "You've never really thought . . . ?" I don't finish the question. Maybe I really don't want to know his answer.

"Hell, I'm not sure what I've been thinking lately," he says. "That's the truth. But what am I going to do, Doc?"

"Do? About what?" I don't know what he means.

He shrugs and gets choked up. I can't believe it. Marino is about to cry. "If you quit." His voice rises and he clears his throat and fumbles for his Lucky Strikes. He cups his huge hands around my hand and lights a cigarette for me, his skin rough against mine, the hairs on the back of his wrists whispering against my chin. He smokes, staring off, heartbroken. "Then what? I'm supposed to go down to the fucking morgue and you ain't there anymore? Hell, I wouldn't go down to that stink-hole half as much as I do if it wasn't for you being there, Doc. You're the only damn thing that gives any life to that joint, no kidding."

I hug him. I barely come up to his chest, and his belly separates the beat of our hearts. He has raised his own barriers in this life and I am over-whelmed by an immeasurable compassion and need for him. I pat his broad chest and let him know, "We've been together for a long time, Marino. You're not rid of me yet."

CHAPTER 21

TEETH HAVE THEIR OWN stories. Your dental habits often reveal more about you than jewelry or designer clothes and can identify you to the exclusion of all others, providing you have premortem records for comparison. Teeth tell me about your hygiene. They whisper secrets about drug abuse, early childhood antibiotics, disease, injury and how important your appearance was to you. They confess if your dentist was a crook and billed your insurance company for work that was never done. They tell me, for that matter, if your dentist was competent.

Marino meets me at the morgue before daylight the next morning. He has in hand the dental records of a twenty-two-year-old James City County man who went out jogging yesterday near the campus of William & Mary and never returned home. His name is Mitch Barbosa. William

& Mary is but a few miles from The Fort James Motel, and when Marino talked to Stanfield last night and was given this latest information, my first thought was, "How odd." Marino's shifty attorney son, Rocky Caggiano, went to William & Mary. Life offers up yet one more eerie coincidence.

It is six-forty-five when I roll the body out of the X-ray room and over to my station inside the autopsy suite. Again, it is quiet. It is Christmas Eve and all state offices are closed. Marino is suited up to assist me, and I don't expect another living person—except the forensic dentist—to show up here right now. Marino's part will be to help me undress the stiff, unwilling body and lift it to and from the autopsy table. I would never allow him to assist in any medical procedure—not that he has ever volunteered. I have never asked him to scribe and won't because his slaughter of Latin medical words and terms is remarkable.

"Hold him on either side," I direct Marino. "Good. Just like that."

Marino grips either side of the dead man's head, trying to hold it still as I work a thin chisel into the side of the mouth, sliding it between molars to pry open the jaws. Steel scrapes against enamel. I am careful not to cut the lips, but it is inevitable that I chip the surfaces of the back teeth.

"It's just a damn good thing people are dead

when you do shit like this to them," Marino says. "Bet you'll be glad when you got two hands again."

"Don't remind me." I am so sick of my cast, I have had thoughts of cutting it off myself with a Stryker saw.

The dead man's jaws give up and open, and I turn on the surgical lamp and fill the inside of his mouth with white light. There are fibers on his tongue, and I collect them. Marino helps me break the rigor mortis in the arms so we can get the jacket and shirt off, and then I take off shoes and socks, and finally the warm-up pants and running shorts. I PERK him and find no evidence of injury to his anus, nothing so far to suggest homosexual activity. Marino's pager goes off. It is Stanfield again. Marino has not said a word about Rocky this morning, but the specter of him hovers. Rocky is in the air, and the effect this has on his father is subtle but profound. A heavy, helpless anguish radiates from Marino like body heat. I should be worried about what Rocky has in store for me, but all I can think about is what will happen to Marino.

Now that my patient is naked before me, I take in the full picture of who he was physically. He is five-foot-seven and a lean one hundred and thirty-eight pounds. He has muscular legs but little muscle development in his upper body, which is consistent with a runner. He has no tattoos, is circumcised and clearly cared about his grooming, based on his neatly manicured fingernails and toenails and clean-shaven face. So far, I find no evidence of injury externally, and X rays reveal no projectiles, no fractures. He has old scars on his knees and left elbow, but nothing fresh except the abrasions from being bound and gagged. What happened to you? Why did you die? He remains silent. Only Marino is talking in a blunt, loud way to disguise how unsettled he is. He thinks Stanfield is a dolt and treats him as such. Marino is more impatient, more insulting than usual.

"Yeah, well, it *sure* would be nice if we knew that," Marino blasts sarcasm into the wallphone. "Death don't take no holiday," he adds a moment later. "You tell whoever I'm coming and they *will* let me in." Then, "Yeah, yeah, yeah. 'Tis the season. And Stanfield? Keep your mouth shut, okay? You got that? I read about this in the goddamn paper one more time . . . Oh really, well, maybe you didn't see the Richmond paper yet. I'll make sure and tear out this morning's article for you. All this Jamestown shit, hate crime shit. One more peep and I'm gonna get tear-ass. You never seen me tear-ass and you don't want to."

Marino pulls on fresh gloves as he returns to the gurney, his gown flapping around his legs. "Well, it just gets more squirrelly, Doc. Assuming this guy here's our disappeared jogger, it appears we're dealing with a garden-variety truck driver. No record. No trouble. Lived in a condo with a girl-friend who's ID'ed him by photo. That's who Stanfield talked to late last night, apparently, but she ain't answering the phone so far this morning." He gets a lost look on his face, not certain how much he has already told me.

"Let's get him on the table," I say.

I parallel-park the gurney next to the autopsy table. Marino gets the feet, I grab an arm, and we pull. The body bangs against steel and blood trickles from the nose. I turn on water and it drums into the steel sink, the dead man's X rays glowing from light boxes on the wall, revealing perfectly pristine bones, and the skull from different angles, and the zipper of the warm-up jacket snaking down each side of gracefully bowed ribs. The buzzer sounds out in the bay as I run a scalpel from shoulder to shoulder, then down to the pelvis, making a small detour around the navel. I observe Dr. Sam Terry's image on closed-circuit TV and hit a button with my elbow to open the bay door. He is one of our odontologists, or forensic dentists, whose bad luck it is to be on call Christmas Eve.

"I'm thinking we need to drop by and pay her a visit while we're in the area," Marino goes on. "I got her address, the girlfriend. The condo where they live." He glances down at the body. "Lived, I guess."

"And you think Stanfield can keep his mouth shut?" I reflect back tissue with staccato cuts of the scalpel, awkwardly gripping forceps in the gloved fingertips of my plaster-bound left hand.

"Yeah. Says he'll meet us at the motel, which ain't being real friendly, moaning and groaning it's Christmas Eve and they don't want any more attention because it's already hurt their business. Something like ten cancellations because of people hearing about it on the news. Yeah, like bullshit, is what I say. Most the people who stay in that dump probably don't know shit about what's happened around here or care."

Dr. Terry walks in, his scuffed black doctor's bag in hand, a fresh surgical gown untied in back and billowing as he heads to the counter. He is our youngest and newest odontologist and is almost seven feet tall. Legend has it that he could have had a career with the NBA but wanted to continue his education. The truth, and he'll tell you if you ask, is he was a mediocre guard at Virginia Commonwealth University, that the only good shooting he has ever done is with guns, the only good rebounding is with women and he only went into dentistry because he couldn't get into medical school. Terry desperately wanted to be a forensic pathologist. What he's doing as basically a volunteer is as close as he will ever get.

"Thank you, thank you," I tell him as he begins arranging his paperwork on a clipboard. "You are a good man to come help us out this morning, Sam."

He grins, then jerks his head at Marino and says in his most exaggerated New Jersey accent, "How'ya doin', Marino?"

"You ever seen the Grinch steal Christmas? 'Cause if you haven't, just hang out with me for a while. I'm in a mood to take back little kids' toys and pat their mamas on the ass on my way up the chimney."

"Don't you be trying to go up no chimneys. You'll get stuck for sure."

"Hell, you could look out the top of a chimney and still have your feet in the fireplace. You still growing?"

"Not as much as you are, man. What you weighing in these days?" Terry thumbs through the dental charts Marino brought in. "Well, this won't take long. He's got a rotated right maxillary second premolar, the distal surface lingual. Annnndddd . . . lots of restorations. Saying this guy"—he holds up the charts—"and your guy are one and the same."

"How about them Rams beating Louisville?" Marino calls out above the drumming of running water.

"Were you there?"

"Nope, and you wasn't either, Terry, which is why they won."

"Probably true."

I pluck a surgical knife off the cart as the phone rings.

"Sam, you mind getting that?" I ask.

He trots to the corner, snaps up the phone and announces, "Morgue." I cut through the costochondral cartilage junctions, removing a triangle of sternum and parasternal ribs. "Hold on," Terry says to whoever has him on the line. "Dr. Scarpetta? Can you talk to Benton Wesley?"

The room becomes a vacuum that sucks out all light and sound. I freeze, staring, stunned, the steel surgical knife poised in my bloody, gloved right hand.

"What the fuck?" Marino blurts out. He strides over to Terry and snatches the phone from him. "Who the hell is this?" he yells into the mouthpiece. "Shit." He tosses the receiver back into the cradle on the wall. Obviously, the person hung up. Terry looks stricken. He has no idea what just happened. He hasn't known me long. There is no reason for him to know about Benton unless someone else told him, and apparently no one has.

"What exactly did the person say to you?" Marino asks Terry.

"I hope I didn't do something wrong."

"No, no." I find my voice. "You didn't," I reassure him.

"Some man," he replies. "All he said is he wanted to speak to you and he said his name was Benton Wesley."

Marino picks up the phone again and swears and fumes because there is no Caller ID. We have never had occasion to need Caller ID in the morgue. He hits several buttons and listens. He writes down a number and dials it. "Yeah. Who's this?" he demands over the line to whoever has picked up. "Where? Okay. You see someone else using this phone just a minute ago? The one you're talking on. Uh huh. Yeah, well, I don't believe you, asshole." He slams down the receiver.

"You think it's the same one who just called?" Terry asks him in confusion. "What'd you do, hit star sixty-nine?"

"A pay phone. At the Texaco on Midlothian Turnpike. Supposedly. I don't know if it's the same person who called. What was his voice like?" Marino pins Terry with a stare.

"He sort of sounded young. I think. I don't know. Who's Benton Wesley?"

"He's dead." I reach for the scalpel, pushing the point down on a cutting board, snapping in a new blade and dropping the old in a bright red bio-hazard plastic container. "He was a friend, a close friend."

"Some squirrel playing a sick joke. How would anybody know the number down here?" Marino is upset. He is furious. He wants to find the caller and pound him. And he is considering that his malevolent son may be behind this. I can read it in Marino's eyes. He is thinking about Rocky.

"Under state government listings in the phone book." I begin cutting blood vessels, severing the carotids very low at the apex, moving down to the iliac arteries and veins of the pelvis.

"Don't tell me it says *morgue* in the goddamn phone book." Marino starts up his old routine again. He is blaming me.

"I think it's listed under funeral information." I cut through the thin flat muscle of the diaphragm, loosening the bloc of organs, freeing it from the vertebral column. Lungs, liver, heart, kidneys, and spleen shimmer different hues of red as I lay the bloc on the cutting board and wash off blood with a gentle hosing of cold water. I notice pe-techial hemorrhages, dark areas of bleeding no bigger than pin pricks scattered over the heart and lungs. I associate this with persons who had difficulty breathing at or about the time of death.

Terry carries his black bag over to my station and sets it on the surgical cart. He gets out a dental mirror and goes inside the dead man's mouth. We work in silence, the weight of what has just occurred pressing down hard. I reach for a bigger knife and cut sections of organs, slicing through the heart. The coronary arteries are open and clear, the left ventricle one centimeter wide, the valves normal. Other than a few fatty streaks in the aorta, the heart and vessels are healthy. The only thing wrong with it is the obvious: It quit. For some reason, this man's heart stopped. I find no explanation anywhere I look.

"Like I said, this one's easy," Terry says as he makes notes on a chart. His voice is nervous. He wishes he had never answered the phone.

"He's our guy?" I ask him.

"Sure is."

The carotid arteries lie like rails in the neck. Between them are the tongue and neck muscles, which I flip down and peel away so I can examine them closely on the cutting board. There are no hemorrhages in deep tissue. The tiny, fragile U-shaped hyoid bone is intact. He wasn't strangled. When I reflect back his scalp, I find no contusions or fractures hiding underneath. I plug a Stryker saw into the overhead cord reel and realize I need more than one hand. Terry helps me steady the head as I push the whining, vibrating semicircular blade through the skull. Hot, bony dust drifts on the air, and the skullcap lifts off with a soft sucking sound, revealing the convoluted horizon of the brain. On gross examination, there is nothing wrong with it. Slices gleam like creamy agate with gray ruffled edges as I rinse them on the cutting board. I will save the brain and heart for further special studies, fixing them in formalin and sending them to the Medical College of Virginia.

My diagnosis this morning is one of exclusion. Having found no obvious, pathological cause of death, I am left with one that is based on whispers. Tiny hemorrhages on heart and lungs and burns and abrasions from bondage suggest Mitch Barbosa died from stress-induced arrhythmia. I also postulate that at some point he was holding his breath or his airway was obstructed—or for some reason his breathing was compromised to the extent that he partially asphyxiated. Perhaps the gag, which would have gotten wet from saliva, is to blame. Whatever the truth, I am getting a picture that is simple and ghastly and calls for demonstration. Terry and Marino are handy.

First I cut off several lengths of the thick white twine that we routinely use to suture up Y-incisions. I tell Marino to push up the sleeves of his surgical gown and hold out his hands. I tie one segment of twine around one wrist and a second strand around the other, not too tight, but snug. I instruct him to hold his arms up in the air and direct Terry to grab the loose ends of twine and pull up. Terry is tall enough to do this without a chair or footstool. The bindings immediately dig into the underside of Marino's wrists and are angled up toward the knots. We try this in different positions, with variations of the arms close together and spread wide crucifixion-style. Of course, Marino's feet remain squarely on the floor. In no instance is he hanging or even dangling.

"The weight of a body on outstretched arms interferes with exhalation," I explain. "You can inhale but it's difficult exhaling because the intercostal muscles are compromised. Over a period of time, this would lead to asphyxia. You add that to the shock of pain from torture, you add fear and panic, and you could certainly suffer from an arrhythmia."

"What about the nosebleed?" Marino holds out his wrists and I examine the indentations the twine has left in his skin. They are angled up similarly to those on the dead man.

"Increased intracranial pressure," I say. "In a breath-holding situation, you can get nosebleeds. In the absence of injury, that's a good guess."

"My question is whether someone *meant* to kill him?" Terry poses.

"Most people aren't going to string someone up

and torture him and then let him go to tell the story," I reply. "I'll pend his cause and manner for now until we see what tox has to say." My eyes light on Marino's. "But I believe you'd best treat this as a homicide, a very awful one."

We contemplate this later in the morning as we drive toward James City County. Marino wanted to take his truck, and I suggested we follow Route 5 east along the river, through Charles City County where eighteenth-century plantations fan out from the roadside in vast fallow fields that lead to the awesome brick mansions and outbuildings of Sherwood Forest, Westover, Berkeley, Shirley and Belle Air. There isn't a tour bus in sight, no logging trucks or roadwork, and country stores are closed. It is Christmas Eve. The sun shines through endless arches of old trees, shadows dapple pavement and Smoky the Bear asks for help from a sign in a gracious part of the world where two men have died barbarically. It does not seem that anything so heinous could happen here until we get to The Fort James Motel and Camp Ground. Tucked off Route 5 in the woods, it is a hodgepodge of cabins, trailers and motel buildings that are rusting and paint-peeled, reminding me of Hogan's Alley at the FBI Academy: cheaply constructed facades where shady people are about to get raided by the law.

The rental office is in a small frame house overwhelmed by scrubby pines that have carpeted the roof and earth in brown tags. Soft-drink and ice machines in front glow through overgrown bushes. Children's bicycles lie wounded in leaves, and ancient seesaws and swings aren't to be trusted. A homely mixed-breed dog that sags with a history of chronic breeding rises to her old feet and stares at us from the sloping porch.

"I thought Stanfield was meeting us here." I open my door.

"Go figure." Marino climbs out of the truck, his eyes moving everywhere.

A veil of smoke drifts out the chimney and streams almost horizontally with the wind, and through a window I catch winking, gaudy Christmas lights. I feel eyes on us. A curtain moves, the sounds of a television muted from deep within the house as we wait on the porch and the dog sniffs my hand and licks me. Marino announces our arrival with a fist pounding the door, and finally calls out, "Anybody home? Hey!" Banging his fist hard. "Police!"

"I'm coming, I'm coming," an impatient woman's voice sings out. A hard, tired face fills the space of the opening door, the burglar chain still anchored and taut.

"You Mrs. Kiffin?" Marino asks her.

"Who are you?" she asks him back.

"Captain Marino, Richmond P.D. This is Dr. Scarpetta."

"What you bringing a doctor for?" Brow furrowing, she glances at me from her shadowy crack. A stirring at her feet, and a child peeks out at us and smiles like an imp. "Zack, you go back inside." Small bare arms, hands with dirty nails wrap around mama's knee. She shakes him loose. "Go on!" He disconnects and is gone.

"Going to need you to show us the room where the fire was," Marino tells her. "Detective Stanfield with James City County should be here. You seen him?"

"No police been here this morning." She pushes the door shut and the burglar chain rattles as she removes it, then the door opens again, this time wide, and she steps out on the porch, pushing her arms into the sleeves of a lumberjack's red plaid coat, a ring of keys jingling in her hand. She yells into the house, "Y'all stay! Zack, don't you get into the cookie dough! I'll be right back." She shuts the door. "Never seen anybody love cookie dough like that boy," she tells us as we go down the steps. "Sometimes I buy the premade in rolls and one day I catch Zack eating one, wrapper peeled down like a banana. Ate half of it by the time I caught him. I told him, You know what's in it? *Raw eggs*, that's what."

Bev Kiffin is probably no more than forty-five, her prettiness hard and garish like truck-stop cafes and late-night diners. Her hair is dyed bright blond and is curly like a French poodle, her dimples deep, her figure ripe on the way to matronly. She has a defensive, obstinate air about her that I associate with people who are used to being worn down and in trouble. I would also call her shifty. I am about to distrust every word she says.

"I don't want problems out here," she lets us know. "As if I don't have enough going on, especially this time of year," she says as she walks. "All these people pulling in here morning, noon and night to gawk and take pictures."

"What people?" Marino asks her.

"Just people in cars, pulling up in the drive, staring. Some of them getting out and roaming around. Last night I woke up when someone drove through. It was two A.M."

Marino lights a cigarette. We follow Kiffin through the shade of pines along an overgrown path of churned-up snow, past old campers that list like unseaworthy ships. Near a picnic table is a nest of personal belongings that at first glance look like trash from a campsite someone didn't clean up. But then I see the unexpected: an odd collection of toys, dolls, paperback books, sheets, two pillows, a blanket, a double baby carriage— items that are soggy and dirty not because they were worthless and deliberately pitched but because they have been inadvertently exposed to the elements. Scattered throughout are shredded plastic wrappers that instantly connect with the fragment I found clinging to the first victim's burned back. The fragments are white, blue and bright orange and are ripped in narrow strips, as if whoever did it has a nervous habit of picking things to pieces.

"Someone sure left in a hurry," Marino comments.

Kiffin is watching me.

"Maybe skipped without settling the bill?" Marino says.

"Oh no." She seems in a hurry to move on to the small tawdry motel showing through trees ahead. "They paid up front like everyone else. A family with two little ones staying in a tent and all of a sudden they hightailed it out of here. Don't know why they left all that. Some of it, like the baby buggy's pretty nice. Course, then it snowed on everything."

A gust of wind scatters several bits of wrappers like confetti. I wander closer and nudge a pillow with my foot, turning it over. A pungent, sour odor rises to my nostrils as I squat and take a closer look. Clinging to the underside of the pillow is hair—long, pale hair, very fine hair that has no pigmentation. My heart thuds like the sudden, unexpected kick of a bass drum. I move the shredded wrappers around with my finger. The plasticized material is pliable but tough, so it doesn't tear easily unless you start at a crinkled edge where the wrapper was heat-sealed together. Some of the fragments are large and easily recognizable as having come from PayDay peanut-caramel candy bars. I can even make out the website address for Hershey's Chocolate. More hair on the blanket, short, dark hair, a pubic hair. And several more of the long, pale hairs.

"PayDay candy bars," I say to Marino. I look at Kiffin as I open my satchel. "Know anybody out here who eats a lot of PayDay candy bars and picks apart the wrappers?"

"Well, it didn't come from my house." As if we have accused her, or maybe Zack and his sweet tooth.

I do not carry my aluminum crime scene case to scenes where there is no body. But I always keep an emergency kit in my satchel, a heavy-duty freezer bag filled with disposable gloves, evidence bags, swabs, a tiny vial of distilled water and gun-shot residue (GSR) kits, among other items. I remove the cap from a GSR kit. It is nothing more than a small, clear plastic stub with an adhesive tip that I use to collect three hairs from the pillow and two from the blanket. I seal the stub and the hairs inside a small transparent plastic evidence bag.

"You don't mind my asking?" Kiffin says to me. "What are you doing that for?"

"Think I'll just bag all this crap, the whole campsite, and take it in to the labs." Marino is suddenly low-key, calm like a seasoned poker player. He knows how to handle Kiffin, and now she has to be handled because he also knows all too well that hypertrichotic people have unique hair, fine, unpigmented, rudimentary, baby-like hair. Only baby hair is not six or seven inches long like the hair Chandonne shed at his crime scenes. It is possible that Jean-Baptiste Chandonne has been to this campground. "You manage this place by yourself?" Marino asks Kiffin.

"Pretty much."

"When did the family in the tent leave? It's not exactly tent weather."

"They were here right before it snowed. Late last week."

"You ever find out why they left in such a hurry?" Marino keeps probing in his bland tone.

"Haven't heard from them, not a word."

"We're going to need to take a better look at what all they left behind."

Kiffin blows on her bare hands to warm them and hugs herself, turning away from the wind. She looks back at her house and you can almost see her contemplating what kind of trouble life holds for her and her family this time. Marino motions for me to follow him. "Wait here," he tells Kiffin. "We'll be right back. Just gonna get something out of my truck. Don't touch nothing, all right?"

She watches us walk off. Marino and I talk in low voices. Hours before Chandonne appeared at my front door, Marino was out with the response team searching for him, and they discovered where he was hiding in Richmond in the mansion under major renovation on the James River, very close to my neighborhood. Since he rarely if ever went out during daylight hours, we assume, his comings and goings went undetected as he hid in the house and helped himself to whatever was there. Until this moment, it never occurred to any of us that Chandonne might have stayed anyplace else.

"You think he scared off whoever was in that tent so he could use it?" Marino unlocks his truck and reaches in the back of the cab where I know, for one thing, he keeps a pump-action shotgun. "Because I gotta tell ya, Doc. Something we noticed when we went inside that house on the James was junk food wrappers everywhere. A lot of candy bar wrappers." He lifts out a red tool box and shuts the door of the truck. "Like he's got a real sugar thing."

"Do you remember what kind of junk food?"

I remember all the Pepsis Chandonne drank while Berger was interviewing him.

"Snickers bars. I don't remember if there were PayDays. But candy. Peanuts. Those little bags of Planter's peanuts, and now that I think of it, the wrappers were all tore up."

"Christ," I mutter, suddenly chilled to the marrow. "I wonder if he might have low blood sugar." I try to be clinical, to regain my balance. Fear returns like a swarm of bats.

"What the hell was he doing out here?" Marino says, and he keeps staring in the direction of Kiffin in the distance, making sure she isn't tampering with anything in a campsite that has now become part of a crime scene. "And how the hell did he get here? Maybe he did have a car."

"Any vehicles at the house where he was hiding?" I ask as Kiffin watches our return, a solitary figure in red plaid, breath emerging in smoky puffs.

"The people that own the mansion, they didn't keep any cars there while all the work was going on," Marino tells me in a voice Kiffin can't hear. "Maybe he stole something and kept it parked somewhere it wasn't going to be noticed. I just assumed the squirrel didn't even know how to drive, seeing as how he pretty much lived in the dungeon in his family's house in Paris."

"Yes. More assumptions," I mutter, remembering Chandonne's claiming he drove one of those green motorcycles to clean Paris sidewalks, doubting the story but not much else any longer. We are back at the picnic table, and Marino sets down the toolbox and opens it. He gets out leather work gloves and puts them on, then shakes open several fifty-gallon heavy-duty garbage bags and I hold them open. We fill three bags, and he cuts open a fourth and drapes sections of black plastic over the baby carriage and tapes them together. While he is doing this, he explains to Kiffin that it is possible someone scared off the family who was staying in this tent. He suggests that maybe a stranger claimed squatter's rights at this site, even if for only a night. Did she at any point have a sense of anything out of the ordinary, including an unfamiliar vehicle in the area prior to last Saturday? He poses all this as if it would never occur to him that she would tarnish the truth.

We know, of course, that Chandonne could not have been here after Saturday. He has been in custody since then. Kiffin is no help. She claims she was aware of nothing out of the ordinary except that early one morning she went out for firewood and noticed the tent was gone but the family's belongings were still here, or at least part of them. She can't swear to it, but the more Marino prods her, the more she believes she noticed the tent gone around eight A.M., last Friday. Chandonne murdered Diane Bray on Thursday night. Did he then flee afterward to James City County to hide? I imagine him appearing at the tent, a couple and their small children inside. One look at him and it is believable they would have jumped into their car and sped off without bothering to pack.

We carry the trash bags to Marino's truck and put them in back. Again, Kiffin awaits our return, hands in the pockets of her jacket, her face rosy from the cold. The motel is straight ahead through pine trees, a small, boxy white structure, two stories with doors painted the color of evergreens. Behind the motel are more woods, then a wide creek that branches off from the James River.

"How many people you got staying here right now?" Marino asks the woman who runs this dreadful tourist trap.

"Right now? Maybe thirteen, depending on whether anybody else's checked out. Lot of people just leave their key in the room and I don't know they're gone until I go in to clean up. You know, I left my cigarettes in the house," she says to Marino without looking at him. "You mind?"

Marino sets down his toolbox on the path. He shakes a cigarette loose from the pack and lights it for her. Her upper lip crinkles like crepe paper when she sucks in smoke, inhaling deeply and blowing out one side of her mouth. My lust for tobacco stirs. My fractured elbow complains about the cold. I can't stop thinking about the family in the tent and their terror—if it is true that Chandonne showed up and the family exists. If he did come directly here after murdering Bray, what happened to his clothes? He had to have gotten blood all over himself. Did he leave Bray's house and come out here covered with blood and frighten strangers out of their tent, and no one called the police or said a word to anyone?

"How many people were staying here night before last, when the fire started?" Marino picks up his toolbox and we start walking again.

"I know how many were checked in." She is vague. "Don't know who was still here. Eleven had checked in, including him."

"Including the man who died in the fire?" It is my turn to ask questions.

Kiffin throws a look at me. "That's right."

"Tell me about his checking in," Marino says to her as we walk and pause to look around, and then walk on. "You see him drive up like we just did? Appears to me cars just pull right up to the front of your house."

She starts shaking her head. "No sir. Didn't see no car. There was a knock on the door and I opened it. Told him to go next door to the office and I'd meet him there. He was a nice-looking man, well-dressed, didn't look like the usual I get, that much stands out clear as day."

"He tell you his name?" Marino asks her.

"Paid cash."

"So if someone pays cash, you don't get them to fill out nothing."

"Can if they want. Don't have to. I have a registration pad you can fill out and then I tear off the receipt. He said he didn't need a receipt."

"He have an accent or anything?"

"He didn't sound like he was from these parts."

"Could you place where he sounded from? Northern? Maybe foreign?" Marino keeps on as we pause again beneath pines.

She looks around, thinking and smoking as we follow her along a muddy path that leads to the motel parking lot. "Not deep South," she decides. "But he didn't sound like he was from a foreign country. You know, he didn't say much. Said as little as he had to. I got a feeling, you know. like he was in a hurry and sort of nervous, and he sure wasn't chatty." This sounds completely fabricated. Her tone of voice actually changes.

"Anybody staying in these campers?" Marino then asks.

"I rent 'em out. People don't come with their own campers right now. It's off-season for camping."

"Anybody renting them now?"

"No. Nobody."

In front of the motel, a chair with ripped up-holstery has been placed near a Coke machine and pay phone. There are several cars in the lot, American-made, not new. A Granada, an LTD, a Firebird. There is no sign of whoever might own them.

"Who do you get this time of year?" I inquire.

"A mixture," Kiffin goes on as we cross the parking lot to the south end of the building.

I scan wet asphalt.

"Folks who aren't getting along. That's a lot of it this time of year. People fussing and one or the other walks out or gets kicked out and needs a place to stay. Or people driving a long distance to visit family and need a place for the night. Or when the river floods like it did a couple months back, some people come here because I allow pets. And I get tourists."

"People seeing Williamsburg and Jamestown?" I ask.

"A fair number of people here to see Jamestown. That's picked up quite a bit since they started digging up the graves out there. Funny how people are."

CHAPTER 22

ROOM SEVENTEEN IS ON THE first level at the very end. Crime scene tape is a bright yellow ribbon across the door. The location is remote, at the edge of thick woods that buffer the motel from Route 5.

I am especially interested in any vegetation or debris that might be on the asphalt directly in front of the room, where rescuers would have dragged the body. I note dirt and bits of dead leaves and cigarette butts. I am wondering if the fragment of candy bar wrapper I found adhering to the dead man's back came from inside the room or from out here in the parking lot. If it came from inside the room, that could mean the killer tracked it in, or it could mean that the killer walked through or close to the abandoned camp-site at some point prior to the murder, unless the bit of paper had been inside the room for a while, perhaps tracked in by Kiffin herself when she came in to clean after the last guest checked out. Evidence is tricky. You always have to consider its origin and not draw conclusions based on where the evidence ended up. Fibers on a body, for example, might have been transferred from the killer, who picked them up from a carpet where they were deposited originally by someone who tracked them into a house after yet another individual left them on a car seat.

"Did he ask for a particular room?" I ask Kiffin as she goes through keys on the ring.

"Said he wanted something private. Seventeen didn't have anybody on either side or above, so that's what I gave him. What'd you do to your arm?"

"Slipped on ice."

"Oh, that's too bad. You got to wear that cast a long time?"

"Not much longer."

"You get the sense he might have had anybody with him?" Marino asks her.

"Didn't see anybody else." She speaks tersely with Marino but is friendlier toward me. I feel her glancing at my face frequently and have the sinking feeling she has seen my photograph in the papers or on television. "What kind of doctor did you say you are?" she quizzes me.

"I'm a medical examiner."

"Oh." She brightens. "Like Quincy. Used to

love that show. You remember that one where he could tell everything about a person from one bone?" She turns the key in the lock and opens the door and the air turns acrid with the dirty stench of fire. "I just thought that was the most amazing thing. Race, gender, even what he did for a living and how big he was, and exactly when and how he died, all from one little bone." The door opens wide onto a scene that is as dark and filthy as a coal mine. "Can't tell you how much this is going to cost me," she says as we move past her and step inside. "Insurance won't ever cover something like this. Never does. Damn insurance companies."

"I'm going to need you to wait outside," Marino says to Kiffin.

The only light is what spills through the open doorway, and I make out the shape of the double bed. In the center of it is a crater where the mattress burned down to the bed springs. Marino turns on a flashlight and a long finger of light moves through the room, starting with the closet just right of where I am standing near the doorway. Two bent wire hangers dangle from the wooden rod. The bathroom is just left of the door, and against the wall opposite the bed is a dresser. Something is on top of the dresser, a book. It is open. Marino walks closer to illuminate the pages. "Gideon Bible," he says.

The light moves on to the far end of the room, where there are two chairs and a small table before a window and a back door. Marino opens the curtains and wan sunlight seeps into the room. The only fire damage I can see is to the bed, which smoldered and produced a lot of dense smoke. Everything inside the room is covered with soot, and this is an unexpected forensic gift. "The entire room's been smoked," I marvel out loud.

"Huh?" Marino shines the light around as I dig out my portable phone. I see no evidence that Stanfield tried looking for latent prints in here, not that I blame him. Most investigators would assume the intense soot and smoke damage would obliterate fingerprints, when in fact, the opposite is true. Heat and soot tend to process latent prints, and there is an old laboratory method called *smoking* used on nonporous objects such as shiny metals, which tend to have a Teflon effect when traditional dusting powders are applied. Latent prints are actually transferred to an object because the friction ridge surfaces of fingers and palms have oily residues on them. It is these residues that end up on some surface: a doorknob, a drinking glass, a window pane. Heat softens the residues, and smoke and soot then adhere to them. During cooling the residues become fixed or firm and the soot can be gently brushed away like dusting powder. Before Super Glue fuming and alternate light sources, it was not uncommon to conjure up prints by burning tarry pine chips, camphor and magnesium. It is very possible that beneath the patina of soot in this room there is a galaxy of latent fingerprints that have already been processed for us.

I call fingerprints section chief Neils Vander at home and explain the situation, and he says he will meet us at the motel in two hours. Marino is caught up in other preoccupations, his attention fixated on some spot above the bed, where he is shining the light. "Holy shit," he mutters. "Doc, would you look at this?" He illuminates two sooty eyebolts screwed into the drywall ceiling about three feet apart. "Hey!" he calls through the doorway to Kiffin.

She peers inside the room and looks where he shines the light.

"You got any idea why these bolts are in the ceiling?" he asks her.

She gets a strange expression on her face, her voice going up a note, the way it does when she is being evasive, I think. "Never seen them before. Now I wonder how that happened?" she declares.

"Last time you were in this room was when?" Marino asks her.

"A couple days before he checked in. When I cleaned it after the last person checked out, the last person before him, I mean."

"The bolts weren't here then?"

"I didn't notice, if they were."

"Mrs. Kiffin, you just hang outside there in case we got more questions."

Marino and I put on gloves. He splays his fingers, rubber stretching and snapping. The window next to the back door overlooks a swimming pool that is filled with dirty water. Across from the bed is a small Zenith television on a stand, a note taped to it reminding guests to turn the TV off before they go out. The room is rather much what Stanfield described, but he did not mention the Gideon Bible open on the dresser, or that to the right of the bed near the floor there is an electrical outlet with two unplugged cords on the carpet next to it, one to the lamp on the bedside table, the other to the clock radio. The clock radio is old. It isn't digital. When it was unplugged, the hands stopped at 3:12 P.M. Marino tells Kiffin to step inside the room again. "What time did you say he checked in?" he asks.

"Oh, 'round three." She is just inside the doorway, staring blankly at the clock. "Looks like he came in and unplugged the clock and the lamp, now doesn't it? That's kind of strange, unless maybe he was plugging something else in and needed the outlet. Some of these business types have those laptop computers."

"Did you notice if he had one?" Marino glances at her.

"I didn't notice he had anything except what looked like a car key and his wallet."

"You didn't say nothing about a wallet. You saw a wallet?"

"Pulled it out to pay me. Black leather, as I recall. Expensive looking, like everything else he had. Might have been alligator or something," she adds to her story.

"How much cash he pay you and in what kind of bills?"

"A hundred-dollar bill and four twenties. He told me to keep the change. The total was one hundred and sixty dollars and seventy cents."

"Oh yeah. The sixteen-oh-seven special," Marino says in a monotone. He doesn't like Kiffin. He certainly doesn't trust her worth a damn, but he keeps it to himself, playing her like a hand of cards. If I didn't know him so well, he might fool even me.

"You got some kind of stepladder around here?" Marino says next.

She hesitates. "Well, I guess so." She is gone again, the door left standing wide open.

Marino gets down to take a closer look at the outlet and unplugged cords. "You think they plugged the heat gun in here?" He ponders this out loud.

"It's possible. *If* we're talking about a heat gun," I remind him.

"I've used them to thaw my pipes and to get ice off my front steps. Works like a charm." He is looking under the bed with the flashlight. "Never had a case where one was used on a person. Jesus. He must've been gagged pretty good for no one to hear anything. Wonder why they unplugged both things, the lamp and the clock?"

"Maybe so it didn't throw the circuit breaker?"

"In a joint like this, yeah, maybe. A heat gun's probably about the same voltage as a blow-dryer. One-twenty, one-twenty-five. And a blow-dryer would probably knock out the lights in a dump like this."

I move over to the dresser and look at the Bible. It is open to the sixth and seventh chapters of Ecclesiastes, and the exposed pages are sooty, the area of dresser under the Bible spared, indicating this was the position the Bible was in when the fire started. The question is whether the Bible was open like this before the victim checked in, or does it even belong with the room, for that matter? My eyes wander down lines and stop at the first verse of the seventh chapter. *A good name is better than precious ointment; and the day of death than the day of one's birth.* I read it to Marino. I tell him that this section of Ecclesiastes is about vanity.

"Kind of fits with the queer thing, don't it?" he comments as aluminum scrapes outside and Kiffin returns with a rush of wintry air. Marino takes a paint-spattered, bent ladder from her and opens the legs. He climbs up and shines the flashlight on the bolts. "Damn, I think I need new glasses. I can't see nothing," he says as I hold the ladder steady.

"Want me to look?" I offer.

"Help yourself." He climbs back down.

I take a small magnifying lens from my satchel and up I go. He hands me the light and I examine the eyebolts. I can't see any fibers. If there are any, we are not going to have any luck collecting them here. The problem is how to preserve one type of evidence without ruining another, and there are three possible types of evidence that might be associated with the eyebolts: finger-prints, fibers and tool marks. If we dust off soot to look for latents, we might lose fibers that could match the ligature that might have been threaded through the eyebolts, which we also can't un-screw without risking the introduction of new tool marks, assuming we use a tool such as pliers. The biggest threat is inadvertently eradicating any possible prints. In fact, the conditions and light-ing are so bad that we shouldn't be examining anything here, really. I get an idea. "If you can hand me a couple baggies," I tell Marino. "And tape."

He hands me two small, transparent plastic bags.

I slip one over each eyebolt and carefully wrap tape around the top of the bag, careful not to touch any part of the bolt or the ceiling. I climb back down while Marino opens his tool box. "Hate to do this to you," he says to Kiffin, who hovers outside the door, hands deep in her pockets, trying to keep warm. "But I'm gonna have to cut out part of the ceiling."

"Like that's gonna make much difference at this point," she says in a voice of resignation, or is it indifference I detect? "May as well," she adds.

I am still wondering why the fire only smoldered. This has really got me stuck. I ask Kiffin what type of linens and mattress cover were on the bed.

"Well, they were green," she seems sure of herself on this point. "The bedspread was dark green, sort of like the color the doors are painted. Not that we know what happened to the linens. The sheets were white."

"Do you have any idea what they were made of?" I ask.

"I'm pretty sure the bedspreads are polyester."

Polyester is so combustible that I try to remember never to wear synthetic materials when I fly. If we have a crash landing and there is a fire, the last thing I want against my flesh is polyester. I may as well douse myself with gasoline. If a polyester bedspread had been on the bed when the fire was set, more than likely the entire room would have gone up in flames, and quickly. "Where did you get the mattresses?" I ask her.

She hesitates. She doesn't want to tell me. "Well," she finally gets around to what I believe is the truth, "new ones are awfully expensive. I get secondhand ones when I can."

"From where?"

"Well, from that prison they closed down in Richmond a few years back," she tells me.

"Spring Street?"

"That's right. Now, I didn't get anything that I wouldn't sleep on myself." She defends her choice in fine bedding. "Got the newest ones from them."

This might explain why the mattress only smoldered and never really caught fire. In hospitals and prisons, mattresses are treated heavily with flame retardants. This also suggests that whoever set the fire wouldn't have had any reason to know he was trying to burn a mattress specially treated with flame retardants. And of course, common sense would have it that this person also did not hang around long enough to know that the fire went out on its own. "Mrs. Kiffin," I say, "is there a Bible in every room?"

"The one thing folks don't steal." She avoids my question, taking on a suspicious tone of voice again.

"Do you know why this one in here is open to Ecclesiastes?"

"Now I don't go around opening them. I just leave them on the dresser. I didn't open it." She hesitates, then announces, "He must have been murdered or everybody wouldn't be going to all this trouble."

"We have to look into every possibility," Marino remarks as he climbs back up the ladder, a small hacksaw in hand that is helpful at scenes like this because the teeth are hardened and aren't angled. They can cut elements *in situ*, or in place, such as trim molding, baseboard, pipes or, in this instance, joists.

"Business has been hard," Mrs. Kiffin says. "I'm on my own because my husband's on the road all the time."

"What does your husband do?" I inquire.

"A truck driver for Overland Transfer."

Marino begins popping out drywall tiles from the ceiling around the ones the eyebolts are screwed through.

"I don't imagine he's home much," I say.

Her lower lip trembles almost imperceptibly and her eyes brighten with pain. "I don't need a murder. Oh Lord, it's going to hurt me bad."

"Doc, you mind holding the light for me?" Marino doesn't respond to her sudden need for sympathy.

"Murder hurts many people." I train the flashlight on the ceiling, my good arm steadying the ladder again. "That's a sad, unfair fact, Mrs. Kiffin."

Marino starts sawing, wood dust drifting down.

"I've never had anybody die here," she whines some more. "Not much worse can happen to a place."

"Hey," Marino quips to her above the noise of sawing, "you'll probably get business from the publicity."

She gives him a black look. "Those types can just stay the hell away."

FROM THE PHOTOGRAPHS STANFIELD showed me, I recognize the area of wall where the body was propped up and I get the general idea where the clothing was found. I imagine the victim nude on the bed, his arms strung up by rope threaded through the eyebolts. He might be kneeling or even sitting—only partially hoisted up. But the crucifixion position and gag would impair his breathing. He is panting, fighting for breath, his heart palpitating furiously in panic and pain as he watches someone plug in the heat gun, as he hears air blow out when the trigger is pulled. I have never related to the human desire to torture. I know the dynamics, that it is all about control, the ultimate abuse of power. But I can't

comprehend deriving satisfaction, vindication and
certainly not sexual pleasure out of causing any
living creature pain.

My central nervous system spikes and surges,
my pulse pounds. I am sweating beneath my coat
even though it is cold enough inside the room to
see our breath. "Mrs. Kiffin," I say as Marino
strokes the saw, "five days—a business special?
This time of year?" I pause as confusion dances
across her face. She is not inside my mind. She
does not see what I see. She can't begin to imagine the horror I am reconstructing as I stand inside this cheap motel with its secondhand prison
mattresses. "Why would he check in for five days
the week of Christmas?" I want to know. "Did he
say anything at all that might have given you a hint
as to why he was here, what he was doing, where
he was from? Aside from your observation that he
didn't sound local?"

"I don't ask." She watches Marino work.
"Maybe I should. Some people talk a lot and tell
you more than you want to know. Some don't
want you in their business."

"What feeling did you get from him?" I keep
prodding her.

"Well, Mr. Peanut didn't like him."

"Who the hell is Mr. Peanut?" Marino reaches
down with a ceiling tile that is attached by an eyebolt to a four-inch section of joist.

"Our dog. You probably noticed her when you came in. I know it's kind of a funny name for a female that's had as many puppies as that one, but Zack named her. Mr. Peanut just barked her head off right when that man showed up at the door. Wouldn't come near him, the fur just standing up on her back."

"Or maybe your dog was barking and upset because someone else was around? Someone you didn't see?" I suggest.

"Could be."

A second ceiling tile drops, and the ladder shakes as Marino descends. He goes back into his toolbox for a roll of freezer paper and evidence tape and begins wrapping the ceiling tiles in neat packages as I walk into the bathroom and shine the light around. Everything is institutional white, the top of the counter scarred with yellowish burns, probably from guests parking lit cigarettes while they shave or put on makeup or fix their hair. I see something else Stanfield missed. A single strand of dental floss dangles inside the toilet. It is draped over the edge of the bowl and trapped under the seat. With a gloved hand, I pick it up. It is about a foot long, several inches of it wet from toilet water, and the midsection of it pale red, as if someone flossed his teeth and his gums bled. Because this latest find isn't perfectly dry, I don't seal it in plastic. I place it in a square of freezer paper which I fold into a jeweler's envelope. We probably have DNA. The question is, whose?

Marino and I return to his truck at one-thirty, and Mr. Peanut flies out of the house when Kiffin yanks open the front door to go back inside the house. The dog chases us as we pull out, barking. I watch in the side mirror as Kiffin yells at her dog. "You get here right now!" She angrily claps her hands. "Come here now!"

"Some asshole take time out from torture to floss his teeth?" Marino starts in. "Like what the hell is that about? Or more likely, it's been hanging out in the toilet since last Christmas."

Mr. Peanut is now right by my door, the truck bumping over the unpaved drive that leads through woods to Route 5.

"Come here now!" Kiffin bellows as she comes down the steps, hands *smack-smack-smack*.

"Goddamn dog," Marino complains.

"Stop!" I am afraid we are going to run over the poor animal.

Marino stamps the brakes and the truck lurches to a halt. Mr. Peanut jumps up barking, her head bobbing in and out of my window. "What in the world?" I am baffled. The dog was scarcely interested in us when we first showed up a few hours ago.

"Get back here!" Kiffin is coming after her dog. Behind her, a child fills the doorway, not the little boy we saw earlier, but someone as tall as Kiffin.

I get out of the truck and Mr. Peanut starts wagging her tail. She nuzzles my hand. The poor, wretched creature is dirty and smells bad. I get her by the collar and tug her in the direction of her family, but she doesn't want to leave the truck. "Come on," I talk to her. "Let's get you home before you get run over."

Kiffin strides up, just livid. She pops the dog hard on top of the head. Mr. Peanut bleats like an injured lamb, tail tucked, cowering. "You learn to mind, you hear me?" Kiffin furiously wags her finger at her dog. "Get in the house!"

Mr. Peanut sneaks behind me.

"Get!"

The dog sits down in the dirt behind me, pressing its trembling body against my legs. The person I saw in the doorway has vanished, but Zack has emerged on the porch. He is dressed in jeans and a sweatshirt that are way too big. "Come 'ere, Peanut," he sings out, snapping his fingers. He sounds as frightened as the dog.

"Zack! Don't you make me tell you again to get your butt inside the house!" Zack's mother shouts at him.

Cruelty. Leave, and the dog will be beaten. Maybe the child will. Bev Kiffin is an out-of-control, frustrated woman. Life has made her feel powerless, and beneath her skin she seethes with hurt and anger, the unfairness of it all. Or maybe she is just plain bad, and maybe poor Mr. Peanut is running after Marino's truck because the dog wants us to take her with us, to save her. That fantasy enters my mind. "Mrs. Kiffin," I say in the calm voice of authority—that cool, cool voice I reserve for times when I intend to threaten the living shit out of somebody. "Don't you touch Mr. Peanut again unless you do it gently. I have this special thing about people who hurt animals."

Her face darkens and anger glints. I fix my stare dead center on her pupils.

"There are laws against cruelty to animals, Mrs. Kiffin," I say. "And beating Mr. Peanut is not a good example to set in front of your children." I hint that I spotted a second child she has failed to mention to us thus far.

She steps back from me, turns and walks off toward the house. Mr. Peanut sits, looking up at me. "You go home," I tell her as my heart breaks. "Go on, sweetie. You need to go home."

Zack comes down the steps and runs up to us. He takes the dog by the collar, squats and scratches between her ears, talking to her. "Be good, don't go making mama mad, Mr. Peanut. Please," he says, looking up at me. "She just don't like it 'cause you're taking her baby buggy."

This jolts me, but I don't let it show. I get down

to Zack's level and pet Mr. Peanut, trying to block out that her musky stench triggers memories of Chandonne again. Nausea twists my stomach and makes my mouth water. "The baby buggy's hers?" I ask Zack.

"When she has puppies, I take them on rides in it," Zack tells me.

"Why was it over there by the picnic table, Zack?" I ask. "I thought maybe some campers might have left it there."

He shakes his head, petting Mr. Peanut. "Uh uh. It's Mr. Peanut's buggy, isn't it, Mr. Peanut? I gotta go in." He gets up, glancing back furtively at the open front door.

"I tell you what." I get up, too. "We just need to look at Mr. Peanut's buggy, but when we're done I promise to bring it back."

"Okay." He tugs the dog after him, half running, half yanking. I stare after them as they go inside the house and shut the door. I stand in the middle of the dirt drive in the shadow of scrub pines, hands in my pockets, watching, because I have no doubt Bev Kiffin is watching me. On the street it is called signifying, making your presence known. My business isn't finished here. I'll be back.

CHAPTER 23

WE HEAD EAST ON ROUTE 5 and I am mindful of the time. Even if I could conjure up Lucy's helicopter, I would never make it back to Anna's house by two. I pull out my wallet and find the card Berger wrote her phone numbers on. There is no answer at her hotel, and I leave a message for her to pick me up at six P.M. Marino is silent as I slip the cell phone back inside my satchel. He stares straight ahead, his truck rumbling loudly along the winding, narrow road. He is processing what I just told him about the baby carriage. Bev Kiffin, of course, lied to us.

"The whole thing out there, wow," he finally says, shaking his head. "Talk about a creepy feeling. Like there were all these eyes watching everything we were doing. Like that place has a whole life of its own nobody knows nothing about."

"She knows," I reply. "She knows something.

That much is obvious, Marino. She made a point of telling us the baby carriage was left by the people who abandoned the campsite. She volunteered that without pause. Wanted us to think it. Why?"

"Those people don't exist, whoever was supposedly staying out in that tent. If the hairs turn out to be Chandonne's, then I'm gonna have to entertain the idea she let him stay out there, and that's why she got all hinky about it."

The vision of Chandonne showing up at her motel office and asking for a place to stay for the night shorts out my imagination. I can't picture it. Le Loup-Garou, as he calls himself, would not take such a chance. His modus operandi, as we know it, was not to show up at anyone's door unless he intended to murder and maul that person. *As we know it.* As we know it, I keep thinking. The truth is, we know less than we did two weeks ago. "We have to start all over," I tell Marino. "We've defined someone without information, and now what? We made the mistake of profiling him and then believing our projection. Well, there are dimensions to him we've completely missed, and even though he's locked up, he isn't."

Marino gets out his cigarettes.

"Do you understand what I'm saying?" I go on. "In our arrogance, we decided what he's like. Based it on scientific evidence and came up with what, in truth, is an assumption. A caricature. He's not a werewolf. He's a human being, and no matter how evil he is, he has many facets, and now we're finding them. Hell, it was obvious on the videotape. Why are we so damn slow on the uptake? I don't want Vander going to that motel alone."

"Good point." Marino reaches for the phone. "I'll go to the motel with him and you can take my truck back to Richmond."

"There was someone in the doorway," I say. "Did you see him? He was big."

"Huh," he says. "I didn't see anyone. Just the little kid, what's his name? Zack. And the dog."

"I saw someone else," I insist.

"I'll check it out. You got Vander's number?"

I give it to him and he calls. Vander is already on his way and his wife gives Marino a cell phone number. I stare out the window at wooded residential developments with large Colonial homes set back far from the streets. Elegant Christmas decorations shine through trees.

"Yeah, there's some strange shit out there," Marino is telling Vander by cell phone. "So yours truly here's gonna be your bodyguard." He ends the call and we are quiet for a moment. Last night seems to fill the rumbling space between us in the truck.

"How long have you known?" I finally ask Marino one more time, not at all satisfied with what he told me in Anna's driveway when I walked him out to his truck after midnight. "When exactly did Righter tell you he was instigating a special grand jury investigation and what was his reason?"

"You hadn't even finished her damn autopsy yet." Marino lights a cigarette. "Bray was still on your table, to be exact. Righter gets me on the phone and says he don't want you doing her post, and I tell him, 'So what you want me to do? Walk in the morgue and order her to drop her scalpel and put her hands up in the air?' The dumb shit." Marino blows out smoke as my dismay folds into a scary shape inside my brain. "That's why he didn't ask your permission to come snoop around your house, either," Marino adds.

The snooping part, at least, I had already figured out.

"He wanted to see if the cops came across anything." He pauses to tap an ash. "Like a chipping hammer. Especially one with maybe Bray's blood on it."

"The one he tried to attack me with may very well have her blood on it," I reply reasonably, calmly as anxiety inches through me.

"Problem is, the hammer with her blood on it was found in your house," Marino reminds me of a fact.

"Of course it was. He brought it to my house so he could use it on me."

"And yeah, it does have her blood on it," Marino keeps talking. "They already did the DNA. Never seen the labs move so fast as they are these days, and you can guess why. The governor's got his eye on everything going on—in case his chief medical examiner turns out to be some whacko murderer." He sucks on the cigarette and glances over at me. "And another thing, Doc. Don't know if Berger might have mentioned this to you. But the chipping hammer you say you bought at the hardware store? It ain't been found."

"What?" I am incredulous, then furious.

"So the only one at your house is the one with Bray's blood on it. One hammer. Found at your house. And it's got Bray's blood." He makes his point, not without some reluctance.

"You know why I bought that hammer," I reply as if my argument is with him. "I wanted to see if it matched up with the pattern of her injuries. And it was definitely in my house. If it wasn't there when you guys went through everything, then either you overlooked it or someone took it."

"You remember where you had it last?"

"I used it in the kitchen on chicken to see what the injuries looked like, and also what kind of pattern the coiled handle would leave if I put something on it and pressed the handle against paper."

"Yeah, we found pounded-up chicken in the

garbage. And a pillowcase with barbecue sauce on it, like maybe from your rolling the handle around." He doesn't think such an experiment is odd. He knows I engage in a lot of unusual research when I am trying to figure out what happened to somebody. "But no chipping hammer. We didn't find that. Not with or without barbecue sauce," Marino goes on. "So I'm wondering if asshole Talley swiped it. Maybe you ought to get Lucy and Teun to turn their secret squirrel organization on him and see what they find out, huh? The Last Precinct's first big investigation. I'd like to run a credit check on the bastard and see where he gets all his money from, for starters."

I keep glancing at my watch, timing our drive. The subdivision where Mitch Barbosa lived is ten minutes from The Fort James Motel. Taupe clapboard townhouses are new and there is no vegetation, just raw earth sprinkled with dead young grass and patched with snow. I recognize unmarked police vehicles in the lot when we pull in, three Ford Crown Victorias and a Chevrolet Lumina parked in a row. It doesn't escape my attention or Marino's that two of these vehicles have Washington, D.C., plates.

"Oh shit," Marino says. "I smell the feds. Oh boy," he says to me as we park, "this ain't good."

I notice a curious detail as Marino and I follow the brick walkway to the townhouse where

Barbosa lived with his alleged girlfriend.
Through an upstairs window I see a fishing rod.
It leans against the glass, and I don't know why
it strikes me as out of place except that this isn't
the time of year for fishing, just as it isn't the time
of year for camping. Again, I think of the mysterious if not mythical people who fled the
campground, leaving behind many of their pos-
sessions. I return to Bev Kiffin's lie and feel I am
moving deeper into a dangerous airspace where
there are forces I can't see or understand moving at incredible speeds. Marino and I wait at the
front door of townhouse D, and he rings the bell
again.

Detective Stanfield answers and greets us dis-
tractedly, his eyes darting everywhere. Tension
between him and Marino is a wall between them.
"Sorry I didn't make it by the motel," he announces curtly as he steps aside to let us in.
"Something's come up. You'll see that in a
minute," he promises. He is in gray corduroys
and a heavy wool sweater, and he won't meet my
eyes, either. I am not sure if this is because he
knows how I feel about his leaking information
to his brother-in-law, Representative Dinwiddie,
or if there is some other reason. It flashes across
my thoughts that he might know I am being investigated for murder. I try not to think about that
reality. It serves no good purpose to worry right

now. "Everybody's upstairs," he says, and we follow him up.

"Who's everybody?" Marino asks.

Our feet thud quietly on carpet. Stanfield keeps moving. He doesn't turn around or pause when he replies, "ATF and the FBI."

I notice framed photographs arranged on the wall to the left of the staircase and take a moment to peruse them, recognizing Mitch Barbosa grinning with tipsy-looking people in a bar and hanging out the window of the cab of a transfer truck. In one photograph, he is sunbathing in a bikini on a tropical beach, maybe Hawaii. He holds up a drink, toasting the person behind the camera. Several other poses are with a pretty woman, perhaps the girlfriend he lives with, I wonder. Halfway up is a landing and the window the fishing pole leans against.

I stop, a strange sensation lightly whispering across my flesh as I examine, without touching, a Shakespeare fiberglass rod and Shimano reel. A hook and split-shot weights are attached to the fishing line, and on the carpet next to the rod's handle is a small blue plastic tackle box. Nearby, as if set down when someone entered the townhouse, are two empty Rolling Rock beer bottles, a new pack of Tiparillo cigars and some change. Marino turns around to see what I am doing. I join him at the top of the stairs and we emerge into a brightly lit living area that is attractively decorated in spare modern furniture and Indian rugs.

"When's the last time you went fishing?" I ask Marino.

"Not freshwater," he replies. "Not around here these days."

"Exactly." I am cut off by an awareness that I know one of the three people standing near the picture window in the living room. My heart jumps when the familiar dark head turns to me and suddenly I am facing Jay Talley. He doesn't smile, his glance sharp as if his eyes are tipped like arrows. Marino makes a barely audible noise that is like a groan from a small, primitive animal. It is his way of letting me know that Jay is the last person he wants to see. Another man in a suit and tie is young and looks Hispanic, and when he sets down his coffee cup, his jacket falls open and reveals a shoulder holster holding a large caliber pistol.

The third person is a woman. She doesn't demonstrate the devastated, confused demeanor of a person whose lover has just been killed. She is upset, yes. But her emotions are well contained beneath the surface, and I recognize the flare in her eyes and angry set of her jaw. I have seen the look in Lucy, in Marino and others who are more than bereft when something bad happens to a person they care about. Cops. Cops are offended and in *an eye for an eye* mode when something happens to one of their own. Mitch Barbosa's girlfriend, I suspect right away, is law enforcement, probably undercover. In a matter of minutes, the scenario has dramatically shifted.

"This is Bunk Pruett, FBI," Stanfield makes introductions. "Jay Talley, ATF." Jay shakes my hand as if we have never met. "And Jilison McIntyre." Her handshake is cool but firm. "Ms. McIntyre's ATF."

We find chairs and arrange them so all of us can look at each other and talk. The air is hard. It is flinty with anger. I recognize the mood. I have seen it so many times when a cop is killed. Now that Stanfield has set the stage, he slips behind a curtain of sullen silence. Bunk Pruett takes charge, typical FBI. "Dr. Scarpetta, Captain Marino," Pruett begins. "I want to state the obvious right off. This is highly, highly sensitive. To be honest, I hate saying anything about what's going on, but you got to know what you're dealing with." His jaw muscles bunch. "Mitch Barbosa is—was—undercover FBI, working a big investigation here in this area, which now of course we have to dismantle, at least to a certain degree."

"Drugs and guns," Jay says, glancing from Marino to me.

CHAPTER 24

Is INTERPOL INVOLVED?" I don't understand why Jay Talley is here. Barely two weeks ago, he was working in France.

"Well, you should know," Jay says with a trace of sarcasm, or maybe I imagine it. "The unidentified case you just contacted Interpol about, the guy who died in the motel down the road? We have an idea who he might be. So yes, Interpol's involved. Now we are. You bet."

"I wasn't aware we'd gotten a response from Interpol." Marino barely tries to be civil to Jay. "So you're telling me the guy from the motel's some sort of international fugitive, maybe?"

"Yes," Jay replies. "Rosso Matos, twenty-eight-year-old native of Colombia, as in South America. Last seen in Los Angeles. Also known as the Cat because he's such a quiet guy when he goes in and out of places, killing. That's his specialty. Taking people out, a hit man. Matos has a reputation for liking very expensive clothes, cars—and young men. I guess I need to talk about him in the past tense." Jay pauses. No one responds beyond looking at him. "What none of us understands is what he was doing here in Virginia," Jay adds.

"What exactly is the operation here?" Marino asks Jilison McIntyre.

"Started four months ago with a guy speeding along Route Five just a couple miles from here. A James City cop pulls him." She glances at Stanfield. "Runs his tag and finds out he's a convicted felon. Plus the officer happens to notice the handle of a long gun protruding from under a blanket in the back seat, turns out to be a MAK-90 with the serial number ground off. Our labs in Rockville managed to restore the SN and traced the weapon to a shipment from China—a regular shipment to Richmond. As you know, a MAK-90's a popular knock-off of the AK-47 assault rifle, going rate of a thousand, two thousand bucks on the street. Gang members love the MAK, made in China, regularly shipped to local ports in Richmond, Norfolk, legitly in crates accurately marked. Other MAKs are being smuggled in from Asia along with heroin, in all kinds of crates marked everything from *electronics* to *Oriental rugs.*"

In an all-business voice that only occasionally

reveals the strain she feels, McIntyre describes a smuggling ring that, in addition to area ports, involves the James City County trucking company where Barbosa was undercover as a driver and she was undercover as his girlfriend. He got her a job in the company's office, where bills of lading and invoices were falsified to disguise a very lucrative operation that also involves cigarettes en route from Virginia to New York and other destinations in the Northeast. Some weapons are being sold through a dirty gun dealer in this area, but a lot of them end up in backroom sales at gun shows, and we all know how many gun shows Virginia has, McIntyre says.

"What's the name of the trucking company?" Marino asks.

"Overland."

Marino's eyes dart to me. He runs his fingers through his thinning hair. "Christ," he says to everyone. "That's who Bev Kiffin's husband works for. Jesus Christ."

"The lady who owns and runs The Fort James Motel," Stanfield explains to the others.

"Overland's a big company and not everybody is involved in illegal activity," Pruett is quick to be objective. "That's what makes this so tough. The company and most people in it are legit. So you could pull their trucks all day and never find anything hot inside a single one of them. Then on another day, a shipload of paper products, televisions, whatever, heads out and stashed inside boxes are assault rifles and drugs."

"You think someone put the dime on Mitch?" Marino asks Pruett. "And the bad guys decided to whack him?"

"If so, then why is Matos dead, too?" It is Jay who speaks. "And it appears Matos died first, right?" He looks at me. "He's found dead in these really weird circumstances, in a motel right down the road. Then the next day, Mitch's body is dumped in Richmond. Plus, Matos is an eight-hundred-pound gorilla. I don't see what his interest would be here—even if someone out there dimed Mitch, you don't send in a hit man like Matos. He's pretty much reserved for big prey in powerful crime organizations, guys hard to get to because they are surrounded by their own heavily armed thugs."

"Who does Matos work for?" Marino asks. "Do we know that?"

"Whoever will pay," Pruett replies.

"He's all over the map," Jay adds. "South America, Europe, this country. He's not associated with any one network or cartel, but is a lone operator. You want someone taken out, you hire Matos."

"Then someone hired him to come here," I conclude.

"We have to assume that," Jay replies. "I don't think he was in the area to check out Jamestown or the Christmas decorations in Williamsburg."

"We also know he didn't kill Mitch Barbosa," Marino adds. "Matos was already dead and on the Doc's table before Mitch went out jogging."

There are nods around the room. Stanfield is picking at a fingernail. He looks lost in space, extremely uncomfortable. He keeps wiping sweat off his brow and drying his fingers on his pants. Marino asks Jilison McIntyre to tell us exactly what happened.

"Mitch likes to run midday, before lunch," she begins. "He went out close to noon and didn't come back. This was yesterday. I went out in the car looking for him around two o'clock and when there was still no sign, I called the police, and of course, our guys. ATF and FBI. Agents came in from the field and started looking, too. Nothing. We know he was spotted in the area of the law school."

"Marshall-Wythe?" I inquire, taking notes.

"Right, at William and Mary. Mitch usually ran the same route, from here along Route Five, then over on Francis Street and to South Henry, then back. Usually an hour or so."

"Do you remember what he was wearing and what he might have had with him?" I ask her.

"Red warm-up suit and a vest. He had on a

down vest over his warm-up. Uh, gray, North Face. And his butt pack. He never went anywhere without his butt pack."

"He had a gun in it?" Marino assumes.

She nods, swallowing, face stoical. "Gun, money, portable phone. House keys."

"He wasn't wearing the down jacket when his body was found," Marino informs her. "No butt pack. Describe the key."

"Keys," she corrects him. "He has the key for here, for the townhouse, and his car key on a steel ring."

"What does the key for your townhouse look like?" I ask, and I feel Jay staring at me.

"Just a brass key. A normal-looking key."

"He had a stainless steel key in the pocket of his running shorts," I say. "It has two-three-three written on it in permanent Magic Marker."

Agent McIntyre frowns. She knows nothing about it. "Well now, that's really strange. I have no idea what that key might be to," she replies.

"So we gotta figure he was taken somewhere," Marino says. "He was tied up, gagged, tortured, then driven to Richmond and dumped in the street in one of our lovely projects, Mosby Court."

"Hot drug-trafficking area?" Pruett asks him.

"Oh yeah. The projects are big into economic development. Guns and drugs. You bet." Marino knows his turf. "But the other nice thing about places like Mosby Court is people don't see nothing. You want to dump a body, don't matter if fifty people were standing right there. They get temporary blindness, amnesia."

"Someone familiar with Richmond, then," Stanfield finally offers an opinion.

McIntyre's eyes are wide. She has a stricken expression on her face. "I didn't know about torture," she says to me. Her professional resolve shivers like a tree about to fall.

I describe Barbosa's burns and go into detail about the burns Matos had, as well. I talk about the evidence of ligatures and gags, and then Marino talks about the eyebolts in the motel room ceiling. All present get the picture. Everyone can envision what was done to these two men. We have to suspect the same person or persons are involved in their deaths. But this doesn't begin to tell us who or why. We don't know where Barbosa was taken, but I have an idea.

"When you go back there with Vander," I say to Marino, "maybe you ought to check out the other rooms, see if another one has eyebolts in the ceiling."

"Will do. Got to go back there anyway." He glances at his watch.

"Today?" Jay asks him.

"Yup."

"You got any reason to think Mitch was drugged like the first guy?" Pruett asks me.

"I didn't find any needle marks," I reply. "But we'll see what comes up on his tox results."

"Jesus," McIntyre mutters.

"And both of them wet their pants?" Stanfield says. "Doesn't that happen when people die? They lose control of their bladders and wet their pants? Just a natural thing, in other words?"

"I can't say losing urine is rare. But the first man, Matos, took his clothes off. He was nude. It appears he wet his pants and then disrobed."

"So that was before he got burned," Stanfield says.

"I would assume so. He wasn't burned through his clothing," I reply. "It's very possible both victims lost control of their bladders due to fear, panic. You get scared badly enough, you wet your pants."

"Jesus," McIntyre mutters again.

"And you see some asshole screwing eyebolts in the ceiling and plugging in a heat gun, that's enough to scare the piss right out of you," Marino abundantly illustrates. "You know damn well what's about to happen to you."

"Jesus!" McIntyre blurts out. "What the fuck is this about?" Her eyes blaze.

Silence.

"Why the fuck would someone do something

like that to Mitch? And it's not like he wasn't careful, not like he would just get in someone's car or even get close to some stranger trying to stop him on the road."

Stanfield says, "Makes me think of Vietnam, the way they did things to prisoners of war, tortured them to make them talk."

Making someone talk can certainly be one reason for torture, I respond to what Stanfield has just said. "But it's also a power rush. Some people are into torture because they get off on it."

"You think that's the case here?" Pruett says to me.

"I have no way of knowing." Then I ask McIntyre, "I noticed a fishing pole when I was coming up the walk."

Her reaction is a flicker of confusion. Then she realizes what I am talking about. "Oh, right. Mitch likes to fish."

"Around here?"

"A creek over near College Landing Park."

I look at Marino. That particular creek is at the edge of the wooded camping area at The Fort James Motel.

"Mitch ever mention to you the motel over there by that creek?" Marino asks her.

"I just know he liked to fish over there."

"He know the lady who runs the joint? Bev Kiffin? And her husband? Maybe you both know him since he works for Overland?" Marino says to McIntyre.

"Well, I do know that Mitch used to talk to her boys. She has two young boys and sometimes they'd be out there fishing when Mitch was. He said he felt for them because their dad was never around. But I don't know anybody named Kiffin at the trucking company, and I do their books."

"Can you check that out?" Jay says.

"Maybe his last name's different from hers."

"Yeah."

She nods.

"You remember the last time Mitch went fishing out there?" Marino asks her.

"Right before all the snow," she replies. "It was pretty nice weather up until then."

"I noticed some change, a couple beer bottles and some cigars on the landing," I say. "Right by the fishing pole."

"You sure he hasn't been fishing out there since it snowed?" Marino picks up my thought.

The expression in her eyes makes it evident that she isn't sure. I wonder just how much she really knows about her undercover boyfriend.

"Any illegal shit going on at the motel that you and Mitch are aware of?" Marino asks her.

McIntyre starts shaking her head. "He never mentioned anything about that. Nothing like that.

His only connection to the place was fishing and being nice to the two boys, on occasion, if he saw them."

"Just if they happened up when he was fishing?" Marino keeps pushing. "Any reason to think Mitch might have ever wandered over to the house to say hi to them?"

She hesitates.

"Mitch a generous guy?"

"Oh yes," she says. "Very much so. He might have wandered over. I don't know. He really likes kids. Liked them." She tears up again and at the same time simmers.

"How did he identify himself to people around here? He say he was a truck driver? What did he say about you? You supposed to be a career woman? Now, you two weren't really boyfriend and girlfriend. That was just part of the front, right?" Marino is on to something. He is leaning forward, his arms braced on his knees, staring intensely at Jilison McIntyre. When he gets like this, he fires questions so rapidly, people often don't have time to answer. Then they get confused and say something they regret. She does that this very moment.

"Hey, I'm not a fucking suspect," she snaps at him. "And our relationship, I don't know what you're getting at. It was professional. But you can't help being close to someone when you live in the same damn townhouse and act like you're involved, make people think you are."

"But you weren't involved," Marino says. "Or at least he wasn't with you. You guys were doing a job, right? Meaning, if he wanted to pay attention to a lonely woman with two nice little boys, he could do that." Marino leans back in his chair. The room is so silent, it seems to hum. "Problem is, Mitch shouldn't have done that. Dangerous, fucking stupid in light of his situation. He one of those types who had a hard time keeping his pants on?"

She doesn't answer him. Tears jump out.

"You know what, folks?" Marino scans the room. "It just might be that Mitch got tangled up in something that doesn't have a damn thing to do with your undercover operation here. Wrong place, wrong time. Caught something he sure as hell wasn't fishing for."

"You got any idea where Mitch was at three o'clock Wednesday afternoon, when Matos checked into the motel and the fire started?" Stanfield is putting the pieces together. "Was he here or out somewhere?"

"No, he wasn't here," she barely says, wiping her eyes with a tissue. "Gone. I don't know where."

Marino blows out in disgust. He doesn't need to say it. Undercover partners are supposed to keep track of each other, and if Agent McIntyre didn't always know where Special Agent Barbosa was, then he was up to something that maybe wasn't germane to their investigation.

"I know you don't even want to think it, Jilison," Marino goes on in a milder tone, "but Mitch was tortured and murdered, okay? I mean, the guy was fucking *scared to death*. Literally. Whatever someone was doing to him, it was so awful, he had a fucking heart attack. He wet his fucking pants. He was taken somewhere and strung up, gagged and then has a weirdo key put in his pocket, planted, what for? Why? He into anything we ought to know about, Jilison? He fishing for more than bass out there in that creek by the campground?"

Tears are rolling down McIntryre's face. She wipes them away roughly with the tissue and sniffles loudly. "He liked drinking and women," she barely says. "Okay?"

"He ever go out at night, barhopping and that sort of thing?" Pruett asks her.

She nods. "It was part of his cover. You saw . . ." Her eyes jump to me. "You saw him. His dyed hair, the earring, all the rest. Mitch played the role of a sort of, well, wild party guy and he did like the women. He never pretended to be, uh, faithful to me, to his so-called girlfriend. It was part of his cover. But it was also him. Yeah. I worried about it, okay? But that was Mitch. He was a good agent. I don't think he did anything dishonest, if that's what you're asking. But he didn't tell me everything, either. If he got onto something going on at the campground, for example, he might have started poking around. He might have."

"Without letting you know," Marino confirms.

She nods again. "And I was out doing my thing, too. It's not like I was here every minute waiting for him. I was working in the office at Overland. Part-time, anyway. So we didn't always know what the other was up to every hour of every day."

"I'll tell you this much," Marino decides. "Mitch stumbled onto something. And I'm just wondering if he wasn't out at the motel around the time Matos showed up, and maybe whatever Matos was into, Mitch had the misfortune of being spotted in the area. Maybe it's just that simple. Somebody thinks he saw something, knew something, and next thing, he gets picked up and gets the treatment."

No one argues. Marino's theory, actually, is the only one so far that makes any sense.

"Which brings us back to what Matos was doing here to begin with," Pruett comments.

I look at Stanfield. He has wandered out of the conversation. His face is wan. He is a nervous wreck. His eyes drift to me and quickly move away. He wets his lips and coughs several times.

"Detective Stanfield," I feel compelled to say to him in front of everyone. "For God's sake, don't tell any of this to your brother-in-law." Anger sparks in his eyes. I have humiliated him and don't care. "Please," I add.

"You want to know the truth?" he angrily retorts. "I don't want nothing to do with any of this." He slowly draws himself to his feet and looks around the room, blinking, his eyes glazing over. "I don't know what this is all about, but I don't want no part—I mean, no part of it. You feds are in it already, up to your eyeballs, so you can just have it. I quit." He nods. "You heard me right, I quit."

Detective Stanfield, to our amazement, collapses. He falls so hard the room shakes. I spring up. Thank God, he is breathing. His pulse is running wild, but he is not in the grips of a cardiac arrest or anything life-threatening. He simply has fainted. I check his head to make sure he hasn't injured himself. He is all right. He comes to. Marino and I help him to his feet and get him on the couch. I make him lie down and prop several pillows under his neck. Most of all, he is embarrassed, acutely so.

"Detective Stanfield, are you diabetic?" I ask. "Do you have a heart condition?"

"If you just got a Coke or something, that would be good," he says, weakly.

I get up and head into the kitchen. "Let me see what I can do," I say as if I live here. Inside the refrigerator, I get out orange juice. I find peanut butter in a cabinet and scoop out a big spoonful. It is while I am looking for paper towels that I notice a prescription bottle by the toaster oven. Mitch Barbosa's name is on the label. He was taking the antidepressant Prozac. When I return to the living room, I say something about this to McIntyre and she tells us that Barbosa went on Prozac several months ago because he was suffering anxiety and depression, which he blamed on the undercover assignment, on stress, she adds.

"That's interesting," is all Marino has to say about it.

"You said you're going back to the motel when you leave here?" Jay asks Marino.

"Yeah, Vander's going to see if we might have any luck with prints."

"Prints?" Stanfield murmurs from his sickbed.

"Jesus, Stanfield," Marino blurts out in exasperation. "They teach you anything in detective school? Or did you get sent ahead several grades because of your goddamn brother-in-law?"

"He *is* a goddamn brother-in-law, you want to know the truth." He says this so pitifully and with such candor that everybody laughs. Stanfield perks up a little bit. He sits higher against the pillows. "And you're right." He meets my eyes. "I shouldn't have told him one peep about this case. And I won't tell him nothing else, not a word, because it's all politicking to that one. It wasn't me who dragged in this whole Jamestown thing, just so you know."

Pruett frowns. "What Jamestown thing?"

"Oh, you know, the dig out there and the big celebration the state's planning. Well, thing is, if the truth be known, Dinwiddie got no more Indian blood in him than I do. All this horse crap about him being a descendent of Chief Powhatan. Pshaw!" Stanfield's eyes dance with resentment that I doubt he rarely touches. He probably hates his brother-in-law.

"Mitch has Indian blood," McIntyre says somberly. "He's half Native American."

"Well, for Christ's sake, let's hope the newspapers don't find that out," Marino mutters to Stanfield, not buying for one second that Stanfield is going to keep his mouth shut. "We got a gay guy and now an Indian. Oh boy, oh boy." Marino shakes his head. "We got to keep this out of politics, out of circulation and I mean it." He stares right at Stanfield, then at Jay. "Because guess what? We can't talk about what we think is really going on, now can we? About the big undercover operation. About Mitch being undercover FBI. And that maybe in some fruitloop way, Chandonne is all wrapped around whatever the shit's going on out here. So if people get all caught up in this hate crime shit, how do we turn that around when we can't tell the truth?"

"I don't agree," Jay says to him. "I'm not ready to say what these murders are about. I'm not prepared to accept, for example, that Matos and now Barbosa aren't related to gun smuggling. I do think without a doubt their murders are connected."

No one disagrees. The modi operandi are too similar for the deaths not to be related, and in fact, committed by the same person or persons.

"I'm also not prepared to totally ignore the idea that they're hate crimes," Jay goes on. "A gay male. A Native American." He shrugs. "Torture's pretty damn hateful. Any injuries to their genitalia?" He turns to me.

"No." I hold his gaze. It is odd to think we were intimate, to look at his full lips and graceful hands and to remember their touch. When we walked the streets of Paris, people turned to stare at him.

"Hmmm," he says. "I find that interesting and maybe important. I'm not a forensic psychiatrist, of course, but it does seem in hate crimes the perpetrators rarely injure the victims' genitals."

Marino gives him an incredible look, his mouth parting in blatant disdain.

"Because you get some redneck homophobic sort, and the last thing he's going to go near is the guy's genitals," Jay adds.

"Well, if you really want to go around this mul-
berry bush," Marino acidly says to him, "then
let's just connect it to Chandonne. He never went
near his victims' genitals either. Shit, he didn't
even take their fucking pants off, just beat and bit
the shit out of their faces and breasts. Only lower
body thing he did at all was to take off their shoes
and socks and bite their feet. And why? The guy's
afraid of female genitalia because his own's as deformed as the rest of him." Marino surveys the
faces around him. "One good thing about the
bastard being locked up is we got to find out what
the rest of him looks like. Right? And guess what?
He ain't got a dick. Or let's just say that what he's
got I wouldn't call a dick."

Stanfield is sitting straight up on the couch now,
his eyes wide in amazement.

"I'll go with you to the motel," Jay says to
Marino.

Marino gets up and looks out the window.
"Wonder where the hell Vander is," he says.

He gets Vander on the cell phone and we head
out minutes later to meet in the parking lot. Jay
walks with me. I feel the energy of his desire to talk
to me, to somehow come to a consensus. In this
way, he is like the stereotype of a woman. He wants
to talk, to settle matters, to have closure or to rekin-
dle our connection so he can then play hard to get
again. I, on the other hand, want none of it.

"Kay, can I have a minute?" he says in the parking lot.

I stop and look at him as I button my coat. I notice Marino glancing our way as he gets the trash bags and baby carriage out of the back of his truck and loads them into Vander's car.

"I know this is awkward, but is there some way we can make it easier? For one thing, we have to work together," Jay says.

"Maybe you should have thought about that before you told Jaime Berger every detail, Jay," I reply.

"That wasn't against you." His eyes are intense.

"Right." .

"She asked me questions, understandably. She's just doing her job."

I don't believe him. That is my fundamental problem with Jay Talley. I don't trust him and wish I never had. "Well, that's curious," I comment. "Because it appears people started asking questions about me before Diane Bray was even murdered. Right about the time I was with you in France inquiries began, as a matter of fact."

His expression darkens. Anger peers out before he can hide it. "You're paranoid, Kay," he says.

"You're right," I reply. "You're absolutely right, Jay."

CHAPTER 25

I HAVE NEVER DRIVEN MAR-
ino's Dodge Ram Quad Cab pickup truck,
and were circumstances not so strained I
would probably find the scenario comical. I am
not a big person, barely five foot five, slender, and
there is nothing funky or extreme about me. I do
wear jeans, but not today. I suppose I dress like a
proper chief or lawyer, usually in a tailored skirt
suit or flannel trousers and a blazer, unless I am
working a crime scene. I wear my blond hair
short and neatly styled, am light on makeup and,
other than my signet ring and watch, jewelry is
an afterthought. I don't have a single tattoo. I
don't look like the sort who would be roaring
along in a monster macho truck that is dark blue
with pinstriping, chrome, mud flaps, scanner and
big, swooping antennas that go with the CB and
two-way radios.

I take 64 West back to Richmond because it is

quicker, and I pay close attention to my driving because it is a lot to handle a vehicle this size with only one arm. I have never spent a Christmas Eve like this and I am increasingly depressed over the notion. Usually, by now I have stocked the refrigerator and freezer, and have cooked sauces and soups and decorated the house. I feel utterly homeless and alien as I drive Marino's truck along the interstate, and it occurs to me that I don't know where I will sleep tonight. I guess at Anna's, but I dread the necessary chill between us. I didn't even see her this morning, and a helpless feeling of loneliness settles over me and seems to push me down in my seat. I page Lucy. "I've got to move back into my house tomorrow," I tell her on the phone.

"Maybe you should stay in the hotel with Teun and me," she suggests.

"How about you and Teun stay with me?" It is so hard for me to express a need, and I need them. I do. For a lot of reasons.

"When do you want us there?"

"We'll have Christmas together in the morning."

"Early." Lucy has never stayed in bed past six on Christmas morning.

"I'll be up, and then we'll go to the house," I tell her.

December 24. Days have gotten as short as they

can, and it will be a while before light savors the hours and burns off my heavy, anxious moods. It is dark by the time I reach downtown Richmond, and when I pull up to Anna's house at five minutes past six, I find Berger waiting for me in her Mercedes SUV, headlights penetrating the night. Anna's car is gone. She is not home. I don't know why this unsettles me so completely unless it is that I am suspicious she somehow knows Berger is meeting me and chose not to be here. Considering such a possibility reminds me that Anna has talked to people and may one day be forced to reveal what I have told her during my most vulnerable hours in her home. Berger climbs out as I open the truck door, and if she is taken aback by my transportation, she makes no indication of it.

"Do you need anything from inside the house before we go?" she asks.

"Give me just a minute," I tell her. "Was Dr. Zenner here when you arrived?"

I feel her stiffen a little. "I got here just a few minutes before you did."

Evasion, I think as I climb the front steps. I unlock the door and turn off the burglar alarm. The foyer is dark, the great chandelier and Christmas tree lights off. I write Anna a note and thank her for her friendship and hospitality. I need to return to my own home tomorrow and know she will understand why I must. Mostly, I want her to believe I am not upset with her, that I realize she is as victimized by circumstances as I am. I say *circumstances* because I am no longer sure who is holding a gun to Anna's head and ordering her to divulge confidences about me. Rocky Caggiano may be next in line, unless I am indicted. If that should happen, I will be no factor in Chandonne's trial, not hardly. I leave the note on Anna's immaculately made Biedermeier bed. Then I get in Berger's car and begin to tell her about my day in James City County, about the abandoned campsite and the long, pale hairs. She listens intently, driving, knowing where she is going as if she has lived in Richmond all of her life.

"Can we prove the hairs are Chandonne's?" she finally asks. "Assuming there are no roots, as usual. And there weren't roots with the ones found at the crime scenes, right? Your crime scenes. Luong and Bray."

"No roots," I say, rankled by the reference to *my* crime scenes. They aren't my crime scenes, I silently protest. "He shed those hairs, so there are no roots," I tell Berger. "But we can get mitochondrial DNA from the shafts. So yes, we can definitely know if the hairs from the campground are his."

"Please explain," she says. "I'm not an expert on mitochondrial DNA. Or an expert on hair for that matter, especially the kind of hair he has."

The subject of DNA is a difficult one. Explaining human life on a molecular level tells most people far more than they can understand or care to know. Cops and prosecutors love what DNA can do. They hate to talk about it scientifically. Few of them understand it. The old joke is, most people can't even spell DNA. I explain that *nuclear* DNA is what we get when cells with nuclei are present, such as with blood, tissue, seminal fluid and hair roots. Nuclear DNA is inherited equally from both parents, so if we have someone's nuclear DNA we have, in a sense, all of him, and can compare his DNA profile to any other biological sample this same person has left at, say, another crime scene.

"Can we just compare the hairs from the campground to the hairs he left at the murder scenes?" Berger asks.

"Not successfully," I reply. "Examining microscopic characteristics in this instance won't tell us much because the hairs are unpigmented. The most we will be able to say is their morphologies are similar or consistent with each other."

"Not conclusive to a jury." She thinks out loud.

"Not in the least."

"If we don't do a microscopic comparison anyway, the defense will bring that up," Berger considers. "He'll say, *Why didn't you?*"

"Well, we can microscopically compare the hairs, if you want."

"The ones from Susan Pless's body and the ones from your cases."

"If you want," I repeat.

"Explain hair shafts. How does DNA work with those?"

I tell her that mitochondrial DNA is found in the walls of cells and not in their nuclei, meaning mitochondrial DNA is the anthropological DNA of hair, fingernail, tooth and bone. Mitochondrial DNA is the molecules that make up our mortar and stone, I say. The limited usefulness lies in that mitochondrial DNA is inherited only through the female lineage. I use the analogy of an egg. Think of mitochondrial DNA as the egg white, while nuclear DNA is the yolk. You can't compare one to the other. But if you have DNA from blood, you have the whole egg and can compare mitochondrial to mitochondrial—egg white to egg white. We have blood because we have Chandonne. He had to give up a blood sample while in the hospital. We have his complete DNA profile and can compare the mitochondrial DNA of unknown hairs to the mitochondrial DNA from his blood sample.

Berger listens without interruption. She has taken in what I am saying and seems to understand. As usual, she takes no notes. She asks, "Did he leave hair at your house?"

"I'm not sure what the police found."

"As much as he seems to shed, I would think he left hair at your house or certainly out in the snow in your yard when he was thrashing about."

"You would think so," I agree with her.

"I've been reading about werewolves." Berger leaps to the next topic. "Apparently, there have been people who really thought they were werewolves or tried all sorts of bizarre things to turn themselves into werewolves. Witchcraft, black magic. Satan worship. Biting. Drinking blood. Do you think it's possible Chandonne really believes he is a loup-garou? A werewolf? And maybe even wants to be one?"

"Thus not guilty by reason of insanity," I reply, and I have assumed all along this would be his defense.

"There was a Hungarian countess in the early sixteen hundreds, Elizabeth Bathory-Nadasdy, also known as the Blood Countess," Berger goes on. "She supposedly tortured and murdered some six hundred young women. Would bathe in their blood, believing it would keep her young and preserve her beauty. Familiar with the case?"

"Vaguely."

"As the story goes, this countess kept young women in her dungeon, fattened them up, would bleed them and bathe in their blood and then force other imprisoned women to lick all the blood off her body. Supposedly because towels were harsh on her skin. Rubbing blood in her skin, all over her body," she ponders. "Accounts of this have left out the obvious. I'd say there was a sexual component," she adds dryly. "Lust murders. Even if the perpetrator truly believed in the magical powers of blood, it's about power and sex. That's what it's about whether you're a beautiful countess or some genetic anomaly who grew up on the Île Saint-Louis."

We turn on Canterbury Road, entering the wooded, wealthy neighborhood of Windsor Farms, where Diane Bray lived on the outer edge, her property separated by a wall from the noisy downtown expressway.

"I would give my right arm to know what's in the Chandonne library," Berger is saying. "Or better put, what sorts of things Chandonne's been reading over the years—aside from the histories and other erudite materials he says his father gave him, yada, yada, yada. For example, does he know about the Blood Countess? Was he rubbing blood all over his body in hopes it might magically heal him of his affliction?"

"We believe he was bathing in the Seine and then here in the James River," I reply. "Possibly for that reason. To be magically healed."

"Sort of a biblical thing."

"Maybe."

"He might read the Bible, too," she offers. "Was he influenced by the French serial killer Gilles Garnier, who killed little boys and ate them and bayed at the moon? There were a lot of so-called werewolves in France during the Middle Ages. Some thirty thousand people charged with it, can you imagine?" Berger has been doing a lot of research. This is evident. "And there's the other weird idea," she goes on. "In werewolf folklore it was believed if you were bitten by a werewolf, you would turn into one. Possible Chandonne was trying to turn his victims into werewolves? Maybe so he could find a bride of Frankenstein, a mate just like him?"

These unusual considerations begin to form a composite that is far more matter-of-fact and pedestrian than it might seem. Berger is simply anticipating what the defense is going to do in her case, and an obvious ploy is to distract the jury from the heinous nature of the crimes by preoccupying them with Chandonne's physical deformity and alleged mental illness and downright bizarreness. If the argument can be successfully made that he believes he is a paranormal creature, a werewolf, a monster, then it is highly unlikely the jury will find him guilty and sentence him to life in prison. It occurs to me that some people might even feel sorry for him.

"The silver-bullet defense." Berger alludes to the superstition that only a silver bullet can kill a werewolf. "We have a mountain of evidence, but then so did the prosecution in the O.J. case. The silver bullet for the defense will be that Chandonne is deranged and pitiful."

DIANE BRAY'S HOUSE IS A WHITE cape cod with a gambrel roof, and although the police have secured and cleared the scene, the property has not returned to life. Not even Berger can enter without permission of the owner, or in this case, the person acting as custodian. We sit in the driveway and wait for Eric Bray, the brother, to appear with a key.

"You may have seen him at the memorial service." Berger reminds me that Eric Bray was the man carrying the urn containing his sister's cremains. "Tell me how you think Chandonne got an experienced policewoman to open the door." Berger's attention flows far away from monsters in medieval France to the very real slaughterhouse before our eyes.

"That's a little wide of my boundaries, Ms. Berger. Maybe it's better if you restrict your questions to the bodies and what my findings are."

"There are no boundaries right now, only questions."

"Is this because you assume I may never be in court, at least not in New York, because I'm tainted?" I go ahead and open that door. "In fact, they don't get much more tainted than I am right this minute."

I pause to see if she knows. When she says nothing, I confront her. "Has Righter given you a hint that I may not prove very helpful to you? That I'm being investigated by a grand jury because he has this cockeyed notion that I had something to do with Bray's death?"

"I've been given more than a hint," she quietly replies as she stares out at Bray's dark house. "Marino and I have talked about it, too."

"So much for secret proceedings," I sardonically say.

"Well, the rule is, nothing that goes on inside the grand jury room can be discussed. Nothing's gone on yet. All that's happening is Righter is using a special grand jury as a tool for gaining access to everything he can. About you. Your phone bills. Your bank statements. What people have to say. You know how it works. I'm sure you've testified in your share of grand jury hearings."

She says all this as if it is routine. My indignation rises and spills over in words. "You know, I do have feelings," I say. "Maybe murder indictments are everyday matters to you, but they aren't to me. My integrity is the one thing I've got that

I can't afford to lose. It's everything to me, and of all people to accuse of such a crime. Of all people! To even consider that I would do the very thing I fight against every waking minute of my life? Never. I don't abuse power. Never. I don't deliberately hurt people. Never. And I don't take this bullshit in stride, Ms. Berger. Nothing worse could happen to me. Nothing."

"Do you want my recommendation?" She looks at me.

"I'm always open for suggestions."

"First, the media's going to find out. You know that. I'd beat them to the draw and have a press conference. Right away. The good news is, you haven't been fired. You haven't lost the support of the people who have power over your professional life. A fucking miracle. Politicians are usually quick to run for cover, but the governor has a very high opinion of you. He doesn't believe you killed Diane Bray. If he makes a statement to that effect, then you should be all right, providing the special grand jury doesn't come back with a true bill, an indictment."

"Have you discussed any of this with Governor Mitchell?" I ask her.

"We've had contact in the past. We're acquainted. We worked a case together when he was AG."

"Yes, I know that." It also isn't what I asked.

Silence. She stares out at Bray's house. There are no lights on inside, and I point out that it was Chandonne's MO to unscrew the lightbulb over the porch or pull out the wires, and when his victim opened the door, he was hidden by darkness.

"I would like your opinion," she then says. "I'm confident you have one. You're a very observant, seasoned investigator." She says this firmly and with an edge. "You also know what Chandonne did to you—you are intimately familiar with his MO in a way no one else is."

Her reference to Chandonne's attack on me is jarring. Even though Berger is simply doing her job, I am offended by her blunt objectivity. I am also put off by her evasiveness. I resent that she decides what we will discuss and when and for how long. I can't help it. I am human. I want her to show at least a hint of compassion toward me and what I have endured. "Someone called the morgue this morning and identified himself as Benton Wesley." I drop that one on her. "You heard from Rocky Marino Caggiano yet? What's he up to?" Anger and fear sharpen my voice.

"We won't hear from him for a while," she says as if she knows. "Not his style. But it sure wouldn't surprise me if he's up to his old tricks. Harassment. Hurting. Terrorizing. Going for the sensitive spots as a warning, if nothing else. My guess is you'll have no direct contact with him or even catch a whiff of him until closer to the trial. If you ever see him at all. He's like that, the son of a bitch. Behind the scenes all the way."

Neither of us speaks for a moment. She is waiting for me to lower the gate. "My opinion or speculation, all right," I finally say. "That's what you want? Fine."

"That's what I want. You'd make a pretty good second seat." A reference to a second D.A. who would be her co-counsel, her partner during a trial. Either she has just paid me a compliment or she is being ironical.

"Diane Bray had a friend who came over quite often." I take my first step out of bounds. I begin deducing. "Detective Anderson. She was obsessed with Bray. Bray seriously teased her, so it appears. I think it's possible Chandonne watched Bray and gathered intelligence. He observed Anderson come and go. On the night of the murder, he waited until Anderson left Bray's house"—I stare out at it—"and immediately went up to it, unscrewed the porch light, then knocked on the door. Bray assumed it was Anderson returning to resume their argument or make up or whatever."

"Because they'd been fighting. They fought a lot," Berger carries along the narrative.

"By all appearances, it was a tempestuous relationship," I keep heading deeper into restricted airspace. I am not supposed to enter this part of an investigation, but I keep going. "Anderson had stormed off and come back in the past," I add.

"You sat in on the interview with Anderson after the body was found." Berger knows this. Someone has told her. Marino, probably.

"Yes, I did."

"And the story of what happened that night while Anderson was eating pizza and drinking beer at Bray's house?"

"They got into an argument—this is according to Anderson. So Anderson left angry and soon after there is a knock on the door. The same pattern of knocking that Anderson always did. He imitated the way she knocked just as he imitated the police when he came to my house."

"Show me." Berger looks at me.

I knock on the console between the front seats. Three times, hard.

"This is how Anderson always knocked on the door? She didn't use the doorbell?" Berger asks.

"You've been around cops enough to know that they hardly ever ring doorbells. They're used to neighborhoods where doorbells don't work, if they exist."

"Interesting that Anderson didn't come back," she observes. "What if she had? Do you think Chandonne somehow knew she wasn't going to come back that night?"

"I've wondered that, too."

"Maybe just something he sensed about her demeanor when she left? Or maybe he was so out of control he couldn't stop," Berger ponders. "Or maybe his lust was stronger than his fear that he might be interrupted."

"He may have observed one other important thing," I say. "Anderson didn't have a key to Bray's house. Bray always let her in."

"Yes, but the door wasn't locked when Anderson came back the next morning and found the body, right?"

"Doesn't mean it wasn't locked when he was inside attacking Bray. He hung out a closed sign and locked the convenience store while he was killing Kim Luong."

"But we don't know for a fact that he locked the door behind him when he entered Bray's house," Berger reiterates.

"*I* certainly don't know it for a fact."

"And he might not have locked up." Berger is into it. "He might have shoved his way in and the chase begins. The door is unlocked the entire time he is mutilating her body in the bedroom."

"That would suggest he was out of control and taking big risks," I point out.

"Hmmm. I don't want to go down the road of *out of control*." Berger seems to talk to herself.

"Out of control isn't at all the same thing as insane," I remind her. "All people who murder, except out of self-defense, are out of control."

"Ah. Touché." She nods. "So Bray opens the door, and the light is out and there he is in the dark."

"This is also what he did to Dr. Stvan in Paris," I tell Berger. "Women were being murdered over there, same MO, and in several cases Chandonne left notes at the crime scenes."

"That's where the name Loup-Garou comes from," Berger interjects.

"He also wrote that name on a box inside the cargo container where the body was found—the body of his brother, Thomas. But yes," I say, "he apparently began leaving notes, referring to himself as a werewolf when he began murdering over there, in Paris. One night, he showed up at Dr. Stvan's door, not realizing that her husband was home sick. He works at night as a chef, but on this particular occasion, he was home unexpectedly, thank God. Dr. Stvan opens the door and when Chandonne hears her husband call out from another room, he flees."

"She get a good look at him?"

"I don't think so." I conjure up what Dr. Stvan told me. "It was dark. It was her impression that he was dressed neatly in a long, dark coat, a scarf, his hands in his pockets. He spoke well, was gentlemanly, using the ruse that his car had broken down and he needed a phone. Then he realized she wasn't alone and ran like hell."

"Anything else she remembered about him?"

"His smell. He had a musky smell, like a wet dog."

Berger makes a strange sound at that comment. I am becoming familiar with her subtle mannerisms, and when a detail is especially weird or disgusting, she sucks the inside of her cheek and emits a quiet rasping squeak like a bird. "So he goes after the chief medical examiner there, and then goes after the one here. You," she adds for emphasis. "Why?" She has turned halfway around in her seat and is resting an elbow on the steering wheel, facing me.

"Why?" I repeat, as if it is a question I can't possibly answer—as if it is a question she shouldn't ask me. "Maybe someone should tell me that." Again, I feel the heat of anger rise.

"Premeditation," she replies. "Insane people don't plan their crimes with this sort of deliberation. Picking the chief medical examiner in Paris and then the one here. Both women. Both autopsied his victims and therefore in a perverse way are intimate with him. Perhaps more intimate with him than a lover, because you have, in a sense, *watched*. You see where he has touched and bitten. You put your hands on the same body he did. In a way, you have watched him make love with these women, for this is how Jean-Baptiste Chandonne makes love to a woman."

"A revolting thought." I find her psychological interpretation personally offensive.

"A pattern. A plan. Not the least bit random. So it's important we understand his patterns, Kay. And do so without personal revulsion or reaction." She draws out a pause. "You must look at him dispassionately. You can't indulge in hate."

"It's hard not to hate someone like him," I reply honestly.

"And when we truly resent and hate someone, it's also hard to give them our time and attention, to be interested in them as if they are worth figuring out. We have to be interested in Chandonne. Intensely interested. I need you to be more interested in him than you have in anyone else in your life."

I don't disagree with what Berger is saying. I know she is pointing out a significant truth. But I desperately resist being interested in Chandonne. "I've always been victim-driven," I tell Berger. "I've never spent my time trying to get into the soul and mind of the assholes who do it."

"And you've never been involved in a case like this, either," she counters. "You've never been a suspect in a murder, either. I can help you with your mess. And I need you to help me with mine.

Help me get into Chandonne's mind, into his heart. I need you not to hate him."

I am silent. I don't want to give Chandonne any more of myself than he has already taken. I feel tears of frustration and fury and blink them back. "How can you help me?" I ask Berger. "You have no jurisdiction here. Diane Bray is not your case. You can drag her into your Molineux motion in Susan Pless's murder, but I'm left hanging out to dry when it comes to a Richmond special grand jury. Especially if certain people are trying to make it appear that I killed her, killed Bray. That I'm deranged." I take a deep breath. My heart races.

"The key to your clearing your name is my same key," she replies. "Susan Pless. How could you possibly have had anything to do with that death? How could you have tampered with that evidence?"

She waits for my answer, as if I have one. The thought numbs me. Of course, I had nothing to do with Susan Pless's murder.

"My question is this," Berger goes on. "If the DNA from Susan's case matches your cases here and possibly the DNA in the Paris cases, doesn't that mean it has to be the same person who killed all these people?"

"I guess jurors don't have to believe it beyond a reasonable doubt. All they need is probable cause," I reply, playing devil's advocate in my own dilemma. "The chipping hammer with Bray's blood on it—found in my house. And a receipt showing that I bought a chipping hammer. And the chipping hammer I actually bought has vanished. All sort of sticks out like a smoking gun, Ms. Berger, don't you think?"

She touches my shoulder. "Answer me this," she says. "Did you do it?"

"No," I reply. "No, I didn't do it."

"Good. Because I can't afford for you to have done it," she says. "I need you. *They* need you." She stares out at the cold, empty house beyond our windshield, indicating Chandonne's other victims, the ones who didn't survive. They need me. "Okay." She returns us to why we are waiting in this driveway. She returns us to Diane Bray. "So he comes through her front door. There's no sign of a struggle and he doesn't attack her until they are all the way to the other end of the house, in her bedroom. It doesn't appear she attempted to escape or defend herself in any way. She never went for her gun? She's a policewoman. Where's her gun?"

"I know when he forced his way into my house," I reply, "he tried to throw his coat over my head." I am trying to do what she wants. I act as if I am talking about someone else.

"Then maybe he nets Bray with a coat or something else he threw over her head, and forced her back to the bedroom?"

"Maybe. The police never found Bray's gun. Not that I know of," I reply.

"Huh. Wonder what he did with that?" Berger muses.

Headlights shine in the rearview mirror and I turn around. A station wagon slows at the driveway.

"There was also money missing from her house," I add. "Twenty-five hundred dollars, drug money Anderson had just brought over earlier that evening. According to her, to Anderson." The station wagon pulls up behind us. "From the sale of prescription pills, if Anderson's telling the truth."

"Do you think she was telling the truth?" Berger asks.

"The whole truth? I don't know," I reply. "So maybe Chandonne took the money and he may have taken her gun, too. Unless Anderson took the money when she came back to the house the next morning and found the body. But after seeing what was in the master bedroom, it's frankly hard for me to imagine she did anything but run like the wind."

"Based on the photographs you've shown me, I would tend to agree," Berger replies.

We get out. I can't see Eric Bray well enough to recognize him, but my vague impression is of a well-dressed, attractive man who is close in age to his slain sister, maybe forty or so. He hands Berger a key attached to a manila tag. "The alarm code's written on it," he says. "I'm just going to wait out here."

"I'm really sorry to put you to all this trouble." Berger gathers a camera and an accordion file from the backseat. "Especially on Christmas Eve."

"I know you people have to do your job," he says in a dull, flat tone.

"Have you been inside?"

He hesitates and stares off at the house. "Can't do it." His voice rises with emotion and tears cut him off. He shakes his head and climbs back inside his car. "I don't know how any of us . . . Well," he clears his throat, talking to us through the open car door, the interior light on, the bell dinging. "How we're ever going to go in and deal with her things." He focuses on me, and Berger introduces us. I have no doubt he already knows very well who I am.

"There are professional cleaning services in the area," I delicately tell him. "I suggest you contact one and have them go in before you or any other family member does. Service Master, for example." I have been through this many times with families whose loved ones have died violently inside the residence. No one should have to go in and deal with their loved one's blood and brains everywhere.

"They can just go in without us?" he asks me. "The cleaning people can?"

"Leave a key in a lock box at the door. And yes, they'll go in and take care of things without you present," I reply. "They're bonded and insured."

"I want to do that. We want to go on and sell this place," he tells Berger. "If you're not needing it anymore."

"I'll let you know," she replies. "But you, of course, have the right to do whatever you want with the property, Mr. Bray."

"Well, I don't know who will buy it after what happened," he mutters.

Neither Berger nor I comment. He is probably right. Most people do not want a house where someone has been murdered. "I already talked to one realtor," he goes on in a dull voice that belies his anger. "They said they couldn't take it on. They're sorry and all that, but they didn't want to represent the property. I don't know what to do." He stares out at the dark, lifeless house. "You know, we weren't real close to Diane, no one in the family was. She wasn't what I would call really into her family or friends. Mostly just into herself, and I know I probably shouldn't say that. But it's the damn honest truth."

"Did you see her very often?" Berger asks him.

He shakes his head, no. "I guess I knew her best because we're only two years apart. We all knew she had more money than we could understand. She stopped by my house on Thanksgiving, pulled up in this brand new red Jaguar." He smiles bitterly and shakes his head again. "That's when I knew for sure she was into something I probably didn't want to know a damn thing about. I'm not surprised, really." He takes a deep, quiet breath. "Not surprised really that it's ended up like this."

"Were you aware of her involvement in drugs?" Berger shifts her file to her other arm.

I am getting cold standing out here, and the dark house pulls at us like a black hole.

"The police have said some things. Diane never talked about what she did and we didn't ask, frankly. As far as we know, she didn't even have a will. So now we've got that mess, too," Eric Bray tells us. "And what to do with her things." He looks up at us from the driver's seat and the dark can't hide his misery. "I really don't know what to do."

So much eddies around a violent death. These are hardships that no one sees in the movies or reads about in the newspapers: the people left behind and the wrenching concerns they bear. I give Eric Bray my business card and tell him to call my office if he has any further questions. I go through my usual routine of letting him know the Institute has a booklet, an excellent resource called *What to Do When the Police Leave* written by Bill Jenkins, whose young son was murdered during the mindless robbery of a fast-food restaurant a couple years back. "The book will answer a lot of your questions," I add. "I'm sorry. A violent death leaves many victims in its wake. That's the unfortunate reality."

"Yes, ma'am, that's for damn sure," he says. "And yes, I'd like to read anything you got. I don't know what to expect, what to do about any of this," he repeats himself. "I'm out here if you have any questions. I'll be right here inside the car."

He shuts his door. My chest is tight. I am touched by his pain, yet I can't feel sorrow for his slain sister. If anything, the portrait he paints of her makes me like her even less. She wasn't even decent to her own flesh and blood. Berger says nothing as we climb the front steps and I sense her never-ending scrutiny. She is interested in my every reaction. She can tell that I still resent Diane Bray and what she tried to do to my life. I make no effort to hide it. Why bother at this point?

Berger is looking up at the porch light, which is faintly illuminated by the headlights of Eric Bray's car. It is a simple glass fixture, small and globe-shaped, supposed to be held into the fixture by screws. Police found the glass globe in the grass near a boxwood where Chandonne apparently tossed it. Then it was simply a matter of unscrewing the bulb, which "would have been hot," I tell Berger. "So my guess is he covered it with something to protect his fingers. Maybe he used his coat."

"No fingerprints on it," she says. "Not Chandonne's prints, according to Marino." This is news to me. "But that doesn't surprise me, assuming he covered the bulb so he didn't burn his fingers," she adds.

"What about the globe?"

"No prints. Not his." Berger inserts the key in the lock. "But he might have his hands covered when he unscrewed that, too. Just wonder how he reached the light. It's pretty high up." She opens the door and the alarm system begins beeping. "Think he climbed up on something?" She goes to the key pad inside and enters the code.

"Maybe he climbed up on the railing," I suggest, suddenly the expert on Jean-Baptiste Chandonne's behavior and not liking the role.

"What about at your house?"

"He could have done that," I reply. "Climbed up on the railing and steadied himself against the wall or the porch roof."

"No prints on your light fixture or the bulb, in

case you don't know," she tells me. "Not his, at any rate."

Clocks tick-tock in the living room, and I remember how surprised I was when I walked into Diane Bray's house for the first time, after she was dead, and discovered her collection of perfectly synchronized clocks and her grand but cold English antiques.

"Money." Berger stands in the living room and looks around at the scroll-end sofa, the revolving bookcase, the ebonized sideboard. "Oh yes, indeed. Money, money, money. Cops don't live like this."

"Drugs," I comment.

"No fucking kidding." Berger's eyes move everywhere. "User and dealer. Only she got others to be her mules. Including Anderson. Including your former morgue supervisor who was stealing prescription drugs that you assumed were being disposed of down the morgue sink. Chuck what's-his-name." She touches gold damask draperies and looks up at the valances. "Cobwebs," she observes. "Dust that didn't just appear during these last few days. There are other stories about her."

"There must be," I reply. "Selling prescription drugs on the street can't account for all this and a new Jaguar."

"Brings me back to a question I keep asking everyone who will stand still long enough for me to talk to them." Berger moves on toward the kitchen. "Why did Diane Bray move to Richmond?"

I have no answer.

"Not for the job, no matter what she said. Not for that. No way." Berger opens the refrigerator door. There is very little inside: Grape-Nuts cereal, tangerines, mustard, Miracle Whip. The two percent milk passed its expiration date yesterday. "Rather interesting," Berger says. "I don't think this lady was ever home." She opens a cupboard and scans cans of Campbell's soup and a box of saltine crackers. There are three jars of gourmet olives. "Martinis? I wonder. She drink a lot?"

"Not the night she died," I remind her.

"That's right. Point-oh-three alcohol level." Berger opens another cupboard and another until she finds where Bray kept her liquor. "One bottle of vodka. One of Scotch. Two Argentine cabernets. Not the bar of someone who drank a lot. Probably was too vain about her figure to ruin it with booze. Pills at least aren't fattening. When you came to the scene, was that the first time you'd ever been to her house—to this house?" Berger asks.

"Yes."

"But your house is only a few blocks away."

"I'd seen this house in passing. From the street. But no, I'd never been inside. We weren't friends."

"But she wanted to be friends."

"I'm told she wanted to have lunch or whatever. To get to know me," I reply.

"Marino."

"That's what Marino told me," I confirm, getting used to her questions by now.

"Do you think she was sexually interested in you?" Berger asks this very casually as she opens a cabinet door. Inside are glasses and dishes. "There are plenty of intimations that she played both sides of the net."

"I've been asked that before. I don't know."

"Would it have bothered you if she was?"

"It would have made me uncomfortable. Probably," I admit.

"She eat out a lot?"

"It's my understanding she did."

I am noting that Berger asks questions I suspect she already has answered. She wants to hear what I have to say and weigh my perceptions against those of others. Some of what she explores carries the echo of what Anna asked me during our fireside confessionals. I wonder if it is remotely possible that Berger has talked to Anna, too.

"Reminds me of a store that's a front for some illegal business," Berger says as she checks out what's beneath the sink: a few cleansers and several dried sponges. "Don't worry," she seems to read my mind. "I'm not going to let anyone ask you these sorts of things in court, about your sex life or whatever. Nothing about her personal life, either. I realize that's not supposed to be your area of expertise."

"Not supposed to be?" It seems an odd comment.

"Problem is, some of what you know isn't hearsay, but knowledge you got directly from her. She did tell you"—Berger opens a drawer—"that she often ate out alone, sat at the bar at Buckhead's."

"That's what she told me."

"The night you met her there in the parking lot and confronted her."

"The night I tried to prove that she was in collusion with my morgue assistant, Chuck."

"And she was."

"Unfortunately, she certainly was," I reply.

"And you confronted her."

"I did."

"Well, good ol' Chuck's in lockup where he belongs." Berger walks out of the kitchen. "And if it's not hearsay," she returns to that topic, "then Rocky Caggiano is going to ask you and I can't object. Or I can, but it will get me nowhere. You need to realize that. And how it makes you look."

"Right now, I'm more worried about how

everything makes me look to a special grand jury," I pointedly answer her.

She stops in the hallway. At the end of it, the master bedroom is behind a door that is carelessly ajar, adding to the ambiance of neglect and indifference that chills this place. Berger meets my eyes. "I don't know you personally," she says. "No one seated on that special grand jury is going to know you personally. It's your word against a murdered policewoman's that it was she who harassed you and not the other way around, and that you had nothing to do with her murder—even though you seem to think the world is better off without her."

"Did you get that from Anna or Righter?" I bitterly ask her.

She starts down the hallway. "Pretty soon, Dr. Kay Scarpetta, you're gonna get a thick skin," she says. "I'm making that my mission."

CHAPTER 26

BLOOD IS LIFE. IT BEHAVES like a living creature.

When the circulatory system is breached, the blood vessel contracts in a panic, making itself smaller in an attempt to diminish the blood flowing through it and out of the tear or cut. Platelets immediately rally to plug the hole. There are thirteen clotting factors and together they instigate their alchemy to stop blood loss. I have always thought that blood is bright red for a reason, too. It is the color of alarm, of emergency, of danger and distress. If blood were a clear fluid like sweat, we might not notice when we are injured or when someone else is. Bright red boasts of blood's importance, and it is the siren that sounds when the greatest of all violations has occurred: when another person has maimed or taken a life.

Diane Bray's blood cries out in drips and

droplets, splashes and smears. It tattles on who did what and how and in some instances, why. The severity of a beating affects the velocity and volume of blood flying through the air. Cast-off blood from the backswing of a weapon tells the number of blows, which in this case were at least fifty-six. That is as precisely as we can calculate, because some blood spatters overlay other spatters and sorting out how many might be on top of each other is like trying to figure out how many times a hammer struck a nail to drive it into a tree. The number of blows mapped in this room are consistent with what Bray's body told me. But again, so many fractures overlaid others and so much bone was utterly crushed that I, too, lost count. Hate. Incredible lust and rage.

There has been no attempt to clean up what happened in the master bedroom, and what Berger and I find contrasts profoundly with the stillness and sterility of the rest of the house. First, there is what looks like a massive bright pink web spun by crime scene technicians who have used a method called stringing to find the trajectories of blood droplets that are simply everywhere. The objective is to determine distance, velocity and angle, to conjure up through a mathematical model the exact position of Bray's body when each blow was struck. The results look like a strange modern art design, a weird fuchsia geometry that leads the eye to walls, ceiling, floor, antique furniture and the four ornate mirrors where Bray once admired her spectacular, sensual beauty. Coagulated puddles of blood on the floor are now hard and thick like dried molasses, and the king-size bed where Bray's body was so crudely displayed looks as if someone dashed cans of black paint across the bare mattress.

I feel Berger's reaction as she stares. She is silent as she absorbs what is ghastly, truly incomprehensible. She becomes charged with a peculiar energy that only people, especially women, who battle violence for a living can really understand. "Where are the bed linens?" Berger opens the accordion file. "Were they turned in to the labs?"

"We never found them," I reply, and I am reminded of the motel room at the campground. Those bed linens are missing, too. Chandonne claims bed linens disappeared from his apartment in Paris, I recall his saying.

"Removed before or after she was killed?" Berger slips photographs out of an envelope.

"Before. That's apparent from the bloody transfers on the bare mattress." I step inside the room, moving around strings that point accusingly at Chandonne's crime like long slender fingers. I show Berger unusual parallel smears on the mattress, the bloody stripes transferred by the coil handle of the chipping hammer when Chandonne set it down on the mattress between or after blows. Berger doesn't see the pattern at first. She stares, slightly frowning as I decipher a chaos of dark stains that are handprints and smears where I believe Chandonne's knees may have been as he was straddling the body and acting out his horrific sexual fantasies. "These patterns wouldn't have been transferred to the mattress if there were linens on the bed at the time of the attack," I explain.

Berger studies a photograph of Bray on her back, sprawled across the middle of the mattress, black corduroy pants and belt on, but no shoes and socks, naked from the waist up, a smashed gold watch on her left wrist. A gold ring on her battered right hand is driven into the bone of her finger.

"So either there were no linens on the bed at the time, or he removed them for some reason," I add.

"I'm trying to envision that." Berger scans the mattress. "He's in the house. He's forcing her down the hallway, back to this area, to the bedroom. There's no sign of a struggle—no evidence he injured her until they get in here and then boom! All hell breaks loose. My question is this: He gets her back here and then says, 'Hey, wait a second while I strip the bed'? He takes time to do that?"

"By the time he got her on the bed, I seriously doubt she was talking or able to run. If you look here and here and here and here." I refer to segments of string taped to blood droplets that begin at the bedroom's entrance. "Cast-off blood from the backswing of the weapon—in this case, the chipping hammer."

Berger follows the bright pink string design and tries to correlate what it indicates with what she is seeing in photographs she goes through. "Tell me the truth," she says. "Do you really put a lot of credence in stringing? I know cops who think it's bullshit and a huge waste of time."

"Not if the person knows what he's doing and is faithful to the science."

"And the science is?"

I explain to her that blood is ninety-one percent water. It adheres to the physics of liquid, and it is affected by motion and gravity. A typical drop of blood will fall 25.1 feet per second. Stain diameter increases as the dropping distance increases. Blood dripping into blood produces a corona of spatters around the original pool. Splashed blood produces long, narrow spatters around a central stain, and as blood dries, it goes from bright red to reddish-brown to brown to black. I know experts who have spent their entire careers affixing medicine droppers of blood to ring stands, using plumb lines, squeezing or dripping or pouring or projecting blood onto a variety of target surfaces from a variety of angles and heights, and walking through puddles and stamping and slapping, and experimenting. Then, of course, there is the math, the straight-line geometry and trigonometry for figuring out point of origin.

The blood in Diane Bray's bedroom, at a glance, is a videotape of what happened, but it is in a format that is unreadable unless we use science, experience and deductive reasoning to sort it out. Berger also wants me to use my intuition. Again, she wants me to edge beyond my clinical boundaries. I follow dozens of strands of string that connect spatters on the wall and the door frame and converge to a point in mid-air. Since you can't tape string to thin air, the crime scene technicians moved an antique coat rack in from the foyer and taped the string some five feet from the base of it to determine the point of origin. I show Berger where Bray probably was standing when Chandonne struck the first blow.

"She was several feet inside the door," I say. "See this void area here?" I point out a space on the wall where there is no blood, just spatters in an aura all around it. "Her body or his blocked blood from hitting that part of the wall. She was upright. Or he was. And if he was upright, we can assume she was because you don't stand straight up and beat someone who is on the floor." I stand straight up and show her. "Not unless you have arms six feet long. Also, the point of origin is more than five feet off the floor, implying this is where the blows were connecting with their target. Her body. Most likely, her head." I move several feet closer to the bed. "Now she's down."

I point out smears and drips on the floor. I explain that stains produced from a ninety-degree angle are round. If, for example, you were on your hands and knees and blood was dripping straight down to the floor from your face, those drips would be round. Numerous drips on the floor are round. Some are smeared. They cover an approximate two-foot area. Bray was, for a brief time, on her hands and knees, perhaps trying to crawl as he kept on swinging.

"Did he kick or stomp?" Berger asks.

"Nothing I found would tell me that." It is a good question. Stomping and kicking would add other shadings to the emotions of the crime.

"Hands are more personal than feet," Berger remarks. "That's been my experience in lust murders. Rarely do I see kicking, stomping."

I walk around, pointing out more cast-off blood and satellite spatters before moving to a hardened puddle of blood several feet from the bed. "She bled out here," I tell her. "This may be where he tore off her blouse and bra."

Berger shuffles through photographs and finds the one of Bray's green satin blouse and black underwire bra on the floor several feet from the bed.

"This close to the bed and we begin finding brain tissue." I keep deciphering the gory hieroglyphics.

"He places her body on the bed," Berger interpolates. "Versus forcing her on it. Question is, is she still conscious when he gets her on the bed?"

"I really don't think so." I point out tiny bits of blackened tissue adhering to the headboard, the walls, a bedside lamp, the ceiling over the bed. "Brain tissue. She doesn't know what's going on anymore. That's just an opinion," I offer.

"Still alive?"

"She's still bleeding out." I indicate dense black areas of the mattress. "That's not an opinion. That's a fact. She still has a blood pressure, but it's very unlikely she's conscious."

"Thank God." Berger has gotten out her camera and begins taking photographs. I can tell she is skilled and has been properly trained. She walks out of the room and starts shooting as she comes back in, recreating what I have just walked her through and capturing it on film. "I'll get Escudero back here and videotape it," she lets me know.

"The cops videoed it."

"I know," she replies as the flash goes off again and again. She doesn't care. Berger is a perfectionist. She wants it done her way. "I'd love to have you on tape explaining all this, but can't do it."

She can't, not unless she wants opposing counsel to have access to the same tape. Based on the resounding absence of note-taking, I am certain that she doesn't want Rocky Caggiano to have access to a single word—written or spoken—that goes beyond what is on my standard reports. Her caution is extreme. I am shaded by suspicions that I have a hard time taking seriously. It really hasn't penetrated that anyone might seriously think I murdered the woman whose blood is all around us and under our feet.

BERGER AND I FINISH WITH THE bedroom. Next we explore other areas of the house that I paid little if any attention to when I was working the scene. I did go through the medicine cabinet in the master bedroom. I always do that. What people keep to alleviate bodily discomforts tells quite a story. I know who has migraines or mental illness or is obsessive about health. I know that Bray's chemicals of choice, for example, were Valium and Ativan. I found hundreds of pills that she had put in Nuprin and Tylenol PM bottles. She had a small amount of BuSpar, too. Bray liked sedatives. She craved soothing. Berger and I explore a guest bedroom down the hall. It is a room I have never stepped inside, and unsurprisingly, it is unlived-in. It isn't even furnished, but instead is cluttered with boxes that Bray apparently never unpacked.

"Are you getting the sensation that she wasn't planning on staying here long?" Berger is beginning to talk to me as if I am part of her prosecution team, her second seat in the trial. "Because I sure am. And you don't take on a major position in a police department without assuming you're going to stick it out for at least a few years. Even if the job is nothing but a stepping stone."

I look around inside the bathroom and note there is no toilet paper, no tissues, not even soap. But what I find inside the medicine cabinet surprises me. "Ex-Lax," I announce. "At least a dozen boxes."

Berger appears in the doorway. "Well, I'll be damned," she says. "Maybe our vain friend had an eating disorder."

It is not uncommon with people who suffer from bulimia to use laxatives to purge themselves after bingeing. I lift the toilet seat and find evidence of vomit that has splashed up on the inside of the rim and the bowl. It is a reddish color. Bray supposedly ate pizza before she died, and I recall that she had very little stomach contents: traces of ground meat and vegetables.

"If someone threw up after eating and then died maybe a half hour or hour later, would you expect his stomach to be totally empty?" Berger follows what I am piecing together.

"There would still be traces of food clinging to the stomach lining." I lower the toilet seat. "A stomach isn't totally empty or clean unless the person has drunk huge amounts of water and purged. Like a lavage or a repeated infusion of water to wash out a poison, let's say." Another section of footage plays before my eyes. This room was Bray's dirty, shameful secret. It is closed off from the regular flow of the house and no one but Bray ever came back here, so there was no fear of discovery, and I know enough about eating disorders and addictions to be very aware of the person's desperate need to hide his shameful ritual from others. Bray was determined that no one would ever catch even the slightest hint that she was bingeing and purging, and perhaps her problem explains why she kept so little food in the house. Perhaps the medications helped control the anxiety that is inevitably part of any compulsion.

"Maybe this is one of the reasons she was so quick to run Anderson off after eating," Berger conjectures. "Bray wanted to get rid of the food and wanted privacy."

"That would be at least one reason," I reply. "People with this affliction are so overwhelmed by the impulse it tends to override anything else that might be going on. So yes, she might have wanted to be alone to take care of her problem. And she might have been back here in this bathroom when Chandonne showed up."

"Thus adding to her vulnerability." Berger takes photographs of the Ex-Lax inside the medicine cabinet.

"Yes. She would have been alarmed and paranoid if she was in the middle of her ritual. And her first thought would have been about what she was doing—not about any imminent danger."

"Distracted." Berger bends over and photographs the toilet bowl.

"Extremely distracted."

"So she hurries to finish what she's doing, vomiting, " Berger reconstructs. "She rushes out of here and shuts the door and goes to the front door. She's assuming it's Anderson who's out there knocking three times. Very possibly, Bray's rattled and annoyed and might even start saying something angry as she opens the door and . . ." Berger steps back out in the hallway, her mouth grimly set. "She's dead."

She lets this scenario hang pregnantly as we seek out the laundry room. She knows I can relate to the distraction and mind-searing horror of opening the front door and having Chandonne suddenly rush in from the darkness like a creature out of hell. Berger opens hall closet doors, then finds a door that leads to the basement. The laundry area is down here, and I feel strangely unsettled and unnerved as we walk about in the harsh glare of naked overhead lightbulbs that are turned on by tugging strings. I have never been in this part of the house, either. I have never seen the bright red Jaguar I have heard so much about. It is absurdly out of place in this dark, cluttered, dismal space. The car is gorgeously bold and an on-the-nose symbol of the power Bray craved and flaunted. I am reminded of what Anderson angrily said about her being Bray's "gofer." I seriously doubt Bray ever drove to the carwash herself.

The basement garage looks the way I imagine it did when Bray bought the house: a dusty, dark, concrete space frozen in time. There is no sign of improvements. Tools hanging on a pegboard and a push lawn mower are old and rusting. Spare tires lean against a wall. The washer and dryer are not new and although I feel certain the police checked them, I see no sign of it. Both machines are full. Whenever Bray did laundry last, she didn't bother to empty either the washer or dryer, and lingerie, jeans and towels are hopelessly wrinkled and smell sour. Socks, more towels and work-out clothes in the washer were never put through the cycle. I pull out a Speedo running shirt. "Did she belong to a gym?" I ask.

"Good question. Vain and obsessive as she was, I suspect she did something to keep in shape." Berger digs through clothes in the washer and pulls out a pair of panties that are spotted with blood in the crotch. "Talk about airing some-one's dirty laundry," she ruefully comments. "Even I feel like a voyeur sometimes. So maybe she had her period recently. Not that it necessar-ily has anything to do with the price of tea in China."

"It might have," I reply. "Depends on how it affected her moods. PMS could certainly make her eating disorder worse, and mood swings couldn't have helped her volatile relationship with Anderson."

"Pretty amazing to think about the common, mundane things that can lead to catastrophe." Berger drops the panties back into the machine. "I had a case one time. This man has to pee and decides to pull off Bleecker Street and relieve himself in an alleyway. He can't see what he's doing until another car goes by and illuminates the

alleyway just enough for the poor old guy to realize he's peeing on a bloody dead body. The guy
peeing has a heart attack. A little later, a cop in-
vestigates this car illegally parked, goes in the alleyway and finds a dead Hispanic with multiple
stab wounds. Next to him is a dead older white
male with his dick hanging out of his unzipped
pants." Berger goes to a sink and rinses her hands,
shakes them dry. "Took a little while to figure that
one out," she says.

CHAPTER 27

WE FINISH WITH BRAY'S house at half past nine, and although I am tired, it would be impossible for me to even think about sleeping. I am energized in a strung-out way. My mind is lit up like a huge city at night and I almost feel feverish. I would never want to admit to anyone how much I actually enjoy working with Berger. She misses nothing. She keeps even more to herself. She has me intrigued. I have tasted the forbidden fruit of straying from my bureaucratic boundaries and I like it. I am flexing muscles I rarely get to use because she is not limiting my areas of expertise, and she is not territorial or insecure. Maybe I also want her to respect me, too. She has encountered me at my lowest point, when I am accused. She returns the house key to Eric Bray, who has no questions for us. He doesn't even seem curious but just wants to be on his way.

"How are you feeling?" Berger asks me as we drive off. "Holding up?"

"Holding up," I affirm.

She turns on an overhead light and squints at a Post-it on the dash. She dials a number on her car phone, leaving it on speaker. Her own recorded announcement comes on and she hits a code to see how many messages she has. Eight. And she picks up the handset so I can't hear them. This seems odd. Is there some reason she wanted me to know how many messages she has? I am alone with my thoughts for the next few minutes as she drives through my neighborhood, the phone against her ear. She goes through messages quickly and I suspect we share the same impatient habit. If someone is long-winded, I tend to delete the message before it is finished. Berger, I bet, does the same thing. We follow Sulgrave Road through the heart of Windsor Farms, passing the Virginia House and Agecroft Hall—ancient Tudor mansions that were dismantled and crated in England and shipped over here by wealthy Richmonders back in an era when this part of the city was one huge estate.

We approach the guard booth for Lockgreen, my neighborhood. Rita steps out of the booth and I know instantly by her bland expression that she has seen this Mercedes SUV and its driver before. "Hi," Berger says to her. "I have Dr. Scarpetta."

Rita bends over and her face shines in the open

window. She is happy to see me. "Welcome back," she says with a hint of relief. "You're home for good, I hope? It doesn't seem right, you not being here. Seems real quiet these days."

"Coming home in the morning." I experience ambivalence, even fear, as I hear myself say the words. "Merry Christmas, Rita. It looks like all of us are working tonight."

"Gotta do what you gotta do."

Guilt pinches my heart as we drive off. This will be the first Christmas when I haven't remembered the guards in some way. Usually, I bake bread for them or send food to whoever's sad lot it is to be sitting in that small booth when he should be home with family. I have gotten quiet. Berger senses I am troubled. "It's very important that you tell me your feelings," she quietly says. "I know it's completely against your nature and violates every rule you have laid down in your life." We follow the street toward the river. "I understand all too well."

"Murder makes everybody selfish," I tell her.

"No kidding."

"It causes unbearable anger and pain," I continue. "You think only of yourself. I've done much statistical analysis with our computer database, and one day I'm trying to pull up the case of a woman who was raped and murdered. I hit on three cases with the same last name and discover the rest of her family: a brother who died of a drug overdose some years after the murder, then the father who committed suicide several years after that, the mother who got killed in a car accident. We've begun an ambitious study at the Institute, doing an analysis of what happens to the people left behind. They get divorced. They become substance abusers. Are treated for mental illness. Lose their jobs. Move."

"Violence certainly poisons the lake," Berger rather banally replies.

"I'm tired of being selfish. That's what I'm feeling," I say. "Christmas Eve, and what have I done for anybody? Not even for Rita. Here she's working past midnight, has several jobs because she has children. Well, I hate this. He's hurt so many people. He continues to hurt people. We've had two off-the-wall murders that I believe are related. Torture. International connections. Guns, drugs. Bed covers missing." I look over at Berger. "When the hell is it going to stop?"

She turns into my driveway, making no pretense that she doesn't know exactly which one it is. "The reality is, not soon enough," she answers me.

Like Bray's house, mine is completely dark. Someone has turned off all the lights, including the floodlights that are politely hidden in trees or in eaves and pointed down at the ground so they don't light up my property like a baseball park and completely offend my neighbors. I don't feel welcome. I dread walking inside and facing what Chandonne, what the police, have done to my private world. I sit for a moment and stare out my window as my heart sinks lower. Anger. Pain. I am deeply offended.

"What are you feeling?" Berger asks as she stares out at my house.

"What am I feeling?" I bitterly repeat. "So much for *Più si prende e peggio si mangia*." I get out and angrily shut the car door.

Loosely translated, the Italian proverb means *the more you pay, the worse you eat*. Italian country life is supposed to be simple and sweet. It is supposed to be uncomplicated. The best food is made of fresh ingredients and people don't rush away from the table or care about matters that really aren't important. To my neighbors, my sturdy house is a fortress with every security system known to the human race. To me, what I built is a *casa colonica*, a quaint farmhouse of varying shades of creamy gray stone with brown shutters that warm me with reassuring, gentle thoughts of the people I come from. I only wish I had roofed my house with *coppi*, or curved terra-cotta tiles, instead of slate, but I didn't want a red dragon's back on top of rustic stone. If I couldn't reasonably find materials that were old, at least I chose ones that blend with the earth.

The essence of who I am is ruined. The simple beauty and safety of my life is sullied. I tremble inside. My vision blurs with tears as I climb the front steps and stand beneath the overhead lamp that Chandonne unscrewed. The night air bites and clouds have absorbed the moon. It feels like it might snow again. I blink and take in several breaths of cold air in an effort to calm myself and shove down overwhelming emotion. Berger, at least, has the good grace to give me a moment of peace. She has dropped back as I insert my key into the deadbolt lock. I step inside the dark, cool foyer and enter the alarm code as an awareness raises the hair on the back of my neck. I flip on lights and blink at the steel Medeco key in my hand and my pulse picks up. This is crazy. It can't be. No way. Berger is quietly coming through the door behind me. She looks around at the stucco walls and vaulted ceilings. Paintings are crooked. Rich Persian rugs are rumpled and disturbed and filthy. Nothing has been restored to its original order. It seems contemptuous that no one bothered to clean up dusting powder and tracked-in mud, but this isn't why I have a look on my face that pins Berger's complete attention.

"What is it?" she says, her hands poised to open her fur coat.

"I need to make a quick phone call," I tell her.

I DON'T TELL BERGER WHAT I AM thinking. I don't let on what I fear. I don't divulge that when I stepped back outside the house to use my cell phone in private, I called Marino and asked him to come here right now.

"Everything all right?" Berger asks when I return and shut the front door.

I don't answer her. Of course, everything isn't all right. "Where do you want me to start?" I remind her we have work to do.

She wants me to reconstruct exactly what happened the night Chandonne tried to murder me, and we wander into the great room. I begin with the white cotton sectional sofa in front of the fireplace. I was sitting there last Friday night, going through bills, the television turned down low. Periodically, a newsbreak would come on, warning the public about the serial killer who calls himself Le Loup-Garou. Information had been released about his supposed genetic disorder, his extreme deformity, and as I remember that evening it almost seems absurd to imagine a very serious anchor on a local channel talking about a man who is maybe six feet tall, has weird teeth and a body covered with long baby-fine hair. People were advised not to open the door if they weren't sure who was there.

"At about eleven," I tell Berger, "I switched over to NBC, I think, to watch the late news and moments later my burglar alarm went off. The zone for the garage had been violated, according to the display on the keypad, and when the service called, I told them they'd better dispatch the police because I had no idea why the thing had gone off."

"So your garage has an alarm system," Berger repeats. "Why the garage? Why do you think he tried to break into it?"

"To deliberately set off the alarm so the police would come," I repeat my belief. "They show up. They leave. Then he shows up. He impersonates the police and I open my door. No matter what anybody says or what I heard on the videotape when you interviewed him, he spoke English, perfect English. He had no accent at all."

"Didn't sound like the man in the videotape," she agrees.

"No. Certainly not."

"So you didn't recognize his voice in that tape."

"I didn't," I reply.

"You don't think he was really trying to get inside your garage, then. That this was just for the purpose of setting off the alarm," Berger probes, as usual writing nothing down.

"I doubt it. I think he was trying to do exactly what I said."

"And how do you suppose he knew your garage had an alarm system?" Berger inquires. "Rather unusual. Most homes don't have an alarm system in the garage."

"I don't know if he knew or how he knew."

"He could have tried a back door instead, for example, and been assured that the alarm would go off, assuming you had it on. And I fully believe he knew you would have it on. We can assume he knows you are a very security-minded woman, especially in light of the murders going on around here."

"I have no clue what would go through his mind," I say rather tersely.

Berger paces. She stops in front of the stone fireplace. It gapes empty and dark and makes my house seem unlived-in and neglected like Bray's. Berger points a finger at me, "You *do* know what he thinks," she confronts me. "Just as he was gathering intelligence on you and getting a feel for how you think and what your patterns are, you were doing the same thing to him. You read about him in the wounds of the bodies. You were communicating with him through his victims, through the crime scenes, through everything you learned in France."

CHAPTER 28

MY TRADITIONAL ITALIAN white sofa is stained pink from formalin. There are footprints on a cushion, probably left by me when I jumped over the sofa to escape Chandonne. I will never sit on that sofa again and can't wait to have it hauled away. I perch on the edge of a nearby matching chair.

"I must know him to dismantle him in court," Berger goes on, her eyes reflecting her inner fire. "I can only know him through you. You must make that introduction, Kay. Take me to him. Show him to me." She sits on the hearth and dramatically lifts her hands. "Who is Jean-Baptiste Chandonne? Why your garage? Why? What is special about your garage? What?"

I think for a moment. "I can't begin to say what might be special about it to him."

"All right. Then what's special about it to you?"

"It's where I keep my scene clothes." I begin trying to figure out what might be special about my garage. "And an industrial-size washer and dryer. I never wear scene clothes inside my house, so that's rather much my changing room, out there in the garage."

Something shines in Berger's eyes, a recognition, a connection. She gets up. "Show me," she says.

I turn on lights in the kitchen as we pass on through to the mud room, where a door leads into the garage.

"Your home locker room," Berger comments.

I flip on lights and my heart constricts as I realize the garage is empty. My Mercedes is gone.

"Where the hell's my car?" I ask. I scan walls of cabinets, and the specially ventilated cedar locker, and neatly stored yard and gardening supplies, the expected tools, and an alcove for the washer, dryer and a big steel sink. "No one has said anything about taking my car anywhere." I look accusingly at Berger and am rocked by instant distrust. But either she is quite an actor, or she has no clue. I walk out into the middle of the garage and look around, as if I might find something that will tell me what has happened to my car. I tell Berger my black Mercedes sedan was here last Saturday, the day I moved to Anna's. I haven't seen the car

since. I haven't been here since. "But you have,"
I add. "Was my car here when you were here last?
How many times have you been here?" I go ahead
and ask her that.

She is walking around, too. She squats before
the garage door and examines scrapes on the rubber strip where we believe Chandonne used some
type of tool to pry the door up. "Could you open
the door, please?" Berger is grim.

I press a button on the wall and the door loudly
rolls up. The temperature inside the garage instantly drops.

"No, your car wasn't here when I was." Berger
straightens up. "I've never seen it. In light of circumstances, I suspect you do know where it is,"
she adds.

The night fills the large empty space and I walk
over to where Berger is standing. "Probably im-
pounded," I say. "Jesus Christ."

She nods. "We'll get to the bottom of it." She
turns to me and there is something in her eyes I've
never before seen. Doubt. Berger is uneasy.
Maybe it is wishful thinking on my part, but I
sense she feels bad for me.

"So now what?" I mutter, looking around my
garage as if I have never seen it before. "What am
I supposed to drive?"

"Your alarm went off around eleven o'clock
Friday night," Berger is all business again. She is

firm and no-nonsense again. She returns to our mission of retracing Chandonne's steps. "The cops arrive. You take them in here and find the door open about eight inches." Obviously, she has seen the incident report of the attempted breaking and entering. "It was snowing and you found footprints on the other side of the door." She steps outside and I follow. "The footprints were covered with a dusting of snow, but you could tell they led around the side of the house, up to the street."

We stand on my driveway in the raw air, both of us without coats. I stare up at the murky sky and a few flakes of snow coldly touch my face. It has started again. Winter has become a hemophiliac. It can't seem to stop precipitating. Lights from my neighbor's house shine through magnolias and bare trees, and I wonder how much peace of mind the people of Lockgreen have left. Chandonne has tainted life for them, too. I wouldn't be surprised if some people move.

"Can you remember where the footprints were?" Berger asks.

I show her. I follow my driveway around the side of the house and cut through the yard, straight out to the street.

"Which way did he go?" Berger looks up and down the dark, empty street.

"Don't know," I reply. "The snow was churned

up and it was snowing again. We couldn't tell which way he went. But I didn't stay out here looking, either. I guess you'll have to ask the police." I think about Marino. I wish he would hurry up and get here, and I am reminded of why I called him. Fear and bewilderment crackle up my spine. I look around at my neighbors' houses. I have learned to read where I live and can tell, by windows lit up, by cars in the driveway and newspaper deliveries, when people are home, which really isn't often. So much of the population here is retired and wintering in Florida and spending hot summer months on the water somewhere. It occurs to me that I have never really had friends in my neighborhood, only people who wave when we pass each other in our cars.

Berger walks back toward the garage, hugging herself to keep warm, the moisture in her breath freezing and puffing out white. I remember Lucy as a child coming to visit from Miami. Her only exposure to the cold was Richmond, and she would roll up notebook paper and stand out on the patio, pretending to smoke, tapping imaginary ashes, not knowing I was watching through a window. "Let's back up," Berger is saying as she walks. "To Monday, December sixth. The day the body was found in the container at the Richmond Port. The body that we believe was Thomas Chandonne, allegedly murdered by his brother, Jean-Baptiste. Tell me exactly what happened that Monday."

"I was notified about the body," I begin.

"By whom?"

"Marino. Then minutes later, my deputy chief, Jack Fielding, called. I said I would respond to the scene," I begin.

"But you didn't have to," she interrupts. "You're the chief. We have a stinky, nasty decomposing body on an unseasonably warm morning. You could have let, uh, Fielding or whoever respond."

"I could have."

"Why didn't you?"

"It was clearly going to be a complicated case. The ship was out of Belgium and we had to entertain the possibility that the body originated in Belgium, thus adding international difficulties. I tend to take the hard cases, the ones that will get a lot of publicity."

"Because you like the publicity?"

"Because I don't like it."

We are inside my garage now and both of us are thoroughly chilled. I shut the door.

"And maybe you wanted to take this case because you'd had an upsetting morning?" Berger walks over to the large cedar locker. "You mind?" I tell her to help herself as I marvel again at the details she seems to know about me.

Black Monday. That morning, Senator Frank Lord, chairman of the judiciary committee and an old, dear friend, came to see me. In his possession was a letter Benton had written to me. I knew nothing about this letter. It would never occur to me that while Benton was on vacation at Lake Michigan some years ago, he had written me a letter and instructed Senator Lord to give it to me should he—Benton—die. I remember recognizing the penmanship when Senator Lord delivered the letter to me. I will never forget the shock. I was devastated. Grief finally caught up with me and seized my soul, and this was precisely what Benton had intended. He was the brilliant profiler to the end. He knew exactly how I would react should something happen to him, and he was forcing me out of my workaholic denial.

"How do you know about the letter?" I numbly ask Berger.

She is looking inside the locker at jumpsuits, rubber boots, waders, heavy leather gloves, long underwear, socks, tennis shoes. "Please bear with me," she says almost gently. "Just answer my questions for now. I'll answer yours later."

Later isn't good enough. "Why does the letter matter?"

"I'm not sure. But let's start with state of mind."

She lets that sink in. My state of mind is the

bull's-eye of Caggiano's target, should I end up in New York. More immediately, it is what everyone else seems to be questioning.

"Let's assume if I know something, the opposing counsel does, too," she adds.

I nod.

"You get this letter out of the blue. From Benton." She pauses and emotion flickers across her face. "Let me just say . . ." She looks away from me. "That would have undone me, too, totally. I'm sorry for what you've been through." She meets my eyes. Another ploy to make me trust her, bond with her? "Benton is reminding you a year after his death that you've probably not dealt with his loss. You've run like hell from the pain."

"You can't have seen the letter." I am stunned and outraged. "It's locked in a safe. How do you know what it says?"

"You showed it to other people," she reasonably replies.

I realize with the little bit of objectivity I have left that if Berger hasn't talked to everyone around me, including Lucy and Marino, she will. It is her duty. She would be foolish and negligent if she didn't. "December the sixth," she resumes. "He wrote the letter on December the sixth, nineteen-ninety-six, and instructed Senator Lord to deliver it to you on the December the sixth following

Benton's death. Why was that date special to Benton?"

I hesitate.

"Thick skin, Kay," she reminds me. "Thick skin."

"I don't know the significance of December the sixth, exactly—except Benton mentioned in the letter that he knew Christmas is hard for me," I reply. "He wanted me to get the letter close to Christmas."

"Christmas is hard for you?"

"Isn't it hard for everybody?"

Berger is silent. Then she asks, "When did your intimate relationship with him begin?"

"In the fall. Years ago."

"Okay. In the fall, years ago. That's when you began your sexual relationship with him." She says this as if I am avoiding reality. "When he was still married. When your affair with him began."

"That's right."

"Okay. This past December the sixth, you get the letter and later that morning responded to the scene at the Richmond port. Then you came back here. Tell me exactly what your routine is when you come straight home from a crime scene."

"My scene clothes were double-bagged in the trunk of my car," I explain. "A jumpsuit and tennis shoes." I keep staring at the empty space where my car should be. "The jumpsuit went into the washing machine, the shoes into a sink of scalding water with disinfectant." I show her the shoes. They are still parked on the shelf where I left them to dry more than two weeks ago.

"Then?" Berger walks over to the washing machine and dryer.

"Then I stripped," I tell her. "I took off everything and put it in the washing machine, started it up and went inside the house."

"Naked."

"Yes. I went back to my bedroom, to the shower, without stopping. That's how I disinfect if I come straight home from a scene," I conclude.

Berger is fascinated. She has a theory going, and whatever it is, I am feeling increasingly uncomfortable and exposed. "I just wonder," she muses. "Just wonder if he somehow knew."

"Somehow knew? And I really would like to go inside, if it's all right with you," I say. "I'm freezing."

"Somehow knew your routine," she persists. "If he was interested in your garage because of your routine. It was more than setting off the alarm. *Maybe he really was trying to get in.* The garage is where you take off your death clothes—in this instance, clothes sullied by a death he caused. You were nude and vulnerable, even if ever so briefly." She follows me back inside and I shut the mud room door behind us. "He might have a real sexual fantasy about that."

"I can't see how he could know a damn thing about my routine." I resist her hypothesis. "He didn't witness what I did that day."

She raises an eyebrow as she looks at me. "Can you say that as fact? Any possibility he followed you home? We know he was at the port at some point, because that's how he got to Richmond—aboard the *Sirius*, where he'd covered himself with a white uniform, shaved visible areas of his body, and stayed in the galley most of the time, working as the cook and keeping to himself. Isn't that the theory? I certainly don't buy what he said when I interviewed him—that he stole a passport and wallet and flew coach."

"It's a theory that he arrived at the same time his brother's body showed up," I reply.

"So Jean-Baptiste, caring guy that he is, probably hung around in the ship and watched all you people scurrying around when the body was found. Greatest show on earth. These assholes love to watch us work their crimes."

"How could he have followed me?" I get back to that outrageous thought. "How? He had a car?"

"Maybe he did," she says. "I'm getting around to entertaining the possibility that Chandonne wasn't the lone, wretched creature who just happened upon your city because it was convenient or even random. I'm no longer sure what his connections are, and I'm beginning to wonder if perhaps he might have been part of a grander scheme that has to do with the family business. Perhaps even with Bray herself, since she clearly was involved in an underworld of crime. And now we have other murders, one of the victims clearly involved in organized crime. An assassin. And an undercover FBI agent working a gun-smuggling case. And the hairs at the campground that might be Chandonne's. This is all adding up to something more than a man who killed his brother, took his place on a ship bound for Richmond—all to get out of Paris because his nasty little habit of murdering and mutilating women was becoming increasingly inconvenient to his powerful criminal family. Then he starts killing here because he can't control himself? Well." Berger leans against the kitchen counter. "There are just too many coincidences. And how did he get to the campground if he didn't have a car? Assuming those hairs turn out to be his," she repeats.

I sit down at the table. There are no windows inside my garage, but there are small windows in the garage door. I consider the possibility that Chandonne did follow me home and peeped through the garage door at me while I was cleaning up and undressing. Maybe he had help finding the abandoned house on the river, too. Maybe Berger is right. Maybe he isn't alone and never has been. It is almost midnight, almost Christmas, and Marino still isn't here and Berger's demeanor tells me she could keep going until dawn.

"Alarm goes off," she resumes. "Cops come and go. You return to the great room." She motions me to follow her there. "You're sitting where?"

"On the sofa."

"Right. TV on, going through bills, and around midnight what?"

"There's a knock on the front door," I reply.

"Describe the knock."

"A rapping with something hard." I try to remember every detail. "Like a flashlight or tactical baton. The way police knock. I get up and ask who's there. Or I think I ask. I'm not sure, but a male voice identifies himself as police. He says a prowler has been spotted on my property and asks if everything's okay."

"And that makes sense because we know a prowler was there about an hour earlier, when someone tried to force open your garage door."

"Exactly." I nod. "I turn off the alarm and open

the door, and he is there," I add as if I am talking about nothing more threatening than trick-or-treaters.

"Show me," Berger says.

I WALK THROUGH THE GREAT ROOM, past the dining room and to the entrance hall. I open the door, and just the act of recreating a scenario that almost cost me my life causes a visceral reaction. I feel sick. My hands begin to tremble. My front porch light is still out because the police removed the bulb and fixture and submitted them to the labs to be processed for fingerprints. No one has replaced them. Exposed wires dangle from the porch ceiling. Berger is waiting patiently for me to continue. "He rushes inside," I say. "And back-kicks the door shut behind him." I shut the door. "He has this black coat and he tries to put it over my head."

"Coat on or off when he came in?"

"On. He was grabbing it off as he came through the door." I am standing still. "And he tried to touch me."

"Tried to touch you?" Berger frowns. "With the chipping hammer?"

"With his hand. He reached out his hand and touched my cheek, or tried to touch it."

"You stood there while he did that? Just stood there?"

"It all happened so fast," I say. "So fast," I repeat. "I'm not sure. I just know he tried to do that and was snatching off his coat and trying to throw it over my head. And I ran."

"What about the chipping hammer?"

"He had it out. I'm not sure. Or he got it out. But I know he had it out when he was chasing me into the great room."

"Not out at first? He didn't have the chipping hammer out at first? You're sure?" She presses me on this point.

I try to remember, to envision it. "No, not at first," I decide. "He tried to touch me first with his hand. Then net me. Then he pulled out the chipping hammer."

"Can you show me what you did next?" she asks.

"Run?"

"Yes, run."

"Not like that," I say. "I'd have to have the same adrenaline rush, the same panic, to run like that."

"Kay, walk me through it, please."

I move out of the entrance hall, past the dining room and back into the great room. Straight ahead is the yellow Jarrah coffee table I discovered at that wonderful shop in Katonah, New York. What was the name? Antipodes? The rich blond wood glows like honey and I try not to notice the dusting powder all over it, or that somebody left a 7-Eleven coffee cup on it. "The jar of formalin was here, on this corner of the table," I tell Berger.

"And it was there because . . . ?"

"Because of the tattoo in it. The tattoo I'd removed from the back of the body that we believe is Thomas Chandonne."

"The defense is going to want to know why you brought human skin to your house, Kay."

"Of course. Everyone's been asking me that." I feel a rush of annoyance. "The tattoo is important and created many, many questions because we just couldn't figure out what it was. Not only was the body badly decomposed, thus making it very difficult to even see the tattoo, but then it turned out that it was a cover-up tattoo. One tattoo covering up another, and it was crucial, especially, that we determine what the original tattoo was."

"Two gold dots that were covered up with an owl," Berger says. "Every member of the Chandonne cartel has two gold dots tattooed on him."

"That's what Interpol told me, yes," I say, and by now I have accepted that she and Jay Talley have spent a lot of quality time together.

"Brother Thomas was screwing his family, had his own side business, was diverting ships, falsifying bills of lading, running his own guns and drugs. And the theory is the family caught on. He changed his tattoo into an owl and began using aliases because he knew the family would kill him if they found him," I recite what I have been told, what Jay told me in Lyon.

"Interesting." She touches a finger to her lips, looking around. "And it appears the family did kill him. The other son did. The jar of formalin. Why did you bring it home? Tell me again."

"It wasn't really deliberate. I went to a tattoo parlor in Petersburg to have the tattoo from the body looked at by someone who's an expert, a tattoo artist. I came straight home from there and left the tattoo in my office here. It was just a chance situation that the night he came here . . ."

"Jean-Baptiste Chandonne."

"Yes. The night he came here I had carried the jar in here, in the great room, and was looking at it while I was doing other things. I set it down. He pushes his way into my house and I run. By now he has the chipping hammer out and has it raised to strike me. It was just a panicked reflex that I see the jar and grab it. I jump over the back of the sofa and unscrew the lid and throw the formalin in his face."

"A reflex because you know very well how caustic formalin is."

"You can't smell it every day and not know. It's accepted in my profession that exposure to formalin is a chronic danger, and all of us fear being splashed," I explain, realizing how my story may sound to a special grand jury. Contrived. Unbelievable. Grotesquely bizarre.

"Have you ever gotten it in your eyes?" Berger asks me. "Ever splashed yourself with formalin?"

"No, thank God."

"So you dashed it in his face. Then what?"

"I ran out of the house. On my way, I grabbed my Glock pistol off the dining room table, where I'd left it earlier. I go outside, slip on the icy steps and fracture my arm." I hold up my cast.

"And what's he doing?"

"He came out after me."

"Instantly?"

"It seems like it."

Berger moves around to the back of the sofa and stands at the area of antique French oak flooring where formalin has eaten off the finish. She follows the lighter areas of hardwood. The formalin apparently splashed almost to the entrance of the kitchen. This is something I didn't realize until this moment. I only remember his shrieks, his howls of pain as he grabbed at his eyes. Berger stands in the doorway, staring in at my kitchen. I go to her, wondering what has caught her interest.

"I have to stray off subject and say I don't think I've ever seen a kitchen quite like this," she comments.

The kitchen is the heart of my house. Copper

pots and pans shine like gold from racks around
the huge Thirode stove that is central to the room
and includes two grills, a hot water bath, a grid-
dle, two hot plates, gas tops, a charbroiler and an
oversized burner for the huge pots of soup I love
to make. Appliances are stainless steel, including
the Sub-Zero refrigerator and freezer. Racks of
spices line the walls and there is a butcher block
the size of a twin bed. The oak floor is bare, and
there is an upright wine cooler in a corner and a
small table by the window that offers a distant
view of a rocky bend in the James River.

"Industrial," Berger mutters as she walks around
a kitchen that, yes, I must admit, fills me with
pride. "Someone who comes in here to work but
loves the finer things in life. I've heard you're an
amazing cook."

"I love to cook," I tell her. "It gets my mind off
everything else."

"Where do you get your money?" she boldly
asks.

"I'm smart with it," I reply coolly, never one to
discuss money. "I've been lucky with investments
over the years, very lucky."

"You're a smart businesswoman," Berger says.

"Try to be. And then when Benton died, he left
his Hilton Head condo to me." I pause. "I sold it,
couldn't stay there anymore." I pause again. "Got
six-hundred-and-something thousand for it."

"I see. And what's this?" She points out the Milano Italian sandwich maker.

I explain.

"Well, when this is all over, you'll have to cook for me sometime," she says rather presumptuously. "And rumor has it that you cook Italian. Your specialty."

"Yes. Mostly Italian." There is no rumor involved. Berger knows more about me than I do. "Do you suppose he might have come in here and tried to wash his face in the sink?" she then asks.

"I don't have any idea. All I can tell you is I ran out and fell, and when I looked up he was staggering out the door after me. He came down the steps, still screaming, and dropped to the ground and started rubbing snow in his face."

"Trying to wash the formalin out of his eyes. It's rather oily, isn't it? Hard to wash out?"

"It wouldn't be easy," I reply. "You would want copious amounts of warm water."

"And you didn't offer that to him? Made no effort to help him?"

I look at Berger. "Come on," I say. "What the hell would you have done?" Anger spikes. "I'm supposed to play doctor after the son of a bitch has just tried to beat my brains out?"

"It will be asked," Berger matter-of-factly answers me. "But no. I wouldn't have helped him, either, and that's off the record. So he's in your front yard."

"I left out that I hit the panic alarm when I was running out of the house," I remember.

"You grabbed the formalin. You grabbed your gun. You hit the panic alarm. You had pretty damn good presence of mind, didn't you?" she comments. "Anyway, you and Chandonne are in your front yard. Lucy pulls up and you have to talk her out of shooting him point-blank in the head. ATF and all the troops show up. End of story."

"I wish it were the end of the story," I say.

"The chipping hammer," Berger gets back to that. "Now you figured out what the weapon was because you went to a hardware store and just looked around until you found something that might have made a pattern like the one on Bray's body?"

"I had more to go on than you might think," I reply. "I knew Bray was struck with something that had two different surfaces. One rather pointed, the other more square. Actual punched-out areas of her skull clearly showed the shape of what struck her, and then the pattern on the mattress that I knew was made when he set down something bloody. Which most likely was the weapon. A hammer or pickax-type weapon of

some sort, but unusual. You look around. You ask
people."

"And then of course when he came to your
house, he had this chipping hammer inside his
coat or whatever and tried to use it on you." She
says this dispassionately, objectively.

"Yes."

"So there were two chipping hammers at your
house. The one you bought in the hardware store
after Bray had already been murdered. And a second hammer, the one he brought with him."

"Yes." I am stunned by what she has just indicated. "Good God," I mutter. "That's right. I
bought the hammer after she was murdered, not
before." I am so confused by what has passed, by
the days, by all of it. "What am I thinking? The
date on the receipt . . ." My voice fades. I remember paying cash in the hardware store. Five
dollars, something like that. I don't have a receipt, I am fairly sure, and I feel the blood drain
from my face. Berger has known all along what I
have forgotten: that I didn't buy the hammer before Bray was beaten to death, but the day after.
But I can't prove it. Unless the clerk who waited
on me in the hardware store can produce the cash
register tape and swear I am the one who bought
the chipping hammer, there is no proof.

"And now one of them is gone. The chipping

hammer you bought is gone," Berger is saying as my mind reels. I tell her I am not privy to what the police found.

"But you were there when they were searching your house. Were you not in your house while the police were?" she asks me.

"I showed them whatever they wanted to see. I answered their questions. I was there on Saturday and left early that evening, but I can't say I saw everything they did or what they took, nor were they finished when I left. Frankly, I don't even know how long they were in my house or how many times." I am touched by anger as I explain all this, and Berger senses it. "Christ, I didn't have a chipping hammer when Bray was murdered. I've been confused because I bought it the day her body was found, not the day she died. She was murdered the night before, her body found the next day." I am rambling now.

"What exactly is a chipping hammer used for?" Berger next asks. "And by the way, hate to tell you, but no matter when you say you bought the chipping hammer, Kay, there remains the minor problem that the one—the only one—found at your house happened to have Bray's blood on it."

"They're used for masonry. There's a lot of slatework in this area. And stonework."

"So probably used by roofers? And the theory is that Chandonne found a chipping hammer at the house he had broken into. The place under construction where he was staying?" Berger is relentless.

"I believe that's the theory," I reply.

"Your house is made of stone and has a slate roof," she says. "Did you closely supervise when it was being built? Because you seem the sort who would. A perfectionist."

"You're foolish not to supervise if you're building."

"I'm just wondering if you might have ever seen a chipping hammer while your house was being built. Maybe at the construction site or in a workman's tool belt?"

"Not that I recall. But I can't be sure."

"And you never owned one prior to your shopping expedition at Pleasants Hardware on the night of December seventeenth—two weeks ago exactly and almost twenty-four hours after Bray was murdered?"

"Not before that night. No, I never owned one before then, not that I am aware of," I tell her.

"What time was it when you bought the chipping hammer?" Berger asks as I hear the deep thunder of Marino's truck parking in front of my house.

"Sometime around seven. I don't know exactly. Maybe between six-thirty and seven, that Friday night, the night of December seventeenth," I reply. I am not thinking clearly now. Berger is wearing me down and I can't imagine how any lie could stand up to her long. The problem is knowing what is a lie, and what isn't, and I am not convinced she believes me.

"And you went home right after the hardware store?" she goes on. "Tell me what you did the rest of the night."

The doorbell rings. I glance at the Aiphone on the wall in the great room and see Marino's face looming on the video screen. Berger has just asked *the* question. She has just tested the alchemy that I am sure Righter will use to turn my life to shit. She wants to know my alibi. She wants to know where I was at the exact time Bray was murdered on Thursday night, December sixteenth. "I'd just come in from Paris that morning," I reply. "Ran errands, got home around six P.M. Later that night, around ten, I drove to MCV to check on Jo— Lucy's former girlfriend, the one who got in the shooting with her in Miami. I wanted to see if I could help out in that situation because the parents were interfering." My doorbell rings again. "And I wanted to know where Lucy was, and Jo told me Lucy was at a bar in Greenwich Village." I start walking toward the door. Berger is staring at me. "In New York. Lucy was in New York. I came home and called her. She was drunk." Marino rings the bell again and pounds on the door. "So to answer your question, Ms. Berger, I have no alibi for where I was between six and maybe ten-thirty Thursday night because I was either in my home or in my car—alone, absolutely alone. No one saw me. No one talked to me. I have no witnesses to the fact that where I *wasn't* between seven-thirty and ten-thirty was at Diane Bray's house beating her to death with a goddamn chipping hammer."

I open the door. I can feel Berger's eyes burning into my back. Marino looks as if he is about to fly apart. I can't tell if he is furious or scared to death. Maybe both. "What the hell?" he asks, his eyes going from me to her. "What the shit's going on?"

"I'm sorry for making you stand out in the cold," I tell Marino. "Please come in."

CHAPTER 29

MARINO TOOK SO LONG getting here because he had stopped by the property room at headquarters. I had asked him to pick up the stainless-steel key I found in the pocket of Mitch Barboso's running shorts. Marino tells Berger and me that he rooted around for quite some time inside that small room behind wire mesh where Spacesaver shelves are crowded with bar-coded bags, some of which hold items the police took from my house last Saturday.

I have been in the property room before. I can picture it. Portable phones ring from inside those bags. Pagers go off as unwitting people keep trying to call associates who are either locked up or dead. There are also locked refrigerators for the storage of Physical Evidence Recovery Kits and any other evidence that might be perishable—such as the raw chicken I pounded with the chipping hammer.

"Now, why did you pound raw chicken with a chipping hammer?" Berger wants further clarification on this part of my rather odd story.

"To see if the injuries correlated to the ones on Bray's body," I reply.

"Well, the chicken's still inside the evidence refrigerator," Marino says. "Gotta say, you sure beat the hell out of it."

"Describe in detail exactly what you did to the chicken," Berger prods me, as if I am on the witness stand.

I face her and Marino inside my entrance hallway and explain that I placed raw chicken breasts on a cutting board and beat them with every side and edge of the chipping hammer to note the pattern of injuries. The wounds from both the blunt-bladed tip and the pointed tip were identical in configuration and measurement to those on Bray's body, particularly to the punched-out areas in her cartilage and skull, which are excellent for retaining the shape—or tool mark—of whatever penetrated them. Then I spread out a white pillowcase, I explain. I rolled the coiled handle of the chipping hammer in barbecue sauce. What kind of barbecue sauce? Berger wants to know, of course.

I recall it was Smokey Pig barbecue sauce that I had thinned to the consistency of blood, and then I pressed the sauce-coated handle against the cloth to see what that transfer pattern looked like. I got the same striations that were left in blood on Bray's mattress. The pillowcase with its barbecue sauce imprints, Marino says, were turned in to the DNA lab. I remark that this is a waste of time. We don't test for tomatoes. I am not trying to be funny but am sufficiently frustrated to emit a spark of sarcasm. The only result the DNA lab will get from the pillowcase, I promise, is *not human*. Marino is pacing the floor.

I am screwed, he says, because the chipping hammer I bought and did all these tests with is gone. He couldn't find it. He looked everywhere for it. It isn't listed in the evidence computer. It clearly was never turned in to the evidence room, nor was it picked up by forensic technicians and receipted to the labs. It is gone. Gone. And I have no receipt. By now I am sure of this.

"I told you from my car phone that I had bought it," I remind him.

"Yeah," he says. He remembers my calling him from my car after I left Pleasants Hardware store, sometime between six-thirty and seven. I told him I believed a chipping hammer was what had been used on Bray. I said I had bought one. But, he points out, that doesn't mean I didn't buy such a tool after Bray's murder to fabricate an alibi. "You know, to make it look like you didn't own one or even know what she was killed with until after the fact."

"Whose goddamn side are you on?" I say to him. "You believe this Righter bullshit? Jesus. I can't take any more of this."

"This isn't about sides, Doc," Marino grimly replies as Berger looks on.

We are back to there being only one hammer: the one with Bray's blood on it found inside my house. Specifically, in my great room on the Persian rug, exactly seventeen and a half inches to the right of the Jarrah Wood coffee table. Chandonne's hammer, not my hammer, I keep saying as I imagine cheap brown paper bags with a voucher number and bar code that represent Scarpetta—me, behind wire mesh on Spacesaver shelves.

I lean against the wall inside my entry hallway and feel lightheaded. It is as if I am having an out-of-body experience, looking down on myself after something terrible and final has happened. My undoing. My destruction. I am dead like other people whose brown paper bags end up in that evidence room. I am not dead, but maybe it is worse to be the accused. I hate even to suggest the next stage of my undoing. It is overkill. "Marino," I say, "try the key in my door."

He hesitates, frowning. Then he slips the clear plastic evidence bag out of the inner pocket of his old leather jacket with its balding fleece lining. Cold wind punches into the house as he opens the front door and slides the steel key—easily slides it—into the lock, and clicks the lock, and the dead bolt slides open and shut.

"The number written on it," I quietly tell Marino and Berger. "Two-thirty-three. That's my burglar alarm code."

"What?" Berger, for once, is almost speechless.

The three of us go into my great room. This time I perch on the cold hearth, like Cinderella. Berger and Marino avoid sitting on the ruined couch, but situate themselves near me, looking at me, waiting for any possible explanation. There is but one, and I think it is rather obvious. "Police and God knows who else have been in and out of my house since Saturday," I begin. "A drawer in the kitchen. In it are keys to everything. My house, my car, my office, file cabinets, whatever. So it's not like someone didn't have easy access to a spare key to my house, and you guys had my burglar alarm code, right?" I look at Marino. "I mean, you weren't leaving my house unarmed after you left it. And the alarm was on when we came in a little while ago."

"We need a list of everybody who's been inside this house," Berger grimly decides.

"I can tell you everybody I know about," Marino answers. "But I haven't been here every time somebody else has. So I can't say I know who everybody is."

I sigh and lean my back against the fireplace. I start naming cops I saw with my own eyes, including Jay Talley. Including Marino. "And Righter's been in here," I add.

"As have I," Berger replies. "But I certainly didn't let myself in. I had no idea what your code is."

"Who let you in?" I ask.

Her answer is to look at Marino. It bothers me that Marino never told me he was Berger's tour guide. It is irrational for me to feel stung. After all, who better than Marino? Who do I trust more than him? Marino is visibly agitated. He gets up and strolls through the doorway leading into my kitchen. I hear him open the drawer where I keep the keys, then he opens the refrigerator.

"Well, I was with you when you found that key in Mitch Barbosa's pocket," Berger starts to think out loud. "You couldn't have put it there, couldn't have planted it." She is working this out. "Because you weren't at the scene. And you didn't touch the body unwitnessed. I mean, Marino and I were right there when you unzipped the pouch." She blows out in frustration. "And Marino?"

"He wouldn't," I cut her off with a weary wave of my hand. "No way. Sure, he had access, but no way. And based on his account of the crime scene, he never saw Barbosa's body. It was already being loaded into the ambulance when he pulled up on Mosby Court."

"So either one of the cops at the scene did it . . ."

"Or more likely," I finish her thought, "the key was placed in Barbosa's pocket when he was killed. At the crime scene. Not where he was dumped."

Marino walks in drinking a bottle of Spaten beer that Lucy must have bought. I don't remember buying it. Nothing about my house seems to belong to me anymore, and Anna's story comes to mind. I am beginning to understand the way she must have felt when Nazis occupied her family home. I realize, suddenly, that people can be pushed beyond anger, beyond tears, beyond protest, beyond even grief. Finally, you just sink into a dark mire of acceptance. What is, is. And what was, is past. "I can't live here anymore," I tell Berger and Marino.

"You got that right," Marino fires back in the aggressive, angry tone he seems to wear like his own skin these days.

"Look," I say to him, "don't bark at me anymore, Marino. We're all angry, frustrated, worn out. I don't understand what's happening, but it's clear someone connected to us is also involved in the murder of these two recent victims, these men who were tortured, and I guess whoever planted my key on Barbosa's body wants to either implicate me in those crimes, as well, or more likely, is sending me a warning."

"I think it's a warning," Marino says.

And where's Rocky these days? I almost ask him.

"Your dear son Rocky," Berger says it for me.

Marino takes a slug of beer and wipes his mouth with the back of his hand. He doesn't respond. Berger glances at her watch and looks up at us. "Well," she says, "Merry Christmas, I guess."

CHAPTER 30

ANNA'S HOUSE IS DARK AND still when I come in at nearly three A.M. She has thoughtfully left on a light in the hallway and one in the kitchen near a crystal tumbler and the bottle of Glenmorangie, just in case I need a sedative. At this hour, I decline. A part of me wishes Anna were awake. I am halfway tempted to rattle around in hopes she will wander in and sit down with me. I have become oddly addicted to our sessions even if I am now supposed to wish they had never taken place. I make my way to the guest wing and start thinking about transference and wonder if I am experiencing this with Anna. Or maybe I just feel lonely and gloomy because it is Christmas and I am wide awake and frazzled in someone else's house after investigating violent death all day, including one I am accused of committing.

Anna has left a note on my bed. I pick up the elegant creamy envelope and can tell by its weight and thickness that whatever she has written is lengthy. I leave my clothes in a pile on the bathroom floor and imagine the ugliness that must linger in their very fabrics because of where I have been and what I have done the past twenty hours. I do not realize until I am out of the shower that the clothes carry with them the dirty fire smell of the motel room. Now I ball them up in a towel so I can forget about them until they can go to the dry cleaner. I wear one of Anna's thick robes to bed and am edgy as I pick up the letter again. I open it and unfold six stiff pages of watermarked engraved stationery. I begin to read, willing myself not to go too fast. Anna is deliberate and wants me to take in every word, because she does not waste words.

Dearest Kay,

As a child of the war, I learned that truth is not always what is right or good or best. If the SS came to your door and asked if you had Jews inside, you did not tell the truth if you were hiding Jews. When members of the Totenkopf SS occupied my family home in Austria, I could not tell the truth about how much I hated them. When the SS commander of Mauthausen came into my bed so many nights and asked me if I enjoyed what he did to me, I did not tell the truth.

He would tell vile jokes and hiss in my ear, imitating the sound of the Jews being gassed, and I laughed because I was afraid. He would get very drunk sometimes when he came back from the camp, and once he bragged he had killed a 12-year-old village boy in nearby Langenstein during an SS hunting raid. Later I learned this was not so, that the Leitstelle—Chief of Staatspolizei in Linz—was the one who shot the boy, but I believed what I was told at the time and my fear was indescribable. I, too, was a civilian child. No one was safe. (In 1945 that same commander died in Gusen and his body was displayed to the public for days. I saw it and spat. That was the truth about how I felt—a truth I could not tell earlier!)

Truth is relative, then. It is about timing. It is about what is safe. Truth is the luxury of the privileged, of people who have plenty of food and are not forced to hide because they are Jews. Truth can destroy, and therefore it is not always wise or even healthy to be truthful. A strange thing for a psychiatrist to admit, yes? I give you this lesson for a reason, Kay. After you read my letter, you must destroy it and never admit it existed. I know you well. Such a small covert act will be hard for you. If you are asked, you must say nothing about what I am telling you here.

My life in this country would be ruined if it was known that my family gave food and shelter to the SS, no matter that our hearts were not in it. It was to survive. I also think you would be greatly harmed if people should know that your best friend is a Nazi sympathizer, as I am certain I would be called. And oh, what a terrible thing to be called, especially when one hates them as I do. I am a Jew. My father was a prescient man and very aware of what Hitler intended to do. In the late thirties, my father used his banking and political connections and wealth to secure entire new identities for us. He changed our name to Zenner and moved us from Poland to Austria when I was too young to be aware of much.

So you might say that I have lived a lie since I can remember. Perhaps this helps you understand why I do not want to be interrogated in a legal proceeding and why I will avoid this if I can. So Kay, the real reason for this long letter is not to tell my story. At last I talk to you about Benton.

I am quite certain you do not know that for a while he was my patient. About three years ago, he came to see me in my office. He was depressed and had many work-related difficulties that he could not speak of to anyone, including you. He said that throughout his career with the FBI he had seen the worst of the worst—the most aberrant acts imaginable, and although he had been haunted by them and suffered in many ways because of this exposure to what he called "evil," he had never felt truly afraid. Most of those bad people were not interested in him, he said. They meant him no personal harm, and in fact enjoyed the attention he paid to them when he interviewed them in prison. As for the many cases he helped police solve, again, he was in no personal danger. Serial rapists and killers were not interested in him.

But then strange things began to happen to him some months before he came to see me. I wish I could remember better, Kay, but there were odd events. Phone calls. Hang-ups that could not be traced because they were made by satellite (I guess he meant cell phones). He got crank mail that made very terrible references to you. There were threats made toward you, again untraceable. It was clear to Benton that whoever was writing the letters knew something about both of you personally.

Of course, he was very suspicious of Carrie Grethen. He kept saying, "We haven't heard the last from that woman." But at the time, he did not see how she could be making the calls and sending the mail because she was still locked up in New York—in Kirby.

I will sum up six months of conversations with Benton by saying he had a very strong premonition that his death was imminent. He suffered subsequent depression, anxiety, paranoia and began to struggle with alcohol. He said he hid bouts of heavy drinking from you and that his problems were causing a deterioration in his relationship with you. As I listened to some of what you told me during our talks, Kay, I can see that his behavior at home did change. Now perhaps you understand some of the reasons why.

I wanted to put Benton on a mild antidepressant but he would not let me. He worried constantly about what would happen to you and Lucy if something happened to him. He wept about it openly in my office. It was I who suggested he write the letter that Senator Lord delivered to you several weeks ago. I said to Benton, "Imagine you are dead and have one last chance to say something to Kay." So he did. He said to you the words you read in his letter.

During our sessions, I suggested to him repeatedly that perhaps he knew more about
who was harassing him and perhaps denial
was preventing him from facing the truth. He
hesitated. I remember so well I had a feeling
he possessed information he could not or
would not say. Now I am beginning to think
I might know. I have reached the conclusion
that what began happening to Benton several
years ago and what is now happening to you
are connected to Marino's Mafia son. Rocky
is involved with very powerful criminal people and he hates his father. He would hate
everyone who matters to his father. Can it be
a coincidence that Benton got threatening
letters and was murdered, and then this terrible killer, Chandonne, ends up in Richmond and now Marino's terrible son is
Chandonne's lawyer? Is this tortuous road
not winding, at last, to some dreadful conclusion that is meant to bring down everyone good in Marino's life?

In my office, Benton often referred to a
Tlip file. In it he kept all the strange, menac-
ing letters and other records of communications and incidents that he had begun to
receive. For months, I thought he was saying *Tip* file, as in police tips. But one day I
made mention of his Tip file and he cor-

rected me and said the file was actually his *T-L-P* file which he pronounced *tlip*. I next asked what TLP stood for, and he said *The Last Precinct*. I asked him what he meant by that and his eyes filled with tears. His exact words to me were this: "The Last Precinct is where I will end up, Anna. It is where I'll end up."

You cannot imagine my feeling when Lucy mentioned that this is also the name for the investigative consulting company that she has now gone to work for in New York. When I was so upset last night, it was not simply over the subpoena delivered to my house. What happened was the following: I got the subpoena. I called Lucy because I thought she should know what was happening to you. She said her "new boss" (Teun McGovern) was in town and mentioned The Last Precinct. I was shocked. I still am shocked and do not understand what all this means. Does Lucy perhaps know about Benton's file?

Again, can this be coincidence, Kay? Did she just happen to think up the same name that Benton called his secret file? Can all these connections be coincidences? Now there is something called The Last Precinct and it is located in New York and Lucy is moving to New York, the trial of Chandonne has moved to New York because he killed in New York two years ago while Carrie Grethen was still incarcerated in New York, and Carrie's former murderous partner Temple Gault was killed (by you) in New York, and Marino began his police career in New York. And Rocky lives in New York.

Let me close by telling you I feel so badly over any hand I might have in making your current situation worse, although you can be sure I intend to say nothing that can be twisted. Never. I am too old for this. Tomorrow, on Christmas Day, I will leave for my house in Hilton Head, where I will stay until it is all right to return to Richmond. I do this for several reasons. I do not intend to make it easy for Buford or anyone else to get to me. Most important, you need some place to stay. Do not go back to your house, Kay.

Your devoted friend,
Anna

I read and reread. I feel sick as I imagine Anna growing up in the poisonous air of Mauthausen and knowing what went on there. I feel the deepest sorrow that all her life she has listened to references to Jews and bad jokes about Jews and learned more of the atrocities committed against Jews, all the while knowing she is a Jew. No matter how she rationalizes it, what her father did was cowardly and wrong. I suspect he also knew Anna was being raped by the SS commander he wined and dined, and Anna's father did nothing about that, either. Not one thing.

I realize it is now almost five o'clock in the morning. My eyelids are heavy, my nerves buzzing. There is no point in trying to sleep. I get up and go into the kitchen to make coffee. For a while I sit before the dark window looking out toward a river I can't see and contemplate everything Anna has revealed to me. So much about Benton's last years now makes sense. I think of days when he claimed to have a tension headache, and I thought he looked hung over and now I suspect he probably was. He was increasingly depressed and distant and frustrated. In a way, I understand his not telling me about the letters, the phone calls, the Tlip file, as he referred to it. But I don't agree with him. He should have told me.

I have no recollection of having come across such a file when I was going through his belongings after his death. But then, there is so much I don't remember about that time. It was as if I were living under the earth, moving ever so heavily and slowly, and unable to see where I was going or where I had been. After Benton's death, Anna helped me sort through his personal effects. She cleaned out his closets and went through his drawers while I was in and out of rooms like a crazed insect, helping one minute, ranting and weeping the next. I wonder if she came across that file. I know I must find it, if it still exists.

The first morning light is a hint of deep blue as I fix coffee for Anna and carry it back to her bedroom. I listen outside her door to see if I hear any sign of her being awake. All is still. I quietly open her door and carry her coffee in. I set it down on the oval table by her bed. Anna likes night-lights. Her suite is lit up like a runway, lights inserted in almost every receptacle. When I first became aware of this, I thought it odd. Now I begin to understand. Perhaps she associates utter darkness with being alone and terrified in her bedroom, waiting for a drunken, stinking Nazi to come in and overpower her young body. No wonder she has spent her life dealing with damaged people. She understands damaged people. She is as much a student of her past tragedies as she has said I am of mine.

"Anna?" I whisper. I see her stir. "Anna? It's me. I've brought you coffee."

She sits up with a start, squinting, her white hair in her face and sticking up in places.

Merry Christmas, I start to say. I tell her "happy holidays" instead.

"All these years I celebrate Christmas while I am secretly Jewish." She reaches for her coffee. "I am not known for a sweet disposition early in the morning," she says.

I squeeze her hand, and in the dark she seems suddenly so old and delicate. "I read your letter. I'm not sure what to say but I can't destroy it, and we must talk about it," I tell her.

For an instant she pauses. I think I catch relief in her silence. Then she gets stubborn again and waves me off, as if by a mere gesture she can dismiss her entire history and what she has told me about my own life. Night-lights cast exaggerated, deep shadows of Biedemeier furniture and antique lamps and oil paintings in her large, gorgeous bedroom. Thick silk draperies are drawn. "I probably should not have written any of that to you," she says firmly.

"I wish you'd written it to me sooner, Anna."

She sips her coffee and pulls the covers up to her shoulders.

"What happened to you as a child isn't your fault," I say to her. "The choices were made by your father, not you. He protected you in one way and didn't protect you at all. Maybe there was no choice."

She shakes her head. "You do not know. You cannot know."

I am not about to argue with that.

"There are no monsters to compare with them.

My family had no choice. My father drank a lot of schnapps. He was drunk most the time on schnapps and they would get drunk with him. To this day I cannot smell schnapps." She clutches the coffee mug in both hands. "They all got drunk, it did not matter. When Reichsminister Speer and his entourage visited installations at Gusen and Ebensee, they came to our *schloss,* oh yes, our quaint little castle. My parents had this sumptuous banquet with musicians from Vienna and the finest champagne and food, and everyone was drunk. I remember I hid in my bedroom, so afraid of who would come next. I hid under the bed all night and several times there were footsteps in my room and once someone yanked the covers back and swore. I stayed on the floor under the bed all night dreaming of the music and of one young man who made such sweetness flow from his violin. He looked at me often and made me blush and as I hid under my bed later that night, I thought of him. No one who made such beauty could be unkind. All night I thought of him."

"The violinist from Vienna?" I asked. "The one you later . . . ?"

"No, no." Anna shakes her head in the shadows. "This was many years before Rudi. But I think it is when I fell in love with Rudi, in advance, having never met him. I saw the musicians in their black cutaways and was mesmerized by the magic they made, and I wanted them to steal me from the horror. I imagined myself soaring on their notes into a pure place. For a moment, I was returned to Austria before the quarry and the crematorium, when life was simple, the people decent and fun and had perfect gardens and such pride in their homes. On sunny spring days we would hang our goose-down duvets out windows to be scrubbed by the sweetest air I have ever breathed. And we would play in rolling fields of grass that seemed to lead right up to the sky while father would hunt in the woods for boar and mother would sew and bake." She pauses, her face touched by sweet sadness. "That a string quartet could transform the most dreadful of nights. And then later, my magical thinking carries me into the arms of a man with a violin, an American. And I am here. I am here. I escaped. But I have never escaped, Kay."

DAWN BEGINS TO LIGHT UP THE drapes and turn them the color of honey. I tell Anna I am glad she is here. I thank her for talking to Benton and for finally letting me know. In some ways the picture is more complete because of what I now understand. In some ways, it isn't. I can't sharply outline the progression of moods and changes that preceded Benton's murder, but

I do know that about the time he was seeing Anna, Carrie Grethen was looking for a new partner to replace Temple Gault. Carrie had worked in computers earlier in her life. She was brilliant and incredibly manipulative and talked her way into gaining access to a computer at the forensic psychiatric hospital, Kirby. This was how she cast her web back out into the world. She linked up with a new partner—another psychopathic killer named Newton Joyce. She did this through the Internet, and he helped her escape from Kirby.

"Perhaps she met certain other people through the Internet, too," Anna suggests.

"Marino's son. Rocky?" I say.

"I am thinking it."

"Anna, do you have any idea what happened to Benton's file? The Tlip file, as he called it?"

"I have never seen it." She sits up straighter, deciding it is time to get out of bed, and the covers settle around her waist. Her bare arms look pitifully thin and wrinkled, as if someone has let the air out of them. Her bosom sags low and loose beneath dark silk. "When I helped you sort through his clothing and other personal belongings, I did not see a file. But I did not touch his office."

I remember so little.

"No." She pulls back the covers and lowers her feet to the floor. "I would not. That was not something I would go into. His professional files."

She is up now and slips on a robe. "I just assumed you would have gone through those." She looks at me. "You have, yes? What about his office at Quantico? He had already retired, so I suppose he had cleaned that out already?"

"That was cleaned out, yes." We walk down the hallway toward the kitchen. "Case files would have stayed there. Unlike some of his compatriots who retire from the FBI, Benton didn't believe cases he worked belonged to him," I add ruefully. "So I know he didn't take any case files away from Quantico when he retired. What I don't know is if he would have left the Tlip file with the Bureau. If so, I'll never see it."

"That was his file," Anna points out. "Correspondence to him. When he spoke about it to me, he never referred to what was happening to him as Bureau business. He seemed to take the threats, the crank calls, as something personal, and I am not aware that he ever shared these things with other agents. He was so paranoid, mostly because some of the threats involved you. I was led to believe I am the only person he told. I know this. I said to him many times that I believed he should tell the FBI." She shook her head. "He would not," she says again.

I empty the coffee filter into the trash and feel a spike of old resentment. Benton kept so much from me. "A shame," I reply. "Maybe if he'd told some of the other agents, none of this would have happened."

"Would you like more coffee?"

I am reminded that I did not go to bed last night. "I guess I'd better," I reply.

"Some Viennese coffee," Anna decides, opening the refrigerator and picking through bags of coffee. "Since I am feeling nostalgic for Austria this morning." She says this with a hint of sarcasm, as if she is silently berating herself for divulging details of her past. She pours beans into the grinder and the kitchen is filled briefly with noise.

"Benton got disillusioned with the Bureau in the end," I think out loud. "I'm not sure he trusted people around him anymore. Competitiveness. He was the unit chief and knew everybody was going to fight over his job the minute he even mentioned he was ready to retire. Knowing him, he handled his problems in total isolation—the same way he worked his cases. If nothing else, Benton was a master of discretion." I am running through every possibility. Where would Benton have kept the file? Where might it be? He had his own room in my house where he stored his belongings and plugged in his laptop. He had file drawers. But I have been through those and never saw anything even similar to what Anna has described.

Then I think of something else. When Benton

was murdered in Philadelphia, he was checked into a hotel. Several bags of his personal effects were returned to me, including his briefcase, which I opened. I went through it just as the police had. I know I didn't see anything like this Tlip file, but if it is true Benton was suspicious that Carrie Grethen might have had something to do with the crank calls and notes he was getting, might he not have carried the Tlip file with him when he was working new cases possibly connected to her? Wouldn't he have brought the file to Philadelphia?

I go to the phone and call Marino. "Merry Christmas," I say. "It's me."

"What?" he blurts out, half asleep. "Oh shit. What time is it?"

"A few minutes past seven."

"Seven!" Groan. "Hell, Santa ain't even come yet. What you calling me so early for?"

"Marino, this is important. When the police went through Benton's personal effects in the hotel room in Philadelphia, did you go through them?"

A big yawn and he blows out loudly. "Damn, I gotta quit staying up so late. My lungs are killing me, got to quit smoking. Me and some of the guys and Wild Turkey hung out last night." Another yawn. "Hold on. I'm coming to. Let me switch channels. One minute it's Christmas, next you're asking about Philadelphia?"

"That's right. The stuff you guys found in Benton's hotel room."

"Yeah. Hell, yeah I went through it."

"Did you take anything? Anything, for example, that might have been in his briefcase? A file, for example, that might have had letters in it?"

"He had a couple files in there. Why do you want to know?"

I am getting excited. My synapses are firing, clearing my head and pumping energy into my cells. "Where are these files now?" I ask him.

"Yeah, I remember some letters. Weirdo shit that I thought I should pay some attention to. Then Lucy blew Carrie and Joyce out of the air and turned them into fish chum, and that exceptionally cleared the case, I guess you could say. Shit. I still can't believe she had a fucking AR-fifteen in the damn helicopter and . . ."

"Where are the files?" I ask him again and I can't keep the urgency out of my voice. My heart is pounding. "I need to see a file that had the weird letters. Benton called it his Tlip file. T-L-P. As in The Last Precinct. Maybe where Lucy got the idea for the name."

"The Last Precinct. You mean where Lucy's going to work—McGovern's place in New York? What the hell's that got to do with some file in Benton's briefcase?"

"Good question," I tell him.

"Okay. It's somewhere. I gotta find it, and I'll be over."

Anna has gone back to her bedroom, and I occupy myself with thinking about our holiday meal as I wait for Lucy and McGovern to get here. I start pulling food out of the refrigerator as I replay what Lucy told me about McGovern's new company in New York. Lucy said the name *The Last Precinct* started out as a joke. *Where you go when there is nowhere left.* And in Anna's letter, she said Benton told her The Last Precinct is where he would end up. Cryptic. Riddles. Benton believed his future was somehow connected to what he was putting in that file. The Last Precinct was death, I then consider. Where was Benton going to end up? He was going to end up dead. Is this what he meant? Where else might he have ended up?

Days ago, I promised Anna I would cook Christmas dinner if she did not mind an Italian in her kitchen who does not go near a turkey or what people stuff in turkeys during the holidays. Anna has made a valiant effort at shopping. She even has cold-pressed olive oil and fresh buffalo mozzarella. I fill a large pot with water and go back to Anna's bedroom to tell her she can't go to Hilton Head or anywhere else until she has eaten a little *cucina Scarpetta* and sampled a little wine. This is a family day, I tell her as she brushes her teeth. I don't care about special grand juries or prosecutors or anything else until after dinner. Why doesn't she make something Austrian? At this she almost spits out toothpaste. Never, she says. If both of us were in the kitchen at the same time, we would kill each other.

For a while, the mood seems to lift in Anna's house. Lucy and McGovern appear around nine and gifts are piled under the tree. I start mixing eggs and flour and work it all together with my fingers on a wooden cutting board. When the dough is the right consistency, I wrap it in plastic and start looking for the hand-cranked pasta machine Anna claims to have somewhere as I jump from thought to thought, barely hearing what Lucy and McGovern are chatting about.

"It's not that I can't fly when it's not VFR conditions." Lucy is explaining something about her new helicopter, which apparently has been delivered to New York. "I have my instrument rating. But I'm not interested in having an instrument-rated single-engine helicopter because with only one engine, I want to see the ground at all times. So I don't want to be flying above the clouds on crappy days."

"Sounds dangerous," McGovern comments.

"It's not in the least. The engines never quit in these things, but it pays to always consider the worst-case scenario."

I begin kneading the dough. It is my favorite part of making pasta, and I always refrain from using food processors because the warmth of the human touch gives a texture to fresh pasta that is unlike anything agitating steel blades can effect. I get into a rhythm, pushing down, folding over, giving half-turns, pressing hard with the heel of my good hand as I, too, think of worst-case scenarios. What might Benton have believed was the worst-case scenario for him? If he was thinking that his metaphorical Last Precinct was where he would end up, what would have been the worst-case scenario? This is when I decide he didn't mean death when he said he would end up in The Last Precinct. No. Benton of all people knew there are far worse things than death.

"I've given her lessons off and on. Talk about a quick study. But people who use their hands have an advantage," Lucy is saying to McGovern, talking about me.

It is where I will end up. Benton's words shine my mind.

"Right. Because it takes coordination."

"Got to be able to use both hands and both feet at the same time. And unlike fixed wing, a helicopter is intrinsically unstable."

"That's what I'm saying. They're dangerous."

It is where I'll end up, Anna.

"They aren't, Teun. You can lose an engine at a thousand feet and fly it right down to the ground. The air keeps the blades turning. Ever heard of autorotating? You land in a parking lot or someone's yard. You can't do that with a plane."

What did you mean, Benton. Goddamn it, what did you mean? I knead and knead, always turning the ball of dough in the same direction, clockwise because I am leading with my right hand, avoiding my cast.

"Thought you said you never lose an engine. I want some eggnog. Is Marino making his famous eggnog this morning?" McGovern says.

"That's his New Year's Eve thing."

"What? It's against the law on Christmas? I don't know how she does that."

"Stubborn, that's how."

"No kidding. And we're just standing here doing nothing."

"She won't let you help. No one touches her dough. Trust me. Aunt Kay, isn't that making your elbow hurt?"

My eyes focus as I look up. I am kneading with my right hand and the fingertips of my left. I glance at the clock over the sink and realize I have lost track of time and have been kneading for almost ten minutes.

"God, what world were you just in?" Lucy's light spirit turns to lead as she searches my face.

"Don't let all this eat you alive. It's going to be all right."

She thinks I am worrying about the special grand jury, when ironically, I am not thinking about that at all this morning.

"Teun and I are going to help you, *are* helping you. What do you think we've been doing these last few days? We've got a plan we want to talk to you about."

"After eggnog," McGovern says with a kind smile.

"Did Benton ever talk to you about The Last Precinct?" I am out with it, almost accusing in the fierce way I look at both of them, then realizing by their confused expressions they don't know what I am alluding to at all.

"You mean what we're doing now?" Lucy frowns. "The office in New York? He couldn't have known about that unless you mentioned to him you were thinking about going into your own business." This she says to McGovern.

I divide the dough into smaller parts and begin kneading again.

"I've always thought about going private," McGovern replies. "But I never said anything about it to Benton. We were pretty consumed with the cases up there in Pennsylvania."

"Understatement of the century," Lucy adds blackly.

"Right." McGovern sighs and shakes her head.

"If Benton didn't have a clue about the private enterprise you planned to start," I then say, "is it possible he'd heard you mention The Last Precinct—the concept, the thing you say you used to joke about? I'm trying to figure out why he would label a file with that name."

"What file?" Lucy asks.

"Marino's bringing it over." I finish kneading one portion of dough and wrap it tightly in plastic. "It was in Benton's briefcase in Philadelphia." I explain to them what Anna told me in her letter and Lucy helps clarify at least one point. She feels certain she mentioned the philosophy of The Last Precinct to Benton. She seems to recall that she was in the car with him one day and was asking him about the private consulting he had begun doing in his retirement. He told her it was going all right but it was difficult handling the logistics of running his own business, that he missed having a secretary and someone else answering the phone, that sort of thing. Lucy wistfully replied that maybe all of us ought to get together and form our own company. That was when she used the term The Last Precinct—sort of "a league of our own," she says she told him.

I spread clean, dry dish towels over the countertop. "Did he have any idea you might be serious about really doing that some day?" I ask.

"I told him if I ever got enough money, I was going to quit working for the fucking government," Lucy replies.

"Well." I fit thinning rollers in the pasta machine and set them at the largest opening. "Anybody who knows you would figure it was only a matter of time before you made money doing something. Benton always said you were too much a maverick to last in a bureaucracy forever. He wouldn't be the least bit surprised over what's happening to you now, Lucy."

"In fact, it had already started happening to you from the start," McGovern points out to my niece. "Which is why you didn't last with the FBI."

Lucy isn't insulted. She has at least accepted that she made mistakes early on, the worst one being her affair with Carrie Grethen. She no longer blames the FBI for backing away from her until she finally quit. I flatten a piece of dough with my palm and crank it through the machine. "I'm wondering if Benton used your concept as the name of his mysterious file because he somehow knew The Last Precinct—meaning us—would investigate his case some day," I offer. "That *we* are where he would end up, because whatever was begun with those harassing letters and all the rest of it wasn't going to stop, even with his death." I turn the dough back through the machine again and again until I have a perfect strip of pasta to lay flat over a towel. "He knew. Somehow he did."

"Somehow he always knew everything." Lucy's face is touched by deep sadness.

Benton is in the kitchen. We feel him as I make Christmas pasta and we talk about the way his mind worked. He was very intuitive. He always thought far ahead of where he was. I can imagine him projecting himself into a future after his death and imagining how we might react to everything, including a file we might find in his briefcase. Benton would know for a fact that if something happened to him—and he clearly feared something would—then I most certainly would go through his briefcase, which I did. What he may not have anticipated was that Marino would go through the briefcase first and remove a file that I would not learn about until now.

By noon, Anna has her car packed for the beach and her kitchen countertops are covered with lasagna noodles. Tomato sauce simmers on the stove. Parmesan reggiano and aged asagio cheeses are grated in bowls and fresh mozzarella rests in a towel and surrenders some of its moisture. The house smells like garlic and wood smoke, and Christmas lights glow while smoke drifts out the chimney, and when Marino arrives with all his typical noise and gaucheness he finds more happiness than he has seen from any of us for a while. He is dressed in jeans and a denim shirt and laden with gifts and a bottle of Virginia Lightning moonshine. I catch the edge of a file folder peeking out from behind wrapped packages in a bag, and my heart skips.

"Ho! Ho! Ho!" he bellows. "Merry fucking Christmas!" It is his standard holiday line, but his heart isn't into it. I have a feeling he didn't spend the past few hours merely looking for the Tlip file. He has been through it. "I need a drink," he announces to the house.

CHAPTER 31

IN THE KITCHEN, I SET THE oven and cook pasta. I mix grated cheeses with ricotta and begin layering it and meat sauce between noodles in a deep dish. Anna stuffs dates with cream cheese and fills a bowl with salted nuts while Marino, Lucy and McGovern pour beer and wine or mix whatever holiday potion they want, which in Marino's case is a spicy Bloody Mary made with his moonshine.

He is in a weird mood and well on his way to getting drunk. The Tlip file is a black hole, still in the bag of presents, ironically under the Christmas tree. Marino knows what's in that file, but I don't ask him. Nobody does. Lucy begins getting out ingredients for chocolate-chip cookies and two pies—one peanut butter, the other key lime—as if we are feeding the entire city. McGovern uncorks a Chambertin Grand Cru red burgundy while Anna sets the table, and the file pulls silently and with great force. It is as if all of us have made an unspoken agreement to at least drink a toast and get dinner going before we start talking about murder.

"Anybody else want a Bloody?" Marino talks loudly and hangs out in the kitchen doing nothing helpful. "Hey, Doc, how 'bout I mix up a pitcher?" He yanks open the refrigerator and grabs a handful of Spicy Hot V8 juices and starts popping open the small cans. I wonder how much Marino had to drink before he got here and the safety comes off my anger. In the first place, I am insulted that he put the file under the tree, as if this is his idea of a tasteless, morbid joke. What is he implying? This is my Christmas present? Or is he so callous it didn't even occur to him that when he rather unceremoniously stuck the bag under the tree the file was still in it? He bumps past me and starts pressing lemon halves into the electric juicer and tosses the rinds in the sink.

"Well, I guess nobody's gonna help me so I'll just help myself," he mutters. "Hey!" he calls out as if we aren't in the same room with him. "Anybody think to buy horseradish?"

Anna glances at me. A collective bad mood begins to settle in. The kitchen seems to get darker and chillier, and my anger itches. I am going to fire at Marino any minute, and I am trying so hard to hold back. It is Christmas, I keep telling myself. It is Christmas. Marino grabs a long wooden spoon and makes a big production of stirring his pitcher of Bloody Marys as he slops in an appalling amount of moonshine.

"Gag." Lucy shakes her head. "At least use Grey Goose."

"Ain't a way in hell I'm drinking *French* vodka." The spoon clacks as he stirs and then taps it on the lip of the pitcher. "French wine, French vodka. Hey. What happened to things Italian?" He exaggerates a New York–Italian accent. "What happened to the neigh-ba-hood?"

"Nothing Italian about that shit you're mixing," Lucy tells him as she gets a beer out of the refrigerator. "You drink all that, Aunt Kay will take you to work with her in the morning. Only you'll be lying down in a bag."

Marino chugs a glass of his dangerous concoction. "That reminds me," he says to no one in particular. "I die, she ain't cutting on me." As if I am not standing right there. "That's the deal." He pours another glass, and by now, all of us have stopped what we are doing. We stare at him. "That's been bothering me for ten fucking years now." Another swallow. "Damn, this stuff will warm your toes. I don't want her slamming me around on one of those damn steel tables and cutting me up like I'm a fish from the fucking market. Huh. I got a deal with the girls up front." A reference to my clerks in the front office. "No passing my pictures around. Don't think I don't see what goes on up there. They compare dick sizes." He chugs half a glass and wipes his mouth with the back of his hand. "I've heard 'em do it. Especially Clit-ta." He makes a lewd play on Cleta's name.

He starts for the pitcher again and I put out my hand to stop him as my anger rushes forth in an army of harsh words. "That's enough. What the hell's gotten into you? How dare you come here drunk and then get drunker. Go sleep it off, Marino. I'm sure Anna can find a spare bed. You're not driving anywhere and none of us care to be subjected to you right now."

He gives me a defiant, mocking stare as he lifts his glass again. "Least I'm being honest," he retorts. "Rest of you can pretend all you want that it's a good damn day because it's fucking Christmas. Well, so fucking what? Lucy's quit her job so she don't get fired because she's a smart-ass queer."

"Don't, Marino," Lucy warns him.

"McGovern quit her job, and I dunno what *her* deal is." Pokes a thumb at her, insinuating she may be of Lucy's same persuasion. "Anna's gotta move outta her own fucking house because you're here and being investigated for murder, and now you're quitting your job. No small fucking god-damn wonder, and we'll just see if the governor keeps you around. A private consultant. Yeah." He slurs his words and sways in the middle of the kitchen, his face blotchy red. "That'll be the day. So guess who's left? Me, myself and I." He slams the glass down on the counter and walks out of the kitchen, bumping into a wall, knocking a painting crooked, stumbling into the living room.

"My God." McGovern quietly lets out a big breath.

"Redneck bastard," Lucy says.

"The file." Anna stares after him. "That is what is wrong with him."

MARINO IS IN A DRUNKEN COMA ON the living room couch. Nothing stirs him. He does not move, but his snoring alerts us that he is both alive and not aware of what is going on in-side Anna's house. The lasagna is cooked and stay-ing warm in the oven, and a key lime pie chills inside the refrigerator. Anna has set out on the eight-hour drive to Hilton Head, despite my protests. I did all I could to encourage her to stay, but she felt she should go on. It is midafternoon. Lucy, McGovern and I have been sitting at the dining room table for hours, place settings moved out of the way, gifts still unopened under the tree, the Tlip file spread out before us.

Benton was meticulous. He sealed each item in clear plastic, and purple stains on some of the letters and envelopes indicate ninhydrin was used to process latent fingerprints. The postmarks are Manhattan, all with the same first three digits of a zip code, 100. It is not possible to know which branch posted the letters. All a three-digit prefix indicates is which city and that the mail wasn't processed through a home or business postage meter machine or at some rural station. In those instances, the postmark would be five digits.

There is a table of contents in the front of the Tlip file and it lists a total of sixty-three items dating from the spring of 1996 (about six months before Benton wrote the letter he wanted delivered to me after his death) to the fall of 1998 (mere days before Carrie Grethen escaped from Kirby). The first item is labeled Exhibit 1, as if it is physical evidence for a jury to see. It is a letter posted in New York on May 15, 1996, unsigned and computer-printed in an ornate, hard-to-read WordPerfect font that Lucy identifies as "Ransom."

Dear Benton,
I'm the president of the Ugly Fan Club and

you've been picked to be an honorary member! Guess what? Members get to be ugly for
free! Aren't you excited? More later . . .

This was followed by five more letters, all
within weeks of each other, all making the same
references to an Ugly Fan Club and Benton's becoming the newest member. The paper was plain,
same Ransom font, no signature, same New York
zip code, clearly the same author for all. And a
very clever one until this person mailed the sixth
letter and made a mistake, a rather obvious one to
the investigative eye, which is why I am baffled
that Benton didn't seem to catch it. On the back
of the plain white envelope are writing impressions that are noticeable when I tilt the envelope
and catch light at different angles.

I get a pair of latex gloves out of my satchel and
put them on as I wander into the kitchen to find
a flashlight. Anna keeps one on the counter by the
toaster. Back in the dining room, I slip the envelope out of its plastic cover, hold it up by the
corners and shine the flashlight on the paper
obliquely. I catch the shadow of the indented
word *Postmaster* and it becomes instantly clear to
me what the author of this letter did.

"Franklin D.," I make out more words. "Is there
a Franklin D. Roosevelt post office in New York?
Because this definitely says N-Y, N-Y."

"Yes. The one in my neighborhood," McGovern says, her eyes getting wide. She comes over to my side of the table to get a closer look.

"I've had cases where people try to create alibis," I say, shining the light from different angles. "An obvious, shopworn one is you were in a different, very distant location at the time of the murder and therefore couldn't have done it. An easy way to do that is have mail posted from some remote location at or around the time the murder happens, thereby making it seem the killer couldn't be you because you can't be in two places at once."

"Third Avenue," McGovern says. "That's where the FDR post office is."

"We've got part of a street address; some of it's obliterated by the flap. *Nine*-something. *Three A-V.* Yes, Third Avenue. What you do is address the letter, put on the appropriate postage, then enclose it in another envelope addressed to the postmaster of whatever post office you want your letter mailed from. The postmaster is obliged to mail your letter for you, postmarked in that city. So what this person did was tuck this letter inside another envelope, and when he addressed that outer envelope, the impressions of what he wrote were left on the envelope underneath."

Lucy has come behind me, too, and is leaning close to see. "Susan Pless's neighborhood," she says.

Not only that, but the letter, which is by far the most vile, is dated December 5, 1997—the same day Susan Pless was murdered:

Hey Benton,
How are you, soon-to-be-ugly boy. Just wondering—Got any idea what it's like to look in the mirror and want to commit suicide? No? Will soon. Wiiiilllll soooonnnnn. Gonna carve you up like a Christmas turkey and same goes for the Chief Cunt you screw when you got time off from trying to figure out people like me & you. Can't tell you how much I'm-a-gonna (to quote Southerners) like using my big blade to open her seams. Quid pro quo, right? When you gonna learn to mind your own business?

I imagine Benton receiving these sick, crude missives. I imagine him in his room at my house, sitting at the desk with laptop opened and plugged into a modem line, his briefcase nearby, coffee within reach. His notes indicate he determined the font was Ransom and then contemplated the significance. *To obtain release by paying a price. To buy back. To deliver from sin,* I read his scribbles. I might have been down the hallway in my study or in the kitchen at the very moment he was reading this letter and looking up "ransom" in the dictionary, and he never said a word. Lucy volunteers that Benton wouldn't have wanted to burden me, and nothing helpful would have come from my knowing. I couldn't have done anything about it, she adds.

"Cactus, lilies, tulips," McGovern goes through pages of the file. "So someone was anonymously sending him flower arrangements at Quantico."

I start picking through dozens of message slips that simply have "hang-up" written on them and the date and time. The calls were made to his direct line at the Behavioral Science Unit, all tracing back to *out of area* on Caller ID, meaning they were probably made on a cell phone. Benton's only observation was *pauses on the line before hanging up.* McGovern informs us that flower orders were placed with a Lexington Avenue florist that Benton apparently checked out, and Lucy calls directory assistance to see if that same florist is still in business. It is.

"He makes a note here about payment." It is so hard for me to look at Benton's small, snarled penmanship. "Mail. The orders were placed by mail. Cash, he has the word 'cash.' So it sounds like the person sent cash and a written order." I flip back to the table of contents. Sure enough, exhibits fifty-one through fifty-five are the actual orders received by the florist. I turn to those pages. "Computer-generated and unsigned. One small arrangement of tulips for twenty-five dollars with instructions to send it to Benton's Quantico address. One small cactus for twenty-five dollars, and so on, envelopes postmarked New York."

"Probably the same thing," Lucy says. "They were mailed through the New York postmaster. Question is, where were they mailed from originally?"

We can't know that without the outer envelopes, which certainly would have been tossed into the trash the instant post office employees opened them. Even if we had those envelopes, it is highly unlikely the sender wrote out his return address. The most we could have hoped for was a postmark.

"Guess the florist just assumed he was dealing with some nutcase who doesn't believe in charge cards," McGovern comments. "Or someone having an affair."

"Or an inmate." I am, of course, thinking of Carrie Grethen. I can imagine her sending out communications from Kirby. By slipping the letters in an outer envelope addressed to a postmaster, at the very least she prevented the hospital staff from seeing who she was sending the letters to, whether it was to a florist or to Benton directly. Using a New York post office makes sense, too. She would have had access to various office branches through the telephone directory, and in my gut I don't think Carrie was concerned about anyone's supposing the mail originated in the same city where she was incarcerated. She simply didn't want to alert Kirby staff, and she was also the most manipulative person on this planet. Everything she did had its reason. She was just as busy profiling Benton as he was her.

"If it's Carrie," McGovern somberly remarks, "then you do have to wonder if she in any form or fashion was at least privy to Chandonne and his killings."

"She would get off on it," I reply with anger as I push back from the table. "And she would know damn well that by writing a letter to Benton dated the same day as Susan's murder, it would send him through the ceiling. He'd make that connection, all right."

"And picking a post office located in Susan's neighborhood," Lucy adds.

We speculate, postulate and go on until late afternoon, when we decide it is time for Christmas dinner. After rousing Marino, we tell him what we have discovered and continue to talk as we eat greens, sweet onions and tomatoes drenched in sweet red vinegar and cold-pressed olive oil. Marino shovels in food as if he hasn't eaten in days, stuffing lasagna into his mouth while we debate and speculate and beg the question: If Carrie Grethen was the person harassing Benton and she had some link to the Chandonne family, was Benton's murder more than a simple act of psychopathy? Was his slaying an organized crime hit disguised to seem personal, senseless, deranged, with Carrie the lieutenant who was more than eager to carry it out?

"In other words," Marino says to me with his mouth full, "was his death like what you're accused of."

The table falls silent. None of us quite get his meaning, but then I do. "You're saying, if there was a real motive for his murder but it was disguised to look like a serial killing?"

He shrugs. "Just like you being accused of murdering Bray and disguising it to look like Wolfman did it."

"Maybe why Interpol got so hot and bothered," Lucy considers.

Marino helps himself to excellent French wine he gulps down like Gatorade. "Yeah, Interpol. Maybe Benton got all tangled up with the cartel somehow and . . ."

"Because of Chandonne," I interrupt as my focus sharpens and I think I am on the trail that might just lead to the truth.

Jaime Berger has been our uninvited Christmas guest. She has shaded my thoughts all afternoon. I can't stop thinking about one of the first things she asked when we met in my conference room. She wanted to know if anyone had profiled Chandonne's Richmond murders. She was so quick to bring that up and so clearly believes profiling is important. Certainly, she would have had someone profile Susan Pless's murder and I am increasingly suspicious that Benton very well may have known about that case.

I get up from the table. "Please be home," I say out loud to Berger, and I experience a growing sense of desperation as I dig in my satchel for her business card. On it is her home number and I call from Anna's kitchen where no one can hear what I say. A part of me is embarrassed. I am also frightened and mad. If I am wrong, I will sound foolish. If I am right, then she should have been more open with me, damn it, damn her.

"Hello?" A woman answers.

"Ms. Berger?" I say.

"Hold on." The person calls out, "Mom! For you!"

The minute Berger gets on the line I say, "What else don't I know about you? Because it's becoming patently clear that I don't know much."

"Oh, Jill." She must mean the person who answered the phone. "Actually, they're from Greg's first marriage. Two teenagers. And today I'd sell them to the first bidder. Hell, I'd pay someone to take them."

"No, you wouldn't!" Jill says in the background and laughs.

"Let me get to a quieter spot." Berger talks as she moves into some other area of wherever it is she lives with a husband and two children she has never mentioned to me, even after all the hours we spent together. My resentment simmers. "What's up, Kay?"

"Did you know Benton?" I ask her straight up. Nothing.

"Are you there?" I speak again.

"I'm here," she says and her tone has gotten quiet and serious. "I'm thinking how best to answer you. . . ."

"Why not start with the truth. For once."

"I've always told you the truth," she replies.

"That's ridiculous. I've heard even the best of you lie when you're trying to manipulate someone. Suggesting lie detectors, or the *big needle* truth serum to get people to 'fess up, and there's also such a thing as lying by omission. The whole truth. I demand it. For God's sake, did Benton have something to do with the Susan Pless case?"

"Yes," Berger replies. "Absolutely yes, Kay."

"Talk to me, Ms. Berger. I've just spent the entire afternoon going through letters and other weird things he received before he was murdered.

They were processed in the post office located in Susan's neighborhood."

A pause. "I'd met Benton numerous times and my office has certainly availed itself of the services the behavioral science unit has to offer. Back then, at least. We actually have a forensic psychiatrist we use now, someone here in New York. I'd worked with Benton on other cases over the years, that's my point. And the minute I learned about Susan's murder and went to the scene, I called him and got him up here. We went through her apartment, just as you and I went through the Richmond crime scenes."

"Did he ever indicate to you that he was getting strange mail and phone calls and other things? And that just possibly there was a connection between whoever was doing it and whoever murdered Susan Pless?"

"I see," is all she says.

"See? What the hell do you see?"

"I see you know," she answers me. "Question is, how?"

I tell her about the Tlip file. I inform her that it appears Benton had the documents checked for fingerprints and I am wondering who did that and where and what the results might have been. She has no idea but says we should run any latent prints through the Automated Fingerprint Identification System, known as AFIS. "There are postage stamps on the envelopes," I inform her. "He didn't remove them and he would have had to if he wanted them checked for DNA."

It has only been in recent years that DNA analysis has become sophisticated enough, because of PCR, to make it worthwhile to analyze saliva, and just maybe whoever affixed postage stamps to the envelopes did so by licking them. I am not sure that even Carrie would have known back then that licking a stamp might give up her identity to us. I would have known. Had Benton showed these letters to me, I would have recommended he have the stamps examined. Maybe we would have gotten results. Maybe he wouldn't be dead.

"Back then a lot of people, even those in law enforcement, just didn't think about things like that," Berger is still talking about the postage stamps. "Seems like all cops do these days is follow people for their coffee cups or sweaty towels, Kleenex, cigarette butts. Amazing."

I have an incredible thought. What she is saying has brought to mind a case in England where a man was falsely accused of a burglary because of a cold hit on the Birmingham-based National DNA Database. The man's solicitor demanded a retest of the DNA recovered from the crime, this time using ten loci, or locations, instead of the standard six that had been used. Loci, or alleles, are simply specific locations on your genetic map. Some alleles are more common than others, so the less common they are and the more locations used, the better your chances for a match—which isn't literally a match, but rather a statistical probability that makes it almost impossible to believe the suspect didn't commit the crime. In the British case, the alleged burglar was excluded upon retesting with additional loci. There was a one-in-thirty-seven-million chance of a mismatch, and sure enough, it happened.

"When you tested the DNA from Susan's case, did you use STR?" I ask Berger.

STR is the newest technology in DNA profiling. All it means is we amplify the DNA with PCR and look at very discriminating repeated base pairs called Short Tandem Repeats. Typically, the requirement for DNA databases these days is that at least thirteen probes or loci be used, thus making it highly improbable that there will be any mismatches.

"I know our labs are very advanced," Berger is saying. "They've been doing PCR for years."

"It's all PCR unless the lab is still doing the old RFLP, which is very reliable but just takes forever," I reply. "In 1997, it was a matter of how many probes you used—or loci. Often in first screening of a sample, the lab may not do ten, thirteen or fifteen loci. That gets to be expensive. If only four loci were done in Susan's case, for example, you could come up with an unusual exception. I'm assuming the ME's office still has the extraction left in their freezer."

"What sort of bizarre exception?"

"If we're dealing with siblings. Brothers. And one left the seminal fluid and the other left the hair and saliva."

"But you tested Thomas's DNA, right? And it was similar to Jean-Baptiste's but not the same?" I can't believe it. Berger is getting agitated.

"We also did that just days ago with thirteen loci, not four or six," I reply. "I'm assuming the profiles had a lot of the same alleles, but also some different ones. The more probes you do, the more you come up with differences. Especially in closed populations. And when you think of the Chandonne family, theirs is probably a very closed population, people who have lived on Île Saint-Louis for hundreds of years, probably married their own kind. In some cases, inbreeding—marrying cousins, which might also account for Jean-Baptiste Chandonne's congenital deformity. The more people inbreed, the more they up their chances for genetic glitches."

"We need to retest the seminal fluid from Susan's case," Berger decides.

"Your labs would do that anyway, since he's up on murder charges," I reply. "But you might want to encourage them to make it a priority."

"God, let's hope it doesn't turn out to be someone else," she says in frustration. "Jesus, that would be awful if the DNA doesn't match when they do the retest. Talk about really screwing up my case."

She is right. It certainly would. Even Berger might have a hard time making a jury believe that Chandonne killed Susan if his DNA doesn't match the DNA of the seminal fluid recovered from her body.

"I'll get Marino to submit the stamps and any latent prints to the Richmond labs," she then says. "And Kay, I need to ask you not to look at anything in that file unless it's witnessed; don't look any further. That's why it's best you don't submit any evidence yourself."

"I understand." Another reminder that I am under suspicion for murder.

"For your own protection," she adds.

"Ms. Berger, if you knew about the letters, about what was happening to Benton, then what did you think when he was murdered?"

"Aside from the obvious shock and grief? That he was killed by whoever was harassing him. Yes, first thing that came to mind. However, when it became clear who his killers were and then they

were gunned down, there didn't seem to be anything to pursue further."

"And if Carrie Grethen wrote those harassing
letters, she wrote the worst one, it seems, on the
very day Susan was killed."

Silence.

"I think we must consider there could be a
connection." I am firm on this point. "Susan may
have been Chandonne's first victim in this country, and as Benton started poking around he might
have started getting too close to other things that
point to the cartel. Carrie was alive and in New
York when Chandonne came there and killed
Susan."

"And maybe Benton was a hit?" Berger sounds
doubtful.

"More than maybe," I reply. "I knew Benton
and the way he thought. For starters, why was he
carrying the Tlip file in his briefcase—why did he
take it with him to Philadelphia if he didn't have
some reason to think that the weird stuff in it was
connected to what Carrie and her accomplice
were doing? Killing people and cutting their faces
off. *Making them ugly*. And the notes Benton was
getting made it clear he was going to be made
ugly, and he sure as hell was. . . ."

"I need a copy of that file," Berger dismisses me.
It is obvious by her tone that she suddenly wants

to get off the phone. "I've got a fax machine here in the house." She gives me the number.

I GO INTO ANNA'S STUDY AND SPEND the next half hour photocopying everything in the Tlip file because I can't feed laminated documents into the fax machine. Marino finished the burgundy and is asleep on the couch again when I return to the living room, where Lucy and McGovern sit in front of the fire talking, continuing to paint scenarios that are only getting wilder the more they are influenced by alcohol. Christmas speeds away from us. We finally get around to opening gifts at half past ten, and Marino groggily plays Santa, handing out boxes and trying to be festive. But his mood has gotten only darker and any attempts at humor have a bite. At eleven o'clock, Anna's phone rings. It is Berger.

"*Quid pro quo*?" she launches in, referring to the letter dated December 5, 1997. "How many non-legal-minded people use that term? Just a crazy idea, but wonder if there's a way we could get hold of Rocky Caggiano's DNA. May as well turn over every stone and not be so quick to assume Carrie wrote these letters. Maybe she did. But maybe she didn't."

I can't concentrate as I return to Christmas gifts

beneath the tree. I try to smile and act abundantly thankful, but I don't fool anyone. Lucy gives me a stainless-steel Breitling watch called a B52 while Marino's gift to me is a coupon for a year of firewood that he will personally deliver and stack. Lucy loves the Whirly-Girls necklace I had made for her and Marino loves the leather jacket from Lucy and me. Anna would be pleased with an art glass vase I found for her, but she is somewhere on I-95, of course. Everybody goes through the motions quickly because questions hang heavy in the air. While we gather up rumpled ribbons and torn paper, I motion to Marino that I need a private word with him. We sit in the kitchen. He has been in some stage of drunkenness all day, and I can tell that he is probably getting drunk on a regular basis. There is a reason for it.

"You can't keep drinking like this," I say to him as I pour each of us a glass of water. "It doesn't help anything."

"Never has, never will." He rubs his face. "And that don't seem to make a damn difference when I'm feeling like shit. Right now, everything's shit." His bleary, bloodshot eyes meet mine. Marino looks like he is about to cry again.

"Any reason you might have something that could give us Rocky's DNA?" I come right out and ask.

He flinches as if I have hit him. "What'd Berger

tell you when she called? That it? She call about Rocky?"

"She's just going down the list," I reply. "Anybody connected with us or Benton who might have a link to organized crime. And Rocky certainly comes to mind." I go on and tell him what Berger revealed about Benton and the Susan Pless case.

"But he was getting that whacko shit before Susan was murdered," he says. "So why would someone be jerking him around if he wasn't sticking his nose in anything yet? Why would Rocky, for example? And I assume that's what you're thinking, that maybe Rocky was sending him that weird shit?"

I have no answer. I don't know.

"Well, I guess you're gonna have to get DNA from Doris and me 'cause I don't got anything of Rocky's. Not even hair. You could do that, right? If you got the DNA of the mother and the father then you could compare something like saliva?"

"We could get a pedigree and at least know your son can't be ruled out as a contributor of the DNA on the stamps."

"Okay." He blows out. "If that's what you want to do. Since Anna's split, think I can smoke in here?"

"I wouldn't dare," I reply. "What about Rocky's fingerprints?"

"Forget that. Besides, it didn't look to me like Benton had any luck with the prints. I mean, you can tell he tested the letters for them and that seems to be the end of it. And I know you don't want to hear this, Doc, but maybe you'd better be sure why you're getting into all this. Don't go on a witch hunt 'cause you want to pay back the fucker who might have sent that shit to Benton and maybe had to do with him being killed. It ain't worth it. Especially if you're thinking Carrie did it. She's dead. Let her rot."

"It *is* worth it," I say. "If I can know for sure who sent those letters to him, it's worth it to me."

"Huh. He said The Last Precinct was where he'd end up. Well, looks like he has," Marino muses. "We're The Last Precinct and we're working his case. Ain't that something?"

"Do you think he carried that file to Philadelphia because he wanted to make sure you or I got it?"

"Assuming something happened to him?"

I nod.

"Maybe," he says. "He was worried he wasn't going to be around much longer and he wanted us to find that file if something did happen to him. And it's strange, too. It's not like he says much in it, almost like he knew other people might see it and he didn't want anything in it that maybe the wrong person would see. Don't you find it interesting there ain't any names in it? Like if he had suspects in mind, he never mentioned anybody?"

"The file's cryptic," I agree.

"So who was he afraid might see it? Cops? 'Cause if something happened to him, he would know cops are going through his shit. And they did. Philly cops went through everything in his hotel room and then turned it over to me. He would also figure you're going to see his stuff at some point. Maybe Lucy, too."

"I think the point is he couldn't be sure of who might see the file. So he was cautious, period. And Benton was certainly known for being cautious."

"Not to mention," Marino goes on, "he was up there helping out ATF. So he might have thought ATF would see the file, right? Lucy's ATF. McGovern's ATF and was in charge of the response team working the fires Carrie and her asshole sidekick were setting to disguise the fact they had this nasty little hobby of cutting people's faces off, right?" Marino's eyes narrow. "Talley's ATF," he says. "Maybe we ought to get his DNA, the son of a bitch. Too bad." He gets that look again. I don't think Marino will ever forgive me for sleeping with Jay Talley. "You probably had his fucking DNA, no pun intended. In Paris. I don't guess you got a stain you maybe forgot to wash out?"

"Shut up, Marino," I say softly.

"I'm getting withdrawal." He gets up and goes

to the liquor cabinet. Now it's time for bourbon. He pours Booker's into a glass and comes back to the table. "Wouldn't that just be something if it turns out Talley's involved in everything from soup to nuts. Maybe that's why he wanted you at Interpol. He wanted to pick your brain to see if you knew maybe what Benton knew? 'Cause guess what? Maybe when Benton was poking around after Susan's murder, he started figuring out shit that started pulling him too close to a truth Talley can't afford for nobody to know."

"What are you two talking about?" Lucy is in the kitchen. I didn't hear her walk in.

"Sounds like a job for you." Marino gives her his puffy eyes as he swills bourbon in his glass. "Why don't you and Teun investigate Talley and find out how dirty he is. 'Cause I believe with all my little heart they don't come no dirtier. And by the way." This to me. "In case you didn't hear, he's one of the guys who drove Chandonne up to New York. Now ain't that interesting? He sits in on Berger's interview. He spends six hours in the car with him. Hey, they're probably drinking buddies by now—or maybe they already was."

Lucy stares out the kitchen window, her hands in the pockets of her jeans, obviously put off by Marino and embarrassed by him. He is sweating and profane, and unsteady on his feet, and filled with hate and spite one minute, sullen the next.

"You know what I can't stand?" Marino keeps at it. "I can't stand bad cops who get away with it because everybody's too damn chicken to go after them. And nobody wants to touch Talley or even try because he speaks all these languages and went to Harvard and is a big shot golden boy. . . ."

"You really don't know what you're talking about," Lucy says to Marino, and by now, McGovern has wandered into the kitchen. "You're wrong. Jay's not off limits and you're not the only person on this planet who has doubts about him."

"Serious doubts," McGovern echoes.

Marino shuts up and leans against the counter.

"I can tell you what we know so far," Lucy says to me. She is reluctant and soft-spoken because nobody, really, is quite sure how I feel about Jay. "I kind of hate to, because there's nothing definitive. But it's not looking good so far." She looks at me as if in search of a cue.

"Good," I tell her. "Let's hear it."

"Yeah. I'm all ears," Marino responds.

"I've run him through quite a number of databases. No criminal or civil court records, no liens or judgments, et cetera. Not that we expected him to be a registered sex offender or deadbeat parent or missing or wanted or whatever, and there's no evidence that the FBI, CIA or even ATF has a file on him in their systems of records. But doing a simple search of real estate records raised a red flag.

First of all, he has a condo in New York where he's let certain select friends stay—including high-ranking people in law enforcement," she says to Marino and me. "A three-million-plus place full of antiques, on Central Park. Jay has bragged that the condo is his. Well, it's not. Comes back to a corporate name."

"It's not uncommon for wealthy people to have property in separate corporate names, for privacy reasons and also to protect various assets from litigation," I point out.

"I know. But this corporation isn't Jay's," Lucy replies. "Not unless he owns an air freight company."

"Kind of eerie, right?" McGovern adds. "Considering how much shipping the Chandonne family is involved in. So maybe there's a connection. It's way too soon to say."

"No big surprise," Marino mutters, but his eyes light up. "Yeah, how well I remember him playing the big rich Harvard act, right, Doc? Remember, I wondered why we was suddenly on a Learjet, and next thing we're on the Concorde going to France. I knew Interpol didn't pay for all that shit."

"He never should have bragged about that condo," Lucy remarks. "Obviously he's got the same Achilles' heel other assholes do: ego." She looks at me. "He wanted to impress you, so he flies you out supersonic—says he got the tickets comped because they were for law enforcement. And sure, we know the airlines do that sort of thing on occasion. But we're tracking that, too, to see who made those reservations and what the story was."

"My big question," McGovern goes on, "is obviously whether or not that condo might be owned by the Chandonne family. And you can only imagine how many layers you'd have to go through to get to them."

"Hell, they probably own the whole fucking building," Marino says. "And half of Manhattan to go along with it."

"What about corporate officers?" I ask. "Any interesting names come up?"

"We've got names but they don't mean anything significant yet," Lucy replies. "These paper cases take a lot of time. We run them and then everything and everybody they connect with, on and on it goes."

"And where do Mitch Barbosa and Rosso Matos fit in?" I ask. "Or do they? Because somebody took a key out of my house and put it in Barbosa's pocket. Do you think Jay did?"

Marino snorts and takes a swallow of bourbon. "Gets my vote," he retorts. "That and swiping your chipping hammer. Can't think of anybody else who'd do it. I know every guy who went in there, in your house. Unless Righter did it, and he's too chicken and I really don't think he's dirty."

It isn't that Jay's shadow hasn't crossed our thoughts numerous times before. We know he was in my house. We know he is bitter toward me. We all have considerable questions about his character, but if he did plant the key or steal it from my house and pass it off to someone else, then this directly implicates him in Barbosa's torture-homicide and most likely in Matos's as well. "Where's Jay right now? Anybody know?" I search their faces.

"Well, he was in New York. That was Wednesday. Then we saw him yesterday afternoon in James City County. Got no idea right this very minute," Marino answers.

"There are a couple other things you might want to know." Lucy addresses this to me. "One in particular is real odd but I can't make heads or tails of it yet. On the credit search, I got hits on two Jay Talleys with different addresses and different social security numbers. One Jay Talley was issued his social security number in Phoenix between 1960 and 1961. Which couldn't be Jay unless he's in his forties, and he's what? Not much older than me? Early thirties at the most? A second Jay Talley I got a hit on was issued his social security number between 1936 and '37. No D-O-B, but he'd have to be one of the early timers who got a number shortly after the Social Security Act of 1935, so God knows how old this particular Jay Talley already was when he got his number. He'd have to be at least in his seventies and he sure moves around a lot and uses post office boxes instead of physical addresses. He's also bought a lot of cars, sometimes changing vehicles a couple times a year."

"Did Talley ever tell you where he was born?" Marino asks me.

"He said he spent most of his childhood in Paris and then his family moved to L.A.," I reply. "You were sitting in the cafeteria when he said that. At Interpol."

"No record of either Jay Talley ever living in L.A.," Lucy says.

"And speaking of Interpol," Marino says. "Wouldn't they check him out before letting him work there?"

"Obviously, they might have checked into him, but not extensively," Lucy replies. "He's an ATF agent. You assume he's clean."

"What about a middle name?" Marino asks. "We know his?"

"He doesn't have one. Nothing in his ATF personnel records." McGovern smiles wryly. "And neither does the Jay Talley who got his social security number back before the Great Flood. That alone is unusual. Most people have middle names.

In his file at headquarters it does say he was born in Paris and lived there until he was six. But after that he supposedly moved to New York with his French father and American mother and there's no mention of Los Angeles. On his ATF application he claims to have gone to Harvard, but having looked into that we discovered there's no record of any Jay Talley having ever attended Harvard."

"Jesus," Marino exclaims. "Don't people check out nothing when they go through these applications? They just take your word for it that you went to Harvard or were a Rhodes scholar or pole-vaulted in the Olympics? And they hire you and give you a badge and a gun?"

"Well, I'm not going to give Internal Affairs a heads-up that they may want to check him out a little more closely," McGovern offers. "We've got to be careful someone doesn't tip him off, and it's hard to say who his friends are at headquarters."

Marino lifts his arms in the air and stretches. He cracks his neck. "I'm hungry again," he says.

CHAPTER 32

THE GUEST ROOM IN ANNA'S house faces the river, and over passing days I have fashioned a makeshift desk before the window. This required a small table, which I covered with a cloth so I would not scratch the satin finish, and from the library I purloined an apple-green English leather swivel chair. At first, I was dismayed that I had forgotten my laptop computer, but I discovered an unexpected solace in putting fountain pen to paper and letting thoughts flow through my fingers and shimmer in black ink. My penmanship is awful, and the notion that it has something to do with being a doctor is probably true. There are days when I must sign my name or initials five hundred times, and I suppose scribbling gross descriptions and measurements with bloody gloved hands has taken its toll, too.

I have developed a ritual at Anna's house. Each

morning I slip into the kitchen and pour myself a cup of coffee that was timed to begin dripping at exactly half past five. I return to my room, shut the door and sit at the window writing before a glass square of utter darkness. My first morning here, I was outlining classes I am scheduled to teach at the Institute's next death investigation school. But transportation fatalities, asphyxia and forensic radiology completely left my mind as life on the river was touched by first light.

This morning I have faithfully watched the show once again. At half past six, the darkness lightened to a charcoal gray, and within minutes I could make out the silhouettes of bare sycamores and oaks, then dark plains turned into water and land. Most mornings the river is warmer than the air, and fog rolls over the surface of the James. Right now it looks like the River Styx and I halfway expect a ghostly, gaunt man in rags to pole by in his boat through veils of mist. I don't expect to see animals until closer to eight, and they have become a huge comfort to me. I have fallen in love with the Canada geese that congregate by Anna's dock in a chorus of honking. Squirrels run errands up and down trees, tails curled like plumes of smoke. Birds hover at my window and look me straight in the eye as if to see what I am spying on. Deer run through bare winter woods on the opposite river bank and red-tailed hawks swoop.

At rare, privileged moments I am graced by bald eagles. Their enormous wingspans, white helmets and pantaloons make them unmistakable, and I am comforted because eagles fly higher and alone and don't seem to have the same agendas other birds do. I watch them circle or perch briefly in a tree, never staying in one spot long before suddenly they are gone, leaving me to wonder, like Emerson, if I have just been sent a sign. I have found nature to be kind. The rest of what I live with these days is not.

It is Monday, January 17th, and I remain in exile at Anna's house, or at least this is how I view it. Time has passed slowly, almost stagnantly, like the water beyond my window. The currents of my life are moving in a certain, barely perceptible direction, and there is no possibility of rerouting their inevitable progress. The holidays have come and gone, and my cast has been replaced by Ace bandages and a splint. I am driving a rental car because my Mercedes is being held for further investigation, at Hull Street and Commerce Road, at the impound lot, which is not attended by police twenty-four hours a day and there is no guard dog. On New Year's Eve, someone smashed a window out of my car and stole the two-way radio, the AM-FM radio and CD player and God knows what else. So much for the chain of evidence, I told Marino.

There are new developments in the Chandonne case. As I suspected, when the seminal fluid in Susan Pless's case was originally tested in 1997, only four probes were used. The New York medical examiner's office still uses four probes for the first screening because they are developed in-house and therefore it is more economical to resort to them first. The frozen extraction was retested using fifteen loci, and the result is a non-match. Jean-Baptiste Chandonne was not the donor of the seminal fluid, nor was his brother, Thomas. But there are so many alleles in common, the DNA profiles are so incredibly close, that we can only assume there is a third brother, and it is this brother who had sex with Susan. We are baffled. Berger is on her head. "DNA has told the truth and fucked us," Berger told me over the phone. Chandonne's dentition matches the bite marks and his saliva and hair were on the bloody body, but he did not have vaginal sex with Susan Pless right before she died. That may not be enough for a jury in this day of DNA. A New York grand jury will have to decide if it is enough for an indictment, and it struck me as incredibly ironic when Berger said this. It doesn't seem to require much to accuse *me* of murder, nothing more than rumor and alleged intent and the fact that I conducted experiments with a chipping hammer and barbecue sauce.

For weeks, I have waited for the subpoena. Yesterday it arrived, and the sheriff's deputy was his usual cheerful self when he showed up at my office, not realizing, I suppose, that the case this time involves me as a defendant and not an expert witness. I have been asked to appear in room 302 of the John Marshall Courts Building to testify before the special grand jury. The hearing is set for Tuesday, February 1, at 2 P.M.

At a few minutes past seven, I stand inside the closet, pushing through suits and blouses as I run through all I need to do this day. I already know from Jack Fielding that we have six cases and two of the doctors are in court. I also have a ten o'clock telephone conference with Governor Mitchell. I pick out a black pants suit with blue pinstripes and a blue blouse with French cuffs. I wander into the kitchen for another cup of coffee and a bowl of high-protein cereal that Lucy brought over. I have to smile as I practically break my teeth on her healthy, crunchy gift. My niece is determined that I will emerge from my smoldering life a fit phoenix. I rinse dishes and finish getting dressed and am heading out the door when my pager vibrates. Marino's number shows up on the video display and is followed by 911.

Parked in Anna's driveway is the latest change in my life—the rental car. It is a midnight blue Ford Explorer that smells like ancient cigarettes and will always smell like ancient cigarettes unless I do what Marino suggested and stick an air freshener on the dash. I plug my cell phone into the cigarette lighter and call him.

"Where are you?" he asks right off.

"Heading out the driveway." I turn on the heater and Anna's gates open to let me out. I don't even stop to pick up the newspaper, which Marino next tells me I need to see, because clearly I haven't read it yet or I would have called him right away.

"Too late," I tell him. "I'm already on Cherokee." I harden myself like a little kid flexing his stomach muscles when he dares someone to sock him in the gut. "So go on and tell me. What's in the paper?" I am expecting that the special grand jury investigation has been leaked to the press, and I am right. I drive along Cherokee as recent winter weather continues to dissolve in drips and puddles, and slushy snow sluggishly slides off roofs.

"*Chief Medical Examiner Suspected in Grisly Slaying,*" Marino reads the banner headline on the front page. "It's got a picture of you, too," he adds. "Looks like one maybe that bitch took out in front of your house. The lady that fell on the ice, remember? It shows you climbing in my truck. Pretty good of my truck. Not so hot of you . . ."

"Just tell me what it says," I interrupt him.

He reads the highlights as I hug the hard curves of Cherokee Road. A Richmond special grand jury is investigating me in the murder of Deputy Police Chief Diane Bray, the newspaper says. The revelation is described as *shocking* and *bizarre* and has local law enforcement *reeling*. Although Commonwealth's Attorney Buford Righter refused comment, unnamed sources say Righter instigated the investigation *with great heartache* after witnesses came forth with statements and police produced evidence that was impossible to ignore. Additional unnamed sources claim I was in a heated clash with Bray, who believed I was incompetent and no longer fit to be chief medical examiner of Virginia. Bray was trying to have me removed from office and told people before her murder that I had confronted her on several occasions and had bullied and threatened her. Sources say there are indicators pointing to the possibility that I staged Bray's murder to look like the brutal murder of Kim Luong and on and on and on.

By now I am on Huguenot Road in the thick of rush-hour traffic. I tell Marino to stop. I have heard quite enough.

"It goes on forever," he says.

"I'm sure it does."

"They must have been working on it all during the holidays 'cause it's got all kinds of shit about you and your background." I hear pages turning. "Even stuff about Benton and his death, and Lucy. There's this big sidebar with all your vital statistics, where you went to school. Cornell, Georgetown, Hopkins. The pictures on the inside are good. Even one of you and me together at a crime scene. Oh shit, it's Bray's crime scene."

"What about Lucy?" I ask.

But Marino is bewitched by publicity, by what must be huge photographs that include him and me working together. "I ain't never seen anything like this." More pages turning. "It just goes on and on, Doc. So far I've counted five bylines. They must've had the entire fucking news staff working this thing without our having a clue. Including an aerial shot of your house . . ."

"What about Lucy?" I ask with more force. "What does it say about Lucy?"

"Well, I'll be damned, there's even a photo of you and Bray out in the parking lot at Luong's scene, at the convenience store. Both of you look like you hate each other's guts. . . ."

"Marino!" I raise my voice. It is all I can do to concentrate on my driving. "Okay, enough!"

A pause, then, "I'm sorry, Doc. Jesus, I know it's awful, but I didn't get a chance to look at much beyond the front page before I got hold of you. I had no idea. I'm sorry. I just never seen nothing like this unless somebody really famous suddenly dies."

Tears smart. I don't point out the irony of what he just said. I feel as if I have died.

"Let me look at this Lucy stuff," Marino is saying. "Pretty much what you'd expect. She's your niece but you've always been more like her mother, uh, graduated all-that-laude-shit from UVA, her DUI car wreck, fact she's gay, flies a helicopter, FBI, ATF, yeah, yeah, yeah. And that she almost shot Chandonne in your front yard. I guess that's the fucking point." Marino returns to his irritated self. As much as he picks on Lucy, he doesn't like it one bit if anybody else does. "Don't say she's on admin leave or that you're hiding out at Anna's house. Least there's something those assholes haven't dug up."

I inch closer to West Cary Street. "Where are you?" I ask him.

"HQ. About to head your way," he replies. "Because you're gonna have quite a welcome party." He means the press. "Thought you might like a little company. Plus, I got some stuff to go over with you. Also thought we might try a little trick, Doc. I'll get to your office first and ditch my car. You pull in front on Jackson Street instead of going around to the back lot off Fourth, hop out and go in and I'll park your car. Word from the troops—there's about thirty reporters, photographers, TV guys camping out at your parking place, waiting for you to show up."

I start to agree with him and then have second thoughts. No, I say. I am not about to start the charade of hiding, ducking and holding up files or my coat to hide my face from cameras as if I am a crime boss. Absolutely not. I tell Marino I will see him at my office, but I will park as usual and deal with the media. For one thing, my stubbornness has kicked in. For another, I don't see what I have to lose by going about my business as usual and simply telling the truth, and the damn truth is I didn't kill Diane Bray. I never even thought about it, although I certainly disliked her more than anyone else I have ever met in my life.

On 9th Street I stop at a red light and put on my suit jacket. I check myself in the rearview mirror to make sure I look reasonably glued together. I put on a dab of lipstick and comb my fingers through my hair. I turn on the radio, bracing myself for the first news spot. I anticipate that local stations will interrupt their programs frequently to remind everybody that I am the first scandal of the new millennium.

". . . So, I gotta say this, Jim. I mean, talk about someone who could get away with the *perfect murder.* . . ."

"No kidding. You know, I interviewed her once. . . ."

I switch to a different station and then another one as I am mocked and degraded or simply reported on because someone has leaked to the media what is supposed to be the most secret and sacred of all legal proceedings. I wonder who violated his code of silence, and what is even sadder, several names come to mind. I don't trust Righter. I don't trust anyone he has contacted for telephone or bank records. But I have another suspect in mind—Jay Talley—and I am betting that he has been subpoenaed, too. I compose myself as I pull into my parking lot and see the television and radio vans lining 4th Street and the dozens of people waiting for me with cameras, microphones and notepads.

NOT ONE OF THE REPORTERS NO-tices my dark blue Explorer because they aren't expecting it, and this is when I realize I have made a serious tactical error. I have been driving a rental car for days and it didn't occur to me until this moment that I might be asked why. I turn into my reserved space by the front door and am sighted. The pack moves toward me like hunters after big game, and I will myself to go into my role. I am the chief. I am reserved, poised and unafraid. I have done nothing wrong. I climb out and take my time gathering my briefcase and a stack of folders out of the backseat. My elbow aches beneath layers of elasticized wrappings, and cameras click and microphones point at me like guns cocking and finding their mark.

"Dr. Scarpetta? Can you comment about . . . ?"

"Dr. Scarpetta . . . ?"

"When did you find out a special grand jury is investigating you?"

"Isn't it true you and Diane Bray were at odds . . . ?"

"Where's your car?"

"Can you confirm that you've basically been run out of your home and don't even have your own car right now?"

"Will you resign?"

I face them on the sidewalk. I am silent but steady as I wait for them to get quiet. When they realize I intend to address their questions I catch surprised looks and their aggression quickly settles down. I recognize many faces but can't remember names. I am not sure I have ever known the names of the media's real troops who gather the news behind the scenes. I remind myself they are simply doing their jobs and there is no reason for me to take any of this personally. That's right, nothing personal. Rude, inhumane, inappropriate, insensitive and largely inaccurate, but *not personal*. "I've no prepared statement," I start to say.

"Where were you the night Diane Bray was murdered . . . ?"

"Please," I interrupt them. "Like you, I've recently learned there is a special grand jury investigation into her murder, and I ask you to honor the very necessary confidentiality of such a proceeding. Please understand why I'm not at liberty to discuss it with you."

"But did you . . . ?"

"Isn't it true you aren't driving your own car because the police have it?"

Questions and accusations rip the morning air like shrapnel as I walk toward my building. I have nothing more to say. I am the chief. I am poised and calm and unafraid. I did nothing wrong. There is one reporter whom I do remember, because how could I forget a tall, white-haired, chisel-featured African American whose name is Washington George? He wears a long leather trench coat and presses behind me as I struggle to open the glass door leading inside the building.

"Can I just ask you one thing?" he says. "You remember me? That's not my question." A smile. "I'm Washington George. I work for the AP."

"I remember you."

"Here, let me help you with that." He holds the door and we go inside the lobby, where the security guard looks at me, and I know that look now. My notoriety is reflected in people's eyes. My heart sinks. "Good morning, Jeff," I say as I walk past the console.

A nod.

I pass my plastic ID over the electronic eye and the door leading into my side of the building unlocks. Washington George is still with me, and he is saying something about information he has that he thinks I need to know, but I am not listening. A woman sits in my reception area. She huddles in a chair and seems sad and small amid polished granite and glass blocks. This is not a good place to be. I always ache for anyone who finds himself in my reception area. "Is someone helping you?" I ask her.

She is dressed in a black skirt and nurses' shoes, a dark raincoat pulled tightly around her. She hugs her pocketbook as if someone might steal it. "I'm just waiting," she says in a hushed voice.

"Who are you here to see?"

"Well, I don't rightly know," she stammers, her eyes swimming in tears. Sobs well up inside her and her nose begins to run. "It's about my boy. Do you think I might see him? I don't understand what y'all are doing to him in there." Her chin trembles and she wipes her nose on the back of her hand. "I just need to see him."

Fielding left me a message about today's cases, and I know that one of them is a teenage boy who supposedly hanged himself. What was the name? White? I ask her and she nods. Benny, she gives me his first name. I presume she is Mrs. White and she nods again and explains that she and her son changed their last name to *White* after she got re-married a few years back. I tell her to come on with me—and now she is crying hard—and we will find out what is going on with Benny. Whatever Washington George has to tell me will have to wait.

"I don't think you're going to want it to wait," he replies.

"All right, all right. Come on in with me and I'll get to you as soon as I can." I am saying this as I let us into my office with another pass of my ID key. Cleta is entering cases into our computer, and she instantly blushes when she sees me.

"Good morning," she tries to be her usual cheerful self. But she has that look in her eye, the look I've grown to hate and fear. I can only imag-ine what my staff has been saying among them-selves this morning, and it doesn't escape my attention that the newspaper is folded on top of Cleta's desk and she has tried to cover it with her sweater. Cleta has put on weight over the holi-days and has dark circles under her eyes. I am making everybody miserable.

"Who's taking care of Benny White?" I ask her.

"I think Dr. Fielding is." She looks at Mrs.

White and gets up from her workstation. "Can I take your coat? What about some coffee?"

I tell Cleta to take Mrs. White to my conference room and Washington George can wait in the medical library. I find my secretary, Rose. I am so relieved to see her that I forget about my troubles, nor does she reflect them to me by giving me a look—that secretive, curious, embarrassed look. Rose is just Rose. If anything, disaster irons more starch in her than usual. She meets my eyes and shakes her head. "I'm so disgusted I could spit nails," she says when I show up in her doorway. "The most ridiculous hogwash I've ever heard of my entire life." She picks up her copy of the paper and shakes it at me as if I am a bad dog. "Don't you let this bother you, Dr. Scarpetta." As if it is that simple. "More chicken crap than Kentucky Fried, that damn Buford Righter. He can't come out and just tell you to your face, can he? So you have to find out this way?" Shaking the paper again.

"Rose, is Jack in the morgue?" I ask.

"Oh God, working on that poor kid." Rose gets off the subject of me, and her indignation turns to pity. "Lord, Lord. Have you seen him?"

"I just got here . . ."

"Looks like a little choir boy. Just the most beautiful blue-eyed blond. Lord, Lord. If that was my child . . ."

I interrupt Rose by putting a finger to my lips as I hear Cleta coming up the hallway with the boy's poor mother. I mouth *his mother* to Rose and she gets quiet. Her eyes linger on mine. She is fidgety and high-strung this morning, and dressed severely in black, her hair pulled back and pinned up, reminding me of Grant Wood's *American Gothic*. "I'm okay," I tell her quietly.

"Well, I don't believe that." Her eyes get dewy and she nervously busies herself with paperwork.

Jean-Baptiste Chandonne has decimated my entire staff. Everyone who knows and depends on me is dismayed, bewildered. They don't completely trust me anymore and secretly anguish over what will happen to their lives and jobs. I am reminded of my worst moment in school when I was twelve—like Lucy, precocious, the youngest in my class. My father died that school year on December 23, and the only thing good I can find in his waiting until two days before Christmas is at least the neighbors were winding down from work, most of them home and cooking and baking. In the good Italian-Catholic tradition, my father's life was celebrated with abundance. For several days, our house was filled with laughter, tears, food, drink and song.

When I returned to school after the New Year, I became even more relentless in my cerebral conquests and explorations. Making perfect scores on tests was no longer enough. I was desperate for attention, desperate to please, and begged the nuns for special projects, any project, I didn't care what. Eventually, I was hanging around the parochial school all afternoon, beating chalkboard erasers on the school steps, helping the teachers grade tests, putting together bulletin boards. I got very good with scissors and staplers. When there was a need to cut out letters of the alphabet or numbers and exactly assemble them into words, sentences, calendars, the nuns came looking for me.

Martha was a girl in my math class who sat in front of me and never spoke. She glanced back at me a lot, cold but curious, always trying to catch a peek at the grades circled in red on top of my folded homework and tests, hopeful she had scored better than I had. One day, after an especially difficult algebra test, I noticed that Sister Teresa's demeanor toward me decidedly chilled. She waited until I was cleaning erasers again, squatting outside on stucco steps, pounding, creating clouds of chalk dust in the winter tropical sun, and I looked up. There she was in her habit, towering over me like a giant, frowning Antarctic bird wearing a crucifix. Someone had accused me of cheating on my algebra test, and although Sister Teresa did not identify the source of this lie, I had no doubt of the culprit: Martha. The only way I could prove my innocence was to take the test again and make another perfect score.

Sister Teresa watched me closely after that. I dared never let my eyes stray from what I was doing at my desk. Several days passed. I was emptying the trash baskets, just the two of us alone in the classroom, and she told me I must pray constantly that God would keep me free of sin. I must thank our Heavenly Father for the great gifts I have and look to Him to keep me honest, because I was so smart I could get away with a lot of things. God knows everything, Sister Teresa said. I can't fool God. I protested that I was honest and not trying to fool God and she could ask God herself. I began to cry. "I am not a cheater," I sobbed. "I want my daddy."

When I was at Johns Hopkins in my first year of medical school, I wrote Sister Teresa a letter and recounted that wrenching, unfair incident. I reiterated my innocence, still bothered, still furious that I had been falsely accused and the nuns didn't defend me and never seemed quite as sure of me afterward.

As I stand in Rose's office now, more than twenty years later, I think about what Jaime Berger said the first time we met. She promised that the hurt had only begun. Of course, she was right. "Before everybody leaves today," I say to my secretary, "I'd like to talk to them. If you'd pass that along, Rose. We'll see how the day goes and find a time. I'm going to check on Benny White. Please make sure his mother is all right, and I'll be in shortly to talk to her."

I head down the hallway past the break room and find Washington George in the medical library. "I just have a minute," I tell him in a distracted way.

He is scanning books on a shelf, notepad down by his side like a gun he might use. "I heard a rumor," he says. "If you know it's true, maybe you can verify it. If you don't know, well, maybe you should. Buford Righter's not going to be the prosecutor in your special grand jury hearing."

"I know nothing about it," I reply, masking the indignation I always feel when the press knows details before I do. "But we've worked a lot of cases together," I add. "I wouldn't expect him to want to deal with this himself."

"I guess so, and what I understand is a special prosecutor has been appointed. That's the part I'm getting to. You aware of this?" He tries to read my face.

"No." I am trying to read his face, too, hoping to catch a foreshadowing that might prevent me from being broadsided.

"No one's indicated to you that Jaime Berger's been appointed to get you indicted, Dr. Scarpetta?" He stares me in the eye. "From what I understand, that's one of the reasons she came to town. You've been going through the Luong and Bray cases with her and all that, but I have it from a very good source it's a setup. She's been undercover, I guess you would say. Righter set it up before Chandonne allegedly showed up at your house. I understand Berger's been in the picture for weeks."

All I can think to say is, "Allegedly?" I am shocked.

"Well," Washington George says, "I assume by your reaction that you haven't heard any of this."

"I don't guess you can tell me who your reliable source is," I respond.

"Naw." He smiles a little, somewhat sheepishly. "So you can't confirm?"

"Of course I can't," I say as I gather my wits about me.

"Look, I'm going to keep digging, but I want you to know I like you and you've always been nice enough to me." He goes on. I am barely hearing a word of it. All I can think of is Berger spending hours with me in the dark, in her car, in my house, in Bray's house, and all along she was making mental notes to use against me in the special grand jury hearing. God, no wonder she seems to know so much about my life. She has probably been through my phone records, bank statements, credit reports and interviewed everyone who knows me. "Washington," I say, "I've got the mother of some poor person who just died, and I can't stand here and talk to you any longer." I walk off. I don't care if he thinks I am rude.

I cut through the ladies' room and in the changing area I put on a lab coat and slip paper covers over my shoes. The autopsy suite is full of sounds, every table occupied with the unfortunate. Jack Fielding is splashed with blood. He has already opened up Mrs. White's son and is inserting a syringe with a fourteen-gauge needle into the aorta to draw blood. Jack gives me a rather frantic, wild-eyed look when I walk over to his table. The morning news is all over his face.

"Later." I raise my hand before he can ask a question. "His mother's in my office." I indicate the body.

"Shit," Fielding says. "Shit is all I gotta say about this entire fucking world."

"She wants to see him." I take a rag from a bag on a gurney and wipe the boy's delicately pretty face. His hair is the color of hay and, except for his suffused face, his skin is like rose milk. He has fuzz on his upper lip and the first hint of pubic hair, his hormones just beginning to stir, preparing for an adult life he was not destined to have. A narrow, dark furrow around the neck angles up to the right ear where the rope was knotted. Otherwise, his strong, young body bears no evidence of violence, no hint that he should have had any reason in the world not to live. Suicides can be very challenging. Contrary to popular belief, people rarely leave notes. People don't always talk about their feelings in life and sometimes their dead bodies don't have much to say, either.

"Goddamn," Jack mutters.

"What do we know about this?" I ask him.

"Just that he started acting weird at school right about Christmas." Jack picks up the hose and rinses out the chest cavity until it gleams like the inside of a tulip. "Dad died of lung cancer a few years ago." Water slaps. "That damn Stanfield, Jesus Christ. What we got out there? Some kind of special? Three fucking cases from him in four fucking weeks." Jack rinses off the bloc of organs. They shimmer in deep hues on the cutting board, waiting for their ultimate violation. "He keeps turning up like a fucking bad penny." Jack grabs a large surgical knife from the cart. "So this kid goes to church yesterday, comes home and hangs himself in the woods."

The more times Jack Fielding uses the word "fuck," the more upset he is. He is extremely upset. "What about Stanfield?" I ask darkly. "I thought he was quitting."

"I wish he would. The guy's an idiot. He calls about this case and guess what else? Apparently, he goes to the scene. The kid's hanging from a tree and Stanfield cuts him down."

I have a feeling I know what's coming.

"He cuts *through the knot.*"

I was right. "He took photographs first, let's hope."

"Over there." He nods at the counter on the other side of the room.

I go to look at the photographs. They are painful. It appears Benny didn't even stop to change clothes when he came home from church, but went straight into the woods, threw a nylon rope over a tree branch, looped one end and threaded the other end through it. Then he made another loop with a simple slip knot and put it over his head. In the photographs, he is dressed in a navy blue suit and a white shirt. A red-and-blue-striped clip-on tie is on the ground, either dislodged by the rope or maybe he took it off first. He is kneeling, arms dangling by his sides, his head bent, a typical position for suicidal hangings. I don't have many cases where people are fully suspended, their feet off the ground. The point is to put enough compression on the blood vessels of the neck so that insufficient oxygenated blood reaches the brain. It takes only 4.4 pounds of pressure to compress the jugular veins, and a little more than twice that to occlude the carotids. The weight of the head against the noose is enough. Unconsciousness is quick. Death takes minutes.

"Let's do this." I get back to Jack. "Cover him up. We'll put some plasticized sheets over him so blood won't soak through. And let's give his mother a viewing before you do anything else to him."

He takes a deep breath and tosses his scalpel back on the cart.

"I'll go talk to her and see what else we can find out." I walk off. "Buzz Rose when you're ready. Thanks, Jack." I pause to meet his eyes. "We'll talk later? We've never had that cup of coffee. We never even wished each other Merry Christmas."

I find Mrs. White in my conference room. She has stopped crying and is in a deep, depressed space, staring without blinking, lifeless. She barely focuses on me when I walk in and shut the door. I tell her I just looked at Benny and am going to give her a chance to see him in a few minutes. Her eyes fill with tears again and she wants to know if he suffered. I tell her he would have slipped into unconsciousness rapidly. She wants to know if he died because he couldn't breathe. I reply that we don't know all the answers right now, but it is unlikely that his airway was obstructed.

Benny may have died from hypoxic brain damage, but I am more inclined to suspect that the compression of blood vessels caused a vasovagal response. In other words, his heart slowed down and he died. When I mention he was kneeling, she suggests that maybe he was praying for the Lord to take him home. Maybe, I reply. He very well could have been praying. I comfort Mrs. White as best I can. She informs me that a hunter was looking for a deer he shot earlier and found her son's body, and Benny couldn't have been dead very long because he disappeared right after church, about twelve-thirty, and the police came by her house around five. They told her the hunter found Benny at around two. So at least he wasn't out there all by himself for very long, she keeps saying. And it was a good thing he had his New Testament in his suit pocket because it had his name and address in it. That was how the police figured out who he was and located his family.

"Mrs. White," I say, "was something going on with Benny of late? What about at church yesterday morning? Anything happen that you know about?"

"Well, he's been moody." She is steadier now. She is talking about Benny as if he is sitting out in the reception area waiting for her. "He'll be twelve next month, and you know how that goes."

"What do you mean by 'moody'?"

"He would go in his room a lot and shut the door. Stay in there listening to music with the headphones on. He gets a smart mouth now and again, and he didn't used to be that way. I've been concerned." Her voice catches. She blinks, suddenly remembering where she is and why. "I just don't know why he had to do something like that!" Tears seem to spurt out of her eyes. "I know there're some boys at church he's been having a hard time with. They tease him a lot, calling him *pretty boy*."

"Did anyone tease him yesterday?" I ask.

"That very well could be. They're all in Sunday School together. And there's been a lot of talk, you know, about those killings in the area." She pauses again. She doesn't want to continue down a path that leads to a subject both foreign and aberrant to her.

"The two men killed right before Christmas?"

"Uh huh. The ones they say were cursed, because that's not how America started, you know. With people doing things like that."

"Cursed? Who says they were cursed?"

"It's the talk. A lot of talk," she goes on, taking a deep breath. "With Jamestown being just down the road. There's always been stories about people seeing ghosts of John Smith and Pocahontas and all the rest of it. Then these men are murdered right near there, near Jamestown Island, and all this talk about them being, well, you know. Being *unnatural*, which is why someone killed them, I guess. Or at least that's what I hear."

"Did you and Benny talk about all this?" My heart is getting heavier by the moment.

"Some. I mean, everybody's been talking about those men killed and burned and tortured. People've been locking their doors more than usual. It's been spooky, I must admit. So Benny and I've discussed it, yes we have. To tell you the truth, he's been a lot moodier since all that happened. So maybe that's what had him upset." Silence. She stares at the tabletop. She can't decide which tense to use when she talks about her dead son. "That and the other boys calling him pretty. Benny hated that, and I don't blame him. I'm always telling him, *Just wait until you grow up and are handsomer than all the rest. And the girls are just lining up. That'll teach 'em.*" She smiles a little and starts crying again. "He's real touchy about it. And you know how children can tease."

"Possibly he got teased a lot yesterday at church?" I guide her along. "Do you think maybe the boys made comments about so-called hate crimes, about gays and maybe implied . . . ?"

"Well," she blurts out. "Well, yes. About curses against people who are unnatural and wicked.

The Bible makes itself very clear. 'God gave them up to their own lust,' " she quotes.

"Any possibility Benny's been worried about his sexuality, Mrs. White?" I am very gentle but firm. "That's pretty normal for kids entering adolescence. A lot of sexual identity confusion, that sort of thing. Especially these days. The world's a complicated place, much more complicated than it used to be." The phone rings. "Excuse me a minute."

Jack is on the line. Benny is ready to be viewed. "And Marino's in here looking for you. Says he's got important information."

"Tell him where I am." I hang up.

"Benny did ask me if those men had those awful things done to them because they're . . . He used the word *queer*," Mrs. White is saying. "I said that very well may have been God's punishment."

"How did he react to that?" I ask her.

"I don't remember him saying anything."

"When was this?"

"Maybe three weeks ago. Right after they found that second body and all the news came out about them being hate crimes."

I wonder if Stanfield has any idea how much damage he has caused by leaking investigative details to his goddamn brother-in-law. Mrs. White is chattering nervously as dread builds with her every step down the hallway. I escort her to the front of the office and through a door that takes us into the small viewing room. Inside are a couch and table. There is a painting of a peaceful English countryside on the wall. Opposite the sitting area is a wall of glass. It is covered with a curtain. On the other side is the walk-in refrigerator.

"Why don't you just sit and make yourself comfortable," I tell Mrs. White and touch her shoulder.

She is tense, frightened, her eyes riveted to the drawn blue curtain. She perches on the edge of the couch, her hands tightly clasped in her lap. I open the curtain and Benny is swathed in blue, a blue sheet tucked under his chin to hide the ligature mark. His wet hair is combed back, eyes shut. His mother is frozen on the edge of the couch. She doesn't seem to breathe. She stares blankly, without comprehension. She frowns. "How come his face is all red like that?" she asks almost accusingly.

"The rope prevented the blood from flowing back to his heart," I explain. "So his face is congested."

She gets up and moves closer to the window. "Oh my baby," she whispers. "My sweet child. You're in heaven now. In Jesus' arms in paradise. Look, his hair's all wet like he's just been baptized.

You must have given him a bath. I just need to know he didn't suffer."

I can't tell her that. I imagine when he first tightened the noose around his neck, the roaring pressure in his head was very frightening. He had begun the process of terminating his own life, and he was awake and alert long enough to feel it coming. Yes, he suffered. "Not long," is what I say. "He didn't suffer long, Mrs. White."

She covers her face with her hands and weeps. I draw the curtain and lead her out.

"What will you do to him now?" she asks as she woodenly follows me out.

"We'll finish looking at him and do some tests, just to see if there's anything else we need to know."

She nods.

"Would you like to sit for a while? Can we get you anything?"

"No, no. I'll just go on."

"I'm very sorry about your son, Mrs. White. I can't tell you how sorry. If you have any questions, just call. If I'm not available, someone here will help you. It's going to be hard, and you'll go through a lot of things. So please call if we can help."

She stops in the hallway and grabs my hand. She looks intensely into my eyes. "You're sure someone didn't do this to him? How do we know for a fact he did it to himself?"

"Right now, there's nothing to make us think someone else did this," I assure her. "But we'll investigate every possibility. We're not finished yet. Some of these tests take weeks."

"You won't keep him here for weeks!"

"No, he'll be ready to go in a few hours. The funeral home can come for him."

We are in the front office and I escort her through a glass door, back into the lobby. She hesitates, as if not quite sure what to do next. "Thank you," she says. "You've been very kind."

It isn't often I am thanked. My thoughts are so heavy as I return to my office that I almost run into Marino before I notice him. He is waiting for me just inside my doorway and has paperwork in hand, his face radiating excitement. "You aren't going to fucking believe this," he says.

"I'm to the point of believing just about anything," I grimly reply as I almost fall into the big leather chair behind my piled-up desk. I sigh. I expect Marino has come to tell me that Jaime Berger is the special prosecutor. "If it's about Berger, I already know," I say. "An AP reporter told me she's been appointed to get me indicted. I haven't decided if it's a good thing or a bad thing. Hell, I can't decide if I even care."

Marino has a puzzled expression on his face.

"No kidding? She is? How's she gonna do that? She pass the bar in Virginia?"

"Doesn't have to," I reply. "She can appear *pro hac vice*." The phrase means *for this one particular occasion*, and I go on to explain that at a special jury's request, the court can grant an out-of-state lawyer special permission to participate in a case even if that person is not licensed to practice law in Virginia.

"So what about Righter?" Marino asks. "What will he be doing during all this?"

"Someone from the commonwealth's attorney's office will have to work with her. My guess is he'll be second chair and leave the questioning to her."

"We've had a weird break in The Fort James Motel case." He gives me his news. "Vander's been working like hell on the prints he got inside the room, and you aren't gonna fucking believe it," he says again. "Guess whose popped up? Diane Bray's. I'm not shitting you. A perfect latent by the light switch when you first come in the room—her latent, Bray's damn fingerprint. Of course, we got the dead guy's prints, but no hit on any others except Bev Kiffin, as you'd expect. Her prints are on the Gideon Bible, for example, but not his, not Matos's. And that's kind of interesting, too. It's looking like Kiffin might have been the one who opened the Bible to whatever it was."

"Ecclesiastes," I remind him.

"Yeah. A latent on the open pages, Kiffin's fingerprint. And remember, she said she didn't open the Bible, so I asked her about it over the phone and she still says she didn't open it. So I'm getting mighty suspicious about what her involvement is, especially now that we know Bray was in that very room before the guy was killed in there. What was Bray doing at that motel? You want to tell me that?"

"Maybe her drug-dealing brought her there," I reply. "I can't think of another reason. Certainly, the motel isn't the sort of place you would expect her to stay."

"Bingo." Marino fires his finger at me like a gun. "And Kiffin's husband supposedly works for the same trucking company that Barbosa did, right? Although we still ain't found no record of someone named Kiffin who drives a truck or whatever—can't even track him down at all, which I have to admit is strange. And we know Overland's into smuggling drugs and guns, right? Maybe it's making more sense if it turns out that Chandonne's the one who left those hairs at the campsite. Maybe we're talking his family cartel, huh? Maybe that's what fucking brought him to Richmond to begin with—the family business. And while he was in the area, he just couldn't control his habit of whacking women."

"Might also help explain what Matos was doing there," I add.

"No kidding. Maybe he and John the Baptist were pals. Or maybe someone in the family sent Matos to Virginia to snuff Johnny-boy, take him out of commission so he don't sing to anyone about the family business."

There are endless possibilities. "What none of this explains is why Matos was murdered and who did it. Or why Barbosa was killed," I point out.

"No, but I feel like we're getting warmer," Marino replies. "And I got an itch and I think if we scratch it, we might find Talley. Maybe he's the missing link in all this."

"Well, he apparently knew Bray in Washington," I say. "And he's been living in the same city where the Chandonne family is headquartered."

"And he always manages to be on the scene when John the Baptist is, too," Marino adds. "And I think I saw the asshole the other day. Was pulled up at a red light and there's this big black Honda motorcycle in the lane next to me. Didn't recognize him at first because he had a helmet on with this tinted shield covering his face, but he was staring at my truck. I'm pretty sure it was Talley and he looked away real quick. Asshole."

Rose buzzes me to say that the governor is calling for our ten o'clock telephone appointment. I motion for Marino to shut my office door while

I wait on the line for Mitchell. Reality again intrudes. I am returned to my predicament and its wide broadcast. I have a feeling I know exactly what the governor has on his mind. "Kay?" Mike Mitchell is somber. "I was very sorry to see the paper this morning."

"I'm not happy about it, either," I let him know.

"I'm supportive of you and will continue to be," he says, maybe to ease me into the rest of what he plans to relay, which can't be good. I don't respond. I also suspect he knows about Berger and probably had something to do with her being appointed the special prosecutor. I don't bring it up. There is no point. "I think in light of your current circumstances," he goes on, "that it's best you relinquish your duties until this matter is resolved. And Kay, it's not because I believe a word of it." This is also not the same thing as saying that he thinks I am innocent. "But until things calm down, I believe your continuing to run the medical examiner system for the commonwealth would be unwise."

"Are you firing me, Mike?" I ask him point-blank.

"No, no," he is quick to say, and his tone is gentler. "Let's just get through the special grand jury hearing, and we'll go from there. I haven't given up on you or your idea of being a private contractor, either. Let's just get through this," he says again.

"Of course, I will do whatever you wish," I tell him with all due respect. "But I have to say that I don't think it's in the best interest of the commonwealth for me to withdraw from ongoing cases that still need my attention."

"Kay, it's not possible." He is the politician. "We're only talking two weeks, assuming your hearing turns out all right."

"Good God," I reply. "It has to."

"And I'm sure it will."

I get off the phone and look at Marino. "Well, that's that." I start throwing things in my briefcase. "I hope they don't change the locks the minute I'm out the door."

"Really, what could he do? When you think about it, Doc, what could he do?" Marino has resigned himself to this inevitability.

"I would just like to know who the hell leaked it to the media." I shut my briefcase and snap in the locks. "Have you been subpoenaed, Marino?" I go ahead and ask. "Nothing's confidential. May as well tell me."

"You knew I would be." He has a pained expression on his face. "Don't let the bastards get you, Doc. Don't give up."

I pick up my briefcase and open the office door.

"I'm doing anything but give up. In fact, I've got a lot to do."

His expression asks, *what*? I've just been ordered by the governor to do nothing. "Mike's a good guy," Marino says. "But don't push him. Don't give him a reason to fire you. Why don't you go somewhere for a few days? Maybe go see Lucy in New York. Didn't she head on up to New York? Her and Teun? Just get the hell out of here until the hearing. I wish you would so I don't have to worry about you every other minute. I don't even like you being out there in Anna's house all by yourself."

I take a deep breath and try to tuck in my fury and hurt. Marino is right. There is no point in pissing off the governor and making matters worse. But now I feel run out of town on top of everything else, and I have not heard a word from Anna, and that stings, too. I am almost in tears, and I refuse to cry in my office. I avert my eyes from Marino, but he catches my feelings.

"Hey," he says, "you got every right not to feel good. All of this sucks, Doc."

I cross the hallway and cut through the ladies' room, on my way to the morgue. Turk is sewing up Benny White and Jack is sitting at the counter doing paperwork. I pull out a chair next to my assistant chief and pluck several stray hairs off his scrubs. "You got to quit shedding," I say, trying to hide my upset. "You going to tell me why your hair keeps falling out?" I have been meaning to ask him for weeks. As usual, so much has happened and Jack and I have not talked.

"All you got to do is read the paper," he says, putting down his pen. "That should tell you why my hair's falling out." His eyes are heavy.

I nod as I get his meaning. It is what I expect. Jack has known for a while that I am in serious trouble. Maybe Righter contacted him weeks ago and started fishing, just as he did with Anna. I ask Jack if this is the case, and he admits it. He says he has been a wreck. He hates politics and administration and does not want my job and never will.

"You make me look good," he says. "You always have, Dr. Scarpetta. They might think I should be appointed chief. Then what do I do? I don't know." He runs his fingers through his hair and loses more. "I just wish everything could go back to normal."

"Believe me, so do I," I say as the phone rings and Turk answers it.

"That reminds me," Jack says. "We're getting weird phone calls down here. I tell you about that?"

"I was down here when we got one," I reply. "Someone claiming to be Benton."

"Sick," he says in disgust.

"That's the only one I'm aware of," I add.

"Dr. Scarpetta?" Turk calls out. "Can you take it? It's Paul."

I go to the phone. "How are you, Paul?" I ask Paul Monty, the statewide director of the forensic labs.

"First, I just want you to know everybody in this damn building is pulling for you, Kay," he says. "Bullshit. I read all that bullshit and practically spit my coffee out. And we're working our fannies off." By this he means evidence testing. There is supposed to be an egalitarian order in the workup of evidence—appropriately, no one victim should be more important than another and moved to the front of the line. But there is also an unspoken code, same as in police shootings. People take care of their own. It is a fact. "Got some interesting test results that I wanted to pass on to you personally," Paul Monty goes on. "The hairs from the campground—the ones that you suspect are Chandonne's? Well, the DNA matches. What's of even more interest is that a fiber comparison shows that the cotton linens from that campsite match fibers collected from the mattress in Diane Bray's bedroom."

A scenario forms. Chandonne took Diane Bray's linens after her murder and fled to the campground. Maybe he slept on them. Or maybe he simply disposed of them. But either way, we can definitely place Chandonne at The Fort James

Motel. Paul has nothing more to report at the moment.

"What about the dental floss I found in the toilet?" I ask Paul. "In the room where Matos was killed?"

"No hit on that. The DNA's not Chandonne's or Bray's or any of the usual suspects," he tells me. "Maybe some previous guest at the motel? Could be unrelated."

I return to the counter, where Jack resumes telling me about the strange phone calls. He says there have been several of them.

"One I happened to answer and the person, a guy, asked for you, says he's Benton and then hangs up," Jack reports. "Turk answered the second time. The guy says to tell you he called and will be an hour late to dinner, identifies himself as Benton and hangs up. So add that to the mix. No wonder I'm going bald."

"Why didn't you tell me?" I absently pick up Polaroid photographs of Benny White's body on the gurney before he was unclothed.

"Thought you had enough shit going on. I should have told you. I was wrong."

The sight of this young boy dressed in his Sunday best and inside an unzipped body pouch on top of a steel gurney is so incongruous. I feel deeply saddened as I notice his pants are a little short and his socks don't quite match, one blue, one black. I feel worse. "You find anything un-expected with him?" I have talked enough about my problems. My problems, as a matter of fact, do not seem very important when I look at pho-tographs of Benny and think about his mother in the viewing room.

"Yeah, one thing puzzled me," Jack says. "The story I got is he came home from church and never went inside the house. He gets out of the car and heads out to the barn, saying he'll be right in and is trying to find his pocket knife—thinks it might be in his tackle box and he forgot to take it out when he came home from fishing the other day. He never comes back to the house. In other words, he never ate Sunday dinner. But this little guy had a full stomach."

"Could you tell what he might have eaten?" I ask.

"Yeah. Popcorn, for one thing. And looks like he ate hotdogs. So I call his house and talk to his stepdad. I ask if Benny might have eaten anything at church and am told no. His stepdad's got no idea where the food came from," Jack replies.

"That's very odd," I comment. "So he comes home from church and goes out to hang himself, but stops off someplace to eat popcorn and hot-dogs first?" I get up from the counter. "Some-thing's wrong with that picture."

"If it wasn't for the gastric contents, I'd say it's

a straightforward suicide." Jack remains seated, looking up at me. "I could kill Stanfield for cutting through the knot. The fuckhead."

"Maybe we should take a look at where Benny was hanged," I decide. "Go to the scene."

"They live on a farm in James City County," Jacks says. "Right on the river, and apparently the woods where he was hanged are at the edge of the field, not even a mile from the house."

"Let's go," I tell him. "Maybe Lucy can give us a ride."

IT IS A TWO-HOUR FLIGHT FROM THE hangar in New York to HeloAir in Richmond, and Lucy was more than happy to show off her new company vehicle. The plan is simple. She will pick up Jack and me and land us at the farm, then the three of us will check out where Benny White allegedly killed himself. I also want to see his bedroom. Afterwards, we will drop Jack off in Richmond and I will return to New York with Lucy, where I will stay until the special grand jury hearing. This is all planned for tomorrow morning, and Detective Stanfield has no interest in meeting us at the scene.

"What for?" are the first words out of his mouth. "What you need to go there for?"

I almost mention the gastric contents that don't

make sense. I come close to inquiring as to whether there was anything Stanfield observed that made him suspicious. But I catch myself. Something stops me. "If you can just give me directions to their place," I tell him.

He describes where Benny White's family lives, just off Route 5, I can't miss it because there is a small country store at the intersection, and I need to turn left at that store. He gives me landmarks that will not be helpful from the air. I finally get it out of him that the farm is less than a mile from the ferry near Jamestown, and that's when I realize for the first time that Benny White's farm is very close to The Fort James Motel and Camp Ground.

"Oh yeah," Stanfield says when I ask him about this. "He was right there in the same area as the other ones. That's what had him so upset, according to his mom."

"How far is the farm from the motel?" I ask.

"Right across the creek from it. It's not much of a farm."

"Detective Stanfield, is there any possibility Benny knew Bev Kiffin's children, her two boys? I understand Benny liked to fish." I envision the fishing pole leaning against the upstairs window in Mitch Barbosa's townhouse.

"Now, I know the story about him supposedly getting his pocket knife out of his tackle box, but

I don't think that's what he did. I think he just wanted an excuse to get away from everybody," Stanfield replies.

"Do we know where he got the rope?" I push aside his annoying assumptions.

"His stepdaddy says there's all kinds of rope in the barn," Stanfield replies. "Well, they call it a barn but it's where they just keep junk. I asked him what was in there, and he said just junk. You know, I got a hunch Benny might have run into Barbosa out there, you know, fishing, and we know Barbosa was nice to kids. That sure would help explain it. And his mama did say the boy had been having nightmares and was mighty upset by the killings. Was scared to death, is the way she put it. Now what you're gonna want to do is go straight to the creek. You'll see the barn at the edge of the field, and then the woods right off to the left. There's an overgrown footpath and where he hung himself is maybe fifty feet down that path where a deer stand is. You can't miss it. I didn't climb up it, up the deer stand, to cut down the rope, only cut off the end that was around his neck. So it should still be right where it was. The rope should be right there where it was."

I refrain from showing my complete disgust with Stanfield's sloppy policing. I don't probe any further or suggest to him he ought to do exactly what he threatened: quit. I call Mrs. White to let her know my plans. Her voice is small and wounded. She is dazed and can't seem to comprehend that we want to land a helicopter on her farm. "We need a clearing. A level field, an area where there are no telephone lines or a lot of trees," I explain.

"We don't have a runway." She says this several times.

Finally, she puts her husband on the phone. His name is Marcus. He tells me they have a soybean field between their house and Route 5 and there's a silo painted dark green, too. There isn't another silo in that area, not one painted dark green, he adds. It is fine with him if we land in his field.

The rest of my day is long. I work at the office and catch my staff before they head home. I explain to them what is happening in my life and assure each person that his job is not in jeopardy. I also make it clear that I have done nothing wrong and am confident my name will be cleared. I don't tell them I have resigned. They have suffered enough tremors and don't need an earthquake. I don't pack items in my office or head out with anything other than my briefcase, as if all is well and I'll see everybody in the morning, as usual.

Now it is nine P.M. I sit in Anna's kitchen, picking at a thick slice of cheddar cheese and sipping a glass of red wine, going easy, unwilling to cloud my thinking and simply finding it almost impossible to swallow solid food. I have lost weight. I don't know how much. I have no appetite and have developed a wretched routine of going outside periodically to smoke. Every half hour or so, I try to contact Marino with no success. And I keep thinking about the Tlip file. It has hardly been out of my mind since I looked at it on Christmas Day. The telephone rings at close to midnight and I assume it is Marino finally returning my page. "Scarpetta," I answer.

"It's Jaime," Berger's distinctive, confident voice sounds over the line.

I pause in surprise. But then I remember: Berger seems to have no hesitation in talking to people she intends to send to jail, doesn't matter the hour.

"I've been on the phone with Marino," she starts off. "So I realize you know my situation. Or I guess I should say, *our* situation. And actually you ought to feel all right about it, Kay. I'm not going to coach you, but let me say this. Just talk to the jury the same way you do to me. And try not to worry."

"I think I'm beyond worrying," I reply.

"Mainly I'm calling to pass on some information. We got DNA on the stamps. The stamps from the letters in the Tlip file," she informs me as if she is in my mind again. So now the Richmond labs are dealing directly with her, it occurs to me. "It appears Diane Bray was all over the map, Kay. At least she licked those stamps, and I will assume she wrote the letters and was smart enough not to leave her prints on them. The prints that were left on several of the letters are Benton's, probably from when he opened them before he realized what they were. I assume he knew they were his prints. Don't know why he didn't make a note of it. I'm just wondering if Benton ever mentioned Bray to you. Any reason to think they knew each other?"

"I don't remember him mentioning her," I reply. My thoughts are locked. I can't believe what Berger has just said.

"Well, he certainly could have known her," Berger goes on. "She was in D.C. He was a few miles down the road in Quantico. I don't know. But it baffles me that she would send this stuff to him, and I'm wondering if she wanted it posted in New York so he would go down the path of believing the crank mail was from Carrie Grethen."

"And we know he did go down that path," I remind her.

"Then we also have to wonder if Bray possibly—just possibly—had anything to do with his murder," Berger adds the final touch.

It flashes in my mind that she is testing me

again. What is she hoping? That I will blurt out something incriminating. *Good. Bray got what was coming to her* or *She got what she deserved.* At the same time, I don't know. Maybe it is my paranoia speaking and not reality. Maybe Berger is simply saying what is on her mind, nothing more.

"I don't guess she ever mentioned Benton to you," Berger is saying.

"Not that I recall," I reply. "I don't remember Bray ever saying a word about Benton."

"What I just can't get," Berger goes on, "is this Chandonne thing. If we consider that Jean-Baptiste Chandonne knew Bray—saying they were in business together—then why would he kill her? And in the manner he killed her? That strikes me as a non-fit. It doesn't profile right. What do you think?"

"Maybe you should Mirandize me before you ask me what I think about Bray's murderer," is what I say. "Or maybe you should save your questions for the hearing."

"You haven't been arrested," she replies, and I can't believe it. She has a smile in her tone. I have amused her. "You don't need to be Mirandized." She gets serious. "I'm not toying with you, Kay. I'm asking for your help. You should be goddamn glad it will be me in that room interviewing witnesses and not Righter."

"I'm just sorry anyone will be in that room. No one should be. Not on my account," I tell her.

"Well, there are two key pieces that we've got to figure out." She is impervious and has more to tell me. "The seminal fluid in Susan Pless's case isn't Chandonne's. And now we have this newest information about Diane Bray. It's just instinct. But I don't think Chandonne knew Diane Bray. Not personally. Not at all. I think all of his victims are people he had experienced only from a distance. He watched and stalked and fantasized. And that, by the way, was Benton's opinion, too, when he profiled Susan's case."

"Was it his opinion that the person who murdered her also left the seminal fluid?" I ask.

"He never thought more than one person was involved," Berger concedes. "Until your cases in Richmond, we were still looking for that well-dressed, good-looking guy who ate with her in Lumi. We sure weren't looking for some self-proclaimed werewolf with a genetic disorder, not back then we weren't."

AS IF I AM SUPPOSED TO SLEEP WELL after all this. I don't. I fade in and out, now and then picking up the alarm clock to check the time. Hours advance imperceptibly and weightily, like glaciers. I dream I am in my house and have a puppy, an adorable female yellow Labrador retriever with long, heavy ears and huge feet and the sweetest face imaginable. She reminds me of Gund stuffed animals in FAO Schwarz, that wonderful toy store in New York where I used to pick up surprises for Lucy when she was a child. In my dream, this wounded fiction I spin in my semi-conscious state, I am playing with the puppy, tickling her, and she is licking me, her tail wagging furiously. Then somehow I am walking into my house again, and it is dark and chilled and I sense nobody home, no life, absolute silence. I call out to the puppy—I can't remember her name—and frantically search every room for her. I wake up in Anna's guest room, crying, sobbing, just bawling.

CHAPTER 33

MORNING COMES AND HAZE drifts like smoke as we fly low over trees. Lucy and I are alone in her new machine because Jack woke up with aches and chills. He stayed home, and I have a suspicion that his illness is self-induced. I think he is hung over, and I fear that the unbearable stress I have brought upon the office has encouraged bad habits in him. He was perfectly satisfied with his life. Now everything has changed.

The Bell 407 is black with bright stripes. It smells like a new car and moves with the smooth strength of heavy silk as we fly east, eight hundred feet above the ground. I am preoccupied with the sectional map in my lap, trying to match depictions of power lines, roads and railroad tracks with those we pass over. It isn't that we don't know exactly where we are, because Lucy's helicopter has enough navigational equipment to pilot the Concorde. But whenever I feel the way I do right now, I tend to obsess over a task, any task.

"Two antennas about one o'clock." I show her on the map. "Five hundred and thirty feet above sea level. Shouldn't be a factor, but don't see them yet."

"I'm looking," she says.

The antennas will be well below horizon, meaning they aren't a danger even if we get close. But I have a special phobia of obstructions, and there are more of them going up all the time in this world of constant communication. Richmond air traffic control comes over the air, telling us radar service is terminated and we can squawk VFR. I change the frequency to twelve hundred on the transponder as I barely make out the antennas several miles ahead. They don't have high-intensity strobes and are nothing more than ghostly, straight pencil lines in thick, gray haze. I point them out.

"Got 'em," Lucy replies. "Hate those things." She pressures the cyclic right, curving well to the north of them, wanting nothing personal with antenna guy wires, for the heavy steel cables are the snipers. They will get you first.

"The governor going to be pissed at you if he finds out you're doing this?" Lucy's question sounds inside my headset.

"He told me to take a vacation from the office," I reply. "I'm out of the office."

"So you'll come to New York with me," she says. "You can stay in my apartment. I'm really glad you're leaving the job, giving up being chief, striking out on your own. Maybe you'll end up in New York working with Teun and me?"

I don't want to hurt her feelings. I don't tell her I am not glad. I want to be here. I want to be in my home and working my job as usual, and that will never be possible. I feel like a fugitive, I tell my niece, whose attention is outside the cockpit, eyes never straying from what she is doing. Talking to someone who is piloting a helicopter is like being on the phone. The person really doesn't see you. There is no gesturing or touching. The sun is getting brighter, the haze thinning the farther east we fly. Below us, creeks glisten like entrails of the earth, and the James River shines white like snow. We get lower and slower, passing over the Susan Constant, Godspeed and Discovery, the full-size replicas of the ships that carried one hundred and four men and boys to Virginia in 1607. In the distance, I make out the obelisk peeking up through the trees of Jamestown Island, where archaeologists are raising the first English settlement in America from the dead. A ferry slowly carries cars across the water toward Surry.

"I see a green silo at nine o'clock," Lucy observes. "Think that's it?"

I follow her eyes to a small farm that backs up
to a creek. On the other side of the narrow,
muddy lick of water, rooftops and old campers
peeking out of thick pines become The Fort
James Motel and Camp Ground. Lucy circles the
farm at five hundred feet, making sure there are
no hazards such as power lines. She sizes up the
area and seems satisfied as she lowers the collective and reins us back to sixty knots. We begin our
approach to a clearing between woods and the
small brick house where Benny White spent his
twelve short years. Dead grass storms as Lucy gently sets us down, subtly feeling for the ground,
making sure it is level. Mrs. White comes out of
the house. She stares at us, a hand shielding her
eyes from the sun, and then a tall man in a suit
joins her. They stay on the porch while we go
through the two-minute shutdown. As we climb
out and walk toward the house, I realize that
Benny's parents have dressed up for us. They look
as if they have just come from church.

"Never thought something like that would land
on my farm." Mr. White gazes off at the helicopter, a heavy expression on his face.

"Do come in," Mrs. White says. "Can I get you
some coffee or something?"

We chat about our flight, make small talk, anxiety thick. The Whites know I am here because I must be entertaining ominous scenarios about what really happened to their son. They seem to assume Lucy is part of the investigation and address both of us whenever they speak. The house is very neat and pleasantly furnished with big comfortable chairs, braided rugs and brass lamps. The floor is wide heart of pine, and wooden walls are whitewashed and hung with watercolors of Civil War scenes. By the fireplace in the living room are shelves that are full of cannonballs, minié balls, a mess kit, old bottles and all sort of artifacts that probably are from the Civil War. When Mr. White notices my interest, he explains that he is a collector. He is a treasure hunter and scours the area with a metal detector when he is not busy at the office. He is an accountant. His farm is not an active one, but has been in the family for more than a hundred years, he tells Lucy and me.

"I guess I'm just a history nut," he goes on. "I've even found a few buttons from the American Revolution. Just never know what you're going to find around here."

We are in the kitchen and Mrs. White is getting a glass of water for Lucy.

"What about Benny?" I ask. "Was he interested in treasure hunting?"

"Oh, he sure was," his mother replies. "Of course, he was always hoping to find real treasure. Like gold." She has begun to accept his death and speaks of him in the past tense.

"You know, the old story about the Confederates hiding all this gold that's never been found. Well, Benny thought he was going to find it," Mr. White says, holding a glass of water as if he isn't sure what to do with it. He sets it down on the countertop without drinking a drop. "He loved being outside, that one did. I've often thought it was too bad we don't work the farm anymore because I think he would have really liked it."

"Especially animals," Mrs. White adds. "That child loved animals more than anyone I've ever met. Just so tenderhearted." She tears up. "If a bird flew into a window, he'd go running out of the house to try and find it, and then he'd come in just in hysterics if the poor thing broke its neck, which is usually what happens."

Benny's stepfather stares out the window, a pained expression on his face. His mother falls silent. She is fighting to hold herself together.

"Benny had something to eat before he died," I tell them. "I think Dr. Fielding might have asked you about that to see if he possibly was given something to eat at the church."

Mr. White shakes his head, still staring out. "No, ma'am. They don't serve food at the church except at the Wednesday-night suppers. If Benny had something to eat, I sure don't know where."

"He didn't eat here," Mrs. White adds with emphasis. "I fixed a pot roast for Sunday dinner, and well, he never had his dinner. Pot roast was one of his favorites."

"He had popcorn and hotdogs in his stomach," I say. "It appears he ate them not long before he died." I make sure they understand the oddity of this and that it demands an explanation.

Both parents have baffled expressions. Their eyes light up with both fascination and confusion. They say they have no earthly idea where Benny would have gotten hold of junk food, as they call it. Lucy asks about neighbors, if perhaps Benny might have dropped by someone's house before he went into the woods. Again, they can't imagine him doing something like that, not at dinner time, and the neighbors are mostly elderly and would never give Benny a meal or even a snack without calling his parents first to make certain it was all right. "They wouldn't spoil his dinner without asking us." Mrs. White is certain of this.

"Would you mind if I see his bedroom?" I then say. "Sometimes I get a better feel for a patient if I can see where he spent his private time."

The Whites look a little uncertain. "Well, I guess that would be all right," the stepfather decides.

They take us down a hallway to the back of the house, and along the way we pass a bedroom off to the left that looks like a girl's bedroom, with pale pink curtains and a pink bedspread. There are posters of horses on the walls, and Mrs. White explains that this is Lori's bedroom. She is Benny's younger sister and is at her grandmother's house in Williamsburg right now. She hasn't gone back to school yet and won't until after the funeral, which is tomorrow. Although they don't say it, I infer that they didn't think it was a good idea for the child to be here when the medical examiner dropped in out of the sky and started asking questions about her brother's violent death.

Benny's room is a menagerie of stuffed animals: dragons, bears, birds, squirrels, fuzzy and sweet, many of them comical. There are dozens. His parents and Lucy stay outside the doorway while I walk in and pause in the middle of the room, looking around, letting the surroundings speak to me. Taped to the walls are bright pictures done in Magic Marker, again of animals, and they show imagination and a great deal of talent. Benny was an artist. Mr. White tells me from the doorway that Benny loved to take his sketchpad outside and draw trees, birds, whatever he saw. He was always drawing pictures to give people for presents, too. Mr. White talks on while his wife cries silently, tears rolling down her face.

I am looking at a drawing on the wall to the right of the dresser. The colorful, imaginative picture depicts a man in a small boat. He wears a wide-brim hat and is fishing, his rod bent as if he might just be having some luck. Benny has drawn a bright sun and a few clouds, and in the background, on the shore, is a square building with lots of windows and doors. "Is this the creek behind your farm?" I inquire.

"That's right," Mr. White says, hooking an arm around his wife. "It's all right, sugar," he keeps saying to her, swallowing hard, as if he might start crying, too.

"Benny liked to fish?" Lucy's voice sounds from the hallway. "I'm just wondering, because some people who are big animal lovers don't like to fish. Or else they let everything go."

"Interesting point," I say. "All right to look inside his closet?" I ask the Whites.

"Go right ahead," Mr. White says without hesitation. "No, Benny didn't like to catch anything. Truth is, he just liked to go out in the boat or find him a spot on the shore. Most of the time he'd sit there drawing."

"Then this must be you, Mr. White." I look back at the picture of the man in the boat.

"No, I think that would be his daddy," Mr. White answers somberly. "His daddy used to go out in the boat with him. Truth is, I don't go out in the boat." He pauses. "Well, I don't know how to swim, so I just have this uneasiness about being in the water."

"Benny was a little shy about his drawing," Mrs. White says in a shaky voice. "I think he liked to carry his fishing pole around because, well you know, he thought it made him look like other boys. I don't think he even bothered bringing bait. Can't imagine him killing even a worm, much less a fish."

"Bread," Mr. White says. "He'd take bread, like he was going to roll it up in bread balls. I used to tell him he wasn't going to catch anything very big if all he used for bait was bread."

I scan suits, slacks and shirts on hangers, and shoes lined on the floor. The clothing is conservative and looks as if it was picked out by his parents. Leaning against the back of the closet is a Daisy BB gun and Mr. White says Benny would shoot targets and tin cans. No, he never used the BB gun on birds or anything like that. Of course not. He couldn't even bring himself to catch a fish, both parents make that point again.

On the desk is a stack of schoolbooks and a box of Magic Markers. On top of these is a sketchpad and I ask his parents if they have looked through it. They say they have not. Is it okay if I do? And they nod. I stand at the desk. I don't sit or in any way make myself at home in their dead son's room. I am respectful of the sketchpad and turn pages carefully, going through meticulous drawings in pencil. The first one is a horse in a pasture and it is surprisingly good. This is followed by several sketches of a hawk sitting in a bare tree, water in the background. Benny drew an old broken-down fence. He drew several snow scenes. The pad is half filled, and all of the sketches are consistent with each other until I get to the last few. Then the mood and the subject decidedly change. There is a night scene of a cemetery, a full moon behind bare trees softly illuminating tilting headstones. Next I turn to a hand, a muscular hand clenched in a fist, and then I find the dog. She is fat and homely and is baring her teeth, her hackles up, and she cowers, as if threatened.

I look up at the Whites. "Did Benny ever talk about the Kiffins' dog?" I ask them. "A dog named Mr. Peanut?"

The stepfather gets a peculiar expression, and his eyes brighten with tears. He sighs. "Lori's allergic," he says, as if that answers my question.

"He was always complaining about the way they treated that dog," Mrs. White helps out. "Benny wanted to know if we could take Mr. Peanut. He wanted the dog and said he thought the Kiffins would give it up, but we couldn't."

"Because of Lori," I infer.

"It was an old dog, too," Mrs. White adds.

"Was?" I ask.

"Well, it's real sad," she says. "Right after Christmas, Mr. Peanut didn't seem to be feeling well. Benny said the poor dog was shaking and licking itself a lot, like it was in pain, you know. Then maybe a week ago it must have gone off to die. You know how animals will do that. Benny went out looking for Mr. Peanut every day. It just broke my heart. That child sure did love that dog," Mrs. White adds. "I think that's the main reason he'd go over there—to play with Mr. Peanut—and he just searched high and low for her."

"Was this when his behavior started changing?" I suggest. "After Mr. Peanut disappeared?"

"It was about that time," Mr. White replies, and neither parent seems able to bear stepping inside Benny's room. They cling to the doorway as if holding up the walls. "You don't think he did something like that because of a dog, do you?" He is almost pitiful when he asks.

MAYBE FIFTEEN MINUTES LATER, Lucy and I head out to the woods together, leaving the parents at the house. They have not been to the deer stand where Benny was hanged. Mr. White told me he knew about the stand and has seen it many times when he has been out with his metal detector, but neither he nor his wife can bring themselves to go out there right now. I asked them if they thought other people knew the spot where Benny died—I am worried about the curious having tramped around out there, but the parents don't think anybody knows exactly where Benny's body was found. Not unless the detective told people around here, Mr. White adds.

The field where we landed is between the house and the creek, a barren acre that doesn't appear to have seen a plow in many years. To the east are miles of woods, the silo almost at the shore and jutting up rusty and dark like a tired, thick lighthouse that seems to look out across the water at The Fort James Motel and Camp Ground. As I imagine Benny visiting the Kiffins, I wonder how he got there. There is no bridge across the creek, which is about a hundred feet wide and has no outlet. Lucy and I follow the footpath through the woods, scanning everywhere we step. Tangled fishing line is caught in trees close to the water, and I note a few old shotgun shells and soft drink cans. We have walked no more than five minutes when we come upon the deer blind. It looks like a decapitated tree house that someone threw up in a hurry, with wooden rungs nailed up the trunk. A severed yellow nylon rope dangles from a crossbeam and stirs in a light cold breeze that blows off the water and whispers through trees.

We stop and are silent as we look around. I don't see any trash—no bags or popcorn containers or any sign that Benny might have eaten out here. I get closer to the rope. Stanfield cut it about four feet from the ground and since Lucy is more athletic than I am, I suggest that maybe she could climb up into the stand and remove the rope properly. At least we can take a look at the knot on the other end. I take photographs first. We test the rungs nailed into the tree, and they seem sturdy enough. Lucy is bundled in a thick down-filled jacket that doesn't seem to slow her down as she climbs up, and she is careful as she reaches the platform, pushing and tugging boards to make sure they can bear her weight. "Seems pretty sturdy," she lets me know.

I toss up a roll of evidence tape and she opens a Buck Tool. One thing about ATF agents, they all carry their own portable tool kits that include knife blades, screwdrivers, pliers, scissors. It goes back to needing them at fire scenes, if for no other reason, to pull nails out of the soles of your steel-reinforced boots. ATF agents get dirty. They step in all sorts of hazards. Lucy cuts the rope above the knot and tapes the ends back together. "Just a simple double square knot," she says, dropping the rope and tape down to me. "Just a good ol' Boy Scout knot, and the end's melted. Whoever cut the end, melted it so it wouldn't unravel."

That surprises me a little. I wouldn't expect someone to bother with a detail like that if he were cutting off rope so he could hang himself with it. "Atypical," I comment to Lucy when she climbs down. "Tell you what, I'm going to be bold and take a look."

"Just be careful, Aunt Kay. There are a few rusty nails sticking out. And watch out for splinters," she says.

I am wondering if Benny might have adopted this old stand as a tree fort. I grip weathered gray boards one after the other and work my way up, grateful that I wore khakis and ankle boots. Inside the deer blind is a bench seat where the hunter can sit as he waits for an unsuspecting buck to wander into his sights. I test the seat by pushing against it, and it seems fine, so I sit. Benny was only an inch taller than I am, so I now have his view, assuming he came up here. I have a strong feeling that he did. Someone has been up here. Otherwise the floor of the stand would be thick with dead leaves, and it isn't at all. "You notice how neat it is up here?" I call down to Lucy.

"It's probably still being used by hunters," she replies.

"What hunter is going to bother sweeping out

leaves at five o'clock in the morning?" From this vantage point, I have a sweeping view of the water and can see the back of the motel and its dark and slimy swimming pool. Smoke curls out the chimney of the Kiffin house. I envision Benny sitting up here and spying on life as he sketched and perhaps escaped the sadness he must have felt since his father's death. I can imagine only too well as I remember my own young life. The deer blind would be a perfect spot for a lonely, creative boy, and just a stone's throw ahead at the water's edge is a tall oak tree wearing kudzu around its trunk like spats. I can picture a red-tailed hawk sitting high up on a branch. "I think he might have drawn that tree over there," I say to Lucy. "And he had a damn good view of the campground."

"Wonder if he saw something," Lucy floats this up to me.

"No kidding," I reply grimly. "And someone might have been looking back," I add. "This time of year with no leaves on the trees, he might have been visible up here. Especially if someone had binoculars and had a reason to be looking over this way." Even as I say this, it occurs to me that someone might be looking at us right now. A chill touches my flesh as I climb back down. "You got your gun in that butt pack, don't you?" I say to Lucy when my feet are on the ground. "I'd like to follow this path and see where it goes."

I pick up the rope, coil it and tuck it inside a plastic bag, which I then shove into a coat pocket. The evidence tape goes inside my satchel. Lucy and I start out on the path. We find more shotgun shells and even an arrow from bow season. Deeper into the woods we walk, the path bending around the creek, no sound but trees groaning when the wind gusts and the snap of twigs beneath our feet. I want to see if the path might take us all the way around to the other side of the creek, and it does. It is a mere fifteen-minute hike to The Fort James Motel, and we end up in woods between the motel and Route 5. Benny certainly could have walked over here after church. There are half a dozen cars in the motel parking lot, some of them rentals, and a big Honda touring motorcycle is near the Coke machine.

Lucy and I walk toward the Kiffin house. I point out the campsite where we found the bed linens and baby carriage, and experience a combination of anger and sadness about Mr. Peanut. I don't trust the story about the dog's supposedly going off to die. I worry that Bev Kiffin did something cruel, maybe even poisoned her, and I intend to ask her what happened along with a number of other questions. I don't care how Bev Kiffin reacts. After today, I am grounded, out of commission, suspended from my profession. I can't know for a fact I will ever practice forensic medicine again. I might be fired and branded for life. Hell, I might end up in prison. I feel eyes on us as we climb the Kiffins' front-porch steps.

"Creepy place," Lucy says under her breath.

A face peeks out from behind curtains and then ducks out of sight when Bev Kiffin's older son catches me looking back at him. I ring the bell and the boy answers the door, the same boy I saw when I was here. He is big and heavy-set and has a cruel face speckled with acne. I can't tell how old he is, but I place him at twelve, maybe fourteen.

"You're the lady who was out here the other day," he says to me with a hard look.

"That's right," I reply. "Can you tell your mother that Dr. Scarpetta is here and I need a word with her?"

He smiles as if he knows a mean secret that he thinks is funny. He stifles a laugh. "She ain't in here right now. She's busy." His eyes get harder and wander in the direction of the motel.

"What's your name?" Lucy asks him.

"Sonny."

"Sonny, what happened to Mr. Peanut?" I casually ask.

"That dumb dog," he says. "All we can figure is somebody stole her."

I find it impossible to believe that anyone would have stolen that old, worn-out dog. In the first place, she wasn't friendly to strangers. If anything, I might have expected her to get hit by a car.

"Oh yeah? That's too bad," Lucy answers Sonny. "What makes you think somebody stole her?"

Sonny gets caught on this. He gets a vapid look in his eyes and starts to tell several lies and keeps interrupting himself. "Uh, some car pulled in at night. I heard it, you know, and a door shut and she was barking, then that was it. She was gone. Zack's all tore up about it."

"She disappeared when?" I want to know.

"Oh, I don't know." A shrug. "Last week."

"Well, Benny was pretty torn up about it, too," I comment, watching for his reaction.

That cold look in his eyes again. "The kids at school called him a sissy. And he *was* one, too. That's why he killed himself. Everybody says so," Sonny replies with stunning callousness.

"I thought the two of you were friends?" Lucy is getting aggressive with him.

"He bugged me," Sonny answers. "Always coming over here to play with the dang dog. He wasn't my friend. He was Zack and Mr. Peanut's friend. I don't hang out with no sissies."

A motorcycle engine roars and rumbles to life. Zack's face pops up in the window to the right of the front door, and he is crying.

"Did Benny come over here last Sunday?" I

come right out and ask Sonny. "After church? Maybe twelve-thirty, one o'clock. Did he eat hot-dogs with you?"

Sonny is caught again. He wasn't expecting the detail about hotdogs and now he is in a bind. His curiosity overwhelms his untruthfulness and he says, "How'd you know we had hotdogs?" He frowns as the motorcycle we saw a few minutes ago rumbles and bumps along the dirt path that leads from the motel to the Kiffin house. Who-ever is on it heads right toward us, dressed in red-and-black leather, his face obscured by a dark helmet with a tinted face shield. Yet there is some-thing familiar about the person. The realization stuns me. Jay Talley stops and gets off his motor-cycle, nimbly swinging a leg over the big saddle seat.

"Sonny, get in the house," Jay orders. "Now." He says this with cool ease, as if he knows the boy very well.

Sonny steps back inside the house and the door shuts. Zack has vanished from the window. Jay takes off his helmet.

"What are you doing out here?" Lucy asks him, and in the distance I spot Bev Kiffin walking this way, carrying a shotgun, coming from the direc-tion of the motel, where I can only assume she has been with Jay. Red flags are popping up all over the place inside my head, and neither Lucy nor I make the connection fast enough. Jay is unzipping his thick leather jacket and almost instantly he has a gun in his hand, a black pistol relaxed by his side.

"Christ," Lucy says. "For God's sake, Jay."

"I really wish you hadn't come here," he says to me in a calm, cold way. "I really wish you hadn't." He motions the gun toward the motel. "Come on. We're going to have a little talk."

Run. But there is no place to run. He might shoot Lucy if I run. He might shoot me in the back. He raises the pistol and points it at Lucy's chest as he unfastens her butt pack. He of all people knows what is in it. He takes my satchel and pats me down, making sure he explores my body intimately, to degrade me, to put me in my place, to enjoy the fury that dances across Lucy's face as she has to watch. "Don't," I quietly say to him. "Jay, you can stop now."

He smiles and dark rage sparks in a face that could be Greek. It could be Italian. It could be French. Bev Kiffin reaches us and her eyes narrow as they fix on me. She wears the same red lumberman's jacket she had on the other week, and her hair is tousled as if she has just gotten out of bed. "Well, well," she says. "Some folks just never get the message they aren't welcome, isn't that right?" Her eyes slide to Jay and linger.

I know without being told that they have been sleeping together, and every word Jay has ever told me turns to fable. Now I understand why Agent Jilison McIntyre was perplexed when I said that Bev Kiffin's husband was a truck driver for Overland. McIntyre was undercover. She did the company's books. She would be aware of it if there was an employee named Kiffin. The only connection to that criminal-infested trucking company is Bev Kiffin herself, and the gun and drug smuggling that goes on is connected to the Chandonne cartel. Answers. I have them, and now it is too late.

Lucy walks close to me, her face concrete. She shows no reaction as we are walked at gunpoint past rusty campers that I suspect are unoccupied for a reason. "Drug labs," I say to Jay. "You making designer drugs out here, too? Or maybe just storing assault rifles and other things that end up on the street and kill people?"

"Kay, shut up," he softly says. "Bev, you take care of her." He indicates Lucy. "Find her a nice room and make sure she's comfortable."

Kiffin smiles a little. She taps the back of Lucy's leg with the shotgun. We are at the motel now, and I scan parked cars and find no sign of another human being. Benton flashes in my mind. My heart pounds and the realization roars through my brain. Bonnie and Clyde. We used to refer to Carrie Grethen and Newton Joyce as Bonnie and Clyde. The killing couple. All along we have been so certain they were responsible for Benton's murder. Yet we have never known for a fact who he was meeting that afternoon in Philadelphia. Why did he go off alone and not tell any of us? He was smarter than that. He never would have agreed to meet Carrie Grethen or Newton Joyce or even a stranger with information, because he would never have trusted a stranger with so-called information when he was in a city trying to track down a cunning, evil serial killer like Carrie. I stop in the parking lot as Kiffin opens a door and waits for Lucy to walk ahead of her into one of those rooms. Room 14. Lucy doesn't look back at me, and the door shuts after her and Kiffin.

"You killed Benton, didn't you, Jay." I state it as a fact.

He lays a hand on my back, the pistol pointed and touching me as he pauses behind me and says for me to open the door. We enter room 15, the same room Kiffin showed me when I wanted to see what kind of mattresses and linens she used in this dump. "You and Bray," I say to Jay. "That's why she sent letters from New York, trying to make it seem they were from Carrie, to make Benton assume they were written from up there where she was locked up in Kirby."

Jay shuts the door and waves the gun almost wearily, as if I am tiresome and he is not enjoying this. "Sit down."

My eyes wander up to the ceiling, looking for eyebolts. I wonder where the heat gun is and if it is part of my fate. I keep standing where I am, near the dresser with its Gideon Bible, this one not opened to any special chapter about vanity or anything else. "I just want to know if I slept with the person who killed Benton." I am looking right at Jay. "You're going to kill me? Go ahead. But you already did that when you killed him. So I guess you can kill me twice, Jay." It is odd, I feel no fear, only resignation. My pain, my anguish is over my niece, and I wait for the sound of a shotgun to rock these walls. "Can't you just leave her out of it?" I ask anyway, and Jay knows I mean Lucy.

"I didn't kill Benton," he says, and he has the livid face of people who walk up and shoot a president. Pale, no expression, a zombie. "Carrie and her asshole friend did that. I made the call."

"The call?"

"Called him to meet. That wasn't too hard. I'm an agent," he enjoys reminding me. "Carrie handled it from there. Carrie and that whacko scarface she got hooked up with."

"So you set him up," I say, simply. "Probably helped Carrie escape, too."

"She didn't need much help. Just some," he replies with no inflection. "She was like a lot of people in this business. They get into the goods and fuck up an already fucked-up brain. She started doing her own thing. Years ago. If you guys hadn't solved the problem, we would have. She was at the end of her usefulness."

"Involved in the family business, Jay?" My eyes pin his. The gun is by his side and he leans against the door. He has no fear of me. I am like a bow-string wound too tightly, about to snap, waiting, listening for any sound next door. "All these women murdered—how many of them did you sleep with first? Like Susan Pless." I shake my head. "I just want to know if you helped out Chandonne or did he follow you and help himself to what you left behind?"

Jay's eyes focus more sharply on me. I have probed the truth.

"You know, you're much too young to be Jay Talley, whoever he was," I say next. "Jay Talley with no middle name. And you didn't go to Harvard, and I doubt you ever lived in Los Angeles, not as a child. He's your brother, isn't he, Jay? That horrible deformity who calls himself a werewolf? He's your brother, and your DNA is so close that on a routine screening you could be identical twins. Did you know your DNA is the same as his on a routine screening? At a four-probe level, the two of you are exactly the same."

Anger flashes. Vain, beautiful Jay would never want to think that his DNA was even similar to someone's as ugly and hideous as Jean-Baptiste Chandonne.

"And the body in the cargo container. The one you helped us believe is the brother—Thomas. His DNA had many points in common, too, but not as many as yours does—yours from the seminal fluid you left in Susan Pless's body before she was brutalized. Thomas a relative? Not a brother? What? A cousin? You kill him, too? You drown him in Antwerp or did Jean-Baptiste do that? And then you lure me over to Interpol, not because you need my help with the case, but because you want to see what I know. You want to make sure I don't know what Benton was probably starting to figure out: That you are a Chandonne," I say, and Jay does not react. "You probably mastermind the business for your father and that's why you got into law enforcement, to be an undercover asshole, a spy. God knows how much business you've diverted—knowing everything the good guys are doing and then turning it against them behind their backs." I shake my head. "Let Lucy go," I tell him. "I'll do what you want. Just let her go."

"Can't." He doesn't even begin to argue with what I have said.

Jay glances at the wall, as if he can see through it. I can tell he is wondering what is going on next door, why it is so quiet. My nerves wind tighter.

Please God, please God. Please. Or make it quick, at least. Don't let her suffer.

Jay pushes the lock in and fastens the burglar chain. "Take your clothes off," he says, no longer using my name. It is easier to kill people you have depersonalized. "Don't worry," he bizarrely adds. "I'm not going to do anything. I just have to make it look like something else."

I glance up at the ceiling. He knows what I am thinking. He is pale and sweating as he opens a dresser drawer and pulls out several eyebolts and a heat gun, a red heat gun.

"Why?" I ask him. "Why them?" I refer to the two men I now believe Jay murdered.

"You're going to screw these into the ceiling for me," Jay tells me. "Up there in the crossbeam. Now get on the bed and do it and don't try anything."

He places the eyebolts on the bed and nods for me to pick them up and do what he orders. "It's all about what becomes necessary when people get into something they shouldn't." He gets a rag and rope out of the drawer.

I stand where I am, just looking at him. The eyebolts gleam like pewter on the bed.

"Matos came here to find Jean-Baptiste and it took a little coaxing to know exactly what he had in mind and who gave him the order, which wasn't what you think." Jay takes off his leather jacket and drapes it over a chair. "Not the family, but a first lieutenant who doesn't want Jean-Baptiste to start talking and ruin a good thing for a lot of people. One thing about the family . . ."

"Your family, Jay," I remind him of his family and that I know him by name.

"Yeah." He stares at me. "Fuck yeah, my family. We take care of each other. Doesn't matter what you do, family is family. Jean-Baptiste's a fuck-up, I mean, anybody can look at him and see that, and understand why he's got his problem."

I say nothing.

"Of course we don't approve," Jay goes on as if he is talking about a kid who is shooting out streetlights or drinking too much beer. "But he's blood, our blood, and you don't touch our blood."

"Someone touched Thomas," I reply, and I have not picked up the eyebolts or climbed up on the bed. I have no intention of helping him torment me.

"You want to know the truth? That was an accident. Thomas couldn't swim. He tripped over a rope and fell off the dock, or something like that," Jay tells me. "I wasn't there. He drowned. Jean-Baptiste wanted to get his body a long way from the shipyard, away from other stuff going on there and didn't want him identified."

"Bullshit," I reply. "Sorry, but Jean-Baptiste

left a note with the body. *Bon Voyage Le Loup-Garou.* You do that when you don't want to draw attention to something? I don't think so. Maybe you better recheck your brother's story. Maybe your family takes care of family. Maybe Jean-Baptiste's an exception. Sounds like he doesn't take care of family at all."

"Thomas was a cousin." As if that lessens the crime. "Get up and do what I say." Jay indicates the eyebolts, and he is beginning to get angry, very angry.

"No," I refuse. "Do what you're going to do, Jay," and I keep saying his name. I know him. I am not going to let him do this to me without my saying his name and looking him in the eye. "I'm not going to help you kill me, Jay."

A thud sounds next door, as if something has turned over or fallen to the floor, and then an explosion and my heart lurches. Tears choke me and fill my eyes. Jay flinches and then his face is impassive. "Sit down," he tells me. When I don't comply, he comes closer and shoves me down on the bed as I cry. I cry for Lucy.

"You fucking son of a bitch," I exclaim. "You kill that boy, too? You take Benny out and hang him, a goddamn twelve-year-old kid?"

"He shouldn't have come out here. Mitch shouldn't have. I knew Mitch. He saw me. There was nothing I could do." Jay stands over me as if not sure what to do next.

"Then you killed the boy." I wipe my eyes with the backs of both hands.

Confusion flickers in Jay's eyes. He has a problem with the boy. The rest of us don't bother him, but the boy does.

"How could you stand there and watch him hang? A kid? A kid in his Sunday suit."

Jay swings back his hand and slaps me across the face. It happens so fast I don't even feel it at first. My mouth and nose go numb and begin to sting, and something wet drips. Blood drips into my lap. I let it drip as I tremble all over and stare up at Jay. Now it is easier for him. He has begun the process. He pushes me down on the bed and straddles me, pinning my arms with his knees, and my healing fractured elbow screams in pain as he forces my hands above my head and struggles to tie them with the rope. All the while he is snarling about Diane Bray. He is mocking me, telling me that she knew Benton, and didn't Benton ever tell me that Bray had a thing for Benton? And if Benton had been a little nicer to her maybe she would have left him alone. Maybe she would have left me alone. My head pounds. I barely comprehend.

Did I really think that Benton had an affair only with me? Was I so stupid to think that Benton would cheat on his wife but never on me? How fucking stupid am I? Jay gets up for the heat gun. What people do is what they do, he says. Benton had something with Bray up in D.C., and then when he dumped her, and he did it pretty quickly, to give him credit, she wasn't going to let that pass. Not Diane Bray. Jay is trying to gag me and I keep jerking my head from side to side. My nose is bleeding. I won't be able to breathe. Bray got Benton good, all right, and this is partly why she wanted to move to Richmond, to make sure she ruined my life, too. "Quite a price to pay for fucking somebody a few times." Jay gets up from the bed again. He is sweating, his face pale.

I struggle to breathe through my nose and my heart is hammering like a machine gun as my entire body begins to panic. I try to will myself to calm down. Hyperventilating will only make it harder for me to get air. Panic. I try to inhale and blood is dripping down the back of my throat and I cough and gag as my heart explodes against my ribs like fists trying to pound down a door. Pounding, pounding, pounding and the room turns grainy and I can't move.

CHAPTER 34

Two Weeks Later

THOSE WHO HAVE ASSEMBLED in my honor are ordinary people. They sit quietly, even reverently, almost in shock. It is not possible that they have not heard everything that has been in the news. You would have to live in the hinterlands of Africa not to know what has gone on in recent weeks, especially what happened in James City County at a cesspool of a tourist trap that has turned out to be the eye of a monstrous storm of corruption and evil.

All seemed so quiet in that rundown, overgrown campground. I can't imagine how many people have stayed in tents or in the motel and had no idea what was raging around them. Like a hurricane blown out to sea, the raging forces have fled. As far as we know, Bev Kiffin isn't dead. Neither is Jay Talley. Ironically, he is now considered a red notice by Interpol: The very people he once worked with are after him in a furious full-court press. Kiffin is a red notice, too. The supposition is that Jay and Kiffin have fled the United States and are hiding abroad somewhere.

Jaime Berger stands before me. I am in the witness stand facing a jury of three women and five men. Two are white, five are African-American, one is Asian. The races of all of Chandonne's victims are represented, even though that was not deliberate on anybody's part, I am sure. But it seems just, and I am glad. Brown paper has been taped over the courtroom's glass door to ensure that the curious, the media, can't look in. Jurors and witnesses and I entered the courthouse by an underground ramp the same way prisoners are escorted to their trials. Secrecy chills the air and the jurors stare at me as if I am a ghost. My face is greenish yellow from old bruises, my left arm is in a cast again and I still have rope burns around my wrists. I am alive only because Lucy happened to wear body armor. I had no idea. When she picked me up in the helicopter, she had on a bulletproof vest underneath her down-filled jacket.

Berger is asking me about the night Diane Bray was murdered. It is as if I am a house where different music is playing in every room. I am answering her questions, and yet I am thinking other thoughts and other images are coming to me and I hear other sounds in different areas of my psyche. Somehow I am able to concentrate on my testimony. The cash register tape for the chipping hammer I purchased is mentioned. Then Berger reads from the actual lab report that was turned over to the court as a matter of record, just as the autopsy protocol, the toxicology and all other reports have been. Berger describes the chipping hammer to the jurors and asks me to explain how the hammer's surfaces correlate with Bray's horrendous injuries.

This goes on for a while, and I look at the faces of those here to judge me. Expressions range from passive to intrigued to horrified. One woman gets visibly queasy when I describe punched-out areas of skull and an eyeball that was virtually avulsed, or hanging out of the socket. Berger points out that according to the lab report, the chipping hammer recovered from my house had rust on it. She asks me if the hammer I bought from the hardware store *after Bray's murder* was rusty. I say it wasn't. "Could a tool like this rust in a matter of a few weeks?" she asks me. "In your opinion, Dr. Scarpetta, could blood on the chipping hammer have caused it to be in this condition—in the condition of the one recovered from your house, the one you say Chandonne brought with him when he attacked you?"

"Not in my opinion," I reply, knowing that it is in my best interest to answer such. But it doesn't matter. I would tell the truth even if it were not in my best interest. "For one thing, the police should as a matter of routine make sure the hammer is dry when it is placed in an evidence bag," I add.

"And the scientists who received the chipping hammer for examination say it was rusty, is this not right? I mean, I am reading this lab report correctly, aren't I?" She smiles slightly. She is dressed in a black suit with pale blue pinstripes, and paces in little steps as she works through the case.

"I don't know what the labs have said," I answer. "I haven't seen those reports."

"Of course not. You've not been in the office for ten days or so. And, ummm, this report was just turned in day before yesterday." She glances at the date typed on it. "But it does say the chipping hammer that has Bray's blood on it was rusty. It looked old, and I believe the clerk at Pleasants Hardware Store claims the hammer you bought on the night of December seventeen—almost twenty-four hours *after* Bray's murder—certainly didn't look old. It was brand new. Correct?"

Again, I can't say what the hardware store clerk claimed, I remind Berger from the stand as jurors take in every word, every gesture. I have been excluded from all witness testimony. Berger is simply asking me questions I can't answer so she can tell the jurors what she wants them to know. What

is treacherous and wonderful about any grand
jury proceeding is that defense counsel is not present and there is no judge—no one to object to
Berger's questions. She can ask me anything, and
she does, because in one of the rare instances on
this planet, a prosecutor is trying to show the defendant is innocent.

Berger asks what time I got home from Paris
and went grocery shopping. She mentions my
going to the hospital to visit Jo that night, and the
phone conversation with Lucy afterward. The
window narrows. It gets tighter and tighter. When
did I have time to rush over to Bray's house, beat
her to death, plant evidence and stage the crime?
And why would I bother buying a chipping hammer almost twenty-four hours after the fact unless it was for the very purpose I have stated all
along: to conduct tests? She lets these questions
hover while Buford Righter sits at the prosecution table and studies notes on a legal pad. He
avoids looking at me as much as he can.

I answer Berger point by point. It gets harder
and harder for me to talk. The inside of my mouth
was abraded from the gag, and then the wounds
became ulcerated. I haven't had mouth sores since
I was a child and had forgotten how painful they
are. When my ulcerated tongue hits my teeth as
I speak, it sounds as if I have a speech impediment.
I feel weak and strung out. My left arm throbs, in

a cast again because it was re-injured when Jay wrenched my arms above my head and bound them to the bed's headboard.

"I notice you're having some trouble talking." Berger pauses to point this out. "Dr. Scarpetta, I know this is off the subject." Nothing is off the subject for Jaime Berger. She has a reason for every breath she takes, every step she makes, every expression on her face—everything, absolutely everything. "But can we digress for a moment?" She stops pacing and raises her palms in a shrug. "I think it would be instructive if you would tell the jury what happened to you last week. I know the jury must be wondering why you're bruised and having difficulty speaking."

She digs her hands in the pockets of her trousers and patiently encourages me to tell my story. I apologize for not being the sharpest knife in the drawer at the moment, I say, and the jurors smile. I tell them about Benny and their faces are pained. One man's eyes fill with tears as I describe the boy's drawings that led me up into the deer stand where I believe Benny spent much of his time watching the world and recording it in images on his sketchpad. I express my fears that young Benny may have met up with foul play. His gastric contents, I explain, could not be explained by what we knew about the last few hours of his life.

"And sometimes pedophiles—child molesters—lure children with candy, food, something that will entice them. You've had cases like this, Dr. Scarpetta?" Berger questions me.

"Yes," I reply. "Unfortunately."

"Can you give us an example of a case in which a child was lured by food or candy?"

"Some years ago we got in the body of an eight-year-old boy," I offer a case from personal experience. "On autopsy I determined he had as-phyxiated when the perpetrator forced the boy, this eight-year-old child, to perform oral sex. I re-covered gum from the child's stomach, a rather large wad of chewing gum. It turned out an adult male neighbor had given the boy four sticks of gum, Dentyne gum, and this man did, in fact, confess to the killing."

"So you had good reason, based upon your years of experience, to be concerned when you found popcorn and hotdogs in Benny White's stomach," Berger states.

"That is correct. I was very concerned," I an-swer.

"Please continue, Dr. Scarpetta," Berger says. "What happened when you left the deer stand and followed the footpath through the woods?"

THERE IS A WOMAN JUROR. SHE IS ON the front row of the jury box, second from the left, and she reminds me of my mother. She is very overweight and must be close to seventy, at least, and wears a frumpy black dress with big red flowers on it. She doesn't take her eyes off me, and I smile at her. She seems like a kind woman with a lot of sense, and I am so glad my mother isn't here, that she is in Miami. I don't think she has any idea what is happening in my life. I haven't told her. My mother's health is poor and she doesn't need to worry about me. I keep going back to the juror in the flower-printed dress as I describe what happened at The Fort James Motel.

Berger prompts me to give background information on Jay Talley, how we met and became intimate in Paris. Woven into Berger's prompting and conclusions are the seemingly inexplicable events that transpired after Chandonne attacked me: the disappearance of the chipping hammer I had bought for research purposes; the key to my house found in Mitch Barbosa's pocket—an undercover FBI agent who was tortured and murdered and whom I had never even met. Berger asks if Jay was ever inside my house, and of course, he was. So he would have had access to a key and the burglar alarm code. He would have had access to evidence. Yes, I confirm.

And it would have been in Jay Talley's best interest to frame me and confuse the issue of his brother's guilt, right? Berger stops pacing again, fixing those eyes on me. I am not sure I can answer the question. She moves on. When he attacked me in the motel room and gagged me, I scratched his arms, didn't I?

"I know I struggled with him," I reply. "And after it was over, I had blood under my fingernails. And skin."

"Not your skin? Did you perhaps scratch yourself during the struggle?"

"No."

She goes back to her table and shuffles through paperwork for another lab analysis report. Buford Righter is turned to slate, sitting rigidly, tensely. DNA done on my fingernail scrapings doesn't match my DNA. It does match the DNA of the person who ejaculated inside Susan Pless's vagina. "And that would have been Jay Talley," Berger says, nodding, pacing again. "So we have a federal law enforcement officer who had sex with a woman right before she was brutally murdered. This man's DNA also so closely resembles Jean-Baptiste Chandonne's DNA that we can conclude almost with certainty that Jay Talley is a close relative, most likely a sibling of Jean-Baptiste Chandonne." She walks a few steps, a finger on her lips. "We do know Jay Talley's real name isn't Jay Talley. He is a living lie. He beat you, Dr. Scarpetta?"

"Yes. He struck my face."

"He tied you to the bed and apparently intended to torture you with a heat gun?"

"That was my impression."

"He ordered you to undress, he bound and gagged you, and clearly was going to kill you?"

"Yes. He made it clear he was going to kill me."

"Why didn't he, Dr. Scarpetta?" Berger says this as if she doesn't believe me. But it is an act. She believes me. I know she does.

I look at the juror who reminds me of my mother. I explain that I was having a terribly hard time breathing after Jay tied me up and gagged me. I was panicking and began to hyperventilate, which means, I explain, that I was taking such rapid, shallow breaths, I couldn't get sufficient oxygen. My nose was bleeding and swelling and the gag prevented me from breathing out of my mouth. I went unconscious and when I came to, Lucy was in the room. I was untied, the gag removed, and Jay Talley and Bev Kiffin were gone.

"Now we've already heard Lucy's testimony," Berger says, pensively moving toward the jury box. "So we know from her testimony what happened after you passed out. What did she tell you when you came to, Dr. Scarpetta?" In a trial, for me to say what Lucy said would constitute hearsay. Again, Berger can get away with almost anything in this uniquely private proceeding.

"She told me she'd worn a bulletproof vest, uh, body armor," I answer the question. "Lucy said there was some conversation in the room. . . ."

"Between Lucy and Bev Kiffin," Berger clarifies.

"Yes. Lucy said she was against the wall and Bev Kiffin had the shotgun pointed at her. And she fired it and Lucy's vest absorbed the shot, and although she was badly bruised, she was all right, and she grabbed the shotgun away from Mrs. Kiffin and ran from the room."

"Because her primary concern at this point was you. She didn't stick around to subdue Bev Kiffin because Lucy's priority was you."

"Yes. She told me she started kicking doors. She didn't know which room I was in, so then she ran around to the back of the motel because there are windows in back overlooking the pool. She found my room, saw me on the bed and broke out the window with the butt of the shotgun and came inside. He was gone. Apparently, he and Bev Kiffin went out the front and got on his motorcycle and fled. Lucy says she remembers hearing a motorcycle while she was trying to revive me."

"Have you heard from Jay Talley since?" Berger pauses to meet my eyes.

"No," I say, and for the first time this long day, anger stirs.

"What about from Bev Kiffin? Got any idea where she is?"

"No. No idea."

"So they are fugitives. She leaves behind two children. And a dog—the family dog. The dog Benny White was so fond of. Perhaps even the reason he came to the motel after church. Correct me if my memory is failing me. But didn't Sonny Kiffin, the son, say something about teasing Benny? Something about Benny's calling the Kiffins' house right before church to see if Mr. Peanut had been found? That the dog had, quote, just been for a swim and if Benny came over he could see Mr. Peanut? Didn't Sonny tell Detective Marino all this after the fact, after Jay Talley and Bev Kiffin tried to kill you and your niece and then escaped?"

"I don't know firsthand what Sonny told Pete Marino," I reply—not that Berger really wants me to answer. She just wants the jury to hear the question. My eyes mist over as I think of that old, pitiful dog and what I know for a fact happened to her.

"The dog hadn't been for a swim—not voluntarily—right, Dr. Scarpetta? Didn't you and Lucy find Mr. Peanut as you waited at the campground for the police to come?" Berger goes on.

"Yes." Tears well up.

MR. PEANUT WAS BEHIND THE MO-tel, in the bottom of the swimming pool. She had bricks tied to her back legs. The juror in the flower-printed dress begins to cry. Another woman juror gasps and puts a hand over her eyes. Looks of outrage and even hate pass from face to face, and Berger lets the moment, this painful, awful moment stay in the room. The cruel image of Mr. Peanut is an imagined courtroom display that is vivid and unbearable, and Berger won't take it away. Silence.

"How could anybody do something like that!" the juror in the flower-printed dress exclaims as she snaps shut her pocketbook and wipes her eyes. "What evil people!"

"Sons of bitches is what they are."

"Thank God. The good Lord was looking after you, He sure was." A juror shakes his head, the comment directed at me.

Berger paces three steps. Her gaze sweeps the jury. She looks a long moment at me. "Thank you, Dr. Scarpetta," she quietly says. "There certainly are some evil, awful people out there," she gently says for the jury's benefit. "Thank you for spending this time with us when we all know you're in pain and have been through hell. That's right." She looks back at the jury. "Hell."

Nods all around.

"Hell is right," the juror in the flower-printed dress tells me, as if I don't know. "You've sure been through it. Can I ask a question. We can ask, can't we?"

"Please," Berger replies.

"I know what I think," the juror in the flower-printed dress comments to me. "But you know what? I'll tell you something. The way I grew up, if you didn't tell the truth you got your bottom spanked, and I mean hard." She juts out her chin in righteous indignation. "Never heard of people doing the things you all have talked about in here. I don't think I'll sleep a wink ever again. Now, I'm no nonsense."

"Somehow I can tell," I reply.

"So I'm just going to come right out with it." She stares at me, her arms hugging her big green pocketbook. "Did you do it? Did you kill that police lady?"

"No, ma'am," I say as strongly as I have ever said anything in my life. "I did not."

We wait for a reaction. Everyone sits very quietly, no more talking, no more questions. The jurors are done. Jaime Berger goes to her table and picks up paperwork. She straightens it and gets the edges flush by knocking them on the table. She lets things settle before she looks up. She picks out each juror with her eyes, then looks at me. "I have no further questions," she says. "Ladies and gentlemen." She goes right up to the railing, leaning into the jury as if she is peering into a great ship, and she is, really. The lady in the flower-printed dress and her colleagues are my passage out of troubled, dangerous waters.

"I am a professional truth-seeker," Berger describes herself in words I have never heard a prosecutor use. "It my mission—always—to find the truth and honor it. That is why I was asked to come here to Richmond—to reveal the absolute, certain truth. Now all of you have heard that justice is blind." She waits, acknowledging nods. "Well, justice is blind in that it is supposed to be supremely nonpartisan, impartial, perfectly fair to all people. But"—she scans faces—"we aren't blind to the truth, now are we? We've seen what has gone on inside this room. I can tell you understand what has gone on inside this room and are anything but blind. You would have to be blind not to see what is so apparent. This woman—" she glances back at me and points— "Dr. Kay Scarpetta deserves no more of our inquiries, our doubts, our painful probing. In good conscience, I can't allow it."

Berger pauses. The jurors are transfixed, barely

blinking as they stare at her. "Ladies and gentlemen, thank you for your decency, your time, your desire to do what is right. You can go back to your jobs now, back to your homes and families. You are dismissed. There is no case. Case dismissed. Good day."

The lady in the flower-printed dress smiles and sighs. The jurors start clapping. Buford Righter stares down at his hands clasped on top of the table. I get to my feet and the room spins as I open the saloon-type swinging door and leave the witness stand.

MINUTES LATER

I FEEL AS IF I AM EMERGING from a brownout and avoid eye contact with reporters and others who wait beyond the paper-shrouded glass door that hid me from the outside world and now returns me to it.

Berger accompanies me to the small, nearby witness room, and Marino, Lucy and Anna are instantly on their feet, waiting with dread and excitement. They sense what has happened and I simply nod an affirmation and manage to say, "Well, it's okay. Jaime was masterful." I finally call Berger by her first name as it vaguely registers that although I have been inside this witness room countless times over the past decade, waiting to explain death to jurors, I never imagined I would one day be in this courthouse to explain myself.

Lucy grabs me, hugging me off my feet and I wince because of my injured arm and laugh at the same time. I hug Anna. I hug Marino. Berger waits in the doorway, for once not intruding. I hug her, too. She begins tucking files, legal pads into her briefcase and puts on her coat. "I'm out of here," she announces, all business again but I detect her elation. Goddamn, she is proud of herself and ought to be.

"I don't know how to thank you," I tell her with a heart full of gratitude and respect. "I don't even know what to say, Jaime."

"Amen to that," Lucy exclaims. My niece is dressed in a sharp dark suit and looks like a gorgeous lawyer or doctor or whatever the hell she wants to be. I can tell by the way her eyes fix on Berger that Lucy recognizes what an attractive, impressive woman Berger is. Lucy won't stop looking at her and congratulating her. My niece is effusive. Actually, she is flirting. She is flirting with my special prosecutor.

"Got to head back to New York," Berger tells me. "Remember my big case up there?" she dryly reminds me of Susan Pless. "Well, there's work to be done. How soon can you come up so we can go over Susan's case?" Berger is serious, I think.

"Go," says Marino in his rumpled navy suit, wearing a solid red tie that is too short. Sadness crosses his face. "Go to New York, Doc. Go now. You sure as hell don't want to be around here for a while. Let the hoopla die down."

I don't reply, but he is right. I am rather speechless at the moment.

"You like helicopters?" Lucy asks Berger.

"Never would you get me in that thing," Anna pipes up. "There is no law in physics that accounts for one of those things being able to fly. Not one."

"Yup, and there's no law in physics for why bumblebees can fly, either," Lucy good-naturedly replies. "Big fat things with teeny wings. *Blllbbll-blllblll.*" She imitates a bumblebee flying, both arms going like mad, just giddy.

"Shit, you on drugs again?" Marino rolls his eyes at my niece.

Lucy puts her arm around me and we walk out of the witness room. Berger by now has made it to the elevator, alone, her briefcase under her arm. The down arrow glows and the doors open. Rather unsavory-looking people step out, coming for their judgment day or about to watch someone else go through hell. Berger holds the doors for Marino, Lucy, Anna and me. Reporters are on the prowl, but they don't bother trying to approach me as I make it clear by shakes of my head that I have no comment and to leave me alone. The press doesn't know what just happened in the special grand jury proceeding. The world doesn't know. Journalists were not allowed inside the courtroom, even if they obviously are aware that I was scheduled to appear today. Leaks. There will be more, I am sure. It doesn't matter, but I realize Marino is wise to suggest I get out of town, at least for a while. My mood slowly descends as the elevator does. We bump to a stop on the first floor. I face reality and make a decision.

"I'll come," I quietly tell Jaime Berger as we get out of the elevator. "Let's take the helicopter and go to New York. I'd be honored to help you in any way I can. It's my turn, Ms. Berger."

Berger pauses in the busy, noisy lobby and shifts her fat ratty briefcase to her other arm. One of the leather straps has come off. She meets my eyes. "Jaime," she reminds me. "See you in court, Kay," she says.